WILD TIGRESS

Chris flinched, his hands tightening involuntarily. He had fallen asleep again.

His sudden movement disturbed the woman cradled in his arms. Her eyes opened sleepily as a small contented sigh escaped her. Her head tipped back. She stared dreamily up into his eyes, her parted lips unconsciously inviting.

He kissed her gently, caressing her soft curves. Her breath came quicker as she shifted slightly, arching her back to press herself more firmly against him.

Suddenly she became a tigress. Her nails turned to claws, her warm breath hissed as her teeth clamped down. "Damn you!" she gasped.

His own reflexes, dulled by sleep and lulled by rising passion, barely managed to intercept her. His arms closed tightly around her, squeezing her back against him.

He stared at her, his body stiff as he tried to read the play of expressions across her face.

When the long lashes finally swept upward, they revealed black hatred glaring defiantly.

In that minute he could believe her capable of shooting a man, any man who would assail her. His mouth curled humorlessly. *"Buenos dias, señora."*

SEARING ROMANCE

REBEL PLEASURE   (1672, $3.95)
Mary Martin
Union agent Jason Woods knew Christina was a brazen flirt. But his dangerous mission had no room for clinging vixen. Christina knew Jason for a womanizer and a cad, but that didn't stop the burning desire to share her sweet *Rebel Pleasure*.

SAVAGE STORM   (1687, $3.95)
Phoebe Conn
Gabrielle was determined to survive the Oregon Trail and start a new life as a mail-order bride. Too late, she realized that even the perils of the trail were not as dangerous as the arrogant scout who stole her heart.

GOLDEN ECSTASY   (1688, $3.95)
Wanda Owen
Andrea was furious when Gil had seen her tumble from her horse. But nothing could match her rage when he thoroughly kissed her full trembling lips, urging her into his arms and filling her with a passion that could be satisfied only one way!

LAWLESS LOVE   (1690, $3.95)
F. Rosanne Bittner
Amanda's eyes kept straying to the buckskin-clad stranger opposite her on the train. She vowed that he would be the one to tame her savage desire with his wild *Lawless Love*.

PASSION'S FLAME   (1716, $3.95)
Casey Stuart
Kathleen was playing with fire when she infiltrated Union circles to spy for the Confederacy. But soon she had to choose between succumbing to Captain Donovan's caresses or using him to avenge the South!

Available wherever paperbacks are sold, or order direct from the Publisher. Send cover price plus 50¢ *per copy for mailing and handling to Zebra Books, Dept. 2088, 475 Park Avenue South, New York, N.Y. 10016. Residents of New York, New Jersey and Pennsylvania must include sales tax. DO NOT SEND CASH.*

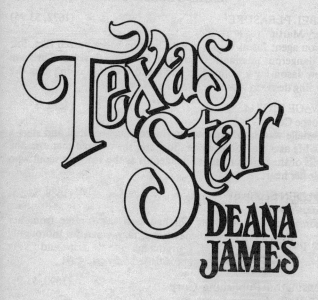

Texas Star

DEANA JAMES

ZEBRA BOOKS
KENSINGTON PUBLISHING CORP.

ZEBRA BOOKS

are published by

Kensington Publishing Corp.
475 Park Avenue South
New York, NY 10016

First printing: June 1987

Printed in the United States of America

To Max Brand and Luke Short
To Randolph Scott and Joel McCrea
To the Lone Ranger and Tonto
To Majesty Hammond and Holly Ripple
To Zane Grey
To Hoot Gibson, Ken Maynard, and Bob Steele
To Belle Starr and Calamity Jane
To Hopalong Cassidy and the Durango Kid
To Silvertip and Nevada and Zorro
To John Wayne
To the Pacing White Stallion and
the Strawberry Roan
To Cochise and Geronimo
To Gabby Hayes and Smiley Burnett
To the Chisholm Trail, the Bar 20,
and the Llano Estacado
To J. Frank Dobie
To the Riders of the Purple Sage and
the Hash Knife Outfit
To Trigger, Champion, and Silver
To the Sheriff's Daughter and the Maverick Queen

To all my heroes and heroines
who filled my dreams and gave me convictions in the
Public Library and the Rio Theatre in
Raymondville, Texas

Prologue

On the bone-pale soil of the corral, a black shadow
twisted and leaped. One shadow. Its shape constantly
changed as slender black appendages snaked out and
shifted the larger whole across the ground. One shadow. Its
edges were fringed now and again with twisting, writhing
tendrils. One shadow.

The creators of that shadow were two. Woman and horse.
In Huasteca Canyon they were Estrella Montejo, the don's
sister, and Humareda, her prancing black mare. North of
the Rio Bravo they would be Star Garner and Cloud of
Smoke. The woman's black hair, as black as the mare's
flowing mane and tail, swirled like a living swatch of silk in
the sun. Tight black trousers encased long slim legs pressed
firmly against the mare's sides. With barely a pressure from
the reins held tightly in the black-gloved left hand, the
animal turned first right, then left "away from the leg."

Smooth skin, like petals at the heart of the magnolia
blossom, glowed with a faint sheen as the sun exacted its
toll on the rider. Estrella's face was perfectly calm, revealing only the concentration necessary to take the horse
through the intricate paces.

The shadow halted in the middle of the corral. Standing

perfectly still; Humareda waited. Only the small ears flicked back and forth. Estrella moved her booted feet gently in the stirrups. The spur chain jingled. Instantly, Humareda's ears cocked back.

The rider drew a deep breath that lifted her bosom against the white silk of her blouse. Her left hand raised the rein, touching the horse's neck on the left at the same time that the right leg touched the horse's right. Humareda spun to the left.

The action was repeated in reverse. Back and forth in a dancing movement, the mare pranced across the corral. A yard from the fence, Estrella raised the reins and shook them lightly. Humareda trotted backward until her haunches were almost against the bars on the opposite side. A twist of the hand accompanied by a forward lean to the slender body of the rider and the horse began the circumference of the corral in a fast, smooth rack, lifting each foot and putting it down alone, one after another.

"Beautiful, lady," the woman crooned. "Beautiful. Smoothly, sweetheart. That's my girl. My beauty."

The black ears flicked back, but the mare's rhythm never faltered.

Again the woman halted the horse, then twisted the reins so the beautiful head pointed out into the corral again.

"Now, Humareda," came the soft voice command. "*Once!*" Tightening her reins, Estrella tilted her upper body forward, shifting her weight. From a standing start the mare leaped forward at a run. Three-quarters of the way across the corral, the rider squeezed her legs and lifted the reins high, still without pulling back on the bit. The mare slid to a standing stop, cutting a pair of perfectly parallel tracks. In the dust behind her was the number eleven, *once*, so beloved of the vaqueros on fiesta days when they wanted to show off their prowess and that of their mounts to the ladies.

"Perfect!" Estrella cried. The black ears flicked backward and the black hide trembled under the mane where her rider's gloved hand patted in pleased approval. "Perfect, sweetheart."

The rider eased her weight in the saddle. A mirage flickered on the horizon, drawing in her eyes and releasing her mind. Pain flashed up from her right hand resting on her slim thigh. Lines around her mouth and across her forehead, shockingly out of place in the youthful face, deepened. Her lips compressed into a thin slit as she struggled for impassivity. The horse, sensing her distraction, shifted impatiently under her.

"Sorry, girl," the woman apologized with a nervous grimace. "How about a drink? I think we both deserve one."

The horse turned at the rider's signal and trotted to the gate. Swinging down from the saddle, Estrella led her mount out of the corral to the concrete water trough, where she removed the bit from the velvet mouth. The mare delicately lipped the water before drinking with a soft sucking sound.

Pushing down on the pump handle, the black-haired girl lowered her mouth to the gushing stream. She took a few tentative sips before drinking long and deeply. Again sharp pain stabbed through her right hand as she exerted more pressure on the metal handle. Hastily she eased up, allowing the water to tail off.

With a grimace she rubbed the base of her thumb with the fingers of her other hand. It still hurt. Would it ever be right?

Like a dark shadow across a bright day, all pleasure disappeared, and in its place came a shuddering cold as she stared down into the black depths of the water. Her eyes closed. What lay there she could not look upon.

Chapter One

The rider tugged off his sweat-stained Stetson to wipe his forehead on the sleeve of his blue chambray shirt. The hot wind ruffled his wet hair where it gleamed whitely in the blaze of noon. His young-old face creased into lines that shielded his eyes from the sun as he scanned the floor of the canyon.

In contrast to the barren crest on which his horse's hooves stirred restlessly, the meandering blue ribbon had created a band of green, winding through Huasteca Canyon. At the bend of the river, like a woman in the arms of her lover, nestled the hacienda and outbuildings. Easily distinguishable along the band was the corral, a wide yellow patch of ground dotted with horses.

The rider's eyes slitted as he studied its proximity to the main building. From the pocket of his shirt he drew a cotton bag and a packet of papers. As the horse shifted its weight he sat loose in the saddle, delicately pouring the grains of tobacco into the tissue, catching the string between his teeth, then rolling his smoke. He hooked one long leg around the horn and scraped a match against the sole of his boot. As the tiny flame flared, he bent to meet it and draw the smoke into his lungs.

11

A couple of horsemen, tiny in the distance, detached themselves from the green canopy and galloped along the white road at a right angle to the river. He straightened alertly in the saddle as he watched their approach. White dust rose behind them and drifted eastward on the hot wind.

The man took a last draw from his cigarette before he pitched the butt away. Tightening his jaw, he settled the Stetson firmly on his head. He made a clicking sound out of the side of his mouth. "Let's go, Al." The horse willingly began to pick a way down the steep trail.

Two Mexicans in dusty garments halted their horses a few yards after the trail leveled out onto the road. With round-brimmed sombreros framing their hostile faces, they stared at him menacingly as he rode toward them. Stolidly ignoring their efforts at intimidation, he did not slow the stallion's pace. He touched his hat brim as he reined his mount slightly to ride past them.

"*A dónde va?*" one growled.

The stranger nodded his head toward the adobe arch crossing the road in the distance. He would have ridden on without speaking, but the one who had spoken reined his horse across the road. His black eyes glittered even as his lips curved back from his stained teeth in a humorless grin. "*Por qué?*"

The rider's eyes, the same blue-gray as gunmetal, were shaded by pale lashes and brows only a shade lighter than his hair. They regarded the inquisitor coolly. The rider eased himself in the saddle, stared off at the horizon for a space, then moved back insolently to the vaquero. He sighed. "I'm looking for a job."

"*Nada.*" The other Mexican spoke for the first time. Of the two his appearance was the more formidable, his eyes piercing, his lips thin. Swiftly he reined his horse in behind the stranger's, thereby catching the man in a box. "No work. They don't need nobody."

"I think I'll ask anyway."

The vaqueros exchanged glances. The one whose horse barred the way narrowed his eyes as he calculated the size and arms of the opposition.

Without waiting, the stranger smoothly guided his mount around the rump of the horse in front, jostling it aside.

"Hey, you waste your time. . . ."

"My time," came the curt reply. The rider touched his spurred heels to the sides of his mount and urged it into a canter. The white dust rose behind him.

The adobe arch was capped by letters of wrought iron proclaiming the entrance to Rancho Montejo. Under the arch he rode, before they caught up to him, flanking him half a length back on either side. Their hands rested on their thighs next to their pistols.

Between the rows of cottonwoods leading up to the front door of the hacienda they trailed him. "Hey, *hombre*," one called. "You want to speak to the *caporal*. He's down at the office. Not here in the hacienda."

The stranger ignored them both. Halting on the crushed limestone drive beside a hitching post, he shifted his weight in the saddle to swing down.

The snick of a pistol being cocked halted him with his leg half-raised from the stirrup. "*Hombre*," the serious one spoke firmly. "I said you should not go to the house."

"What's happening, Miguelito?" a gay voice trilled from the patio. The front of the hacienda consisted of a series of arched windows cut in the adobe brick wall of the patio. A double gate in its center stood open to reveal the shadowy green coolness inside and another door beyond that led into the main house. Out of one of the arches, a young girl leaned on her elbows beside a huge turquoise pot overflowing with trailing jasmine. Her black braids swung down over her shoulders, the bright ribbons at their ends contrasting gaily with her soft white cotton blouse. Her bright,

13

infectious smile touched all three men as her black eyes skipped inquiringly from one to the other.

The one called Miguelito swept off his sombrero with hasty deference. "Doñita Clara, this is not important. A stranger, a gringo, wanting work. He insisted on riding to the office even when I told him there was none."

The young girl looked regretfully at the tanned regular features and the broad shoulders. "I'm afraid Miguelito is right, señor. We are not hiring any riders. I heard my brother say so the other day."

As the girl addressed him, the *Norte Americano* whipped off his Stetson, revealing white-gold hair stunning in contrast to the darkness of his skin.

Her eyes widened, then the lashes dropped coyly to brush her cheeks. "Of course, you could go down to the corral. My brother and sister are there now looking at some new horses." The lashes swept up again, fluttering daintily as she tilted her head to one side. "If there are new horses, perhaps there will be more work. I hope you find luck, señor."

"*Gracias, señorita.*" His Stetson swept across the saddle in an elegant bow. His teeth flashed white and even as he smiled.

"Miguelito," the girl giggled. "Show him the way."

With a disgusted grunt Miguelito reined his horse around the side of the house. "This way," he snarled.

Don Tomas Alejandro de Montejo sat easily atop a magnificent dappled gray Paso Fino stallion with black mane and tail. His black eyes scanned the milling animals in the corral. One brown hand lifted a cheroot to the side of his mouth as he looked up inquiringly at his sister.

The slim woman in the black divided skirt and black cordovan leather boots smiled from her seat on the top rail of the corral. She waved a gloved hand at a black mare with

14

a tiny white star in her forehead. Nervously, the graceful creature wheeled from side to side as she tried to force her way back into the center of the herd and away from the assessing eyes. "Isn't she a little beauty?"

Tomas studied the animal carefully before he confirmed his sister's judgment. "A beauty." He might have said more, but his attention was caught by the three men riding toward them. His eyes narrowed. Between two vaqueros recently hired as guards for the hacienda rode a third man, a stranger.

As the riders drew closer, Tomas lost interest in the riders. His eyes focused on the stallion in the lead. Dust and lathered sweat could not hide the unique qualities of the animal. The grandee plucked the cheroot from between his teeth and whistled thinly. The girl on the corral fence swung her body astraddle and stared also.

From the edge of the cottonwoods screening the back of the hacienda the animal moved in a high-action pace, each knee rising rhythmically almost to the height of its deep breast. It was a dark brown bay, black where sweat stained its neck and shoulders. Its hide was dappled like watered silk taffeta. At the sight of the mares milling in the corral, the animal whickered and tugged eagerly on the reins in the rider's hand.

The Paso Fino stud danced restlessly beneath its rider, its bridle chain jingling. It arched its neck and snorted.

The size of the approaching stallion was unimpressive. It stood only slightly more than fifteen hands, but its close-coupled body with deep broad chest bespoke amazing stamina.

A complacent smile tugged at the corner of the stranger's mouth as he observed the expressions of the brother and sister. "Steady, son." He spoke to the horse softly. Immediately the animal quieted; one small pointed ear flicked back in acknowledgment of the commanding voice.

The dapple-gray stallion laid back its ears as the brown

15

bay approached, but Tomas's hand on the reins settled it. The don plucked the cheroot from his mouth and blew a cloud of smoke from his nostrils. 'State your business, *hombre*."

The smile widened into a friendlier one, although the gray eyes remained unmoved. "I'm looking for work. An *hombre* up north toward Monterrey told me you had a stud going here and might need someone with experience."

Brother and sister glanced at each other, unspoken communication passing between them. "Who told you that?" the man asked suspiciously.

"I forget," came the reply. "Just a rider."

"We aren't hiring any strangers," the girl said swiftly. Her voice was a dry husk, strangely provocative because its tones seemed so out of place coming from her delicate throat.

The man ignored the interruption. His gunmetal eyes never left the don's face. "I rode a long way," he continued. "I'm real interested in horses, especially those Pasos." He nodded toward the corral, where the animals, sensing they were no longer being scrutinized, had stopped milling.

"You know Pasos?"

Peruvian Stepping Horses," the man replied. "Yeah. I know them. That is, I know *of* them. This is only the second time I've ever been close to one." He looked appraisingly at the don's stallion. With a flick of his wrist he reined his animal to the side to study the points of the dapple gray. "Mighty pretty," he drawled after a long look.

His calculated move also gave Tomas an opportunity to study the brown bay stallion. Its small straight head sat proudly atop a short, high-arched neck. Its deep chest and well-sprung ribs bespoke lung power just as the muscular croup guaranteed strength. The legs looked hard, the hocks strong. The stallion was impressive despite its size.

The silence grew as Tomas studied the stallion. His forehead creased into a frown. "I give up," he muttered, gesturing expressively with his cheroot. "What is it?"

The rider did not pretend to misunderstand. "Like it?"

"Maybe."

The stranger pulled off his Stetson, hooking it over the saddle horn, and began to roll a cigarette for himself. "It's for stud. Could do a lot for those Pasos."

Now it was the don's turn to smile sardonically. "I thought perhaps it might be."

The stranger grinned.

"To whom have I the pleasure of speaking?" the don asked with mocking politeness.

"Christopher Stewart's the name."

"I am Tomas de Montejo."

"Tomas, we are not hiring any riders." The woman's husky voice carried an implicit warning.

Her brother threw her an annoyed glance. "Estrella, this is no ordinary rider. Rest easy." His eyes returned to the horse. "Shall we discuss this further, Señor Stewart?"

The stranger took a drag off his cigarette. "My pleasure, Don Tomas."

A pavillion had been erected on a raised platform overlooking the corral. A table and several chairs were set under the cover. There guests and potential buyers could relax in the shade, enjoy refreshment, and study the various horses they might purchase. The don, the woman, and Christopher Stewart mounted the steps.

"May I present my sister, Doña Estrella Luisa Garner y Montejo?" The don made the formal introduction as they seated themselves at the table.

Making her a formal bow, Chris Stewart murmured his name again. Again his smile did not reach his eyes as he ignored the angry glance she cast him. With a toss of her head, she flung her body into her chair. The wicker creaked protestingly.

"Careful, Doña Garner," he whispered for her ears alone as Tomas gave instructions to the two riders who had

17

formed Chris's escort.

She stripped off her gloves, slapping them across her lap in a gesture that made no effort to hide her annoyance. Pulling down the chin button on her flat black hat, she allowed it to slip back off her head. While Tomas leaned over the edge of the pavillion to study the strange horse, a tense silence grew between the man and the woman. At last a servant appeared bearing a tray of nuts, dried fruits, and cool drinks.

Thankfully, Estrella reached for the glass the servant held out to her. Her face suffused with hot, angry color, she was conscious of the stranger's silent scanning of her person.

Her black hair was drawn back tightly from a center part in the middle of her high forehead. The starkness of the style only affirmed the classic line of her face, perfectly sculpted as if from new ivory, stained now with splashes of high color over her cheekbones. Determined not to appear flustered, she pointedly turned her head to return his survey with the full force of her black eyes, glistening with golden flecks like the heart of obsidian. Like duelists, the gray and black gazes took the measure of each other.

When the visitor had been served, the don waved the servant aside and repeated his question. "What stallion do you ride?" His eyes studied the animal as he raised the drink to his lips.

"Alter-Real," came the answer.

The woman stared hard at the horse, then back at the man. His travel-stained clothing was ordinary off-the-shelf stuff. His scuffed boots, store bought. His calloused hands were the hands of a man who worked for a living. The whole picture was unprepossessing. When she turned her attention to his face, she found it closed. His features seemed young enough. Perhaps he was no older than she, but the steely eyes and the hard set of his jaw guarded the secret man behind.

She looked again at the dusty, sweat-stained stallion. "Impossible," she sneered.

Her brother stared into the gunmetal eyes before sitting up straighter. He looked again at the horse. His face took on a calculating expression.

"Do you believe he's impossible?" Stewart asked mockingly.

Slowly, Tomas shook her head, his eyes speculative, his forehead creased. "I remember," he mused. "When I was in Spain at the university, I took a trip to Portugal, to Lisbon. The House of Braganza."

"Could be," came Stewart's agreement. "I don't know about that . . . never having been 'in Spain at the university.' " His tone conveyed a world of sarcasm and contempt.

"But those horses are jealously guarded . . ." Tomas began.

"Of course, they are," his sister interrupted, her husky voice gruffer than usual. "Just because a man rides in on a mustang throwback with dapple-brown hide and announces that it's an Alter-Real, doesn't make it an Alter-Real."

"Have you, too, been 'in Spain at the university'?" The blond man eyed the bowl of nuts carefully before selecting a couple of large salted pecans and tossing them into his mouth.

Her cheeks flushed as she felt the sting of his sarcasm. Then she fixed him with a baleful glare. "No, señor, I have not been in Spain. But I have lived long enough to be wary when a coyote lopes by begging for scraps."

Their glances locked again. Lightning flashed between them.

Prudently ignoring the heated exchange, Don Tomas continued to stare at the stud. "What is your price for his service?"

"Tomas!"

Stewart smiled, raising one eyebrow with mock politeness at the outraged young woman who hissed furiously in reaction to her brother's question.

"A job as *caporal* of your *caponera*, with pay. And a couple of fillies.'

"I already have a foreman."

Stewart shrugged. "I'll work exclusively with your breeding horses if you want. I'm not particular, just so the pay is the same as his."

Tomas studied the stallion again, noting the conformation. "It would take a while to prove the breed."

The horse had lowered his mouth to drink from the water trough. Stewart whistled softly. The fine head came up instantly, ears pricked forward inquiringly. Intelligence, as well as breeding, was incontrovertible in the graceful movement.

Tomas caught his breath. "I'll pay. If everything else is as it should be," he amended hastily.

"You said a couple of fillies. Out of any mares in particular?" The scathing question rasped from the woman's throat.

The blond man smiled in her direction. His smile did not reach his eyes. He recognized the hatred she felt for him. "Funny you should ask that. That *hombre* who told me about this ranch, told me about a black mare that's got real possibilities. Not just a Paso, he said. But something more. Bred up like that stallion there, a real Paso Fino. What do you call him? El Espectro? *Verdad?*"

Tomas studied Stewart closely. "That *hombre* was remarkably well informed about this ranch."

Chris nodded. "Sure was. Seems besides that stallion there's a mare called Humareda."

"Oh, no," Estrella Garner y Montejo slapped her bare hand down on the tabletop so hard the dishes jumped. "Absolutely not," she insisted clearly. The woman's already rough little voice dropped a tone, steeped in bitter finality.

"Humareda's mine. She'll not be bred to some outlaw mustang."

"No?" The blond man seemed to be considering. "Well, in that case . . ." He leaned forward and set his glass on the table. Dusting his hands with elaborate care, he started to rise.

"Just a minute." Tomas turned to his sister. "Will you walk with me, *hermana*," He lifted her to her feet by his grip on her arm.

She did not argue, but her mouth set in hard lines as they went down the steps of the pavilion and walked toward the brown horse.

"Be reasonable, *hermana?*" Tomas hissed in her ear. "This stallion could be important to our plans. The breeding program we have begun here needs a new stallion in a few years. I would have had to journey to Peru or even to Spain. I had planned on an Andalusian. Never in my wildest dreams did I expect such a horse as that one." He nodded his head toward the stallion. "And certainly I never expected a man to come riding in with one and offer me stud service. He even offers to work for me in the bargain."

"It is no bargain. It's a trick. Has he shown you any papers?"

"We haven't discussed papers yet. You know. . . ."

"Tomas, this horse could be stolen. It probably is."

"If it is stolen, then he will have no papers."

"Papers can be forged."

Tomas held up his hand. "I shall ask him to stay and discuss this further. You may be right about all you say. But there is the outside chance, you may be wrong."

They had approached the stud. Cautiously, Tomas ran a hand over the smooth brown hide of the neck. The animal stood for the touch. Down the breast and over the foreleg, Tomas felt the steel under silk beneath the dust and grime. "God," he murmured. "Feel that, Estrella."

"He is a gringo," she pleaded. "He could have been sent

here by . . ." She clasped her right thumb in her left hand and began to massage it. Her face was white beneath the golden tan. "Tomas, you promised. . ."

"And I will keep my promise." He overrode her words. Taking her by the shoulders, he stooped slightly until their eyes were on the same level. "Listen, Estrella, you are my dear sister. I know what you have suffered. I will not let anything happen to you."

"But this man . . ."

He shook her slightly. "I have guards out all around. Did they not see him and come with him?"

"They should have stopped him."

"We cannot shoot every stranger who comes to the ranch. Be reasonable."

She shook her head, refusing to meet his eyes. "That's the second time this morning you've told me to be reasonable. But have you forgotten? We are not dealing with reason."

He clasped her shoulders tighter. "You're right. We are dealing with a madman." He drew in a deep breath. "Listen. I did not tell you this because I knew it would worry you, but the guards turned back a raid of some dozen men the other night. Comancheros and a few Indians. We can easily guess who hired them."

"Oh, Tomas." Her eyes were wide with fear.

"Sssh! They were driven off. Several were killed. No need to think about them. But don't you see? He thinks to take you with a raid of many men. That's his tactic. He's tried it twice now. Soon he will give up, or he will not be able to find anyone to work for him."

"He might try a different tactic," she insisted stubbornly.

Tomas snorted. "Someone else might, but do you really believe he is capable of changing his ways?"

She shook her head reluctantly.

"Then let us thank God that you are here safe on Rancho Montejo and go on with the business of living." He tipped her chin up to look long and lovingly into her eyes. "Look at me, *hermanita*. Smile."

Her mouth curved reluctantly.

"Good." He planted a quick kiss on one corner. "*Hermana*, you are very dear to me. I would let nothing harm you. Don't you know that?"

She nodded her affirmation.

"Then let us see the papers on this horse and talk—at least talk—with this man. At the same time I will set Miguelito and Baca to guard him, night and day. He will not have a minute's privacy until we are absolutely sure of him."

She glanced up at the man sitting on the raised pavillion. His hat was pulled low, but the eyes stared out at the little scene from under the brim. When Tomas turned back to the horse, the gringo grinned at her and popped a pecan into his mouth.

Frustrated and infuriated, she tossed her head, presenting her shoulder to his insolent gaze. Her black eyes raked the stallion, willing a flaw to appear, but with all her experience and training, she could find nothing. Reluctantly, she catalogued his fine points.

Then her brother moved to the foot of the steps. "Señor Stewart, I hope you will stay to dinner, so that we may further discuss this unusual animal and your highly unusual proposition."

The rider repositioned his hat on his head, rose lankily, and sauntered down the steps. "Well, thanks for the hospitality, Don Tomas. I'm much obliged for the invitation. You too, ma'am." He smiled in the face of her obvious hostility.

"Miguelito and Baca will be your guides to the hacienda." The don gestured over his shoulder. The two men who had lounged sourly against the rails of the corral during the exchange straightened up alertly.

"Fellas." Stewart acknowledged them with the same

23

mocking smile he had turned on Estrella.

"May I have a groom take your fine animal to the stable and care for him?"

"Thanks, but no thanks. He's got to make my fortune, so to speak. I wouldn't want to take the chance that someone else might blunder." The tone in Stewart's voice hinted at an unstable past.

Tomas nodded in understanding. "Then show him the stable, Miguelito. "When you are finished, Señor Stewart, you will be shown to the hacienda. Everything will be provided for your comfort."

"*Muchas gracias*, Don Tomas. Doña Estrella."

They watched him walk toward the stables, flanked by the two guards. Tomas smiled in anticipation as he stared at the heavily muscled hindquarters of the stallion. Estrella silently breathed a prayer as Stewart adjusted the holster of the heavy Colt to hang more comfortably on his hip.

Chapter Two

Don Tomas spent the early hours of evening conferring with Christopher Stewart. Determined to be suspicious of every curlicue on the papers, the grandee scrutinized them with minute attention to detail. The stud was described precisely, his name officially inscribed, Santo Estevao el Negro. His ancestry was traced in an unbroken line back to 1750.

When Tomas had read over the line, he whistled softly. "Unbelievable. Magnificent. Never did I expect to see . . ." Then, abruptly, he sat back in his chair, his eyes studying the other man suspiciously. "How did this animal come to you?"

Chris's expression never faltered. "By being in the right place at the right time. My grandfather took a trip to Spain a few years ago to acquire a horse from the Zaragoza stud. In Portugal the Regenerators were in; the Progressives were out. The Regenerators ordered the dissolution of the Braganza stud. So the old horse trader brought home three yearlings, two fillies, and a horse colt."

"Just like that?" Tomas could not keep the incredulity from his voice.

"Just like that." Chris smiled a rare smile with his eyes.

25

"He also brought home a Zaragoza Andalusian."

"My God. He must have all the saints in heaven on his side," Tomas breathed reverently.

"Just about," Chris remarked dryly. He puffed at the cheroot Tomas had offered him, took it out of his mouth, frowned at it. "Are you satisfied?" he asked.

Tomas was far from satisfied, but the manner of his new employee had suddenly become repressive. He leaned forward. "There is much that is not clear," he began.

"Take it or leave it," Stewart interrupted wearily. "It seems simple enough to me. I've got something you want. You've got something I want. I can't build my ranch on a stud. I can't afford your mares. You want my stud to improve your line. Fair exchange."

"But why come to Mexico? Texas has . . ."

"If I cross on a horse in Texas, we both end up with the same thing. Then where's the special thing that makes my horses different?"

Tomas nodded, at last understanding. "What you propose will take at least five years," he pointed out practically.

"I know that. I'm prepared to be patient. It takes a while to build something of value."

"Certainly with a stud."

Chris rose abruptly. "When I leave here, I'll go over a thousand miles away. Your horses and my horses won't compete for the market. We'll each have what we want and I'll have a stake besides."

Tomas stood behind his desk and extended his hand. *"Compañero."*

"Partner." Chris gripped it with his own. "Now what about that bath you were promising me?"

Humareda caracoled, neck arched, lower jaw tucked in only inches from the underside of the gleaming black neck. The slim woman in the black divided skirt easily matched her own movements with the mare's prancing dance. One hand holding the reins, the other lightly tapping the flanks, Estrella smiled in pure pleasure. The delight this mare provided was one of the few delights left in her life. In fact, the only delight.

As unpleasant visions rose in front of her eyes, she tightened her grip on the reins. As she felt the pull on her sensitive mouth, the mare hesitated. One black ear flicked back in inquiry.

"*Mea culpa*, Humareda," Estrella murmured, consciously loosening the reins as she reestablished her concentration. Her business at hand was schooling the mare, she reminded herself sternly.

From the shadow of the stables two men watched her exercise. Miguelito grinned over his shoulder from where he lounged in the doorway. His teeth were dark from too often chewing the mescal buttons. Stewart suspected that Miguelito was more than half Yaqui. Admiringly, he whistled as the mare pranced gracefully from side to side, raising her front legs high. As her rider lifted the reins and shook them, the mare trotted backwards. "She's good, no, *hombre*?"

Chris Stewart stood farther back in the stables. The glaring sun struck only the toes of his black boots. His expression did not change at the man's comment. The continual presence of Miguelito or Baca or both were beginning to wear thin. "*Si. Muy buena*. The horse is good, too."

The Mexican chuckled mirthlessly. "Forget her, gringo," he jeered. "She don't like gringos. No. She could kill them all. She love to get you on the talking end of a pistol." A thundercloud floated in front of the sun, like a white mountain in the blazing blue. The momentary shade made no difference in the atmosphere in the stable.

The blond man did not answer; his eyes never wavered

from the dancing figures in the corral.

Miguelito waited a moment. "You know why?"

"No."

"I tell you why. She just don't like gringos."

"Her name's Garner y Montejo," Chris pointed out.

The Mexican spat in the dust of the stable. His black eyes narrowed as the sun slid out from behind the cloud. "She don't like gringos," he repeated. With a slap of his quirt against his leather leggings, he swayed away from the door and stalked back into the dimness. The forked tongue of his quirt slapped against Chris's leg as he passed.

Stewart did not move. Instead he continued to stare at the girl, his face grim. For two weeks he had observed Estrella Garner y Montejo. In the corral with her horses, in particular the mare Humareda, she seemed happy, her smile, her pleasure evident in her face. In his presence she froze, her mouth tight, her nostrils slightly flared, like those of the high-bred horses she rode.

She had insisted on accompanying the men to the breeding pens when the stallion was put to a mare. Her anger and antipathy were tangible, manifesting themselves in red spots glowing in her high cheekbones and breath coming hoarse and quick from her nostrils. When the mare screamed as the stallion fastened his teeth in her neck and drove her to her knees, the don's sister looked at Christopher Stewart as if *he* were a rapist. He wiped his hand over the lower half of his face and shifted uncomfortably at the memory.

As if she sensed his eyes upon her, Estrella half turned her horse. Sitting in the blazing sunlight, she could see only a shadowy form in the interior of the stable. Nevertheless, despite the dimness, his tall figure was unmistakable. He was watching her! Wherever she went, he watched!

Her control broke. "Open the gate!" she commanded hoarsely. The small boy crouched in the shadow of the boards sprang up at her order. As soon as the opening widened sufficiently, she guided Humareda through. In the churned dust outside, Humareda leaped from a standing start into a run for the river. As Estrella cleared the cluster of buildings, she threw a nervous glance over her shoulder, half expecting him somehow to be following her.

A grove of salt cedars enclosed a small summer pavilion on three sides. The fourth side looked out over the river, its sandy bank only a few feet from the steps. Ground staking Humareda's rein, Estrella strode through the velvety needles that muffled the sound of her boots. The wind soughing through their branches was delightfully cool in contrast to the oppressive heat beyond the grove.

Sighing with relief, she removed her hat and gloves and threw them down beside her stick. Wearily, she stretched out full length upon the bench that circled the latticed wall. On her back, one arm crooked under her head for a pillow, she stared moodily at the pattern of boards that formed the ceiling.

This watching must stop. Miguelito and Baca watched Stewart watch her. Three sets of eyes followed her everywhere. Since Tomas had insisted that Stewart eat his evening meal with the family, she had had little opportunity to speak to her brother. So enchanted was the don with his new employee and the new stallion that he could not be found out of sight and sound of one or the other.

Estrella shifted disgustedly. Tomas was a fool. A naive fool. But he had never been tricked and exploited by gringos as she had. Her brother was unparalled in judging horses and cattle. People were another matter entirely.

The cicadas sang in the salt cedars. The water lapped languidly against the sandy bank. Like so many hairs on a bow, her taut nerves relaxed. Here, at least, she was safe. Safe from everything except her memories and regrets.

She closed her eyes, but the images on the lids frightened her so that she opened them immediately. Alone was no good, either. In the grip of a daymare, she rolled onto her side and drew up her knees into a tight ball.

Her sleep at night was troubled. Only if she worked very hard, to the very point of exhaustion every day, schooling the horses in the blazing sun, riding for hours until she could barely stagger to the house, could she expect to bathe and fall into bed unconscious before she hit the pillow.

But here in the quiet with the insect noises and the sigh of the wind through the trees, the regret mixed with self-castigation returned. How could she have been so foolish? Why had she allowed the beautiful young man to lure her into marriage?

The first night had been a nightmare. Recriminations in the dark. Shame and anguish and finally pain. She clasped her hands, cradling her thumb. Her eyes closed. His face rose before her. Immediately she blinked them open. In the soft afternoon sounds she could hear his breathing. She could almost smell his whiskey-laden breath.

Her hands clawed for the gun strapped to his hip, but his hands were there first. She should have been faster. Why wasn't she faster? He pulled her thumb back toward the top of her wrist. Back and back. She writhed. Back and back. One cruel hand around her throat suppressing her screams. Her sense fading. Then the dull snap of the slender bone. . . .

With a painful jar, her body fell to the floor of the pavilion. Lying on her side, her face on the blue and white tiles, she began to weep. Tired tears slipped from her eyes, tears that no one but she knew she shed. From habit, her left hand massaged her right thumb at its base. Even though the break had been knit for months now, she could still imagine the pain and remember the horror she had felt at the sight of her grotesquely swollen and twisted hand.

Her tears of self-pity changed to tears of anger. Why couldn't she control her thoughts? She was a fool falling off the bench in the summer house and lying here crying like a child. This afternoon was the worst experience she had had since Tomas had taken her away.

Angrily, she pushed herself to a sitting position, rubbing her bruised shoulder. "The gringo is the cause of all this," she groaned, her voice husky and rasping. "I was getting better. Then he came and messed me up again." She had to get rid of him. His intruding presence, his constant watching, were driving her to despair, and to this.

Climbing to her feet, she brushed dust from her skirt and sat down again, directing her mind to think of a solution to her problem rather than regretting the past. The fault lay in the gringo. Somehow, some way she must find a way to be rid of him.

Tomas could not be persuaded to pay him off. That much she was certain of. But perhaps she could.

"Of course!" The perfect solution. Buy the Alter-Real or whatever it was. She had money of her own. She would make a deal with Señor Stewart, purchase the stud as a gift for her brother's birthday, compensate the man with money plus a couple of good Pasos, and send him on his way.

Drifters like him never wanted to stay in one place for too long. To wait from ten months to a year for a filly from one of the mares was not his style; and then to wait another three to five years to see if the breed proved true would certainly require too much patience. She would speak to him tonight after dinner. He should not be hard to find alone, even though he and Tomas spent many evenings talking till after midnight.

Briskly, she put on her hat, setting it at a jaunty angle on her head. Gloves and stick in hand, she paused at the door of the pavilion. It was lovely, even in the heat of summer. The delicate lattice, the river beyond. Her hideaway, her dollhouse, built at her grandfather's order. It served her better now than ever it had in her youth, as a place to retreat and think. She drew the string of her hat tight under the side of her jaw and sprang down the steps. Tonight would see the beginning of the end of Señor Stewart's visit.

Because of her optimism, she allowed herself to relax at the supper table that evening. Because the last of the selected Paso mares had been bred to the stallion, Tomas also laughed and joked with great enthusiasm.

With the tender roast of young kid, he called for a bottle of the fine French burgundy he had laid in on his return from Spain. "A toast." His dark eyes surveyed the table expansively. "A toast to the new breed of Rancho Montejo. I give you the Paso Real."

His young cousin, Clara, lifted her glass eagerly, delighted to have been included in the festivities to the point where wine was offered her for the first time. Estrella smiled indulgently, lifting her glass toward the center of the table.

Christopher Stewart lifted his glass, too, his mouth smiling, his eyes cool. Even at the table he watched her more than the others. He touched the rim of his hosts's glass and the young Clara's, but Estrella withdrew her glass before his could touch hers. Their eyes met, hers cold and hard as *carbonados*, his narrowed as his lips curled mockingly.

"Have you decided on names for your fillies when they arrive, Señor Stewart?" Clara asked eagerly.

He shook his head. His eyes softened at the enthusiasm of the younger girl. "Why don't we just wait until they get here, Clarita? I don't believe in counting my chickens before they're hatched, or my fillies before they're foaled. If you're around—and of a mind to when they come—I

32

might just call on you to supply the names."

"Oh, I would be most honored." Clara's eyes sparkled with anticipation.

"I fear she will hold you to your promise," Tomas warned. "And worry everybody to death about when the foals will be born."

Clara managed to get her enthusiasm in hand, although her cheeks were becomingly flushed. "I shall certainly not, Tomas. I know how long it takes to make a foal. Ten months from now I shall be as patient as anyone here. So there."

Tomas grinned. "So there!" he mocked. "I am put in my place, Cristoforo. See how these women boss me. I never have a moment's peace. Nor the last word in any conversation."

By the time the fruit and sweets were served, Clara was nodding off to sleep.

"Tomas, you must carry her to bed," Estrella chided. "So many toasts and her unused to alcohol. You should have been more prudent. Tomorrow she will be tired and have a headache as well."

"This is her heritage, too, sister," Tomas replied, unperturbed by her criticism. "Such a little pain for so much pleasure. We all pay the price. She will remember this night always. The discomfort of tomorrow she will soon forget."

Estrella's eyes glowed. "You are a good man, Tomas. Father and Mother would be very proud of you."

He lifted his little cousin into his arms, cuddling her close against his shoulder. As she was lifted, her eyelids fluttered sleepily. *"Buenas noches, Cristoforo. Estrella."*

"Close your eyes, Clarita," Tomas whispered.

"Sí."

"The very best of brothers," Estrella smiled. "The very best of men."

The door closed behind him. In silence the two adversaries stared at each other. Cocking one blond eyebrow, Chris reached for a cheroot in his breast pocket. "May I?"

Coolly, she nodded. "Would you like to stroll on the patio? The cheroot will be less of an inconvenience, and the servants can clear away."

"After you, Señora Garner."

His words, delivered in his most sarcastic tone, sent a spurt of angry color to her cheeks, but she said nothing. How she hated his use of that name! How she despised him and all his kind! Gringos! Grinning, mocking, lying, endowed with such barbaric cruelty that a Comanche would pale in comparison. At least the Comanches did not tell a woman that they loved her and respected her. They took what they wanted and left the remains. She had been taken, too, and what was left of her was the remains, but not before her heart had been broken, and her spirit, as well.

Drawing her skirt in toward her body, she preceded him through the double doors into the warm, scented night. The moon, bathing them instantly in its bluish light, had the effect of softening the angry planes of their faces. Beside the fountain she paused, allowing its splashing droplets to mesmerize and soothe her. The rigid carriage of her shoulders relaxed. For just a minute, she forgot him standing tall and hard on the path behind her.

"Star," he whispered softly.

She looked over her shoulder at his face, then glanced upward pretending not to understand. "Did you see one fall?"

"Perhaps," he chuckled. "Have you fallen, Star?"

"My name is Estrella."

"And my name is Chris, but you never use it." He took a long pull from his cheroot, then blew the smoke skyward.

His teasing, flirting talk irritated her. She turned away from him. How dare he! Her fist clenched in the fold of

34

her skirt. How like them all he was! How typical! Because she had suggested a walk around the patio, he considered she had issued an invitation for intimacy. Best set him straight immediately.

"Our relationship is strictly business," she remarked distantly.

"So get on with the business, Mrs. Garner."

"Don't call me that," she snapped.

"Sorry, señora," he chuckled again. He seemed terribly amused this evening.

Drawing a deep, calming breath, she turned to face him, leaning one hand against the fountain's cool rim for support. Her hands were cold and her fingers trembled slightly. "Very well. I would like to buy the Alter-Real as a present for my brother." Her black eyes searched his face for some sign of his feeling. His face, however, was shadowed, since he loomed over her now with the moon at his back.

Too late she realized she had made a mistake in bringing him out into this setting. She should have faced him in the study where the lights would have burned brightly. "The Alter-Real is extremely important to Tomas now." She plunged on blindly, dropping her own lashes over her eyes, so he should have no advantage over her. "You have an agreement with Tomas that you will remain here until the breed has proved true, Señor Stewart, but is that really your intention? Have you thought about the many years that would take? Years that you must work for someone else. How can you be satisfied so long?" She added an interrogatory note to the last word, although it was really not a question.

Still he did not speak.

She hazarded a glance upward, but the dark silhouette afforded her no information. "I would be prepared to offer you a very fair price, especially considering that he is as yet unproven. It will take at least five years to breed the

35

stock, to see the colts, to watch them grow, and then at long last to judge whether the characteristics that you ascribe to this horse," here her husky voice took on a faintly sarcastic tone, "appear consistently in his offspring."

"He'll breed true." Chris interrupted her deprecatory comments.

"But you can't be sure of that."

In a gesture that revealed his irritation with her, he flung his cheroot into the flower bed. The moon limned his profile, with its straight nose, firm lips, and jutting jaw. "The stallion is not for sale."

"The price would be very high. I am quite well off."

He had been looking in the direction he had pitched the smoke. Now his eyes came back to her. Again she found herself trying to pierce the darkness. He waited so long to speak that she began to grow nervous. When he did answer, his voice was a snarl. "I'm sure you are. Did your late husband leave you a wealthy widow?"

The attack drove her back against the edge of the fountain, but she recovered in an instant. "My mother left me a large portion for her wedding dowry as well as for my independent support. What's more, she worked hard for every penny of it."

"I'll just bet. The rich grandee's rich spoiled wife," he sneered.

"Don't malign my mother. You don't know anything about her."

He stopped in the middle of a snarl and inclined his head stiffly. "I apologize to your mother."

She moved away from the fountain. "Clearly this is the wrong time and place to have this conversation."

He caught her arm. "You really want to buy my horse for your brother?" he mocked.

"Yes."

"Sure you don't just want to buy me off to get rid of

36

me?"

She twisted her arm futilely in his grip. "Let me go!"

"Give me a straight answer and I just might."

"My brother means a great deal to me," she insisted. "He is the head of the family."

Chris unclasped her arm. "That he is, but I repeat, the stallion is not for sale." He turned on his heel and strode toward the outer gate.

"Wait," she called. "Wait—I would include other horses in the deal. You would have fine mounts to ride out on. I have heard enough of the conversations at dinner to know that you want to start your own ranch. I could give you more than you bargained for."

"Oh," he turned back, his blond hair glistening silver in the moonlight. "The Pasos are your brother's," he reminded her. "You don't own any of them except Humareda."

"No," she shook her head. "I own several head. Horses you haven't ever seen. Perhaps not so well-trained as Humareda, but certainly as capable of *haute école*."

He leaned against the gate of the patio. "What about the mare?"

"She's not for sale."

He laughed out loud. "You won't sell her. Why should I sell Al?"

She flushed. She had thought of him as heartless, never imagining that he could have the same feelings for his stallion that she had for her mare. She twisted her hands. "Humareda is too small for you," she countered desperately. "You need a larger horse. Your weight would break her down over a long ride."

He appeared to consider her words. "Perhaps you're right."

Her breath escaped in a small sigh of relief. "Of course, I'm right." She moved toward him, putting out her right hand to touch his arm. "Will you ride with me tomorrow

37

to look at my horses? If you see two that meet with your approval, perhaps then we can discuss price again?"

He shook his head.

"Oh, please . . ."

"It's a waste of time, señora." Nevertheless, he shrugged his broad shoulders. "What can I lose? Since you're so all-fired eager to go for a ride with me, the least I can do is oblige." His face split into a grin.

Suddenly she was afraid. "This is strictly business," she reminded him swiftly.

"Oh, sure. And your idea." He laughed again.

"What time tomorrow will be convenient for you, señor?" She withdrew her hand from his arm. Surreptitiously, she rubbed her thumb across the tips of her fingers to rid herself of the warmth of his touch.

"Oh, about ten o'clock will be soon enough for me," he mused. "Give me time to take care of a thing or two."

"Till ten o'clock then, Señor Stewart," she smiled. Her face was upturned to the moonlight. Her smooth, unlined forehead, her cheeks, her chin were the color and texture of magnolia.

Before she knew what he was about, he took a step toward her, bringing his muscular thighs into contact with the rustling starched cotton of her dress. One hard hand caught the fingers she had withdrawn from his arm. His fingers caressed them, his thumb moving over the smoothness of her almond-shaped nails, testing their sharpness, before carrying them to his lips. His breath warmed her knuckles, his lips caressed the skin. Deftly, he turned her palm up to the moonlight.

"Señor Stewart," she gasped, twisting her hand futilely.

"*Paz*, Señora Star." His lips touched the tip of her index finger, her third finger, her ring finger, caressing each sensitive tip with such gentleness that she closed her eyes weakly. She had been so long without a man's touch. Her senses leaped wildly from the depths where they had lain buried. He came to her little finger. His lips closed over it, sliding warmly to take it into his mouth while his tongue caressed its tip. Suddenly, without warning, his teeth closed over the tiny nub of sensitive flesh, nipping it hard.

She cried out, jerking her hand away from him, clasping it in the other. Her face was whiter than ever in the moonlight. She stared at him, trying uselessly to read his purpose in the tiny act of cruelty, if it had been cruelty.

"Damn you, gringo!" The injured hand flashed upward, striking the side of his face.

He did not move. She might have struck a stone or the stiffened leather of her saddle. His stillness frightened her. Then his voice issued out of the dark silhouette. "Good night, señora. I'll see you at ten tomorrow."

She backed away from him and fled into the house.

Chapter Three

He was late!

More anxious than ever to be rid of Chris Stewart, Estrella paced impatiently in the hot dust. The stable boy had saddled Humareda at her request and gone on about his business. The sun crept higher in the sky. Her shadow grew smaller and smaller beneath her feet. The appointment was for ten, damn him!

Seething inside, she slapped her schooling stick against her thigh. She should go back to the house and forget the whole thing. She should take Humareda out and ride off some of her anger. She should go on with the work of schooling the horses. She should do any one of a number of things besides pacing around ruining her boots while waiting for a gringo, an admitted adventurer.

Another slap of the stick accompanied a virulent curse. She had begged Chris Stewart for the privilege of this humiliation. She was every kind of a fool. She was . . ."

The sound of hoofbeats spun her around. Chris Stewart rode toward her at a lazy canter. As he drew rein a few feet from her, his white teeth flashed in a smile. "Didn't keep you waiting too long, I hope?" he inquired pleasantly. Impudently, he surveyed her, from the perspiration on her brow to the dust on her boots. He did not dismount but shifted in the saddle and pulled his Stetson off to wipe his forehead. "Today's going to be another scorcher," he observed.

"Too hot to stand around long," she agreed nastily, fists doubled on her hips. "I don't know whether we ought to go or not. After all, I do have better things to do with my time."

He eyed her narrowly, his face taut. Something flickered there, a trace of shadow perhaps from the cottonwoods that shaded part of the stableyard. Then he shrugged. "Suit yourself."

She hesitated. She really wanted him gone. His presence here was a continual thorn in her side. Night after night of him at the table would drive her mad. "No!"

His peculiarly mirthless grin flashed again. "We can go another time."

"No . . . that is, so long as we're started, we might as well finish it." She spun around, stalking to Humareda's side. She could not credit the violence of her emotions. Her hands were actually trembling as she gathered the reins and swung up. "Follow me," she gritted, touching her heels to the mare's side.

They rode together at a fast lope for several miles south through the green band of trees. Sometimes they rode with their horses' shod feet splashing in the shallows of the river. Sometimes its bluish-green surface merely sparkled and winked at them through the underbrush and salt cedars as they followed a straighter trail than its meandering course.

At last they came to a narrow ford where the water rushed over smooth rocks. Without comment, Estrella guided the mare into its torrent. Midway, the water reached almost stirrup height, presenting no problem to their mounts. "That side of the river is mine," Estrella announced, waving her gloved hand toward the bank

41

ahead of them.

"How come?" Chris asked suspiciously. "I thought a grandee usually left everything to the son."

"My mother gave up a ranch in Texas to come and marry my father," was the reply. "She just gave it up; so he told me. She gave it to her daughter, my half-sister, and came to him without a single thing in her possession, except her horse and her dog. They were married and Tomas was born within the year. When I came on two years later, Father divided the ranch right down the middle of the river and gave half to Mother to leave to me, and half to Tomas."

"What if there'd been some more children?"

"Oh, Mother was too old. She was nearing forty when I was born." Her horse splashed in the shallows, then trotted out on dry land. "This land will never be incorporated into Rancho Montejo by the terms of their wills. It will be my daughter's when she's born, or if I shouldn't have any children, then Clarita's. It's supposed to pass to the oldest female."

Through another grove of salt cedars, she led him, then onto a trail, old and overgrown, but lined with ancient gnarled wild olive trees. The white blossoms peeped out among the gray leaves and sprinkled the ground beneath.

"There's the house," Estrella nodded, pride in her voice. "If I care to live there, it's waiting for me." Smaller than the hacienda across the river, the adobe brick seemed mellower, the walls thicker, the raw umber tiles decorating the arches and fountain more nearly the color of the earth. Around the low encircling wall, bushes of lush bougainvillea entwined their canes, their clusters of flowers brilliant scarlet in the sun.

Forgetting herself and the man she rode with, she smiled at him, her face open and girlish. "Beautiful, isn't it?"

He nodded sincerely, his gray eyes sweeping over the

graceful arches and colorful plants. "Beautiful. Who lives here?"

"Just a caretaker now. My grandfather built the house for Father and Mother after they married. They wanted to be alone here. Eventually, they moved into the big house across the river. That was after Grandfather died. That's when Father gave all this land to Mother."

"She must have been a very lucky woman."

Estrella shot him a look of annoyance. "She wasn't lucky. She was great. She deserved it."

A man limped out of the stables, grinning, his brown face creased in a thousand lines, his moustache and hair a dusty gray.

"*Ramon. Cóm' 'stá?*" she called.

"Señorita Estrella. I am well."

"The hip is not so bad?"

He made a conscious effort to make his steps even as he walked beside the horses to the corral. "No! Not now in the dry weather. Now it is fine. Only in the wet does it cripple me."

She smiled sympathetically. "You must take care this winter."

"*Gracias, señorita.*"

The corral opened up into a pasture where perhaps a dozen Pasos dozed in the sun or cropped grass languidly. All were as black as the mare Humareda or a dark dapple gray, the color of the stallion El Espectro.

Ramon took hold of Humareda's bridle as Estrella lithely swung down and began to climb the boards of the corral. The two horses closest to the fence pricked their ears forward suspiciously. Swinging her legs over the top rail, she made a cooing sound. Immediately one took a step toward her. She held out her hands and snapped her fingers. Chris dismounted and came to stand beside her, draping his arms through the rails.

The nearest mare, a black beauty, almost the twin of the

43

one she rode, came obediently to the call, slipping her soft velvet muzzle into the gloved palm.

"Sweet girl, Sombra," the woman cooed, stroking the mare's nose and patting the arched neck. "Isn't she a beauty? Hand-trained, voice-trained. The sweetest disposition in the world."

A dapple gray who had lingered at the hayrick thrust her nose peremptorily between the black and the gloved hand. "Jealous, Plata, you silly girl." The gloved hand patted the dappled cheek as the horse snuffled noisily at Estrella's boot. "She's a joker," she confided, smoothing the midnight-black forelock over the pale gray forehead. "She'll nip you if you turn your back on her, or if you don't give her the attention she thinks she deserves. Aren't you, girl?"

She let herself down and moved out into the corral, letting them smell her at the same time she patted them. Soon ten mares and two geldings had come up from the pasture. Each nuzzled and nipped for her attention, each received loving caresses, while the woman extolled their virtues and made light of their vices as if they were her children. Sleek and beautiful, they represented some of the best of the breed that Tomas and Estrella were developing.

Chris had a horseman's pleasure at the sight of the beautiful animals, the hard, cynical lines relaxing in his face as he watched the scene. At last when all the horses had been greeted, Estrella walked back across the corral to him. "Can we talk a deal?"

He blinked. The softness disappeared from his face as if it had never been. He nodded shortly.

Ramon opened the corral gate. With a loving pat to the dapple gray Plata, who would have followed her like a dog, she came out. "Come into the hacienda. Lupe will fix us some limeade to cool us."

He shook his head. The planes of his face were set like granite as he stared at her from the toes of her boots to the crown of her hat. "Not necessary. Let's go immediately. I assume you have money in the bank."

She blinked uncertainly. "Why, yes. In Saltillo."

"Then let's go."

"Go?"

"Go get the money."

Confused, she glanced at the horses, then at the house. "How much money do you want?"

"Oh, five thousand in gold will about cover the bill. I'll take that silver mare Plata and the little black mare, Sombra. Have Ramon rustle them up." He turned back to the corral, leaving her blinking and gaping in disbelief. His hand plucked a cheroot from his pocket and lighted it.

Behind him he heard her give the orders. When the two horses were strung on leading lines, he fastened them to his saddle horn and swung into the saddle. "Let's go."

Stunned, she gestured vaguely in the direction of the river. "But we can't ride into Saltillo just like that?"

"Sure we can. We'll come back when I have my five thousand in gold. Then I'll breed the mares to the stallion when they come in season and be on my way."

"But . . ."

"But what?"

She shrugged and swung into the saddle. Dazed by the swiftness of his decision, she led the way along the river toward the south end of the canyon. Something was wrong here, but she could not think what it was. Why had he agreed so rapidly? Why were they taking the mares with them if he was waiting until they came in season to breed them?

The bleached alkali kicked up dust under their horses' hooves as they broke out of the green curtain. Ahead of them across the valley floor rose the rocks of the wall and the slopes of the mountain from which the canyon took its name.

Within its shadow Chris reined in the big Alter-Real.

"Pull up."

Puzzled, she looked around. "What are we . . ."

Her question was never finished. Moving with swift deliberation, he leaned across the saddle. His hard hands seized her own. A leather noose appeared by magic and snapped tightly around her slim wrists. Even as she surged back violently, he looped it three times more around them, tying her as neatly as a calf for branding.

An icy premonition shot through her. She twisted her hands futilely as the rawhide cut painfully into the skin. Panic swept her. The cutting leather around her wrists summoned memory. Its bite was more mental than physical horror. *"Let me go."* Her voice dropped several tones to painful hoarseness.

Chris slid off the back of the stallion, holding the reins of the mare firmly in his grasp, flipping them over the animal's head.

"Damn you!" she screamed, her face contorted. *"Let me go!"*

He ignored her, although his hair stood on the back of his neck at the terrible tones of her voice. She sounded as if each word would literally rip the lining out of her throat. Still hanging on to the mare's reins, he led her into the rocks where he bent over to retrieve a couple of saddlebags.

Turning back, he stared at his captive. She was writhing in panic in the saddle, tears in her eyes, perspiration dripping from her face as she tried to bite through the leather about her wrists.

She shot him a terror-filled glance. "You must untie me," she moaned.

"Now just settle down." Unconsciously, he dropped his voice into the soothing tone he used with his horses. "Settle down." He came to her side and reached up for her elbow.

At the touch of his hand on her arm, she went suddenly

46

still. Perhaps she calmed because of his touch, perhaps because of his voice. He watched her face settle into more normal lines.

She drew a deep, shuddering breath. "Who are you, Christopher Stewart?" Her voice was hardly a voice at all, more like the hiss of a rattler. Her black eyes, hard as obsidian, bored into his face.

Somewhat relieved to see her return to some semblance of sanity, he slung one of the saddlebags over her horse's back and began to tie it to her saddle. His face was beside her thigh, his hat shielding him from her hate-filled stare. "The name's Gillard, Christopher Stewart Gillard," he growled harshly. "Your father-in-law sent me."

With a shriek of rage, she brought her bound hands down with all her considerable force on the top of his head. At the same time she heeled her mare forward with all the strength of her legs.

Gillard dropped to his knees but did not release the reins. As the alarmed mare turned in a tight circle, centrifugal force acted to throw the rider from its back onto the sharp rocks. Their edges tore a sharp cry from Estrella's lips before she rolled into the dust between them, stunned, her limbs sprawled, her cheek pressed against the rough limestone.

Unhurt, her captor righted himself and quieted the excited horse. Sparing only a swift glance in Estrella's direction, he collected the other saddle bag and tossed it onto the back of the Alter-Real, buckling it into place.

When all four horses were quiet, he strode back to his captive who was beginning to stir feebly. Jerking her up to her knees, he shook her roughly. "Try that again," he warned, "and you'll run along behind for a couple of miles until you're too exhausted to give me any trouble."

The shaking cleared her head. Despite the blazing pain all along the side of her body, she tried to raise her arms to fight him off. Her lips curled back from her teeth in a snarl. Ducking her head, she sank her teeth into the fleshy part of his palm below his thumb. Blood flowed into her mouth.

"Damn!" He grabbed her hair in its neat coil and yanked her head back. With his bitten hand, he smacked her hard across the face, leaving a red smear across one cheek.

Both froze.

The pain of his blow shocked her from her hysteria. The sight of the blood on her white face made him sick at his own violence. For a long moment they stared stiffly into each other's eyes.

Then she made a small sound in her throat. "You must let me go," she whispered. "Luke Garner hates me."

Her words recalled him to his original purpose. "What do you expect?" Gillard jeered nastily. "You murdered his only son."

She shook her head wearily. "I don't think. . . ."

"Shot him with his own gun."

The memories he bombarded her with were making her sick. Likewise, the pain from her bruises threatened to overwhelm her. She knew herself to be a rank coward about pain. "I swear . . . please . . . he came toward me. . . ." She could not go on. Her throat blocked with tears. Words would not come to describe the horror of that desperate night.

"The jury found you guilty." He plowed on inexorably.

Her throat closed completely. Only incoherent rasps came from it. She twisted her hands against the rawhide, feeling trickling wetness over her wrists. Her eyes dropped in panic.

Contemptuously, he let go of her, spurning her under his hand, so that she collapsed again into the sharp rocks. Never taking his eyes off her, he collected the reins and led her mare forward. His scuffed boots stopped only inches from her face. He put his hands on his hips, looming over her in a conscious move to intimidate her. His experience had proved that the more roughly he treated his prisoners from the very start, the fewer problems they created later. In this instance he feared he might have overdone the rough stuff.

The eyes she raised to him were glazed with pain. Her legs stirred feebly as she tried to summon the strength to move. The partial numbness caused by the shock of the fall onto the rocks was beginning to wear off. Now she could not draw a deep breath without suffering agonies. Her gloved fist clenched in the fine gravel beneath her.

Not for the world would she reveal that she was broken. Bruised and cracked ribs might clamor for attention, but she must be strong. Only in strength lay hope of escape.

"Get up!" he ordered. "We're going back to Texas. You're guilty as sin. You'll hang."

"Do you really care whether I'm guilty as sin or not?" she gasped, trying to breathe shallowly. "Why should a bounty hunter and chief torturer give a damn?"

He gritted his teeth. "I didn't torture you. Your horse threw you onto those rocks. You've been condemned by a judge and jury in Texas. I'm bringing a murderess to justice."

"Will you get paid to pull the lever, too?

His face whitened slightly. "I'm hired to bring you back. You're an escaped criminal. You shot a man's only son."

"He needed shooting."

"Nobody needs shooting," he denied emphatically. "Mount up, Señora Garner."

"Just don't turn your back, gringo. One of us is not going back to Texas alive," she grated. Blindly, she fumbled for the stirrup, then climbed painfully onto the black mare. Her bound hands clenched around the saddle horn. Her teeth gnawed at her lower lip to keep from moaning.

He bent to pick up the schooling stick where she had

49

dropped it. Then he vaulted into the saddle of the Alter-Real. Reining his horse around beside hers, he slashed the leather and whalebone down hard on Humareda's hindquarters.

Terrified at the pain, the mare buck-jumped, then set off into a bone-jarring run. Chris Gillard held the stallion's nose even with the mare's shoulder to whip her if she slowed. The dapple mare Plata and the black mare Sombra strung out behind them across the plain.

Estrella Garner y Montejo clamped her knees, bent low over the horn, and rode for her life. The rocks and thorns were all around her on either side of the narrow trail. With every stride, the pain in her ribs was a living thing biting and tearing at her like a savage animal. Around the edge of the valley she rode, beneath the shadow of the canyon wall. The pale caliche dust stirred up behind them was almost invisible against the equally pale canyon walls. With a sinking heart, Estrella realized that they could not be seen among the rocks.

The horses were lathered and heaving when Gillard finally allowed them to slow down to a ground-eating gallop, then to a lope. They were heading for the north pass out of Huasteca.

Finally, on the slope of the upward trail, he called a halt. "Dismount," he ordered. "We'll walk the horses to the top. On the other side we can rest and eat."

Dazed, her whole body a mass of pain, she sat her horse. She had long since lost track of time and space and only clung by blind instinct to the saddle.

"Get down." His voice seemed to come from somewhere below her but very far away. Hardly aware that he was touching her, she offered no resistance when his hand closed around her elbow and hauled her from the saddle. Her damaged ribs collided with his lean body. Pain smashed her. With a gasping cry, she collapsed, unconscious.

She revived, cradled in his arms while he bathed her hot, dusty face. As her eyelids flickered open, he held a canteen to her lips, trickling warm water with a metallic taste down her parched throat.

"What's wrong?" he asked huskily, when she could focus. "I thought you were tougher than this."

She let her eyelids droop, refusing to answer. If he did not know her weakness, he could not capitalize on it.

Her eyes flew open again as he lowered her body to the ground and began to inspect it with his hands. Within seconds, his prodding fingers touched her sides, wringing an agonized moan from between her bitten, parched lips.

"Ribs, huh?" He sat back on his haunches. "Cracked them when you hit those rocks back there. That's just dandy, señora."

"Does Luke want me dead or alive?" she gasped, her breathing shallow.

"Alive," he replied shortly, raising her into a sitting position. "Unbutton that blouse and pull it out from your waistband." He threw the command over his shoulder as he went to rummage through his saddlebags.

"Like hell."

He swung around to face her, a clean shirt of blue chambray dangling from his hands. Scowling deeply, he dropped down on his knees beside her. His thumb and third finger closed round her jaw and turned her face up to his. "Listen, señora. I'm going to wrap this shirt around your ribs good and tight, so you'll have some support when you breathe. Likewise, the cracked ends won't rub together when you ride."

"How merciful!" she gritted.

"Mercy doesn't have anything to do with it," he replied harshly. "Like you've already discovered. Luke Garner wants you alive. Only God knows why. If you'd killed my son . . ." He did not finish this statement. "Now, if you don't like the idea of this good, soft cotton against your

51

skin, I can take my reata and do the same thing. The only difference will be the damage to you. I don't give a damn. But I don't aim to take you back with a rib poking through your lung. Now are you going to do as I say, or do I get my reata?"

"Torturer," she muttered.

He began to fold his shirt into a wide bandage, the distance between the cuffs some six feet. "Are you going to get that blouse unbuttoned?"

Humiliated and in pain, she fumbled with the lower buttons. One by one they came free, and she pulled the blouse out of the waistband of her divided skirt.

"Now raise your arms," he ordered. His face inches from hers, he passed his arms round her body and wrapped the material twice around her ribs, drawing it so tightly that she moaned. Her breasts, covered only by the thinnest of cotton chemises, rose as she gasped in pain and embarrassment. She might have been a horse, so impersonally did he knot the sleeves, looking into her face, his eyes holding hers the entire time he ministered to her. At last, his first aid accomplished, he pulled the blouse down and sat back as she lowered her arms. Her face was white to the lips and bedewed with perspiration.

"Have another drink of water," he offered magnanimously.

It tasted like nectar. She could have drunk the whole canteen, but he took it away from her clutching fingers, capped it, and returned it to his saddle horn. Next he withdrew a pair of binoculars from his saddlebags and directed them to the ranchhouse in the valley below.

"No sign of any alarm yet," he informed her. "Must have tied Miguelito and Baca up tighter than I thought."

She called him the filthiest name she could think of.

He chuckled. "Course, you played right into my hands. You didn't tell anyone we were going anywhere, did you? You were going to surprise your brother with my horse, right? So you didn't tell anyone we were going to your place across the river. The old man would have only heard we were going to Saltillo, if he heard anything at all."

She dropped her eyes, staring at the bruised flesh of her wrists. Inside her gloves she could barely feel her fingers.

"You're a real fool, señora," he jeered. "Suppose I'd been a robber or a rapist. I could have smashed your head in on the way back from Saltillo, taken your gold, and rustled all your fine horses. Instead I'm just a poor old bounty hunter looking to make a little money. You knew you were being hunted. You sure are one stupid woman."

Like the lash of a whip, his words tortured her. He was right. She had been unutterably stupid. So anxious to be rid of him, she had not taken proper precautions. Hours would yet pass before Tomas would miss her. They might not even miss her until the next day.

"We can be halfway to the Rio Grande before they even know we've gone," he continued. "Just like taking a baby." He thrust the binoculars back into the saddlebag and went around to her horse. From its bag he drew some tortillas and jerky wrapped in a clean cloth. "Here," he offered her, seating himself cross-legged beside her. "Chew this. The tortillas are wrapped around beans. Taste pretty good. I got your cook to fix me some early this morning. Told him I'd be doing a little exploring about noontime and needed a lunch."

"Liar," she spat.

"Sticks and stones," he replied with a chuckle. "Better eat. You must really be weak, if you can't think of something worse than that to call me. Especially in the light of what you've called me already today."

Recognizing the truth of his statement, she tried to close her numb fingers around the tortilla, but they would not obey her.

For the first time, he saw the condition of her wrists. A muscle flinched in the side of his jaw. Hastily, he bent to untie them, struggling with the stubborn knots that had been pulled to rocklike hardness. When she was free at last, he began to massage her right hand diligently. "Didn't mean to have that happen," he apologized.

She did not acknowledge his concern. Instead, she picked up the tortilla and began to gnaw at it, almost strangling on the tough, dry mess.

When they had finished, he hauled her to her feet. "You're going to have to walk to the top of this pass," he told her, his voice again faintly apologetic. "Too much of a haul for the horses. Wear them out too much. They couldn't be counted on tomorrow."

"I won't take a step," she sneered.

His manner changed instantly. "Oh, I think you will." As she watched him narrowly, he untied the reata from the saddle. "Do you walk," he asked her, shaking out a small loop, "or do I drag you?" He flipped the braided leather over her head, drawing it up around her neck. "Just like a little preview of the noose at the end of the trail."

"Is this how you get your kicks? Or is torture just a characteristic of all male animals?"

He tugged it tighter; the stiff rawhide scratched her neck across the back. She grabbed at it with both hands.

He said no more but gathered the reins of the horses and the rope. Keeping it tight, he started upward. After a hard tug, she followed helplessly.

The sun blazed down upon them. Sweat poured from their bodies. With her ribs stabbing her at every breath, Estrella began to stagger before they had gone twenty feet. Focusing on his back, a couple of yards ahead, she began to list the ways she could kill him. Staking him down on an anthill was seeming to have exceptional merit, when her captor halted in his tracks to stare outward across the valley.

Dust clouds were rising. They had missed her at the rancho. The vaqueros would find the trail. They were already following it south toward Saltillo. Tomas would be leading them. Her brother would not let a gringo have his sister.

When she saw the clouds, she laughed excitedly. "You see! I told you! Run!" She caught up with him and grabbed at his arm. "Run for your life! Take the horses. You can get away. Tomas will be here on this very spot in a couple of hours at the most."

Chapter Four

Christoper Gillard glared at the jubilant girl. The situation would be desperate in minutes. His gunmetal eyes flashed upward along the trail to the summit of the canyon wall. Rapidly, he calculated the amount of time left and the distance to be covered.

"Leave me here," Estrella urged excitedly. "Go on. Take the horses. You can make it over the top."

"Shut up!" He stared at the dust clouds. "He's still got to ride into Saltillo and find out you haven't been there. No one will have heard of you. Then he'll have to send out riders north and south. . . ."

Even as he talked he reeled in the reata, pulling her up to him. "I'll put you up on the gray. She's bigger and rangier than the black."

"No. Don't be a fool!" She pulled back on the line like a fractious colt. The knuckles of her hands showed white around the tough rawhide.

"Here!" he exclaimed. "Don't make me hurt you!" He slung one arm around her shoulders. His other arm slid under the backs of her thighs. "Throw your leg over."

"No . . . oh!"

As he lifted her, the cracked ribs rubbed together.

Excruciating pain made her cry out. Instantly, she was bathed in sick perspiration. Incapable of further resistance, she managed to part her legs. His steely strength bore her upward and mounted her. If not for his grip on her, she would have slid back off as shards of agony slashed through her abused body on contact with the broad back. Her senses dim, she felt one strong hand on her thigh, the other around her elbow.

Was it her imagination, or did she feel his hand tighten on her thigh? She opened her eyes, staring down through a haze of pain and heat exhaustion into his sweat-streaked face. The gray eyes were anxious, his forehead creased in a concerned frown. A wave of fury swept her. Her tongue worked convulsively. Weakly, she spat in his face. "Gringo! Get your damned hands off me!"

The muscles in his face stiffened. His eyes narrowed, the gray gleaming between the lids like steel. With a cold snarl, he wiped the back of his hand across his cheek. "You'll need that spit before we're through," he observed.

Her lips tightened into a sneer, and she looked back over her shoulder at the dust clouds rising in the valley.

Grimly, he gathered the myriad lines—the *jaquimas* on the bareback mares, the reins from the bridles of the saddled mounts, and the reata that he had left around her neck. Taking a deep breath of the hot desert air, he loped rapidly up the trail.

Before he reached the top, he was sure his heart would burst. At the crest his lungs were going like a blacksmith's bellows and his mouth gaped open, vainly trying to extract enough oxygen from the still, hot air. With almost the last remnants of his strength, he managed to lead the horses over the horizon line before his feet slipped out from under him. He slid a dozen feet among the rocks and gravel before coming to a halt.

The stallion nuzzling his cheek with a velvety muzzle brought him to his senses. He stared upward, blinked, then groaned. In a flash he realized he had lost consciousness. The heat from the direct glare of the sun blasted him like a furnace. Abruptly he sat up, although his head reeled and he fought for consciousness.

When the black spots stopped dancing and began gradually to decrease in size, he focused on the horses. "Thanks, Al," he murmured, patting the dark, sweat-streaked hide beneath the black mane. The mares Humareda and Sombra stood with heads bowed, their eyes half-closed. Only Plata stood alert, her ears pricked forward.

Estrella had managed to throw the reata to the ground and now draped herself along the mare's neck, trying desperately to reach the rope on the *jaquima*. The task was proving monumental given her numbed fingers and cracked ribs. Even as he looked, she awkwardly slid forward, her face contorted with pain, and made a futile grab for the cheek strap.

The movement overbalanced her, and she was falling. He staggered to his feet and stumbled up the gravel trail. His outstretched arms broke her fall, but they went down in a heap together, she on top, his arms tight around her.

While the unforgiving sun blazed down, he simply panted, his entire chest heaving. The sweat poured from him, wetting her clothes as he clung to her like a lover.

At last he moved. Wearily, he pushed her aside and crawled up the side of the mare. Drawing a deep breath, he staggered on rubbery legs to the stallion. Unscrewing the top of the canteen, he turned it up to his lips, swallowing once, twice, three times. Over the side of it, he saw her.

She sat up, bracing herself on her stiff arms. She licked her lips as she watched him. He took one more swallow, then capped it. Slinging it back over the saddle, he took off his hat and wiped his forehead on the sleeve of his filthy shirt.

Her eyes were wide with dismay when she realized that he did not intend to share the water with her. Instead, he grinned, his parched lips stretching tightly over his teeth. "Told you so," he reminded her nastily.

Without acknowledging that she knew what he was referring to, she stared back up the way they had come. She could no longer see the valley. Her shoulders slumped wearily.

Behind her, Chris untied the bandanna he wore around his throat and knotted it around his forehead to catch the stinging sweat that was dripping into his eyes. Setting his hat back on his head, he came to get her.

His hands were gentle enough as he lifted her to her feet. But the hated humiliating reata dropped down over her head before he took her upper arm. "Guess we'll put you back up on Humareda for now," he mused. "She's saddled and about as fresh as any of them after being run up the side of a mountain." Suiting action to words, he lifted Estrella by shoulder and thigh. This time she knew enough to make the job easy on herself.

He gathered the assortment of reins and lines and swung into the stallion's saddle. "Now, Señora," he told her grimly. "Hang on."

Down the long slope they dashed. The horses' hooves sprayed fine gravel into the cholla and yucca. Behind them clouds of alkali rose, but not high enough to be seen by men searching for her on the bottom of the canyon floor.

In an hour he stopped, pulling the saddles from Humareda and Al and adjusting them on Sombra and Plata. He cursed roundly at the adjustments necessary to fit his big saddle onto the smaller mare. "I should have asked for a gelding," he panted. "But I figured you'd get suspicious."

Speech was impossible given her swollen tongue and cracked lips. She did not bother to nod, only slumped in weary exhaustion in the weak shade of a stunted mesquite.

When he came to mount her this time, he allowed her a small swallow of water.

By changing mounts regularly, Gillard was able to travel twenty miles before darkness made the going too treacherous for the horses. In the open under the stars, he made dry camp. When he held up his arms, she went into them willingly. After she stood steady on her feet, he untied her hands. Without comment, he massaged the bruised wrists, his thumbs rubbing over and over the welts while she bit her lip to stifle her groans.

Despite hours spent in the saddle every day, Estrella was sure that she had never been so sore. To ease her broken ribs, she had ridden in all sorts of strained attitudes that made cruel demands on her muscles. While he ground-staked the horses, she limped back and forth to the length of her tether. Her heroic effort to keep her body from stiffening proved vain as the desert night shut down cold. Estrella began to shiver as the burning heat of the sun escaped into the clear black void of the sky.

Limping slowly, her arms clasped tightly around her middle, she watched her captor gather dried grasses and sticks together to light a tiny fire. A clod turned under her boot, wringing a groan from her as she staggered to keep her shaky balance. "Enough of this," she muttered.

She dropped down a couple of yards from the fire, drawing her knees up and resting her forearms across them. In this way, she rested her chin and concentrated on breathing as shallowly as possible.

He glanced in her direction, saw the reflection of the fire in her pain-filled eyes, the deep grooves cut in the magnolia skin around her mouth. Hastily, he looked away, steeling himself against stirrings of sympathy. From a saddlebag he dragged cloth-wrapped objects that proved to be jerky and dried apples, from another, a small coffee pot, much dented and misshapen.

Unblinking, she watched him, noting the deft, efficient

movements. Despair threatened to overwhelm her as she observed the evidence of careful planning down to the last detail. Luke Garner's money had bought the best.

She must have dozed. "Estrella. Star." A gentle voice aroused her. She raised her head to stare around her in the darkness. Disoriented, the face beside her a blur, she smiled wearily as she accepted a tin cup full of steaming coffee. Grateful for the stimulant, she murmured her thanks before her memory supplied the identity of her benefactor.

"I've got two bedrolls spread out," he indicated with a sweep of his hand. "Drink your coffee and chew on this jerky."

"Not side by side," she hissed.

"No way else," he replied. "I didn't drag you this far to have you slip away from me while I'm sleeping. And I do intend to get some sleep tonight. My God! I'm tired."

Her outrage abated as she stared at him more closely, seeing for the first time the hollows in his cheeks and about his eyes. He must be exhausted. He had ridden much farther than she today and had run up the side of a mountain while she had ridden Plata. Tentatively, she tested her ribs. The pain that made her gasp might be a blessing. She would not sleep well tonight. The least turning would pain her. Awake in the middle of the night, she might get a chance to slip away.

"Drink up," he commanded. Quizzically, he raised one eyebrow at the sight of her intent stare.

Draining the cup, she handed it to him.

"Now stretch out here." He stood over the nearest blanket.

Gingerly, she hitched herself over to it and propped her shoulders against her saddle for a pillow.

"On your side." Without waiting for her to turn, he clasped the ankle of one leg and looped a piece of rawhide around it twice.

"What are you doing?"

With the same ruthless efficiency, he rolled her over on her side and secured her opposite wrist, bringing the two together with only a couple of inches to spare.

Intense hatred choked her as pain and panic drove her to tug futilely at her bonds. Her eyes willing his death by slow torture, she stared up at him as he rose to his full height and stretched his weary shoulders. His length when viewed from the ground upward was intimidating, but she refused to close her eyes.

Soberly, he met her stare before he stepped over her outstretched leg and lowered himself at her back with a groan. She felt a brief testing tug on the ropes before he pulled her blanket over her.

She initiated a small scuffle when he tried to drop his arm over her body. Indignantly, she pushed it away with her free hand, but he chuckled bitterly in her ear. "I intend to sleep as comfortably as possible, Señora. That means sharing your body warmth."

"No!"

"Yes!" He dropped his arm across her body at the waist and drew her tightly against him. "Now don't wiggle or you'll hurt those ribs."

"For mercy's sake . . ."

"Ssh. If that leg gets to cramping too much," he whispered, "wake me up. I'll change legs for you."

"Savage."

"No," he murmured sleepily. "I don't aim to hurt you more than I have to." So close was he to her body that his breath was hot against her neck. "Just keep you from running off and getting lost."

"You . . ."

Firmly, he covered her mouth with his hand. "Señora, I don't care to listen to what you might have to say. I'm tired and I need my sleep. A gag can be a mighty bad thing. Specially in a mouth that hasn't had much more than a cup of water all day."

Instantly, she was still, subsiding wretchedly against him.

As he felt her body relax, he loosened his grip and placed his arm again at her waist. "Smart lady. Now close your eyes."

Reluctantly, she obeyed. The warmth coupled with the blessed absence of motion acted as a soporific to her abused body, allowing her to drop off to sleep almost immediately.

Chris Gillard awoke to the sound of soft moaning. The pitch blackness and the chill air testified to the time, a little before dawn. Under his hand his prisoner moved restively.

His hand traced her body from shoulder to wrist, discovering the slender arm stretched taut, the wrist gouged by rawhide. As he touched her, her leg jerked reflexively. She whimpered like a small child and jerked again, struggling against confinement even in her sleep.

Mentally, he analyzed his condition, coming to the conclusion that he had probably slept all he was going to for the night. To let her rest better, he fumbled at the knots around her wrist. They were hard as rocks. For a while he was sure he was going to have to take a knife to them, but finally they came loose.

Sliding his hand down her thigh, he drew up his leg and pushed down against her calf. A faint cracking noise reached his ear as her abused joint straightened. Then his thumb and third finger began a circling motion over the ridges on the back of her hand.

Again she moaned, the pain penetrating the deep, exhausted sleep into which she had fallen. "No," she whimpered, her head rolling from side to side. "Please." Her voice was muffled, slurred, fighting out of a dream.

Not wanting her to awaken and thereby force him to retie her, he gathered her into his arms, softly whispering soothing, meaningless phrases. One hand pressed her head against his chest. His fingers brushed back straying tendrils of hair from her cold cheek. The other hand continued its massage of her wrist, gradually working up her arm to the elbow and then the shoulder.

He grinned mirthlessly, sternly reminding himself that she was a murderess. She had shot her young husband in cold blood and fled. She would not hesitate to do the same to him. Any minor pain she might suffer on the trail should not move him to pity so that he would leave himself vulnerable.

Her moans began to quiet and he felt her warm breath caress his skin through the open neck of his shirt. Her curves were undeniably feminine against him. Now was the time to leave bounty hunting behind. He was getting too soft-hearted. With the money he would earn from Garner, he could fix the ranch up the way he wanted it.

She shivered and pulled up her leg. It slid between his, her thigh pressing unknowingly against his crotch. He stirred uneasily, feeling himself swelling. Hastily, he ran his hand down over her waist and hip to push her away. The half caress had the effect of quieting her. She drew warmth from him soothed by the thud of his heart in her ear and the big hand running over her body. He shifted into a more comfortable position and tried to ease her onto her back, but she sighed and clutched at his shirtfront as if to keep him with her.

If she didn't beat all! Luke Garner had described her as a cold, indifferent bitch. Matthew Garner's heart, according to his father, had been broken by her. "I got witnesses," he declared. "I got more'n one who'll testify to the cold way she treated him. Drove him crazy, is what she did."

He had married her because she was the most beautiful

girl he'd ever seen, then been turned away, driven to drink. She had undermined him, laughed at him, then finally, when he had tried to stop her from leaving, she had shot him, ". . . in cold blood." Luke Garner's fists had clenched white. "She killed my boy, my son, my only son. I got a witness. Maudie saw her do it."

Gillard's eyes had flickered over the impassive face of the woman standing silent behind her father's chair. He tried to read her eyes, but they were blank, her face revealing no emotion whatsoever, while her father foamed and frothed. "And the jury found her guilty."

"Guilty as sin," the woman intoned.

"How come she didn't hang?"

Garner cursed. The foul stream of words poured from his thick lips. Chris blinked; his eyes flickered again to the tall, silent woman who still remained unmoved. Suddenly, Garner began to choke. Strangling sounds replaced the vicious words.

For the first time, his daughter moved. Switching around to the side of his chair, she pounded him on the back with one hand while she lifted the stopper from a decanter of whiskey and sloshed a stiff drink into a cloudy glass.

Her father nodded, red-faced, as he downed it in a single gulp. Then he waved a shaking hand at Chris. "The gallows is built; the rope's waiting."

Out in the dusty street, in the middle of the space in front of the courthouse, stood the structure, a skeleton of posts with steps and a platform. A noose whipped in the high, dust-filled wind.

"I had her right there in that cell," Luke Garner continued, specks of white froth collected at the corners of his mouth. "She could look out that barred window and see it waiting for her. But somehow she got word to that brother of hers across the border in Saltillo. He got her out. Got her back into Mexico, where he's got friends and influence. Her dad was part-Indian himself. Fought and died for that Indian Juarez a few years back. The upshot is, I can't get to her with an army."

Chris stirred restively. Now came the part he was interested in. Garner's muddy brown eyes had narrowed as he appraised the young man. "But one man might. You're younger than I expected. But you come with high recommendations. You're not known yet. You could get in there and get her out almost before anybody knew."

"How much is she worth to you?"

Garner chuckled. "Glad you asked that. Makes me real glad to do business with you. I don't exactly trust fellows who want to 'bring criminals to justice.' They said you were starting to make a real good living off bounty hunting." His muddy brown eyes took on a canny questioning look.

A noncommittal shrug was his response.

"So . . . well . . ." Approvingly, his eyes scanned the Colt Peacemaker strapped to Chris's hip and the late-model Winchester slung in its scabbard over his broad shoulder. "Good equipment," he commented.

"To do a good job, a man has to have the right tools."

Garner subsided into silence, lost in memories, his shoulders hunched, his eyes half-closed. At last he roused. "Five thousand now! Five thousand on delivery!" he promised, his voice deadly cold.

Gillard blinked. The amount was unheard of, double what had been offered for Jesse James.

As if reading the bounty hunter's thoughts, Garner chuckled nastily. "Oh, you'll earn every penny. Never fear. Watch her! She's deadly as a Gila monster. She'd just as soon kill you as look at you."

Now Star Garner, the widow Mrs. Matthew Garner, lay nestled in his arms, her hand curled on his chest. He could feel her steady breathing as her breasts pressed against him.

A faint glow began on the eastern horizon; the breeze freshened. A chacalaca cackled sleepily from somewhere in the brush. Chris flinched, his hands tightening voluntarily. He had fallen asleep again.

His sudden movement, accompanied by a grunt, disturbed the woman cradled in his arms. Her eyes opened sleepily as a small contented sigh escaped her. Her head tipped back. She stared dreamily up into his eyes, her parted lips unconsciously inviting.

Perhaps they both forgot.

The man's pale gold head, white in the early dawn, bent. His lips touched hers gently, clung, caressed her softness. Its tip seeking, his tongue slid into the satiny interior of her mouth. The hand on her head steadied her and held her firmly, while the other moved as with a will of its own over her breast. His palm circled the mound of flesh insistently. Suddenly, her nipple hardened. Her breath came quicker as she shifted slightly, arching her back to press herself more firmly against him.

Blood pounded in his ears. He slid one long booted leg across her thighs, rubbing himself against her hip. His hand abandoned her breast to slide down over the arch of her ribs into the valley between her hip bones. His long fingers pressed the joining of her thighs.

In response she moaned deep in her throat, her tongue locking with his, sucking at him. The hand on his shirt clutched convulsively.

Suddenly, he embraced a tigress. The nails turned to claws, the warm breath hissed as her teeth clamped down, missing his tongue by only a fraction of an inch. Her knees rammed upward as her body bowed away from him. "Damn you!"

His own reflexes, dulled by sleep and lulled by rising passion, barely managed to intercept her. His inner thigh absorbed the blow, while his arms closed tightly around her, squeezing her back against him.

A cry of pain ripped from her mouth as his strong arms punished her ribs. Her senses dimmed, black spots dotted her vision. When Estrella opened her eyes, she found her captor hanging over her, his mouth grim, his eyes gleaming in the bright dawn.

Terrified, her courage driven from her by pain, her fists turned to open palms. Prayers and entreaties for mercy flashed through her mind, reflected in the strained white face she turned up to him.

He stared down at her, his body stiff as he tried to read the play of expressions across her face.

Her eyelids closed. As if a shutter had been slammed across a window, the frightened, pleading girl disappeared. When the long lashes swept upward again, they revealed black hatred glaring defiantly. The suppliant palms arched in fierce claws.

In that minute he could believe her capable of shooting a man, any man who would assail her. His mouth curled humorlessly. *"Buenos dias, señora."*

"Bastard!"

He lifted his arm and leg, allowing her to roll away from him in a frantic scramble.

On all fours, one hand pressed against her injured ribs, she spat at him in fury. Her sudden movements had reawakened all the agony of the previous day, accompanied by bruises she had not felt until this morning. Her head swirled dizzily. Only by dint of will was she able to prevent her body from pitching headlong to the hard ground. His face, brightly lighted by the half-risen sun, grinned insolently at her as he slowly lifted his hands to clasp them behind his head.

"Since you rolled out of the blankets first, does that mean you'll fix the coffee?" he jibed.

"Bastardo!" She switched to Spanish. Her voice dropped to a hissing whisper, her forehead wrinkled in pain. *"Gringo bastardo."*

He shrugged mockingly. "I guess that means no in any language."

She pushed herself back on her heels, still clutching her ribs. Her teeth sank into her lower lip. The fear coupled with the unaccustomed sexual responses of her body had confused her. One dazed, trembling hand swept over her eyes and down her cheek.

When next she looked at him, he was gathering more dried grasses to make another tiny fire among the ashes of the night before. Painfully, she staggered to her feet, looking around her vaguely at the flat, dull alkali landscape. She shook her head, finding not a rock nor a tree, only low scraggly sage brush and cactus.

"If you're looking for a little privacy," her captor's voice came clear and mocking, "I won't look over to the right behind me."

Flushing angrily, she longed to scream defiance at him, but her personal needs were too strong. She must trust him. Her past had taught her great distrust of men and all their promises, but in this case she was helpless.

When she returned, he had rolled up the blankets and slung the saddles on the backs of the mare and the stallion. As she stood uncertainly before the campfire, he smiled thinly. "Hunker down there if you want and drink that coffee. We've got another long ride at a fast pace. It'll get you started. And keep your eyes on the fire. I'm going to take advantage of a patch of ground over on the left."

Hastily, she lowered herself to her knees. As she accepted the drink, she carefully avoided touching his hand in the process. As he strode away, she tried to sip the vile brew. Hot and bitter, it left her shuddering and gagging. Tears started from her eyes as she struggled to keep from vomiting.

She did not hear him return until he was suddenly squatted down beside her looking at her curiously.

Wiping her cheeks, she handed him back the coffee. "I

69

can't drink it," she shuddered. "I don't like coffee, anyway. If I drink any more, I'll be sick."

After a quick glance at her pale face, he nodded, taking the cup. Without comment, he lifted it to his lips and drained it down. Reaching for the canteen, he poured the cup half full of water and handed it to her.

Gratefully, she accepted it, sipping it slowly, holding each precious swallow in her mouth before allowing it to slip down her throat.

While she drank it, he drew a handkerchief from his pocket. Wadding it, he moistened it against the neck of the canteen. "Here." He thrust it into her hand, not meeting her surprised expression.

She finished her drink, then set the cup down. Closing her eyes, she wiped the dampened cloth across her forehead, her eyes, her cheeks, nose, lips, and chin. The breeze, not yet risen to its hellish temperature, fanned her face, refreshing her.

He crouched beside her packing the meager utensils away in his saddlebag. How strange he was! He mocked her and punished her ruthlessly, yet displayed this tiny contradictory quality in his nature. This quality of consideration for another person's needs was rare in any man and especially rare in the hard, rough men she was used to.

When Gillard turned back, she thrust the kerchief into his hand. In a low voice she murmured a single word of thanks, although she did not meet his eyes. He tipped the canteen again, then passed the cloth over his face and throat before retying it around his neck.

"Ready, señora?"

She rose. Her fingers trembled and her throat worked as he tied the rawhide around her wrists rather more loosely than the day before. The reata came next. Despite willing herself not to weep, the tears burned beneath the backs of her tight-closed eyelids. She dared not raise her head as the loop slapped down over her shoulders. Through blurred eyes she watched his fist come up under her chin to draw it tighter.

She felt rather than heard the intake of his breath. Then one arm went round her shoulders, the other slipped under her thighs. She lifted her leg and he set her in the saddle in one sweeping, graceful motion.

Almost as if he completed the motion, he spun away. Surreptitiously, he swiped his hand down the leg of his trousers, wiping away the tear that had dripped onto his skin. He swung into his saddle, gathered the lines, and dug his heels into the stallion. The big animal plunged away; the black mare followed, nose on the muscled rump.

Chapter Five

"Dismount, señora!"

Chris's sarcastic tone provoked no comment from his captive. They had ridden only a couple of hours that morning of the third day of her captivity. Her resistance was at its lowest ebb, her pain and discomfort were at their most excruciating. She could barely sit the saddle.

When he came to her side, she slid obediently into his waiting arms, but this time, she did not stand on her feet. Her knees buckled weakly, her head lolled back against his forearm.

"Hey!" Chris swept her up and carried her to the partial shade of a clump of sagebrush. Sternly, he stemmed the flood of pity he felt at the limpness of her body. She might well be faking; but even if she were not, he should be counting his blessings that she had not had the strength to oppose him in the past forty-eight hours. Nevertheless, he tipped the hat back from her forehead, pillowing her on it, to keep the back of her head from contact with the flinty soil.

She kept her eyes closed against the pain he caused as he straightened her limbs. Then she heard him move away. When she opened her eyes, he was rummaging through the saddlebags on the stallion. Curiously, she watched as he pulled out a tiny mirror that flashed in the sun and a tin of shoeblacking. Positioning the mirror against a small rock, he began to rub the stain liberally into his pale hair. Within minutes it was an ugly, greasy blackish-brown. Using his fingertips only, he delicately smeared his upper lip, cheeks, and chin as well. When he looked at her and grinned, she saw he had effectively covered up his pale golden beard.

"What . . . ?" she tried to croak between parched lips. Her throat was so dry that it hurt when she talked. She lapsed into silence.

He recapped the tin of shoe blacking and stowed the gear away in his saddlebags. Pulling forth another piece of rawhide, he came toward her, his face grim.

Helpless to protest, too proud to struggle against the inevitable, she lay back, passively staring at the burning blue sky through the blue-gray leaves while he bound her ankles. When he had pulled the thong tight, he held the canteen to her lips.

"Take a good swallow," he encouraged. "That's a girl. Take some more."

He poured it a little too fast, and some dribbled down her chin. With an apologetic murmur, he wiped it off. His hand left a dirty smear for which he murmured again. He lifted the canteen to her mouth again. "Drink it all," he advised. "Come on. That's a girl."

When the canteen was empty, he pushed her back flat. "Now just lie still." He untied the rawhide around her wrists, then rolled her over onto her face and retied her hands behind her. The reata around her neck he secured to the tiny trunk of the sagebrush. Satisfied, he leaned back on his heels. "Now you stay put right here in the shade." He mocked her. "I'll be back before too long with supplies and a bottle of tequila. Try to rest. If you're real good, I'll bring you a present."

Her eyes spoke her hatred, but she made no protest. The precious water he had poured down her throat was the most she had had since the beginning of this ordeal. She did not intend to waste its effects by arguing uselessly with him.

Swinging up on the gray mare, he looked down at her prone body. "Figure this is the least known of the horses. Still I'm taking a chance. But they'll be looking for a blond man and a dark woman, not one dark man." With a broad, ingratiating grin, he bared his teeth. *"Gracias, señora! Con su permiso, señora! Adios, señora!"*

Her face remained impassive until the ground ceased to vibrate under his horse's hooves. Then she tested the bonds. She could just manage to sit up. The tether around the sage allowed her that much leeway. But what was the point.

She slumped back down on her side, facing the direction he had gone. An insect buzzed past her ear. She felt the sweat trickle down her neck. Stubbornly, she clamped her lips together and closed her eyes.

When Chris dismounted, he found her asleep, her mouth firmly closed. The smear had dried across her chin where he had wiped his hand when he had given her the last of the water. Striving for impassivity, he surveyed his prisoner. Seeing her supine in the light of day was different from stretching out beside her in the dark or ordering her out of the blankets as the sun rose.

He shook his head. She was definitely the worse for wear.

74

Dark circles ringed her eyes. Her lips were cracked and peeling. Stray tendrils of dusty hair hung about her ears and cheeks. Feeling unaccountably guilty, he poured water from the new canteen onto a clean kerchief and bent to wash her face.

Estrella awoke with a start. Delicious coolness spread over her forehead and cheeks. She sighed, then arched her neck to follow the wet cloth as it washed her face.

"Feel good?" a familiar voice inquired gruffly.

Rather than answering, she nodded against his hand.

Chris removed the cloth. Opening her eyes, she watched him while he moistened it again, then draped it across her neck. "Just lie still." His hands fumbled behind her. Then her hands were free. He bent to untie her ankles.

She sat up and moved her stiffened shoulders gingerly.

"Wash your hands and get ready for a feast," he told her heartily as he untied the reata. "I got us some tortillas, a haunch of *cabrito*, and some tequila."

Estrella sniffed experimentally. "I can smell it." Her mouth began to water immediately.

"Then dig in," he invited, bringing a cloth sack from the saddle and sitting down beside her. Crossing his legs Indian style, he began to spread out the meal.

Between them they ate every bite of the thick corn tortillas and shared the leg of the young goat seasoned with *cominos* and chilis and broiled over a mesquite fire. Chris took several pulls off the jug, but Estrella firmly refused after the first taste.

At last replete, he leaned back expansively. Head bowed, she rubbed her wrists, flexing her fingers slowly like a cat sheathing and unsheathing its claws. Once she encircled the base of her thumb.

A buzzard circled high overhead, its great wings outspread to catch the updrafts from the burning desert. Chris sighed and yawned. "I could do with a nap," he confided. "I'm getting too old for this job."

She did not answer, but he saw her shoulders tense. She crossed her hands over each other to clasp her abused wrists.

"Mount up."

Her head flashed up. He met her eyes impassively. She climbed to her feet and walked beside him to the horses. As she stood beside the mare, he lifted her chin, looking deep into her eyes. Then he slapped the reata over her neck and lifted her into the saddle.

Perhaps he was a fool. Perhaps he would damn himself later, but he could not bring himself to wrap rawhide thongs over the scabs and weals that ringed her wrists. To inflict pain on another human being made him sick. Offering no explanation, he mounted Al and picked up the trail to the north.

Two days later they watered the horses in the Arroyo de la Zorra five miles from the Rio Grande. Frustrated and frightened, Estrella stared at the brownish water at her feet. The arroyo emptied into the Rio Grande. They would cross into Texas in less than an hour. The cleverness of her captor had allowed them to evade her brother day after day.

At first, she had scanned the horizon eagerly for dust clouds. But as the barren peaks and vastnesses of the Sierra Madre Oriental closed round them with no sign of Tomas, she had lapsed into despair.

And now the river lay ahead of them, curving deep into Mexico in what Texans called the Big Bend. By tomorrow, if she could not prevent the crossing, he would be leading her on this damned reata onto the Garner ranch.

Would Luke Garner shoot her on sight, or would he take

her into his town, Crossways, Texas, to the gallows he had built for her?

Across the shallow arroyo, a stretch of baked, cracked mud extended for more than half a mile until it blended into a few scraggly trees. Chris cursed roundly as the hooves of the horses turned up great black cakes in the bleached expanse. The trail was clear behind them. Hopefully, she kept turning in her saddle to look over her shoulder. Where was Tomas?

"If I were him, I'd wait at the border," Chris advised her, reading her mind as he caught her searching the horizon. "And I'm counting on us being too far north from Del Rio for his scouts to get word to him."

"But we'll have to cross at Del Rio," she insisted.

"No way. Señora. We'll cross up ahead here in just a few minutes. The Rio Grande will be way down on the west side of the Pecos. The horses can swim. You and I will just hang on." He looked pointedly at her filthy clothing. "The bath will do us both a heap of good."

Into the trees they rode—willowy mesquites with spiky thorns along their rough, snaky limbs. A chaparral cock skittered through the low grass. In the sky to their left, a half-dozen buzzards circled lazily. Their numbers testified to the presence of some animal dying or dead in the wooded area away from the trail.

Finally, Estrella could see the lazy flow of water through the thinning growth. The mesquites became cottonwoods with long straight trunks and heart-shaped leaves. Then the hooves of the horses sank into a sand bar forming the bank of Rio Bravo del Norte—the big river with two names. On the Texas side it was called the Rio Grande. They had reached the border.

A tug on the reata around Estrella's neck directed her to pull her mare to a halt. Chris had put her on Humareda that morning. Absently, Estrella leaned forward to pat the mare's proud neck. The black ear flicked backward in acknowledgment.

Humareda's hide was dusty and sweat-streaked, pathetically different from the polished beauty it had displayed only a few days before. She was thinner too, not gaunt, but run hard. The lack of water had dried the smoothness from her shape, leaving only rippling muscles and spring-steel bone.

As Gillard pulled along side Estrella, his gray eyes scanned the bank intently. While he searched, he reeled in the reata around her neck. "Dismount," he ordered at last. When she slipped from the saddle, he was waiting for her. Ruthlessly, he bound her hands behind her with reata.

"I thought we had done this," she muttered sarcastically.

"Shut up." He turned her to face him. From his shirt pocket, he pulled a white handkerchief she had not seem him use before. "I'm going on a little scouting expedition," he informed her, his eyes not meeting hers. "Can't have you hollering or making a big lot of noise." Before she could draw a breath, he stuffed the gag between her jaws.

He pushed her down gently behind the nearest cottonwood and circled the trunk twice with the reata, passing it above her breasts and about her waist. Tying a quick slip knot at the back, he reached around to pat her on the shoulder. "I won't be long now," he promised with false cheer.

Her black eyes above the white handkerchief were bright with anger as they followed his disappearing figure through the brush. Frantically, she began to struggle, twisting her hands against the tight rawhide and pushing at the constricting cloth with her tongue. If he had seen fit to gag her, he must believe that Tomas might be near.

For less than five minutes she fought before she slumped

back against the tree. Her futile efforts had not only exhausted her but, worse, left her with a feeling of despair. The gag drew the saliva from her mouth. She had to admit that a gag was a wretchedly unpleasant thing. Matthew had never gagged her, preferring to hear her pleas for mercy.

Tears started in her eyes. Life was not fair to a woman. Her strength was so slight that any man, whoever he might be, however ignorant, however bestial, could tie her like an animal. She thought of Matthew—and Luke Garner—and Christopher Stewart Gillard. How she hated them!

A rustle behind her made her stiffen and crane her neck. Her captor crouched at her shoulder. Moving silently, he had made a circuit of the area and returned. "All clear," he muttered as he jerked the slip knot at the base of the tree. "We'll make the crossing now. I'd rather make it at night, but your brother might be tearing hell bent for this spot right now. Those tracks back there as we crossed the flat were mighty easy to read."

He freed her hands and lifted her into the saddle as she drew the sodden handkerchief from her mouth. Suddenly, his hands froze on her body. Looking at him quickly, she realized he was paying no attention to her at all. His eyes were darting back and forth along the bank.

Swift as a cat she struck. Both hands, clasped together in one large fist, slammed down with all her strength on top of his head. In almost the same movement, she kicked him viciously. His breath whooshed out as the toe of her boot caught him just below the ribs on his left side. As he sprawled backward, crashing into the side of the Alter-Real, she yanked the reata and Humareda's reins from his slackening grasp.

Despite the dryness almost tearing the lining from her throat, she gave an inarticulate shout. At the sound the mare sprang forward from a standing start. Out into the burning sunlight she dashed. Shod hooves plowed into the yellow sand of the bank. A grove of low huisache blocked the way. Ruthlessly, she heeled her mount into the cruel thorns. The mare whickered, reared, then jumped sideways. Throwing a glance over her shoulder, Estrella saw Gillard breaking from the trees behind her in hot pursuit.

A dry wash opened on her left. Recklessly, she headed the black mare into it, praying that it would open. The going was rough, the eroded sides creating natural barricades that forced Humareda to turn and twist. The horse stumbled more than once.

A stone and a shower of gravel struck her shoulder. Gillard rode above her!

Damn! Instead of following her, he had climbed the bank and ridden along the flat, driving his stallion ruthlessly through the spiny thickets. She had made a mistake. Unless the wash rose gently, she was trapped like a steer in a chute.

"Pull up!" he yelled. "You can't get away!"

He was right. Her breath caught in her throat. The wash ended in a crumbling bank, some four or five feet high, too steep and soft for her horse to mount without floundering. Quivering with frustration, she reined the mare to a halt. Her eyes rose defiantly to his face. Instantly, she read alarm in it, and her hope returned.

From the trees on the other side of the river galloped horsemen. Tomas led his *vaqueros* into the shallows half a mile upstream.

Ignoring the shards of pain in her ribs, she managed an awkward stand on her saddle bow. From its height she flung herself at the crumbling bank opposite her captor. She struck the side of the bank at the waist. The pain in her ribs made the world darken for a minute, but she held on grimly and managed to throw one leg over the edge. Scrambling upright, she staggered a couple of steps, then righted herself. Drawing a breath as deep as she dared, she began to run back along the top of the wash to the river.

Whirling the Alter-Real, Chris galloped it back along the flat a couple of dozen yards. He turned it again, then leaned forward in the saddle. The stallion sprang forward, its powerful haunches tearing up the sod. At the wash, it rose in the air in response to the commands of hands and heels. Effortlessly, the compact body cleared the space to land on the opposite side without breaking stride.

"Tomas!" she tried to scream. Oh, God! Her voice was a dry croak. He could not possibly hear it. As she stumbled on, her sides on fire, she waved her hand frantically. The thickets of thorns hid them from each other for a space.

The *vaqueros* were nearing the middle of the river, their mounts swimming, the riders clinging to their backs.

The stallion thundered down upon her. With a guttural cry, she dodged. Her effort was wasted. Gillard launched himself from the saddle. His hard hands hooked around her shoulder, grabbing her from behind, bulldogging her. Her knees buckled beneath his weight and she sprawled on the ground.

Straddling his hips, even as she hit, he caught up the reata, still trailing from her neck. At the same time he reached for the Colt strapped to his hip. Then his hard hand jerked her to her feet.

Stunned, in agony with every breath she drew, Estrella submitted tamely as he threw a half-hitch around her wrists. Over his shoulder, her eyes searched feverishly for some sign of her brother. She swallowed violently. Her tongue flicked across her cracked lips. "Tomas! Help!" A dry croak was all she managed.

Instantly her captor closed one hand over her throat.

"One word more and I knock you senseless," he warned.

She shook her head, pulling back against his hand. Her brother was only seconds away. Frantic to escape, she kicked the Texan's shin and tried to cry out again.

He cursed in pain. Still keeping his hand on her throat, he holstered his gun and dragged a soiled bandanna from his hip pocket. This he stuffed between her jaws. In his haste he fumbled. "Goddamn!"

Her teeth snapped to against his knuckle.

The skin broke, but he managed to stuff the handkerchief in anyway, forcing her jaws apart. Then, throwing one arm around her shoulder, Chris caught up the stallion's reins with his bloody hand. Half carrying, half pushing, he hustled her back to the edge of the wash.

The mare stood patiently, head down. Chris leaned far over to grasp the cheek strap on the bridle. In another minute he had guided the animal to a less precipitous slope and helped it up to the flat.

From the direction of the river he could hear the galloping of hooves. "Goddamn!" he breathed. "Oh, damn!" He caught her by her hip and shoulder and tossed her ungently into the saddle.

In an effort to delay him, she tried to go off the saddle on the other side, but his grip on her thigh kept her in place. He jerked the reata roughly, bringing her face down only inches from his. "If you get off that horse, you can damn well run along behind," he snarled.

He threw another couple of turns of the reata around the horn before vaulting into the saddle of the stallion. Throwing a quick glance over his shoulder, he spurred the mount into the thickest part of the *brasado*.

In a mesquite thicket at the box of a tiny canyon less than

a mile downstream, Estrella crouched helpless, her arms and feet tightly bound, her mouth gagged. Gillard's hard body pressed her painfully against him, stilling any movement as she watched her brother ride by.

All around them, indeed on the overhanging ledge they crouched under, *vaqueros* searched. At the sound of the hoofbeats over their heads, Gillard's eyes rolled upward. Carefully, he pulled the hammer back on the Colt, prepared to use it should the Mexican look over the edge.

Beneath him, Estrella went mad. She could not feel the ropes cutting into her wrists. Tomas was so close. Just one sound. Just one! Blinded by tears and sweat, she squirmed violently. The horses' hooves spurned gravel and dust off the overhang. Particles settled on their upturned faces.

She bucked her body upward, but she could not dislodge his weight. It settled more firmly on top of her, pressing her face against his chest. His arm had passed under her thighs, lifting them upward and compressing them against her chest so he forced her into a tight ball. Her ribs protested. She could not breathe. His sweaty shirt blocked her nostrils. Frustration and anger gave way to panic. Then it too dissolved as she lost consciousness.

A piercing call sent the *vaquero* galloping away from the ledge. Tomas and his men had found the spare mounts. The hunt gravitated in that direction.

Gillard relaxed. Drawing a deep breath, he lifted himself slightly from the unconscious woman. Solemnly, he straightened her limbs and body. Inadvertently, she had thwarted her own rescue. Had she not broken through the trees, pursued by him, her brother would have waited until they were out in the river on the other side, then closed in, capturing them efficiently and without fuss. The irony of their escape was not lost on him. He shook his head. Tipping his hat back, he hunkered down beside her to wait out the long, hot afternoon.

"We're going to have to cross at night," he told her when she lay her back, staring up at him with weary eyes. "Damned cold and uncomfortable. Could be dangerous too, for a woman with her hands tied."

Her eyes did not change when he caught her elbow and hauled her to her feet. He heaved her into the saddle again, then tied her hands to the horn.

A bank of clouds slid across the pale half moon. Mounting his own horse, Gillard urged the mounts from the thicket into the shallows of the Rio Grande. With the water black as India ink, their own shapes were undistinguishable.

Gagged, her hands numb from the rawhide, her horse on a tight lead, Estrella made no move except as Chris willed it. As the cold waters touched her legs, she shivered, pressing her elbows in against her sides.

"Going to be cold," he agreed in a tiny whisper. He rode so close beside her that he felt her motion.

Upward the water crept. The mare began to swim. Estrella slipped from the saddle, her legs trailing out behind her. Then her head submerged because she could not use her hands to keep her body afloat. Panicky, she was dragged along, her breath burning into her lungs, the pressure of the water in her nostrils, sending shooting pains into her head. Awkwardly, in her heavy black boots, she kicked. The movement momentarily cleared her head above the water but did not give her sufficient time to clear her nostrils. Even as she drew breath, she was dragged under again. This time her nose filled with water.

He'll never get me back to Texas, was her last conscious thought.

With a curse, Gillard flung himself from his own saddle. He had thought himself so clever until he had looked back to discover she had gone under. Now, in the middle of the Rio Grande, he had no time and no way to release her hands and lift her out.

When he lifted Estrella's head and shoulders above the surface, the mare floundered under their combined weight. Both horse and swimmers sank beneath the surface.

Forced to release his hold on his bound captive, Gillard swam strongly to the mare's head. His heart almost bursting with the effort, he pulled on the bridle, dragging the beast's head out of the water.

The cloud bank slid past the face of the moon, revealing the two of them struggling alone in a pool of churning white water. Estrella's head remained submerged. The stallion swam strongly on several lengths ahead. Even as Gillard sobbed for breath, the hooves of the Alter-Real touched bottom.

Another kick and then another. The mare regained her balance. How much longer, he thought. Frantically, he glanced over his shoulder. Only a few more yards should do it. The stallion was already breasting the waters. The moon streamed its light down on the scene. An agonized glance at the water behind the mare disclosed nothing. Estrella's head was still beneath the surface.

Cold horror gripped his vitals. He had tied a helpless woman to the saddle. Now she was drowning in the murky waters of the Rio Grande. Grinding his teeth in frustration, he kicked fiercely, jerking the mare's head toward the shore. A great groan of relief escaped him when he realized the horse was no longer swimming.

Frantically, he released the bridle and pulled himself back along Humareda's neck. His fingers found the icy ones limply curled around the horn. His hands slid down her arms.

"Estrella," he gasped. "Señora. Star."

Finding his footing, he threw his arm around her waist, lifting her against his chest. She drooped sideways like a dead thing.

"Please," he whispered in her ear. "Please be alive." Anxious to be out of the water, the mare plunged onward toward the shore. Chris stumbled beside the saddle, clutching his captive's body to him. Her feet were dragging now. He scooped her up. Her ivory face turned up to the winking moon. "Star. Star. Star."

Hock-deep in the shallows, Humareda halted at last, sides heaving.

Shuddering with cold and exhaustion, Chris dragged his knife from its sheath. The rawhide was tough. In the dark he worked with agonizing slowness as blood pounded in his ears and his conscience scourged him.

With a final upward slash of the knife, the rawhide parted. Quickly, Chris ducked beneath the girl's limp body, allowing it to fall forward over his shoulder. Head lolling behind his back, arms dangling, she slumped, a dead weight, as he staggered out of the water.

His chest heaved with effort as he slid and struggled at the bank. His feet had hard going finding holds in the slippery clay. Her body rolled heavily on his shoulder, throwing him off balance. Gasping and grunting, he clawed with his free hand high on the bank.

His lungs were on fire when he at last managed to crawl over the top. On his knees, he gently lowered her body to the ground. She was so cold. So still. Merciful God! Please! Praying to all the gods in the universe, he tugged the gag from her mouth.

She coughed.

"Star!" He was surprised at the rush of joyous relief he

felt at the tiny, pathetic sound.

Gasping feebly, her lungs burning, Estrella rolled her head to one side. With one elbow she levered herself onto her side, weakly sobbing as water dripped off her chin and the tip of her nose.

"Señora. Thank God." Chris held her shoulders as spasm after spasm racked her. "Star. I'm sorry. I'm sorry. God, I'm sorry," he babbled. "Believe me, señora. Lord, help me, when you went under . . ." He gasped his protestations and apologies in her ear in a voice of agony.

When she could draw breath into her lungs and think, she nodded weakly. "All right . . ." Her voice was barely a breath. "I'm all right." She shuddered as the breeze rattled the ebony beans. "Cold," she sighed. "Cold . . ."

Wiping the silver-blond mane from his eyes in a distracted motion, he looked around hopelessly. The don's *vaqueros* would be watching from across the river. He dared not build a fire. The soft breeze, so pleasant under ordinary circumstances, plastered his shirt against his chest adding to his discomfort.

Nauseated, Estrella began to vomit, her body twisting and shuddering. Small, gasping cries of pain escaped her. The broken edges of her ribs ground together as one part of her body sought relief at the expense of another.

Pneumonia! He stared down at the dark shape of her body. His hands on her shoulders felt the shivering become more violent. She would have lung fever by morning if he did not act quickly.

The pale clay bank disappeared at the foot of a darker line of trees and brush. Scooping her up in his arms, ignoring her agonized whimper, he carried her into it. Once inside, he realized it was disappointingly thin, but hopefully sufficient to his needs.

He laid her on her side where she instantly curled herself

into a shivering ball, her hands thrust between her thighs.

"I'm going to leave you here for just a minute, Star," he whispered, patting her hip. "Don't be frightened. You'll soon be all right."

The mare had climbed out of the bank downstream and stood with reins dragging, her head resting against the stallion's muscled shoulder. Thanking God for the good fortune that had brought the two horses together, Chris led them deeper into the thicket until the water was nowhere visible through the brush. Loosening their girths and taking the bits out of their mouths, he tied them separately to mesquites. The ground beneath his feet rustled, testifying to the presence of dried grasses. Perhaps they could graze in the early dawn.

That done, he headed back to his captive. He might never have found her had the sound of her agonized breathing, punctuated at intervals by tiny coughs and moans, not drawn him to her side.

"Señora," he whispered as he stretched out beside her, "body heat's all we've got, so I'm going to get a lot closer to you than any man's been in a long, long time."

Chapter Six

Chris pulled the tail of the wet cotton shirt from his waistband. The cool breeze set him to shivering even as it dried his skin. A sense of urgency possessed him. He must act quickly, or his prisoner would have pneumonia.

"Quit fighting me," he advised as Estrella's trembling fingers tried to push his hands away. When her puny efforts disintegrated into a moan of protest, he opened her garments efficiently, peeling back the sodden blouse and the camisole beneath it. His own chambray shirt, used as a bandage to support her ribs, was a sodden roll around her waist. He unwrapped it and tossed it over the limb of the tree.

In her weakness and state of near collapse, Estrella could barely think coherently, much less offer a concentrated resistance. Her mind swung back again to the dark, cold waters of the Rio Grande closing over her head, her hands bound to the saddle, her boots like leaden weights dragging her down. Her head rolled to the side; she coughed weakly.

Her icy nipples, hard as diamonds, stabbed Chris's

chest as he drew her against him, gently pressing their chilled flesh together from naval to shoulder.

"Put your hands on my ribs underneath my shirt," he whispered, as her palms and then her fingernails pushed against the muscles of his shoulders. "God, woman. You take a lot of saving."

The chattering of her teeth made her answer difficult to understand. "I d-don't want to be saved. At least, not by you."

He sighed. His big warm hands slipped inside her blouse under her arms, sliding along her chilled naked skin to meet at her spine. "Ssh." His breath warmed her neck below her earlobe. "Don't fight me. You'll just wear yourself out all the more. Go along with this."

She did not try to answer but caught her breath against the agony as she tried unsuccessfully to twist out of his arms.

"Here now!" he snapped. "Quit that. You'll just hurt yourself." He splayed his fingers over her shoulder blades and began to circle rhythmically. At the same time, he rolled over onto his back and lifted her half on top of him. "Put your head down on my chest if you'd like to," he advised matter-of-factly. "No sense lying there like a turtle with his head rearing up in the air. You'll get a crick in your neck."

After one last wriggle, which sent a shaft of white-hot pain through her side, Estrella dropped her head on his broad chest. Despairing, she lay with her upper body draped across his chest, panting lightly, trying not to add to her pain.

Gradually, she became aware of pleasant sensations. His hands continued to massage her. Curling hair tickled her cheek and lips. His heart beat in her ear with a strong soothing rhythm. His warm male smell filled her nostrils.

As the heat of his body began driving the chill from her own, she felt her muscles loosen. She must have drifted off to sleep for a moment, then jerked awake as her muscles twitched violently.

"Easy there." His voice rumbled suddenly out of his chest.

"Sorry," she murmured, not knowing why she should be. She moved her lower limbs, trying to find a comfortable position for them. Half-asleep, eyes closed, she drew her leg up over the tops of his thighs. Her eyes flashed open as she realized the inside of her thigh had slid up over his belly. Wide awake, too late, she could only make a tiny strangled sound, as his hands slid intimately inside the waistband of her divided skirt. Her buttocks tensed at the intrusion.

"Easy," his voice rumbled again. His fingers splayed over her bottom, clenching, relaxing, kneading firmly. "Nice. Very nice. So smooth."

Ice threaded through her veins. Ice not caused by the river and the cool night, but by fear. A shudder began at the base of her spine. Surely, he did not think she invited him. Half-asleep, uncomfortable, she had moved her leg innocently.

Then his fingertips cupped under her naked curves and shifted her upward. His nails scored her flesh lightly in the crease at the top of her thighs.

The pain was small, but her response was instantaneous. She had learned with Matthew that the more quickly she responded, the less she suffered. Cold as ice, calculating her effect, she twisted in Gillard's arms. The movement rubbed her naked breasts against his chest, rasping their nipples through the curling hair. Instantly, his hands clamped her more tightly; his breath caught in his teeth.

Tears of despair started in her eyes, engendered by

disgust at what lay ahead and shame at her own weakness. With teeth clenched to endure the coming ordeal, she cursed herself silently for lying in the brush waiting for him to find her. Instead, she should have marshalled her forces and tried to slip away.

Tomas searched for her across the river. She should have staggered or crawled to its edge and screamed. If her captor had come for her, she should have thrown herself into the murky waters rather than submit to this degradation one more time.

Mentally she flogged herself for the chance she had missed. Her mother would have missed no such chance. Missed chances never came back. Now the pain would be great or less than what she had known. She did not consider the possibility that he would not hurt her.

The muscular chest beneath her ear rose mightily as he drew in a deep, deep breath. The long fingers splayed as they slipped upward and then his hands were at her waistband where they found the buttons at the back.

"No." The word was no more than a sigh, uttered fearfully, involuntarily. Quickly she bit her tongue and ducked her head.

The flat palm or the clenched fist did not strike her. But neither did he stop. With the same ruthless efficiency that characterized all his movements, her skirt was unbuttoned. His agile fingers pushed aside her clothing, leaving her body naked from breasts to midthigh. Then his hands continued their warming, rhythmic massage. Up and over and down and around. Up, over, down, around.

Far from soothing her, the motions only increased her terror. Teeth sinking into her bottom lip, she held herself rigid. Her muscles trembled as though she shivered, despite the warmth of his hands and body.

At last one big hand cupped her buttock, while the

other tipped her chin up. "You're still cold," he murmured apologetically, his voice deep and slightly hoarse. "I don't dare touch you any harder with those ribs."

His words were a ray of hope. She coughed shallowly and tried to relax. "I'll be all right. Just let go of me."

The hand on her buttock tightened. Instantly, she shut her lips, but a kind of weary, involuntary languor was stealing over her. She was becoming too tired to be afraid. Dead tired, she supposed. His rough palms returned to their massaging. Feeling hypnotized by the rhythm of his heart and his hands and by the rhythmic rise and fall of his chest, she closed her eyes. Her limbs loosened.

As her muscles went soft, she became aware of him hardening, pressing upward into her belly. Fearfully, she stiffened again. Here it comes. Oh, God . . .

The hand at her chin slipped down to caress her breast, the hand on her buttock cupped it and squeezed. "I want you," he whispered. "Want you badly. Lord, woman, your skin is like satin covering your shape."

Her protest caught in her throat. Since he was already excited, perhaps he would not need to beat her to arouse himself. Perhaps. Just perhaps . . .

The hand at her breast began to play with the nipple. Fearfully she waited for him to pinch and twist it. She parted her lips to give a cry of pain. Not too loud, she cautioned herself.

But the pain did not come. Instead his hands were gentle, his fingers warm and firm. She felt his lips on her forehead. "What do you want?" he asked.

She gave a shudder but managed to turn it into a shrug.

"Tell me," he insisted. His hands moved to circle her waist. His middle fingers touched at her spine at the same time his thumbs almost met over her naval. "So slender," he breathed as he kissed the pulse at her temple.

So frail, she thought. So helpless. So damnably helpless. A shaft of white-hot anger seared through her. "Don't!" she gasped, her iron control breaking.

He pulled his hands away from her body, holding them out beside his shoulders. "Hey, I won't hurt you," he promised. Carefully, he resumed his caresses. His right hand slipped up to cup her breast again, his thumb slowly circling her nipple. "Do you like this?"

She dared not answer. If she said she did not, he might continue to do it, becoming ever rougher until she was screaming in pain. If she said she did, he might find some other part of her body to torment. She bit her lip, firmly resolved not to speak again.

His lips slid down from her temple to her cheek, nibbling gently. "Do you like this?" he whispered. "Or this?" His tongue caressed the shape of her ear, then he pursed his lips and blew his hot breath into it.

Despite her determination to remain still, she squirmed. Her movement dragged her soft breasts through the hair on his chest.

He chuckled softly. "At last I found something you like." He cupped the back of her head with one hand and steadied her to receive his caress again.

But this time she was ready for him. He would not take her unawares. She held herself still and stiff.

"What's going on, lady?" he muttered gruffly, nipping her earlobe between his teeth.

Suddenly she knew. How could she have forgotten? Panic welled in her to the extent that she pushed her hands against his shoulders. He was experimenting with her. In just such a manner had Matthew experimented on their wedding night and after.

Strictly reared as a befitted the daughter of a grandee, she had gone to her marriage bed a pure virgin, completely innocent of sensuality. What followed had been a nightmare of torment, both physical and mental.

In despair, she tried to push herself away by pressing her palms into the heavily muscled shoulders. Her struggles jiggled her breasts and excited him more.

For the moment Chris forgot her battered, exhausted state as he felt the warm feminine body rubbing against his chest and belly. "My God!" His gasp was laced with raw passion. His left hand joined his right, grasping her other breast and caressing it with eager roughness. His lips and teeth caressed and nipped at her ear. She cried out, but his mouth found hers, his tongue thrusting hotly.

For longer than he cared to remember, he had remained celibate. Now he burned. His senses swam in the heat he himself had generated. She was warm, she was moving enchantingly, her breasts, small and very firm, almost like a young girl's, were driving him insane.

He drew up his knee to lever her body over onto her back and take her beneath him. Then he remembered. Her ribs would not take his weight. "Sit up!" he commanded, his voice hoarse with excitement.

She hesitated, his words not penetrating the fog of fear. "My God, woman, sit up!" His strong hands on her waist lifted her to her knees. Before she knew what was happening, she was straddling him, swaying groggily in the night breeze that no longer felt the least bit cold to her body.

Gillard's hands left her waist to unbutton the front of his trousers, feeling his swollen staff. His knuckles grazed the insides of her thighs, brushed against the soft hair and ultrasensitive skin at her apex. She shuddered.

He felt the vibration. "Soon," he whispered, completely misinterpreting her involuntary response. "Wait just a second. . . ." He lifted his hips and pushed his trousers

95

down. "Now . . ."

She shook her head, but in the dark he could not see. She felt his hands close hotly over her waist, lifting her again, then bringing her down. His staff impaled her. She twisted to get away, but her thighs trembled with weakness.

His hands tightened inexorably, digging into the soft flesh at her waist.

She moaned. The demand of his hands warned her. Any further protest would be futile and dangerous. He had grasped her body to wring his pleasure from her. She was no stranger to a man's demands.

"Relax," he whispered, his big hands clasping her thighs. His voice came in a gasp as he arched his hips upward to push against her. "I won't hurt you," he promised. "You can believe me. I won't hurt your poor ribs."

He was a liar, she knew. All men were liars. They promised so much; but when their lust blotted out their humanity, they became like the stallion on the mare, demanding the female submission with teeth and hooves and superior weight. Tears of fear filled her eyes as he lanced up into her.

"Come on, Star," he urged. "Move to please yourself, lady. That's my girl." His hands lifted her, demanding that she ride him, teaching her the rhythm through his grip on her thighs.

She gritted her teeth in frustration, knowing what he wanted of her, embarrassed by the oddness of the position.

Restraining himself with an effort, he patted her buttock. "Move, Star. Please, lady. Oh, God . . ."

The pat frightened her inordinately. The next time it would be a slap. Shivering, tears trickling down her cheeks in the darkness, she allowed him to guide her. His hands on the tops of her thighs pushed her upward, then pulled her down.

"That's right," he encouraged through set teeth. "Ah, yes . . ."

Perspiration mixed with the tears that gleamed on her face beneath the brazen moon. Her efforts were tiring her, but a peculiar warmth was curling in her stomach. The hard staff within her grew even harder and bigger. She would not be able to bear it a moment longer, but somehow she did.

His hands squeezed her buttocks again. The pressure lifted her upward as she gasped and moaned. Terrified of what his hands might do to her if she failed to please him, she imitated the responses of passion as she had learned to do with Matthew. Her heart pounded with the exertion. At least he was not inflicting pain on her body. Instead, his warm hands guided her. They moved down her thighs, warming, encouraging. "That's it," he breathed. "Oh, Star. That's right."

She rose, then sank down, pushing her body forcefully against him.

Beneath her, Chris Gillard groaned, then cried out, thrusting upward with the full strength of his thighs and back, lifting her clear of the ground. She cried out in alarm. The whiplash of his motion jarred her ribs.

"Star! Oh, Star . . ."

He was finished. She had done her job and he had not beaten her. She slumped in relief, her body bathed in perspiration. One hand clasped her side. Tipping her face up to the moon, she dropped her other hand palm down on her tired thighs.

The clouds had slipped away toward the horizon, leaving the moon naked to reflect its light. Curiously, she chanced a glance at the man who lay on his back beneath her.

He was beautiful, she noted with impassivity. His chest with its mat of pale gold hair was beautiful. Each curling hair glistened. The fine-textured skin stretched flawlessly across the sculptured bones.

His eyes were half-closed; his jaw, relaxed; his nostrils, flared as he drew more air into his lungs. At these times Matthew would drift off to sleep and she could creep away. Dimly, she realized she did not have the strength to creep away. Instead, she slumped to the side, dragging her clothing more decently around her. When she could do no more without disturbing her captor, she stretched out her cramped limbs, and fell instantly asleep.

The cold dew refreshed the occupants of the thicket at the same time as white swathes of fog drifted up from the river. A sleepy mockingbird trilled softly in the mesquite. The long grass rustled. A jet-eyed armadillo thrust its snout into the little space beneath the tree. Unafraid, it whuffled industriously at the ground before withdrawing. The mockingbird changed its call to a raucous cawing sound.

Chris Gillard stirred, groaned, tightened his arms around the soft form he held against his chest. He had slept too long. Alarmed, he listened breathlessly for sounds of their pursuers. Only the normal sounds of a Texas morning in the brush country reached his ears.

Estrella lay deep in sleep against him, her breathing even, her muscles relaxed.

He closed his eyes, savoring her warmth and shape, then opened them again. The sky was dark gray overhead, the trees clearly silhouetted against it.

Regretfully he placed a hand on her shoulder. She

opened her eyes and moaned softly. Her clothes and hair were still vaguely damp, but she was not uncomfortable. She lifted a hand to her forehead.

"Time to be moving." The sound of his voice brought back all the horrible memories. She jerked in his arms as her muscles spasmed.

"Easy," he advised. "You can take a minute."

"No." She sat up, bracing herself against him with a straight arm and fumbling for her clothing as the chill morning air hit her bare chest. After he had taken her, she had replaced her skirt but had left her upper body bare to press against his chest for warmth. She had draped her shirt over her shoulders. Now she wearily began to push her arms through the sleeves.

The first rays of morning light pinked the horizon. One penetrated the thicket shedding its soft light on Estrella's bare chest.

Chris had rolled over on his side. In the act of fumbling for his own clothing he froze to look at her. By the softness of morning light her breasts were palest cream with pert dark rose nipples.

She caught his expression and hastily dragged her blouse across her chest.

Chris shrugged. "Seems a shame to cover them up," he remarked with a sardonic flash of white teeth. "But I guess we got to head out."

Intense bitterness swept over her, rising in her throat with a sensation akin to strangulation. She felt used. She had been used. Every time a man made love to a woman, he used her. She was recreation, distraction, a receptacle for lust. If she were to confront him with her anger, he would remind her he had saved her life. She should forget that his cruelty had imperiled it in the first place. He then had the right to use her body.

99

He was a bounty hunter. He was being paid to take her to Luke Garner. If he made free with her body, who was to stop him or call him to account later? Certainly not the man who had hired him. She bowed her head to conceal the tears that rose in her eyes.

With her face hidden she managed to shove her useless thoughts to the background, willing her fingers to button her blouse. The wreck of her clothing offered her no consolation. Her divided skirt and boots were caked with mud. The blouse was ripped at both armholes in back and was a dirty reddish-brown from its bath in the Rio Grande. Her hat was crushed, its brim limp and drooping from its soaking.

Furthermore, she was filthy beyond belief. Her hair had come down from its accustomed knot and trailed in a witch's snarl down her back. A tiny hysterical giggle escaped her. Probably, if her captor could have seen her in the light of day, he would not have wanted her.

"What's funny?"

She jumped. Quickly she raised her head to face him defiantly. "Nothing."

For the first time since waking, he stared at her face. The dirt was furrowed by tracks of tears. He stirred uneasily. Had she enjoyed what had happened last night? Hell, she was not a virgin, but a woman, a widow—wedded and bedded. According to her father-in-law, she had run his son ragged with her sexual teasing and denying.

He tried to remember. The feel of her breasts, her moans and gasps as he had caressed her had encouraged him. If she had been cold and resistant, he would not have bothered her. He never forced women. He had never needed to. He had felt her shivers as he had played with her breasts. She had mounted him so easily. Her strong thighs had lifted and lowered her body in such an erotic dance that he had been almost out of his mind with desire. Surely she had been as excited as he.

He waited while she relieved herself behind a clump of cactus. When she returned, he put a hand around her upper arm. "Let's go."

Without demur she allowed him to lead her to the horses. Before he lifted her into the saddle, he turned her to face him. Both hands curved around her shoulders; he stooped to stare directly into her face. "Now, I want you to listen, señora, and you'd better believe what I say. We're going to get on these horses and slip away to the west. Your brother is going to expect us to ride due north to get to Garner's ranch at Crossways. We're going to circle around and *come in* from the north. It'll mean another couple of days of riding, but we'll get there. The only thing we've got to do is slip away from this river."

She listened sullenly, her eyes focused on a spot somewhere to the right of his ear. Her mouth was compressed in a tight, thin line.

"There's one more thing." He brandished an index finger under her nose. "Yesterday you almost got me and then yourself killed by riding out like you did. You keep thinking you can get away from me. But you can't! You need to come to believe that. You can't get away from me!" He enunciated each word with particular emphasis. His gunmetal eyes scanned her face. "I'm being paid ten thousand dollars for you. That's enough to buy the ranch that I want and get my life in order. *Sabe?*"

Still she did not reply.

He went on after a moment. "You have to understand that I don't give a damn about anything except getting you and me back alive. So if anyone, like your brother, for example, gets in my way . . ." he paused for effect,

". . . I'll gun him down."

She paled. Her black eyes met his now. Incredulity in her face, she tried to read his character. "But Tomas has nothing to do with this," she protested.

"His bullet will stop me just as quick as any other's."

"Tomas is the Grandee Montejo."

"Then you don't want him dead." Chris backed off, dropping his hands to his sides.

Her face was a macabre mask, filthy dirty, surrounded by hair like a witch's snarl, but within the trails left by tears the skin was startlingly white. The threat to her brother's life had done the trick.

From between her lips came the foulest names she could think of to call him, names his somewhat limited Spanish did not include.

He grinned and eased back even another step. "Naughty, naughty, señora. Now you're sounding like what I've been led to believe. I was beginning to feel just a little bit sorry for you, like I'd sort of ridden you too hard."

"Don't feel sorry for me," she rasped. Her voice had no tone to it after a night in the cold. "And don't turn your back on me."

Her words wiped the smile off his face. "Oh, don't worry. I wouldn't do that. I like living. Just want you to not make a lot of noise and lead your brother to me. If you do, and he comes riding in at the head of his vaqueros, just remember who I'm going to be aiming my first shot at."

She clenched her fists at her side. Her chest heaved as she drew in her breath with an obvious effort.

He waited no longer. Efficiently, he went about bridling the animals, tightening their cinches, checking the contents of the saddlebags. With a grimace he saw that all the food supplies were ruined. "We're going to get kind of hungry," he remarked over his shoulder.

When all was at last in readiness, he came up beside her. "Mount up," he commanded. As he had done each time, he put one arm around her shoulder and the other beneath her thigh, lifting her easily into the saddle. "I'm not going to tie your hands," he told her. "If you see your brother coming, you'll need both hands to ride away from him as fast as you can. Otherwise, he gets a bullet through the body."

They made ten miles riding almost due west parallel to the river, then turned north. As they watered their horses, Chris stared around him. His eyes never left off scanning the horizon.

Beside him, Estrella shifted wearily in the saddle. "I can tell you one thing," she volunteered, her voice barely above a whisper. "I can't ride much farther without food.

He raised one eyebrow. "So the woman's human after all?"

She shook her head. "What gave you the idea that I wasn't?"

He did not answer that. "When we get a few miles farther on, I'll start looking for some game. There're deer in the brush, and javelina, too. Plenty of meat. Just didn't want to run the risk of a shot until we got way far away."

As if on cue, a small pack of javelina, the wild pigs of the Texas badlands, pushed their way out into the open on the other side of the river. The wind was at their backs, and the little nearsighted eyes could not distinguish the riders.

"Would it be too much to shoot one now?" Estrella asked sarcastically. "Surely a dozen miles is far enough."

"Can't tell about that," he grimaced as he turned the

103

stallion and trotted him upriver. "Might be right on our trail. Besides, those javelina are on the other side of river. No sense in risking another crossing if we don't have to. Don't you agree?"

She shuddered at the thought.

Just at evening, he shot a tiny white-tail deer. As he gutted it and skinned it, she built a fire and boiled water for coffee. The grounds were the worse for their soaking in the river, but the brew was better than nothing.

Chris stripped the tenderloins from the animal and passed them to her to roast on stakes. While they roasted, he cut off a haunch, ran a spit through it, and set it between forked sticks.

With a weary sigh, he lowered himself beside her. She passed him one of the tenderloins. When he bit into it, he was surprised to find it cooked perfectly and flavored by the mesquite smoke. "You're really surprising for a grandee's daughter," he told her between bites.

She did not pretend not to know what he meant. "My father wasn't always a grandee. As a matter of fact, he didn't become one until he was thirty years old. By that time he had learned many things about taking care of himself. My brother and I learned them all."

He waited, but she supplied no more information than that. He chewed reflectively on his meat. She had eaten hers very fast, and now she sat beside him, running her fingers through her hair trying to comb the snarls out of it. From time to time, she made a muffled noise as the tangles jerked on her tender scalp. As the pangs of his own hunger began to recede, he studied her.

She raised her eyes and caught him staring at her. Hastily she looked away, dropping her hands into her lap.

He turned the spit another turn. The sizzling juices dripped into the fire. At last he spoke, his voice low and deep. "Was it good for you last night?"

She shuddered. A cold chill ran up her spine. What did she dare say to him? How was she to answer him? If she said no, he would surely have an excuse to try again. If she said yes, he would take her answer as permission to try again. Her whole body began to tremble.

Suddenly, he stiffened. His hand went to the Colt laid carefully at hand on the ground beside him. In a lithe movement he came to his feet, the weapon cocked even as he rose.

She stared into the darkness beyond the fire, hopeful, fearful. "Tomas?" Her lips formed the single word.

"Easy now, friend," a man's gravelly voice spoke out of the night. "Don't mean no harm. Just thought y' might have a bite for a fella traveler." A man stepped into the circle of firelight.

Chris leaped back too late. The barrel of a rifle slammed against the side of his skull. He pitched forward without a sound, his face in the dirt beside Estrella's hip.

Chapter Seven

"Tomas . . ." Estrella twisted around, eagerly searching the shadows for her brother.

Fast as a rattler, the man who had first stepped into the circle of firelight now leaped across the intervening space. Just as Estrella rose on one knee, he caught her from the back. Her hopeful words changed to a cry of alarm.

"Hold her, Whitey!"

The man who had struck Chris down from the shadows now bent over the fallen body. He lifted Chris's head by the hair. "Out cold," was his callous pronouncement. He began to search his victim's pockets for valuables. His hat hid his face.

"Who are you?" Estrella gasped as the man who held her transferred his hold to her wrist and twisted it up behind her.

"Shut up."

"Are these the right ones?" Whitey grunted.

"Seem to be." The other man rolled Chris over still searching his clothing. He jerked the knife from its scabbard.

"Listen to me." Estrella strove to speak calmly. "I am Dona Estrella Luisa Montejo. My brother is Don Tomas de Montejo of Saltillo, Mexico. He will reward you most generously if you will escort me home."

The man who held her chuckled. The one going through Chris's pockets did not pause.

"Believe me," she continued desperately. "You won't find anything of value on us. But if you take me home, you can be rich men for a year . . . even longer. Believe me. You'll never . . ."

The man called Whitey clamped one hairy hand on her breast to drag her back against him. Shocked speechless, she clawed at his wrist with her free hand. "Can we have a piece first?" Whitey giggled.

"No . . ." Her mouth opened for the word, but she could not make the sound.

The other rose from the still body. "Sure. Why not? Looks like this one ain't gonna wake up no time soon."

"No . . ." This time a harsh rasp came from her throat. She began to twist and buck despite the pain in her wrist and arm.

"Damn!" Whitey pushed his hips against her from behind. "She sure is movin'. I can't wait. . . ." He pushed her down on her knees. Her face was even with the other man's belt buckle. She flashed an imploring look up into his face. Hard, cold eyes looked out of the flickering shadows cast by the small campfire. "Stop him! Oh, please. . . ."

While the other watched, Whitey buried his hand in the layers of cloth covering her breast. With a grunt he ripped downward. Both blouse and camisole were stripped away in his hand.

She might have screamed, but she had no voice. Her throat closed. Before her eyes brown-skinned hands with filthy nails efficiently pushed the greasy leather end through the belt buckle and tugged it free. The shiny steel tongue flipped back and the belt fell open, dangling loosely from the loops on the trousers. The motion was repeated and the gunbelt heavy with pistol and cartridges slid round the man's hips and dangled from his hand. He tossed it carelessly out of the way. One, two, three buttons, and the heavy twill pants slid down around the man's thighs.

"Goddamn it!" Whitey objected. "I get her first."

"You get one end. I get the other," came the thick reply.

"For mercy's sake . . ." she whispered. Her stomach heaved as she caught the odor of his body suddenly exposed inches from her face. The dark brownish-pink object would have brushed against her lips had she not jerked back violently.

Whitey giggled again. "All right by me." He left her blouse to hang in shreds and grasped the waistband of her skirt. "Just let me get her stripped. . . ." He gave a vicious pull. The breath whooshed from her body as the waistband held. "Hell!"

The other man grabbed her wild tangle of hair. "Use both hands. I've got her." His teeth flashed briefly in the dark oval of his face. "Come on, gal. Open up."

She twisted her head from side to side, despite the terrible pain.

"Hold still, gal," he counseled gruffly. "If you suck this off right smart for me, I'll give you a free ride, so you'll go out smiling."

She bared her teeth at him, snapping viciously, clawing at his bare hairy thigh. In her anger and disgust she forgot the man trying to rip the waistband of her skirt, forgot that they had her between them with no hope of escape.

"Goddamn it! Stop that bitin'!"

She did not heed, did not even hear his command. Jaws open in a feral snarl, she lunged at the engorged flesh only

108

inches from her face. He slapped wildly at the side of her head, but not quickly enough. Her teeth grazed him, set off a howl of fear mixed with pain, then sank into the tender skin where belly and thigh joined. At the same time she felt her waistband go.

The bitten man stumbled back howling a curse. His pants down around his thighs hobbled him as his booted feet encountered Chris's outstretched arm and shoulder. He fell on his back in the dirt.

Overbalanced by her wild lunge, Estrella too fell face-down on the ground. The one called Whitey yelled triumphantly as he yanked and pulled at the heavy black broadcloth. At last, with a popping of buttons and ripping of buttonholes, the placket gave way, baring her white hips and thighs to the firelight. "Hot damn!" he yelled. "Look a' that!"

Both her hands were free, but Estrella could not move her left arm. It fell helpless at her side after the merciless twisting. Beneath her midriff Chris's arm was a hard log. Her right hand clawed at the dust as hands like talons fastened in the white flesh of her buttocks.

"Whoo-ee-ee!"

Dust was in her mouth. She struggled to get her right arm under her and turn over. In the act of pushing with preternatural strength, her hand encountered the pistol barrel. Chris had dropped it when he had gone down. Frantically, she clawed at it.

A hard object rammed against the strained flesh between her buttocks. The force of the blow scooted her along the ground. Dust filled her eyes, her nose, her mouth. The flinty soil scraped the skin from her forehead and cheek. The horror, the shame, the fear, the pain, all combined to wring a howl of rage from her tired throat.

"Damn it. Get up and hold her," Whitey grunted to his companion, who still struggled awkwardly with his pants.

For an instant Estrella lost the pistol. Her fingers dabbled frenziedly in the dust. Concentrating all her energies on it and it alone, she managed to locate it again, turning it so that her trembling hand finally closed over the butt, her index finger inside the trigger guard.

Hard, hot, bruising flesh thrust and bored between her buttocks. Frantically, her fighting muscles tensed, refusing to yield to this most hideous of invasions. Her weak right thumb trembled with strain as it fought against the spring mechanism holding down the hammer.

"Loosen up," Whitey growled, striking a sharp blow to her buttock. "Damn you, loosen up!"

Suddenly, the hammer of the Colt Peacemaker slid smoothly back the last quarter of an inch. Breathing a prayer, she closed her eyes as her tormentor reared back on his haunches.

"You asked for it!" he snarled.

She flipped herself over. The gun swung between them, the black hole of the barrel trained directly on him. In the dark he did not see it, or perhaps he did not recognize what it was. Even as he lunged toward her she pulled the trigger, less than a foot from his chest.

The noise, the smoke, the odor of burned cloth, hair, and skin, the recoil, all combined to drive her back flat.

At the same time, Whitey rocked backwards on his heels. He shot a look of pained surprise at the sluice of red. His heart's blood spouted from the wound in his chest, bathing her and him in its hot liquid.

"Goddamn!" An awed voice reminded her of the man behind her.

Flipping back around onto her elbow, she leveled her gun at him. Her finger worked the trigger, but the hammer moved with agonizing slowness. Her thumb trembled. Tears stood in her eyes as she gritted her teeth with the effort.

The second man stared into her face, spattered with shining red, her eyes glittering, her teeth bared. "God-damn!" He vaulted to his feet, hitching his pants up even as he ran. He was already a dark silhouette when she finally had the gun cocked. Acting on instinct alone, she fired, aiming where she looked. A sharp howl answered the shot. The silhouette staggered but did not stop running. In another minute it was gone; the thud of its heavy boots faded into the night.

Estrella blinked.

The pistol fell from her hand. Blindly she stared into the blackness. A shuddering sob released the long pent-up air from her lungs. But she did not cry.

Her thumb hurt her. Unaware of her near nudity, she drew her legs around under her and sat up. With great effort she moved her left arm until she could lift the hand to massage the pain away. She paid no heed to the blood spattered across her breasts and belly. Only the pain of her thumb was real to her. Breathing as if she had been running, she cradled her right hand and began to rub her fingers slowly back and forth across the fragile bones.

Chris stirred slowly. His head felt split open. Pain lanced through him as he lifted an unsteady hand in the general direction of its center. The lump probably felt larger than it really was. Whoever had struck him had not broken the skin, so far as he could tell. His skull must still be pretty much intact, or the lump would have been a cavity. And he would not be feeling it.

Stifling a moan, he opened his eyes to blackness. His ears picked up the sounds of the wind in the sage, the stamp of a horse's hoof as it stirred restlessly in sleep. Nothing more. Normal enough. Then something else. He distinctly heard the sound of raspy breathing very close to

111

him. Gingerly he lifted his head. This time when he opened his eyes, they found the faint red glow from the ashes of the fire. It had almost gone out.

He turned his head, fighting the pain that lanced down into his neck. Beside him sat a figure. He rolled slowly over on his side to face it. The person was breathing hard, huddled over, rocking slightly.

Unable to suppress a slight groan, Chris sat up. The last thing he remembered was the man stepping into the firelight. He had stepped back, drawing his Colt, and then had come the blow to the temple. More than one had jumped him. He cursed his own stupidity in letting them slip up on him. At the same time he wondered vaguely why he was still alive. Warily, he waited for another blow, for some command from the men who had knocked him out.

None came. He drew a deep breath. The pounding at his temple was easing. If they had wanted to kill him, they would already have done so. Therefore, light would do no harm. Climbing to his feet, he staggered to the remains of the little campfire. The pain of his head made him nauseated. He nevertheless poked at the base of the little flame, adding dried grasses and twigs until it blazed brightly.

Then he turned. Estrella sat tailor-fashion on the hard ground, his gun in her lap. Her blouse hung from her shoulders. Her breasts and belly were bare. Her skirt was twisted midway down her thighs. At his gasp of alarm, she did not so much as glance in his direction. Instead, she stared down at her hands moving ceaselessly in her lap.

But the smooth white skin did not excite him. Neither did he see the dusky nipples nor the dark valley between her thighs. Instead the hair rose on the back of his neck. As if some insane painter had swung a loaded brush, Estrella was dappled in hideous crimson. Splotches the size of coins shone on her cheeks, her breasts, the white skin of her belly. His first thought was that she had been shot with a shotgun.

His inspection went beyond her to the body of a man. He lay on his side, his face turned to the fire. His chest had been blown away. His mouth hung slightly open, more fresh blood probably mixed with other fluids draining sluggishly from the corner.

Chris swallowed heavily. He closed his eyes, pressing both hands against his pounding temples. When he opened them, the scene was just as he had imprinted it on his mind.

His first impulse to spring to her side died as his eyes registered the gun in her lap. He guessed she had killed the man sprawled behind her. She had only to lift the Colt to blow the man who had kidnapped her, who was bringing her in for bounty, the man who had nearly drowned her, into the middle of next week.

He stared round him in the blackness. Where was the other man? He was certain there had been two. Was he too lying dead somewhere out in the brush beyond the firelight? He took a step. The toe of his boot nudged the holster of the discarded gunbelt. He bent and lifted it gingerly. His eyes moved back to her with real puzzlement. How had she gotten the other man to discard his weapon?

Star paid no attention to him. A tiny sound escaped her as she rubbed her hand. Warily, he edged around the fire until he was at her back. On cat feet, he came to her, going down on his knees, reaching around her waist. His fingers encountered the cold flesh of her inner thigh as he fumbled for the gun.

She started at his touch, pausing in her rubbing to look vaguely around her. Then the handle was in his hand and he snatched the gun away. Still kneeling behind her, he checked the magazine before returning it to his holster.

Two bullets had been fired.

Carefully, he rested the tips of his fingers on her shoulders. She did not seem to notice. Instead, her eyes found the fire. A slight tremor vibrated through her as if she suddenly realized that she was cold.

Helpless, uncertain what to do, Chris looked behind him at the man this fragile woman had killed. This time his eyes moved from the hideous cicatrice of the dead man's grin past the gaping hole in his chest to the limp organ dangling shrunken from the placket of the overalls.

His face hardened. She had shot in self-defense. The dead man had been out for rape. Had he succeeded? Like most men, he could not understand the enormity of the crime. He patted her clumsily, his sympathy uncertain. "Star," he whispered. "Are you all right?"

She did not answer at first. Her glazed eyes reflected the fire's light. Her hands stilled in their incessant circling, then moved again. This time she lifted the right hand, fanning out the fingers and thumb, staring at them as if she had never seen them.

"Does your hand hurt?" he asked.

"Yes," she murmured reluctantly.

He reached out for it, but she snatched it back, cradling it against her midriff, smearing the darkening red splotches.

"All right," he soothed. "I won't touch it." He shifted over onto all fours, the blood pounding fiercely in his temples at the sudden movement. Swallowing hard, he managed to crawl to his saddle and retrieve the canteen strapped to the horn. Returning, he stripped the kerchief from around his neck and wet it. "Let me just clean you up a bit, Star. . . ."

Her eyes flickered from the fire to his face and then to her body. For a moment she stared uncomprehendingly. Then the storm broke. A harsh sob, then another, then an

114

agonized keening. She swiped at her breasts and belly with her hands.

"Here now. Stop that." He caught one of the flailing arms. "I've got a wet cloth here. Just lie back and close your eyes."

She shook her head, sobbing harder, the palms of her hands and her fingertips stained.

"Star!"

She began to shriek.

His face twisted in a kind of pain of his own. He smacked her lightly across the face with the wet handkerchief. The noise cut off instantly. "Now!" he commanded sternly. "Close your eyes." He waited until she did, then he began to wash her face with the cold water.

She shuddered at the touch, then shivered. Her head fell back on her shoulders; her teeth clenched to still their chattering.

He scrubbed the spots on her breasts with unnecessary vigor. The nipples puckered and hardened at the cold bath. He could hardly keep from moaning as he scrubbed her belly. The curling black hair at the joining of her thighs brushed against the side of his hand. He closed his eyes momentarily. He had to get that smooth white flesh covered up, or he'd be in for a rough time tonight. "Just a little bit more." His voice was low and gentle.

She shut her eyes so tightly that the flesh around them wrinkled. Still, the tears trickled down her cheeks.

"Now lift your hips," he whispered.

Star shuddered. A tiny whimper slipped from between her tight-clamped lips. She and Chris were huddled together in the middle of the night on a Texas prairie. No one could see them, yet shame in the form of vile nausea rose in her throat. The color drained from her face as he pulled her skirt up and fumbled ineffectually with the torn material.

"It's pretty badly torn here at the back," he murmured unsteadily. "Only one button left.

Her fingers fluttered at the waistband, then slipped round to the back where they encountered his. "Can't you d-do something?"

Hesitantly, he squeezed her icy fingers. "Sure," he replied. "I'll just button the one that's left and you can have my shirt. Actually, you've been wearing it more than I have. Might as well give it to you." He opened his saddle bag and pulled out the blue chambray he had wound around her to support her ribs. He had intended to put it back on her after it had dried, but the time had slipped away.

Gently, he drew the shredded rags of her blouse and camisole off her shoulders. When he lifted her left arm, she moaned. "Hurt?"

"One of them . . . That one." She indicated the corpse with a barely perceptible jerk of her head. "He t-twisted it."

A muscle in Chris's jaw flinched. With exquisite care, he arranged the wounded arm and drew the shirt sleeve over it. The long tail fell to the ground, easily long enough to cover the rents in her skirt. Moving around in front of her, he pulled the shirt together across her breasts. "Now, let's get you all buttoned up." He might have spoken to a child. Indeed the smile on his face was the bright, artificial smile a parent might use to distract a hurt baby.

She sat with head dropping, her back bowed as if under intolerable weight. She was unnaturally still while he buttoned the garment. When she was decently covered, he patted her shoulder awkwardly and rose.

He added the last of the kindling to the fire. By its stronger light he flicked a glance at Star's profile; all healthy color seemed to have drained from her face, leaving it deathly white with grayish tints beneath the eyes

116

and around the mouth and nostrils.

A sudden strong flare of the flames revealed the corpse in grisly detail. His first job must be to get rid of that.

Again he glanced at Star. Her inclined profile might have been carved on a cameo. Moving between her and the corpse, he caught the boot heels and dragged it away into the darkness. A decent distance from the campfire, he stopped. The night was light enough to see the white blur where the face of the dead man turned up to the quarter moon.

Chris looked around him. He might have been alone in the Texas desert. Only the normal sounds of soft winds, rustling grasses, faint stirrings of small creatures reached his ears. He stared down at the white blur, then back at the orange glow of the fire about thirty yards away.

With a shrug he made his choice. He found the man's hat, an inky spot in the semidarkness, dragged behind him by the rawhide *barboquejo* under the chin. He laid it over the white blur. "Bad luck, stranger," was the dispassionate eulogy as he turned and hurried back toward the fire.

The haunch of venison was blackened on one side, but not severely damaged. The whole nightmarish incident must have occurred in under an hour. Shaking his head, he rotated the spit and returned to Star's side.

Sweeping up her bedding and saddle, he spread them on the other side of the fire away from the bloodstains. Then he patted her shoulder once more. "Come on now. It's time you went to sleep."

When she did not stir, he slid his hands under her arms and lifted her to her feet. Still she made no move of her own volition, but stood docile. He led her to the blanket and helped her to stretch out. "Now close your eyes."

In this she did not obey him. He pulled the blanket up to her chin, but she turned her head. Her black eyes remained open staring into the fire, its leaping flames

117

reflected in her pupils.

Her screams woke him in the early morning. He sprang to his feet, Colt drawn. The pale streaks of dawn illuminated a bare landscape. He spun around. What had disturbed her?

She sat bolt upright, her eyes wide open, her mouth gaping. Another scream ripped from her throat. He looked in the direction she was looking. Nothing but sagebrush and buffalo grass, a few stunted mesquites, some yucca.

Holstering the weapon, he dropped to his knees beside her. He grasped her shoulders and turned her to face him. Looking directly into his face, she screamed again.

"Star." He shook her gently. "Star!"

Her eyes closed. He slipped his arm around her, supporting her as her fighting muscles relaxed. Lowering her to the saddle, he waited quietly. But as he slipped his hand from under her, she caught at it. Her lips moved.

He bent his ear to them. "Tell me, Star," he urged.

Their motion ceased. Again he tried to pull his hand away, but she only clutched it tighter.

He looked around him. The winds of the morning sprang up, but the landscape was still bathed in gray shadows and mist. Murmuring indistinctly, she shivered. Instantly, he knew his course. Without removing his hand from her possession, he slipped down beside her and gathered her against him, pressing his warm length against her.

She sighed and tucked her cheek into the hollow of his shoulder.

When he awoke again, the sun was up almost an hour on the horizon. A couple of buzzards circled low in the sky directly above them. He shot a glance in the direction he had dragged the body. He must get them both on horses and out of this vicinity before the scavengers reminded her forcefully of the night's horror.

"Star," he called softly. His mouth was only a couple of inches from her ear.

Her eyes flew open. All along his length he felt her body snap to instant alertness. Even as he released her, she was throwing herself out of his arms. "Better get a move on," he said mildly.

She did not face him as she had of old. Instead, she huddled on the edge of her blanket, her back to him.

Patting her shoulder in a manner he meant to be reassuring, he hastily saddled the mare and the stallion and gathered up the camp. The roasted haunch of venison he stored in a cloth bag. They would eat farther down the road, away from the site. For her sake he would call a halt and take the time to build a fire and make coffee.

She rode beside him, her face white, her lips trembling, forced to hold the reins with her right hand. By the time the sun was directly overhead, she looked like a corpse. Her skin stretched tightly over her bones; her eyes were glazed.

Before them was a fork in the trail. To lead her west would take her into the town of Crossways where a gallows waited for her. Before he would hang her, Luke Garner would want to make her suffer. Chris had recognized the man as an inherent bully. Star was in no condition to bear the man's torments.

The thought of her, wounded deeply, cringing and trembling, her spirit in rags, made him ill. He could not take her to Garner in that condition. His common sense told him that he was prolonging her agony, delaying the enactment of justice, playing a sentimental fool. He was doing all those things, yet he could not help himself. She had behaved nobly until faced with more horror than she could bear. Kidnapped and half-drowned first, later her

119

clothes ripped from her body, threatened by rape, she had maintained sufficient control to dispatch one of them at point blank range.

A killer she might be, but she at least deserved the chance to die with some measure of dignity. He knew her to be a proud woman, a grandee's daughter. She would face whatever befell her with calm, if she could have a few days to recuperate from the physical ordeals to which she had been subjected.

His decision made, he turned the stallion toward the north. The black mare followed.

Chapter Eight

The small boy darted out of the small adobe ranchhouse. "Papa! Papa!"

"Duff!" Chris swung down off the dusty stallion. The little boy made a flying leap from the porch of the ranchhouse into the waiting arms. The man staggered back a step. "Whoa, pardner! You've grown a mile since I caught you last. You're getting too heavy to jump on me like that. You'll knock me flat."

The sturdy arms did not release their grip one iota. If anything they tightened as the little boy giggled delightedly. "I have, Papa. I really have. Aunt Neill says I have. She says she's going to have to make me all new shirts and pants."

"Oh, no," Chris groaned. His voice lowered in tone to imitate anger. "Duff. You've been eating and growing behind my back. Every time I come home you cost me money."

Duff giggled. "Silly, Papa! I would have costed you money anyway, 'cause Aunt Neill would have made me pants and shirts whether you came home or not. Besides, the last thing you told me when you left was to eat everything on my plate."

Clearing a lump from his throat, Chris hugged his son a bit tighter. "You're right, son. You're sure right."

"Who's the lady, Papa?" Duff twisted in Chris's arms and looked up at Star, who still slumped silently on her horse.

"Her name is Star." Chris adjusted his son so that the boy's little legs encircled his waist. "She's come to stay with us for a few days so she can get rested up."

"Has she been sick?" Duff looked up sympathetically into her face.

"Yes."

Duff reached out to pat her knee. "I was sick once. Last winter I got a bad cold, but Aunt Neill rubbed Japanese oil on my chest and I got better."

Star smiled faintly, feeling warmed by the show of concern.

"Climb down," Chris invited, holding up his free hand.

Moving stiffly, she threw one leg over the horn and slid to the ground. His hand caught her upper arm and lent her strength. Nevertheless, her knees buckled as her feet touched the ground. Without his support she would have collapsed in the dust in front of the porch. When she had steadied, he passed his arm around her shoulder. With Star leaning against him and Duff chattering in his ear, Chris mounted the porch steps.

"Is supper ready?" he asked his son when they had closed the door behind them. "We're hungry enough to eat a whole javelina apiece."

Duff chortled. "I think so. Let me down. I'll go tell Aunt Neill to hurry." He slid down his father's hip and dashed away.

Chris flexed his arm. "When I'm home, I can almost

122

see him grow. When I'm gone for a few weeks, it's almost like coming home to someone else's son." His voice was gruff with pride. He pointed the way for Star to enter the cool living room.

"Oh, Mr. Gillard, I wish I'd known you were coming." A tall, raw-boned woman with faded red hair bustled into the room. "Duff just told me you were here and brought a lady with you." She looked curiously at their ragged, filthy clothes and exhausted condition. "Glory to God! Did you all take turns dragging each other through the sagebrush and cactus in this heathen land?"

"Just about, Mrs. MacNeill. We need hot water to wash our hands and faces, and then hot food." He steered Star into a chair and went down on one knee beside her.

Mrs. MacNeill leaned slightly to one side trying to catch the expressions on the faces of the man and woman. Chris caught her looking at them, her face avid with curiosity, her mouth slightly open, her eyes gleaming. "The hot water and hot food?" he prodded dryly.

Her eyebrows shot up. "Right away." She stalked out, avoiding Duff as he came charging in.

"Look, Papa. A kitten." Duff thrust the squirming, short-haired calico into his father's hand. "Isn't it grand? Frisky had four. But this one is the prettiest. It's name is Spotty."

Chris regarded the little creature dubiously. Far from being attractive and fluffy, the hair of its coat lay slickly close against its skin. Its orange, black, and white spots were scattered haphazardly over its face and body. It spat indignantly at Chris and raked its tiny claws across the back of his hand. Its long, slick tail whipped angrily back and forth.

"Grand," Chris murmured. He was on the point of handing it back when Duff dashed away again.

123

His voice drifted back to them. "I'll go get you one to hold, Star."

No, Duff. . . ." Chris's command came too late. A door slammed somewhere in the back of the house. "Damn." The wriggling kitten clawed a set of four tiny furrows down the inside of his wrist. "Spotty's about as tame as a bobcat."

Star stirred. A small smile turned up the corners of her mouth as she watched the tiny fighter struggle to climb over the top of the big hand that held it. Tentatively, she put out a single finger and smoothed the fur between the black and orange ears. "She's just scared," she whispered, her throat raw and painful.

"How do you know it's a 'she'?"

"Calicos are always females."

He raised his eyebrows. One side of his mouth turned up as he regarded the kitten quizzically. "I wonder how many more in this litter are females. I'm going to be hip-deep in cats if I'm not careful."

"Here, Star." Duff galloped through the door and plunked an orange-and-yellow-striped kitten down in her lap. "I call this one Sunny."

"That's a nice name," Star replied softly.

"You do got a sore throat," Duff observed, kneeling on the floor and taking the kitten back. "I'll tell Aunt Neill to rub Japanese oil on it for you."

"Thank you."

"The water's ready." Mrs. MacNeill appeared in the doorway. "I've taken towels and hot water to your room, Mr. Gillard, and I've put towels and hot water in my room. If you'll just come with me, ma'am. . . ."

Gillard rose, handing Spotty to Duff. Immediately, he held both kittens side by side up to his face and began kissing their noses, murmuring compliments. The tiny

124

creatures spat and hissed. "Go with Mrs. MacNeill, Star."

She looked around her vaguely, as if she were aware for the first time of her surroundings. "Where am I to go?"

"She'll take you to wash your hands and face." He helped her to her feet.

"A bath?"

"That will come later. While we wash up, she'll put hot food on the table for us."

"What place is this?"

He hesitated. What should he tell her that would alarm her least? He shrugged. "My home."

She looked at the small boy kneeling on the floor between them, kissing the kittens. The boy's white-blond hair was exactly the same shade as Gillard's. "Not Garner's."

"No."

She closed her eyes, swaying where she stood.

He steadied her with a hand under her arm. "Whoa, there. You're not going to pass out on me, are you?"

She opened her eyes and began to move after Mrs. MacNeill. Each step was taken with studied care, as if a sudden jar might fracture something deep within her. In the doorway, she looked back at him. "Do you live near Crossways?"

He frowned slightly. "No."

Even as he watched, she swayed again. Her eyes rolled in her head. Without a sound, she collapsed. He managed to catch her shoulders and keep her head from hitting the floor.

Star awoke to pain. Pain lanced through her ribs. Pain ripped from her throat.

"Star! It's all right! It's all right! Wake up. Wake up,

girl."

She screamed again. Only then did she realize that she had been screaming. She had caused the pain in her throat. But her ribs hurt, too. Hands tightened on her shoulders, shook her. Shards of pain lanced from the abused side into all parts of her body. In the face of it, the nightmare dissolved.

Shivering and sweating, she slumped tiredly.

"Are you awake?" The voice speaking out of the darkness was instantly recognizable as Chris's. Her captivity had lasted only a little over a week. In that time she had shared such an intimacy with her captor that she knew him even in the dark.

"Yes." She thrust her hands out feebly, encountering his chest.

"Can you lie back against the pillows now?"

"Yes."

He lowered her into the midst of a big feather bed. Its fill billowed up around her. Only where he sat did it remain flat.

She located him in the darkness by the pale oval of his blond hair. "Where am I?" she murmured at last.

"In my room."

A dart of fear pricked her. "In your bed?"

"Yes."

She said nothing, merely closed her eyes, too exhausted to think about what would happen in a few minutes. She could only pray that it would be over quickly so she could rest. He had taken her into his home. She could remember the child with the kittens, a child that was unmistakably his son. She could remember his telling her that they were not in Garner's house. She must have passed out. Her head ached faintly.

Gradually she became aware of even breathing. The

126

man on the bed had not moved. Cautiously, she opened her eyes. Blocks of moonlit night lighted the otherwise dark room. By the reflected light she could see his long form stretched out darkly against the sheet. His feet were hanging over the edge. His head and shoulders blended into the darkness at the foot. He was lying on the bed beside her, only he was turned the opposite way. She drew a shuddery breath.

"Shall I get you something for the pain?" His voice spoke again out of the darkness.

"No," she whispered. "It's easing some."

"It must have been pretty bad to wake you up screaming."

"Oh, it wasn't the pain. It was the nightmare."

"The nightmare?"

"Well, a nightmare."

He did not press her. "Duff gets those sometimes."

"I guess everybody does." She stirred uneasily. How strange to be lying here in the darkness talking to a man who lay beside her on a bed! Whenever Matthew had come to her bed, he had not wanted to talk at all.

The silence deepened. Finally, he spoke. "Are you all right now? Can you get back to sleep?"

"I guess so." Her voice disappeared in a hiss when she tried to pronounce the "s's."

"Then I'll leave you." When he rose, the ropes under the mattress creaked. In the moonlight, she could see his dark silhouette stretch as he flexed his wide shoulders. "Call me if you need me. I'll be in the next room."

"What room is this?"

"Mine."

"Where are you sleeping?"

"In the living room."

"But . . ."

"Don't worry. I'm not used to this bed anyway."

"Oh, but, surely . . ."

"I could have put you in with Mrs. MacNeill, but I didn't think you'd sleep well. Her bed's too small. And besides, Duff's in there with her and he tosses and turns. Gallops all night long, she says." He chuckled at the idea of his son rolling and tumbling in his bed, playing rough and tumble games even in his sleep. "Goodnight."

He went out, leaving the door open. She heard the rustle of cloth and the thump of boots. Now she was wide awake, confused over his consideration, his sacrifice. He was every bit as tired as she. He had ridden as far and had been knocked unconscious by a blow to the head. The idea that he would give up his bed to her, his prisoner, was absurd. And yet he had.

She tried to think. Had there been a couch or chaise longue in the living room? She could not remember clearly, but she did not think there had. Was he sleeping on the floor so she might have a bed?

By concentrating on her breathing, she was able to rid herself completely of the pain from her cracked ribs. Her throat was another matter. From the back of her mouth down it felt like an open wound. Right now she would be glad of Duff's Japanese oil if it would give her even the least bit of relief.

She lay very still staring out into the quiet darkness. In the room beyond, the man turned over. His elbow or knee banged against the floor. He did not curse. He was unusual. In her experience men cursed at the least discomfort. She willed herself to relax. But she dared not close her eyes. She might fall asleep and dream again.

Duff was staring at her, his gray-blue eyes, so like his

father's, serious and dark. When she turned her head in his direction, he smiled. "Papa said you were very tired and I was to be quiet so I wouldn't wake you up." He cast a quick look over his shoulder toward the open door. "But you aren't asleep anymore."

"No," Star rasped. She put one elbow under her and raised herself several inches off the bed. When the covers fell away from her shoulder, she realized she was nude. "Maybe you'd better go fetch your father for me. Would you please?"

"Sure." With a grin he darted away. This morning his feet were bare. Probably they explained why he had come stealthily into the room. She had not heard him, had not known he was watching her until she turned her head.

Chris returned at the end of Duff's arm. "Are you feeling better?"

"I need to get up."

"No reason to," he replied equably. "Stay in bed for today. Rest."

"I *need* to get up," she repeated meaningfully.

"Oh, well, we can handle that. Duff, go tell Mrs. MacNeill to bring the breakfast tray." When the boy had dashed off, Chris pulled open the door in the washstand and pulled out the jar. "Use this."

She flushed bright red. "For heaven's sake . . ."

"I'll get out so you can tend to your business. Then I'll be back with your breakfast." He grinned as he turned away.

She caught at his wrist. "Please. You must give me some clothes."

He shook his head. "No need for them today. You're going to stay in bed and get some rest. That's what I brought you here for."

"Why?" But he strode out without answering, snapping

the door behind him.

She scrambled awkwardly from the bed and squatted over the chamber pot. All the time, she kept casting nervous glances at the door, embarrassed that he might return at any moment.

The wall beside the door was occupied by a primitive wardrobe made of cheap yellow pine. Its shiny varnish finish was bare of fingerprints, testimony to Mrs. Mac-Neill's housekeeping. Surely, Chris would have some clothing in there. After all this was his room.

Before she could explore, he knocked. "How about some breakfast?"

"Just a minute." As quickly as her damaged ribs would allow, she climbed back beneath the covers, pulling them high up to her chin and sliding down in the bed. "Now," she called.

He carried the tray himself. Duff trailed him, his face beaming. "I told Aunt Neill about your sore throat and she sent the bottle of Japanese oil." He carried it aloft as if it were a great prize. "Would you like for me to rub it on for you?"

She smiled, touched at his thoughtful efforts on her behalf. She was beginning to suspect that Duff was a most unusual child. "After breakfast maybe," she replied.

"Would you like a kitten to play with?"

"Duff!" Mrs. MacNeill called loudly from the back of the house.

"Coming! She's going to make me dry the dishes." He made a grimace of disgust for his father's benefit before he stomped from the room.

When he was out of hearing, Star raised herself slightly on one elbow. "Where are my clothes?"

"What's left of them, you mean? Mrs. MacNeill's going to try to patch them up for you."

130

Star shrank back against the pillows as Chris came to the side of the bed. "Please let me at least have a shirt."

"Nope."

"Why are you doing this?"

He gave her a calculating look, the smile wiped away in an instant. "Because in my bed I've got you where I want you. I've got a notion you'd be an impossible patient. I brought you here to rest and I expect you to rest. Without any clothes you'll stay in bed."

Her mouth tightened angrily. A flush crept up the sides of her throat. Her eyes skittered away from his face to focus on a spot a couple of yards to the right. "Of course," she said bitterly. She had not misread his seeming kindness. Naked, she could present little resistance when he came to take her. She shuddered at the thought of a man's hands running over her.

He raised an eyebrow quizzically, wondering what she was thinking. "Women are funny creatures. Men, too. Clothes are a sort of armor. Take 'em away and people calm down fast. Right now you're so embarrassed you can't even raise your shoulders off that bed. Afraid I'll see something I've already seen. Who did you think undressed you and put you down last night?"

Her cheeks blazed scarlet with anger. In defiance, she sat bolt upright. The cool air made the skin of her back prickle. At the same time she was careful to hold the sheet across the tops of her breasts to preserve her modesty. She shook back the tangle of black hair and faced him.

A muscle in the corner of his mouth jumped as his eyes were drawn to the outline of her nipples pressed against the rough cotton. Nevertheless, he maintained his serious mien as he placed the tray across her thighs. "Eat it while it's hot," he advised, "and don't give me any arguments."

She refused to answer, but her stomach rumbled loudly

131

as the smell of fresh-baked bread seasoned with bacon grease rose in her nostrils.

"Mrs. MacNeill made an extra batch of sourdough biscuits special this morning just for you since you couldn't eat last night."

Star broke one open and slathered the bottom half with butter. Before it could melt completely, she had it popped into her mouth and the top ready to eat.

He nodded approvingly. "I'll leave you with it. When you finish, just set the tray aside. I've got a pile of business to take care of. I'll try to keep Duff out, so you can rest."

"Wait!" Her mouth was full of crumbs so that she almost choked. "Tell me why. . . ."

"Why you're here?"

She nodded.

He shrugged. "Like I said. 'I've got a pile of business.' "

The next day he came with a shirt of his and a skirt that was much too big and long. "Put these on," he commanded.

Relieved, she shrugged into the garments. He had brought only two. The skirt was so big that she had to bunch it up and hold it at the waist to keep it from sliding off over her hips.

While she was worrying with it, he returned. He took in her worried expression and smiled. "I brought you a comb and brush, too. I thought you might like to sit in a chair in the living room and comb out your hair. It could use some attention."

She flushed. Her free hand rose to the tangled mass. Then it dropped to the front of her skirt. She lifted the hem where it brushed the floor. "Where are my boots?"

He shook his head. "Tomorrow. For today just sit in the chair and brush your hair."

The hour in the living room proved the pleasantest time she had spent in many months. Duff brought all four kittens in to visit. Besides Spotty and Sunny, he showed her Soxy, a black kitten with a white bib and paws, and Blacky, who was solid black without a trace of white. Far from being affectionate pets, the kittens were very nearly feral. They hissed and spat, arched their backs, and tried to skitter away behind the furniture. They kept Duff hopping to keep track of them all.

Far from being distressed, the little boy saw nothing unusual in their behavior. He held each one in turn and talked to it. Finally, he dashed into the kitchen and brought back a saucer of milk. Only with their heads down, their rough pink tongues lapping, did they allow him to pet them without being held.

The tugging and pulling of the comb in her hair brought tears to Star's eyes. She worked on the ends first, gradually getting closer and closer to the scalp. Spots of color stood on her cheekbones and her arms ached before it finally hung straight and smooth in a long black skein reaching below her waist. Gingerly, she rested her head against the high back of the chair with her arms arranged limply in her lap.

"Ready to wash it now." Chris spoke from the doorway.

"Star really has long hair, Papa." Duff informed him, as if the news were an important discovery. "And so black. It's black as Blacky."

Star sat up straight and nodded. "A bath all over would feel wonderful."

"Then come this way. Mrs. MacNeill has the water heated." Chris led her through the house to a small room off the kitchen. "We may not have a large house," Chris temporized, "but Christine always insisted that we have a bathroom."

"Christine?"

"Duff's mother."

Star looked at him questioningly.

"She died when he was born." The words were spoken with no emotion.

"I'm sorry."

"It was a long time ago."

"I'm sorry for Duff," Star elaborated. "I loved my mother very much. I can't imagine what my youth would have been without her."

Chris's expression twisted slightly. "I've always hired a woman to take care of him."

"Mrs. MacNeill?"

"She was Christine's friend. She's been like a mother to Duff."

At that moment, the housekeeper brought two buckets of hot water in from the kitchen. The bathtub was more than just a tub, Star saw as she drew closer. It was thick cedar, copper bound and lined, easily big enough to sit immersed to the waist. The steam rose as the woman poured the water into it. "There's towels in the chest of drawers, ma'am, and soap in the dish on the stool." The woman stepped back, hands on hips. "Best get in before it cools off. When you get clean, call me, and I'll come and pour rinse water over you."

Star sighed deeply. She could hardly wait to sink into the water and let the steam envelop her. Her ribs would not ache quite so much then. Her muscles and nerves would relax, after being tied in knots ever since she had known this Christopher Gillard.

She moved to the edge of the tub, staring down through the steam into the clear, hot water. Then she realized he had not gone. She looked pointedly in his direction.

He folded his arms, grinning broadly. "Don't mind me."

"But I do."

Shrugging, he moved closer behind her. His hands closed over her shoulders in a caress. "I just thought I'd scrub your back for you and help you wash your hair." He parted a lock from her temple and held it out to the side across his palm. "The brushing did it a world of good. It's already black as the wing feathers of a blackbird. I can hardly wait to see it when it's washed."

Her skin prickling with nervousness, she pulled away from him. "Then leave me so I can get it done."

He sighed. "And we could have had such fun." Then, "Give me the clothes."

"No."

"Yes. I've other things to do. I can't stand guard outside the door while you soak and rinse. I've told Mrs. MacNeill to bring in more hot water periodically. I want you to stay in there and get all the kinks out."

"Get out," she hissed.

"The clothes." He held out his hand inexorably.

Her face flamed. She thought about refusing to take a bath, but the water was so warm and her skin itched with filth. Abruptly, she made her decision. Spinning around, she presented him her back. Taking a deep breath, she dropped the skirt. The garment slid over her hips and pooled around her bare feet. Hastily she stepped out of it and scooped it up.

Even as she thrust it behind her, he took it from her hand. She set her teeth against the nerves playing up and down her spine. He stood so close. She could feel his eyes on her legs, on the backs of her thighs. She could not go any farther. She could not. He might . . . He would . . .

"The shirt."

135

Was it her imagination or did his voice sound hoarse? Oh, God. Matthew's voice had roughened when he was excited. Her fingers trembled on her buttons. Yet only seconds elapsed before the shirt hung open.

"Star . . .?"

She quivered, then let the blue chambray slide down her arms. She had no need to thrust it behind her. He was there to take it by the collar and sweep it away.

Only her long black hair reaching almost to the curve of her buttocks veiled her. She could feel his eyes sliding over her form.

Then he sighed and stepped back. "You don't look the worse for wear, lady," he remarked. The door opened behind her and he went out.

Chapter Nine

Star could feel the blush rising, and not only in her cheeks. Her whole body felt on fire with embarrassment. Shivering as though the room were cold, she climbed clumsily into the bathtub, splashing water in her haste to submerge herself. Even though Chris had closed the door behind him, she still needed desperately to hide herself.

Closing her eyes in mortification, she wrapped her arms tightly around her. The warm water rose to her waist; the steam drifted around her in the silent room. Very soon, she stopped trembling. With a sigh, she at last forced herself to open her eyes.

The room was small, bare, and thankfully, windowless. A square of cotton hucking lay folded over the edge of the tub. With fingers that felt weak, she dipped it into the water. Then, with one suspicious eye glaring at the door, she began to sponge away the collected grime of over a week on the trail.

When she was finally clean, she inspected her body by the light of the kerosene lamp. Chris Gillard must not have been looking where she was looking when he had made his parting comment. Hardly a square foot of her body was not bruised or scratched. The skin over her ribs was every color imaginable, from darkest purple to the ugliest yellow-green.

Yet when she pressed on the bruises experimentally, they did not hurt quite so much. They must be healing, despite the bone-jarring rides and constant movement she had been subjected to. Actually, her arm, where the vicious Whitey had twisted it, was much sorer. She used it only with care, experiencing painful twinges if she tried to lift or push.

A copper ewer sat on the floor beside the tub. She filled it and poured the warm water over her scalp and hair. When they were thoroughly wet, she lathered and scrubbed until her arms ached.

Eyes screwed shut against the soap, almost drowned in the streams of water, she nevertheless felt the draft when the door swung open. Fear of her captor made her spine prickle. "Mrs. MacNeill?" she called hopefully.

"Yes, ma'am."

Letting out her breath in a sigh of relief, she parted her hair away from her face. The effort was useless. When she tried to see, the streams of soapy water ran into her eyes.

"Mr. Gillard thought you might need some help rinsing your hair," the woman explained as she pressed the wash cloth into Star's groping fingers.

"How kind." Star's tone conveyed her disbelief.

The housekeeper did not comment immediately. Instead she tilted a bucket of clean hot water and poured a stream into the ewer. "If you'd like to get up on your knees now, ma'am, and swipe all your hair over in front of you, I'll pour this water over it."

The narrow confines of the tub and the weakness of her left arm made her clumsy. In the end Mrs. MacNeill had to steady her in order for Star to maneuver her body up onto her knees. She was trembling with effort and embarrassment by the time the operation was complete.

Mrs. MacNeill, however, seemed to pay no attention to

her charge's naked, bruised skin. "My land, but it's long." she marveled at the length of the ebony fall of hair. "You almost need to stand to keep it from trailing in the soapsuds."

Star sighed at the blissful feel of the clean hot water sluicing over her. The world of pain and fear for the moment was driven out.

When finally the job was done, she stepped out of the tub and into the arms of Mrs. MacNeill, who wrapped a towel around her. Then, with another towel, the house-keeper began to dry Star's hair. "Oh, Mr. Gillard's a hard man," Mrs. MacNeill volunteered out of the blue. "I'd be a liar if I didn't admit that. Maybe he's not all hard. But then, he wouldn't do what he does for a living if he weren't."

"Why do it?" Star asked bitterly.

Mrs. MacNeill shrugged. "Who knows? He wouldn't never confide in me."

"Then how can you say he's not all hard."

"Why the boy! The boy, of course. He fairly worships that child and Duff . . . pshaw! He thinks the sun takes direct orders from his papa before it comes up in the mornings."

"I suppose, no matter how hard a person is, there's always one person he loves."

"Don't know about that, but I do know that Mr. Gillard sent me in here to help you with your hair." She pressed Star back onto the stool, draping one towel across her lap, the other around her shoulders. "My goodness, but you do have a length of it. It's been years since I've seen hair this long. My grandmother had hair almost this long. It was snow white and . . ."

Star closed her eyes as the teeth of the comb pulled through her wet hair. The gentle tug on her scalp, the soothing tone of Mrs. MacNeill's voice, the warm, damp air in the small room made her drowsy.

139

". . . bruises beginning to yellow up."

She realized that Mrs. MacNeill had made some comment that required an answer. Apologetically, she glanced up.

" 'Bout lulled you to sleep, did I?" the housekeeper chuckled.

"I'm afraid so."

"Well, it's almost dry. I'll go get something for you to wear and you can lie down for a nap before the next meal."

"I'll be awake the minute I move," Star protested. "Bring me some clothes."

The last words were uttered with a raised voice in an effort to catch Mrs. MacNeill, who hurried out, leaving the door slightly ajar.

Chris's voice, deep and amused, came from the kitchen. "I think she's gone."

Hastily, Star checked the towels. Both seemed to be in place, but she was acutely aware of the drafts from the open door circulating around her bare feet and over the naked backside. She swallowed in embarrassment. "Where has she gone to? I thought she was supposed to wait outside with my clothes."

"She's gone to get you some things that used to belong to Duff's mother."

"Oh." She waited, half expecting him to volunteer some information about his wife, but he said nothing more. She heard the scuffle of boots on the kitchen floor, the gurgle of liquid being poured.

"Can I fix you a cup of coffee?"

She would have loved to have one. She was tired from her bath. Turning around in the tub had awakened the pain in her side. Her naked state made her wary.

Her captor was moving around in the kitchen right outside the room where she sat helpless. She had no way of knowing whether Mrs. MacNeill would be returning or not. Perhaps the housekeeper had been dismissed to another part of the house. He had seen her naked less than an hour before. He was a man, one of the sex who took what they wanted from the people weaker than they. Perhaps he was even now moving toward the door intending to. . . .

The seconds stretched into minutes. A shudder and then another ran through her body. Her stomach curled within her. She stared hard at the door. "No . . ." Her first attempt at speech failed miserably. She cleared her throat. "No, thank you."

The door swung open.

She clutched convulsively at the towels. Her body went cold as the total vulnerability of her condition weighed her down.

"I had a robe that belonged to Mrs. Gillard put out." Mrs. MacNeill's voice was cross. "Then I couldn't find it. I know absent-mindedness comes with old age, but I didn't think I was that simple. I thought sure I'd hung it up in the wardrobe in her old room after I pressed it. Then I find it hung with Duff's things in his closet." She shook her head in exasperation.

Quivering with relief, Star rose eagerly, stumbling, clutching at the towels as Mrs. MacNeill held the garment out by the shoulders. The robe was heavy dusty rose wool, trimmed with Irish crochet.

"This was the last thing Mr. Gillard bought for Mrs. Gillard before Duff was born." Mrs. MacNeill's voice trembled slightly over the words. "She wore it while she was trying to nurse him those last few days."

In the act of tying the sash around her waist, Star paused to protest. "Surely you could get me my own clothes," she insisted. "This must have painful memories attached to it."

Mrs. MacNeill gathered up the towels with a philosophical shrug. "Don't know about the memories, but I know about the clothes. I'm still working on them. This robe is just going to go to waste. It's a wonder the moths haven't taken it already. Such good serviceable material, too. You really ought to take better care of them. I think I can fix the skirt. But the blouse is gone. I've got rags in better shape."

Star was still trying to puzzle the sense of Mrs. Mac-Neill's speech as she was ushered toward the door. She caught hastily at the neck of the robe, drawing it together across her neck.

Chris was waiting outside in the kitchen, leaning back at the kitchen table, a china mug of coffee in his hand. "Feel better?" He rose and came toward her, bringing his coffee with him.

"Yes." She eyed him warily, her fingers curling in the soft material.

He stared down into her face, noting the mauve circles under huge eyes. The few days on the trail had made a difference in her flesh. A certain softness had gone from her face and figure. She looked fine-drawn. Abruptly, he turned away, stalked to the stove, and poured another cup of coffee. "Have some now?"

She edged around the table, putting it between him and her. "Yes. All right."

"Sit down, the both of you," Mrs. MacNeill insisted. "I'll cut a couple of pieces of pie. It'll tide you over until supper."

They sat in silence until the housekeeper placed the food before them and left to find Duff. Chris's eyes appraised his captive critically.

Star took a sip of her coffee. Carefully, she set the cup down. "Please let me have some clothing." A blush of embarrassment rose from her throat to stain her cheeks. Its heat angered her, making her blush all the more. She dropped her eyes to stare at the coffee as it began to vibrate in the cup. Hastily she pulled her hands off the table and clasped them in her lap.

142

He shook his head. Lazily he reached across the table to tip up her chin. "Drink your coffee and go lie down."

"I'm not tired. I . . ." she began mutinously.

"Go lie down for a nap. After supper we'll talk about it." His opaque gray eyes revealed no emotion. Neither did the set of his jaw.

She wanted to object, but her ribs ached dully and her muscles trembled. Suddenly she felt enervated, as if her hot bath and the accompanying emotional turmoil had exhausted her. But she could not show such weakness. Rebelliously she raised her chin out of his grasp.

Before she could open her lips, he laid his long index finger across them. "Not another word," he ordered gruffly. "Go right now or I'll carry you." Her eyes flickered in sudden alarm. As she pushed back her chair he stood up, looming over her. "If you're too nervous and high-strung to rest, maybe I can do something about calming you down."

She stumbled to her feet. "I'll go."

"Smart lady."

When she awoke, the sun was low in the west. Her body felt languorous, free from pain for the first time in over a week. Slowly she moved her limbs, straightening them and rolling over onto her back. For the moment nothing hurt. Perhaps the rest had been exactly the thing she needed.

A knock sounded on her door. Had there been one before that? Had that been what had awakened her? She sat up on one elbow.

Before she could open her mouth to answer, the door opened. "Almost time for supper," he told her, standing tall in the doorway. His eyes swept from her alarmed face down the gaping V at her neckline to rest on her bare thigh. Moving slowly as her dazed brain commanded, she fumbled for the edge of the robe and pulled it across the exposed skin.

He smiled. "Suppertime," he repeated.

"All right." She did not move immediately. In her bemused state she lay still, staring helplessly at his face.

Raising one eyebrow, he moved toward her. The movement of his body was loose and angular. His hands hung at his sides; the side of his mouth curved upward in a half smile.

She watched him come, her brain sending warning signals that her muscles refused to acknowledge.

Then he was bending over her, one hand braced on the bed beside her, the other tracing the line of her jaw, before threading itself into her hair at the back of her neck.

She watched his mouth come down to find hers. His lips parted; his head tilted to the side to fit hers. Then he kissed her, with lips and tongue. She did not realize until she felt his hot invasion that she had opened her own mouth. Whether in protest or in imitation, she could not tell.

His tongue slid past her lower lip, rasping along the cutting edges of her teeth, before filling her mouth with hot, wet strength. She would have fallen back on the bed before his onslaught had not his hand on the back of her neck kept her within his grasp.

Convulsively, she caught at handfuls of the sheets beneath her. Fear streaked through her mind, but her body did not recognize it. Instead it responded to the sensuality of the bounty hunter's hard body poised above her own.

The kiss went on and on. Other than his hand on her neck and his mouth on hers, he did not touch her. She felt a peculiar heat and a certain loosening of her limbs. Then her brain screamed at her body, with the result that a tiny whimpering sound slipped into his mouth. Instantly he released her and stood back. A satisfied smile curved his lips.

The smile broke the spell. Angrily, she dropped back on

144

the bed and then rolled away to come up on the opposite side from where he was standing. Her stance was almost a crouch, as she clutched at the front of her robe. If he came after her . . .

"Come on," was all he said.

She straightened and took a step back, an obstinate look in her eyes. "I need some clothing."

"Later." He indicated the way with his hand. "After supper I promise I'll take you for a walk."

He was as good as his word. Clad in her boots, cleaned and polished to a high shine; her black wool riding skirt, expertly mended by Mrs. MacNeill, and a blouse that had belonged to Mrs. Gillard, she walked beside him out the back door of the ranchhouse.

The moon bleached the landscape to shades of gray and blue as they strolled toward the corral and shed. There the darker shadows of several horses slept standing, their muzzles within inches of the hayrack.

As they neared the corral fence the stallion, distinguishable from the others by his larger shape, swung his head toward them and whickered softly. The other animals shifted about, half-asleep.

"Is Humareda there?" Star asked.

At the sound of the familiar voice speaking her name, the black mare detached herself from the group and came across the corral at a fast walk. When Star thrust her hands between the rails, the mare put her face into them. "*Buenos noches, querida*," Star whispered as she stroked the velvet muzzle. "Are you still stiff and sore?"

"She's right as rain," Chris commented. "I exercised her this morning. No stiffness, not a sign of unevenness in her gaits."

"She's a sweet lady. Aren't you, beauty?" Star patted the mare's cheek and smoothed the long hair of the

145

forelock.

The stallion swiped a mouthful of hay from the rick and ambled over. He shoved the mare gently aside and thrust his nose between the rails to snuffle at Chris's hands. "Jealous, old son?" Chris chuckled, scratching the soft spot under the Alter-Real's jaw.

Star patted the stallion with one hand at the same time she stroked the soft nose of the mare. "I never knew one that wasn't," she laughed. "At least not one that was hand- and voiced-trained." She began to talk to the stallion and the mare, as Chris had heard her talk to her other horses at the corral among the cottonwoods a few days—or a lifetime—ago.

The stallion stood like a statue, charmed by her voice and touch. He was an aristocrat, a true king of his kind. Beneath the dark hide the powerful muscles rippled with each breath he drew. The mighty heart pounded rhythmically, driving the hot blood through the veins. He could have demolished them all had he unleashed the power of his mighty forehooves. Yet he bowed his neck to stand like a colt for the soft voice and touch of the woman.

Chris felt a sudden tightening in his loins as he listened. Her sweet voice questioned and complimented the pair of horses as if they were children. Hot and vital in his mind rose the memory of the night he had almost killed her, the night they had made love on the banks of the Rio Grande. He raised his hand to lay it on her shoulder, but drew back. Tonight, he promised himself, he would come to her room. Let her enjoy her turn in the fresh air for the moment.

He thrust the eager hand into his pocket. "He's been mine since he was a colt." He found he had to clear his throat. "For the first year, he'd follow me around like a dog. Grandad teased me about it. He said I was just like Grandmother. When she was a girl, she had all the horses named and tamed, so he almost never got her to sell

146

them."

"I know the feeling," Star nodded, turning her attention to Humareda, running her hands up and down the gracefully arched neck. "Your horses become like your children to you."

"Except that you breed them to do certain things," Chris observed. "With your children, you have to take them as you find them and work with what you have."

Star stared at him in the darkness. Was there a note of bitterness in his voice? Surely Duff was everything anyone could want in a child. She dismissed the statement as mere impersonal observation. "You do breed for what you want," she agreed, taking up the thread of the conversation. "And when you get your ultimate product, you still aren't sure. Oh, you're pretty sure the horse you breed has stamina as well as beauty and intelligence, but you're never really certain. To find whether it's true or not, you might have to break the horse. I was worried about Humareda. That was a terrible ride. Especially after you lost the extra mounts to give her a rest. I could just see you leaving her beside the trail. But she kept right on."

"A great mare. Incredible stamina," Chris agreed.

"She'll produce magnificent foals," Star went on enthusiastically. "With her perfect conformation and brain, they'll every one be something special, bred to the right stallion. Tomas had some doubts because of her size, but I knew. . ."

She stopped abruptly, biting her lip.

"Knew what?" Chris prodded in the darkness.

"Nothing." She spun away from the corral. Thrusting her hands into the pockets of the riding skirt, she began walking rapidly away.

"Hey!"

The mare whickered her disappointment, but Star was hurrying now. Tears were prickling the insides of her eyelids. She could not bear to stand weeping in front of

147

this man. Yet her disappointment was so keen. The dreams of her life were nothing. She stumbled over a patch of uneven ground and almost pitched forward on her face.

He caught her arm. "Steady."

"Oh, of course," she lashed out. "Have to be careful. Mustn't fall down in the dark and break my neck. You wouldn't collect your precious reward."

He wrenched her about in his arms. Her body jolted against his. Her breath hissed between her clenched teeth at the stab of pain from the partly healed ribs.

He caught her by the shoulders, unaware of the pain he had caused her, only overwhelmed by his own anger and guilt. "Shut up!" He snarled.

"Bounty hunter," she bit out. She managed to free one hand from between their bodies. With it she slapped him hard across the face.

"Murderess," he countered. His hands tightened on her shoulders, punishing her with his grip until she groaned in agony. "Don't hit at me. I won't take it."

"Then let me go."

With one final squeeze that forced a tiny whimper from between her clenched teeth, he let her go. She stumbled back. Her foot turned under her and she went down on one knee.

With a muttered exclamation, he caught her before she fell. In a voice rough with excitement, he began to apologize. Even as he did so, he transferred his grip to sweep her up in his arms. Holding her high on his chest, he kissed her again. "Don't run away from me," he commanded hoarsely. "I won't hurt you. You'll only hurt yourself."

She tossed her head from side to side, bucking in his arms, slapping at him with bare hands. "Put me down."

Then he did hurt her. His kiss was punitive. He bit at her lip and thrust his tongue into her mouth when she opened it to protest. Her balled fist pummeled his back, while the other pushed at his shoulder.

Her anger only excited him. He did not think what was happening to him. He only felt himself harden. Her mouth was hot and sweet, the taste of her like an aphrodisiac to his senses. Like an aphrodisiac, too, was the feel of her breast pressed hard against his chest. He tightened his arm around her, drawing her more closely against him.

She moaned in anguish, but with the blood pounding in his ears he was oblivious of her pain.

Instead, he took the sound, the vibration of her chest clasped so tightly against his, for her own arousal. He kissed her cheek, her ear, her temple, her hair. "Star. . ." he whispered. "Estrella . . . Estrellita . . . Are you hungry for me too?"

She pushed against him harder than ever.

"Don't fight," he repeated in the same hoarse, demanding voice. He kissed her again and again. The rough skin around his mouth scratched her face, abrading her tender skin. "You want this as much as I do," he insisted between kisses. "I can feel your body heating up."

She shook her head helplessly, even as she let her arms drop limply away from his shoulders. If he felt her body heating, it was feverish with fear. His superior strength terrorized her. Just like Matthew, he had clasped his hard hands about her body and forced her to accept his kisses in her mouth. Her head lolled back across his arm.

Immediately his touch gentled as he took her limpness for consent. Tenderly, never taking his lips from her own, he lowered her until her feet touched the ground. As he rained tiny kisses from the corner of her mouth to her ear, he held her steady. When she could stand alone, he pressed her against his chest and smoothed her hair.

"Listen, Star," he murmured. "God knows I'm burning up for you right here and now, but I want it to be good for us both. We've already made love once on the ground. No need to do it tonight." He waited for her answer.

Terror made her throat dry. She could say nothing, although she shuddered in his arms.

His own body was trembling with suppressed desire. His staff responded instantly to the vibration of her belly against it. "Easy," he hissed. "For God's sake, take it easy. I don't want to take you here in the yard." Setting his teeth, he put her away from him to arm's length and tilted her face up to the moonlight.

"We've got to go back in the house and wait a while until Duff and Mrs. MacNeill get settled for the night," he told her hoarsely. "Duff's the most inquisitive kid in the world. He'd never stop asking questions if he thought we were doing something that he might be interested in . And Mrs. MacNeill . . . Well, she thought the sun rose and set on Duff's mother, so she wouldn't take kindly to me. . . . That is, she's also a real strict Presbyterian. I'd be afraid she'd leave me if I did something that she didn't think was proper."

Star licked her dry lips.

"*Sabe?*" he asked softly.

She did not, could not bring herself to answer.

"*Sabe?*" He shook her urgently.

"Yes. All right." Her voice quavered. "I understand."

He patted her shoulder. "Good girl. Just as soon as the house gets quiet, I'll come to your room."

They walked into the house together. He led her to the most comfortable chair in the living room and patted her shoulder as she sat down.

Mrs. MacNeill smiled beatifically upon them as if they were a young couple courting. Laying aside her mending, she excused herself to go to the kitchen. When she returned in a few minutes, she brought tea in a china pot and a plate of thin-sliced bread spread with persimmon preserves.

Duff had crawled up into his father's lap for a story. When Mrs. MacNeill set the tray in front of him, he crowed with delight. "Is this your birthday, Papa? Aunt Neill, is this Papa's birthday? Why didn't you tell me? I would have given him a present."

"It's not my birthday, son." Chris shared a knowing wink with Star. "I think Aunt Neill is offering some extra-special dessert tonight because we have a guest."

Duff turned happily to Star, sitting white and cold in the big chair. "Isn't this good?" he trilled, his smile wide and sparkling. " 'Simmon 'serves are my favorite thing."

"Along with about fifty other kinds of jellies and jams and candies," Mrs. MacNeill laughed. "Eat yours up then, Duff. It's past your bedtime."

"I don't wanta. . . ."

Chris placed his finger to Duff's lips. "Careful there, son."

"Papa . . ."

"Eat."

"Yes, Papa." Within minutes the little boy's portion was devoured.

"Time for bed," Mrs. MacNeill decreed.

Duff threw one pleading glance at his father who merely nodded in agreement. "Goodnight, Star," Duff sighed. Then, "Goodnight, Papa." He gave his father a sticky kiss on the cheek and slid down. "May I kiss Star, too?"

"If she doesn't mind getting ' 'simmon 'serves' all over her face."

"She doesn't," Duff assured his father with a giggle. "You don't, do you?"

Not trusting herself to speak, Star shook her head and held out her arms. Duff walked into them and hugged her. His kiss was as sticky as Chris had predicted. When Duff drew back, he made a face. "I didn't get them all over your face. Just on one cheek. But it'll wash right off." He looked to Mrs. MacNeill for confirmation.

"Time for bed, Duff," the housekeeper announced. Now that the kisses were over, she was able to take his small hand and lead him away without further protest.

When the door closed behind them, Chris turned the full extent of his gunmetal gaze on Star. "About ready for bed myself," he suggested significantly. "How about you?"

She could only nod dimly. Carefully, wishing for every second to avert the inevitable, she set the plate of tea and sweetened bread untouched on the table beside her.

He rose and extended his hands. "Then go to bed." He kissed her icy cheek. "I'll join you when everything gets still."

Moving stiffly, she nodded and made a move to go. He pulled her back against his chest. His teeth found her earlobe. "Don't wear anything," he commanded. "I love to think of you naked, waiting for me."

Chapter Ten

Star watched the white china doorknob with the desperate fascination of a bird staring at a snake. Her nerves sent pain-filled messages up her spine to the base of her skull. The faint creak of boards in the hall signaled a man's weight moving along them. Then the door opened silently.

Chris Gillard stood transfixed in the doorway, a kerosene lamp in his hand. The yellow light close to his face revealed clearly the firm straight lips, the piercing gray eyes. It glinted off his shoulders and chest with its fleecing of pale hair. It picked out the shadows that defined the muscles and veins of his biceps as well as the faint indentations between the lower ribs. He looked lean as a lobo and every bit as dangerous.

Through dilated pupils she stared at him. The breadth of his chest and the thickness of his upper arms terrified her. The pounding of her heart against her ribs made breathing difficult. Those powerful muscles could kill her very easily if he were too rough. By comparison, Matthew had been slight, his arms and legs thin, a roll of white, soft flesh around his middle. Yet he had had the strength to

153

hurt her terribly.

Her eyes glazed for an instant, then she drew a shuddery breath that made her breasts quiver. She must please him. He must find her body exciting, so he would have his pleasure without beating her. The night beside the Rio Grande, he had been fully aroused by the danger all around them. He had lifted her onto his staff without any effort. His commands accompanied by his hard hands had forced her to perform. She had not been hurt.

But tonight, she feared, would be different. He was tired from a hard day's work. He had eaten a full supper. Tonight she would need all her painfully acquired skills to avoid abuse.

Her fingers which had clutched in instinctive modesty at the edge of the covers, straightened with a jerky, conscious effort. She did not pull the sheet up to hide her bare breasts. In the flickering lamplight her skin shone golden, each aureole darker, with a tint of rose. The nipples themselves were the darkest of all, their shapes clearly defined, perked and hard.

At the sight of her body illumined by the lamp beside the bed, Chris's mouth sagged slightly. He sucked air into his lungs. Even as his heartbeat became more rapid, he let his breath out slowly. Never taking his eyes from her, he closed the door soundlessly behind him.

The sight of her aroused him as he had not been aroused in his entire life. No woman had ever exposed herself to him with such a display. While his body responded to her and hungered for her, one corner of his mind named her a whore. No decent woman would wait naked in a bed for a man. Her brazenness was added to the catalogue of her sins.

He ran his tongue across lips that were suddenly dry. Her eyes locked with his as he came with strange slowness

154

across the room. At the side of the bed, he blew his lamp out and stooped to set it on the floor. Then in one lithe motion he put one knee onto the bed and knelt over her.

She had braided her hair into a long braid that hung over her right shoulder, a jet-black contrast to the flawless golden-cream of her skin. His fingers trembled slightly as he touched the skein of black, his calloused tips sensitive to the silkiness of it. "You're so beautiful. Are you so very eager?" A deep thread of irony laced his voice.

A cold dark pit seemed to be all that remained in the center of her body beneath her ribs. "I . . . I don't know what you mean."

He palmed the thick braid and drew her gently forward until she could feel the heat of him. "Naked," he muttered, his voice thick. "Naked, with the light on."

His chest was only inches from her mouth. "I . . . Don't . . ." she began to stammer as his other hand cupped the back of her head and tilted her face up to him. Her eyes flickered over his stern face. "You told me . . . that is, I thought you said not to put on a nightgown."

His smile mocked the uncertainty in her voice and face. "And, of course, you did what I told you to."

She lowered her lids as a shiver of fear went through her body. In her ears were the sounds of curses and ripping cloth. More than once Matthew had torn her nightgown from her body. Sometimes he had used the strips to tie her to the bedposts. And now, in her desperate effort to avoid pain, she had perhaps invited it by appearing too compliant. She shivered again, despairing at the hopelessness of her situation.

The vibration of her body communicated itself to Chris. She was a passionate little thing playing a tempting whore's game. His smile of anticipation widened. "Kiss me," he invited as he sank back on his haunches and

155

pulled her into his arms.

Her lips trembled in the lamplight. She moistened them as she raised her face. As she touched him, she shivered again.

"Put your arms around me," he breathed as one arm cradled her shoulders, supporting her to receive his kiss. His other hand began a circular motion, chafing the nipple of her breast with his palm.

Her stomach tightened as she swallowed convulsively in an effort to retain its contents. His touch, his nearness, the heat, the scent of him were suffocating her. Above all, the circle of his arm in which she lay was paralyzing her with fear. Only a tiny corner of her mind deplored the way she allowed herself to be used again to satisfy a man's desires. Yet if she protested or struggled in any way, his brute strength would overpower her easily.

His fingers shaped her nipple, tugging at it.

Fear made her anticipate pain where there was none. "No . . . oh, please, no . . ." His tongue slid between her lips, stifling the protest. He kissed her for a long time, tasting the satin interior of her mouth, testing her body's responses. When he had no more air in his lungs, he raised his head. "Wait," he groaned.

Lithely, he rose to unbutton his pants and slide them down over his hips. Freed of the heavy cloth, his staff throbbed almost painfully. In some surprise he glanced down at himself, then up at her to gauge her reaction.

But her eyes were closed. She lay back against the pillows, her hands clenched in the sheets at her sides. A faint sheen of perspiration formed on her upper lip.

He frowned. Her face had taken on a decidedly waxen look. She did not look like a woman eager for love. Then his eyes swept down her body. The flawless skin, the perfect shape of her breasts in the golden light of the lamp

156

made the ache in his loins acutely painful. All conscious thought dissolved in a flood of desire.

He tossed the upper sheet away to the end of the bed. "Put your arms around me," he demanded hoarsely as he laid himself alongside her.

She opened her eyes as his thigh slid over her own. The curling blond hair rasped against her smooth skin even as she felt him pulse against her hip. "Your arms . . ." he prompted as he lowered his mouth to her breast.

Paralyzed, she waited for the pain, but his lips were gentle. First he shaped the nipple, then sucked at it while his tongue laved it. She shivered with anticipation.

He raised his head. "Come on, lady," he groaned. "Give."

Biting her lower lip, she slipped one arm along the side of his ribs, the other up around his neck. She frowned. What did one do now? Matthew had wanted her hands and mouth to do embarrassing, sickening things to him. He had never invited her to put her arms around him.

The blood throbbed in Chris's head. He must satisfy himself soon or explode. His haste making him rough, he bent his head again to her breast. At the same time his fingers slid down across her belly to the tangle of jet-black hair at its base.

Shifting his weight, he pressed his knee between her thighs. There he encountered tense, quivering muscles. Her thighs were squeezed tightly together. His mouth widened in a quick grin at her teasing. He pressed harder, nipping at her breast at the same time. "Don't get coy with me," he growled.

"Oh, no," she gasped. "Oh, I'm not." She clutched at his shoulder convulsively at the same time she spread her legs.

"That's the way. That's right." He rolled over on his

157

hands and knees above her. One knee and then the other he planted between her thighs. His manhood, turgid and heavy, rested in the soft black hair above the entrance to her body.

Hastily, she turned her head away from the light. Any sign that she was fearful or in pain might stir him to more violent actions. But she could not hide from him in this light.

Again he frowned. His fingers tapped gently at the side of her jaw, pushing her face back into the light. "What's wrong?"

She opened her eyes. Involuntary tears slid from their corners to trickle down her temples and into her hair.

He pulled back on his haunches. Experimentally, his hand probed between her legs. Instead of soft, welcoming flesh swollen with heat and moisture, he found only delicate tissue, dry and fragile. "What the hell . . . ?"

She pushed herself up on her elbows. A look of panic flashed from her eyes, to be instantly covered by a smile. She moistened her lips and held out her arms. "Nothing's wrong," she insisted, her voice husky. "Believe me. Nothing's wrong." She caught his forearms and pulled him toward her. Ducking her head to his chest, she kissed his nipple, laving it with her tongue and sucking on it. He gasped as it hardened. Her arms closed round him, hugging him tight. His manhood was between her breasts. "Please," she whispered.

The throbbing of his body crowded the doubts away. "If you're sure . . . "

"Of course." Her teeth nipped the tiny nub of ultrasensitive flesh on his chest. Then she lay back. Her hips rose to meet his.

With a growl of desire, he drove into her.

Every muscle in her body stiffened with shock. The

pain was bad. He was so big, bigger than Matthew, and harder, too. She could not prevent the high, keening cry that escaped from between her clenched teeth. Her fear and her unwillingness had defeated his careful preparations. Consequently, she was not ready. The delicate folds of flesh that ensheathed him could not have been more abused had she been raped.

His own climax came swiftly. She was so incredibly tight. Once inside her, he could only move and move again, impelled by hot instinct, shuddering to his fulfillment. When he convulsed within her, he slumped over her, his head against her breast.

She blinked the salt tears from her eyes. Her chest heaved. It had been better than with Matthew. The pain had been terrible, but brief. Matthew had striven on and on, sometimes failing entirely and then punishing her for his failure. She sighed faintly as she tried to ease a nagging pain in her damaged ribs. At least it was all over.

Then she felt his lips against her breast. "You weren't ready," he whispered huskily, his tone accusatory.

She stiffened. "I . . ." She could think of nothing to say.

He rolled over onto his back to lie staring at the ceiling. The lamp beside her bed suddenly flickered and went out as the last of its fuel was consumed. Still he lay beside her. She thought he had gone to sleep. Cautiously, she reached down to pull the sheet over herself.

"What the hell's going on, lady?" he asked suddenly, a disembodied voice out of the darkness.

She drew back hastily, flattening herself against the bed in the darkness. Pain flared in her side at the sudden movement. She gasped.

"You *were* crying," he accused. "I thought you were. Why?"

"You were pleased," she countered, her throat dry.

159

"You enjoyed it. I felt you . . . I mean . . ." Her voice failed in shamed confusion.

He sat up in the darkness. The ropes creaked beneath the mattress. With eyes now accustomed to the dark, she stared at the white blur of his broad back. He had drawn his knees up and rested his forearms on them. "Why didn't you stop me?"

"Stop you?" She gaped incredulously.

"If you weren't ready, you shouldn't have said what you did."

She would have laughed out loud had she not been so near to tears again. "I did what you told me to," she murmured.

"But, my God, I thought you wanted it as much as I did." He turned toward her, his eyes searching the darkness to find hers.

The room was chilly now that he was no longer covering her with his body. Furtively, she reached again for the sheet, trying to stay low to the bed so he would not see she was moving.

She froze as his hand fumbled on her thigh, patted gently, then cupped it. "I didn't mean to hurt you. I did hurt you, didn't I?"

She lay silent, uncertain how to respond to the gentleness of his touch, the concern in his voice.

"Didn't I?" His hand slid up her thigh until he found her soft hair. It curled wetly about his fingertips. "Are you bleeding?"

She shuddered. The vibration communicated itself through his palm.

He cursed softly. With a violent motion he swung his legs over the side of the bed. Fumbling, he found the lamp where he had set it, stalked around the bed, and struck a match. The light flared.

At the sight of her face, tear-streaked and white, his stomach knotted. Three pain lines bisected her smooth forehead between her eyebrows. Her cheekbones, marred by splotches of pink, seemed to jut out over dark hollows. Her lower lip was swollen and empurpled where she had gnawed it. But worst was the terror in her eyes. She looked like a frightened child, one who had been neglected and starved, then subjected to brutal punishment, and who now feared more punishment.

"My God!" he breathed.

She forced her lips upward in a travesty of a smile. "You—you were so b-big," she quavered.

"Shut up!"

She winced. Raising one trembling hand to her face, she covered her ear as if she would shut out his angry words.

His first impulse was to stalk from the room. He had never hurt a woman before in his life. His initiation of Christine into the rites of womanhood had been a loving, gentle experience that had left her smiling even as she slept, her face flushed with pleasure. In loving her, he had experienced almost as much delight in teaching her as he had in the act of culmination for himself.

Since her death, when he had wanted a woman he had paid for the services of whores or provided a bit of mutual pleasure for a willing widow who ran a boardinghouse at Fort McKavett. She was old enough to be his mother, but she loved a good tumble, and he had been ready to ignore the less-than-perfect body for the comfort and warmth she gave him.

Now as he stared at Star, uncertain what to do, she began to shiver. Ducking her head, she clenched her fists as she tried to get herself under control.

"You're cold." The instant the observation was out, he felt like a fool. The poor woman sat before him naked, her slender frame shaking, her teeth chattering, and he made a bright remark like that.

Even as she shook her bowed head, she stretched forward for the sheet he had thrown to the foot of the bed. The movement exposed her back to the light of the lamp.

He gave an incredulous gasp.

She twisted to look up at him.

His hand fell on her shoulder, keeping her bent forward. "What in hell happened to you?"

She could not imagine what he was talking about. "The bruise on my ribs? When I fell from . . ."

"No." His voice sounded rough and angry. His fingers scrubbed at the skin of her back. "Where'd you get those scars?"

The whip marks! Her fear increased. Would he want to do the same thing? Her control broke. Helpless tears poured from her eyes. A terrible sob burst from her.

He jerked his hand back as if she were a hot stove. "Ah, don't," he begged.

She could not stop. Another sob tore out of her chest. And another. Tears spouted from her eyes. She twisted herself away across the bed, hiding her eyes, even though her sobs and the shaking of her body betrayed her.

He climbed back into bed beside her. "Stop," he begged. "Listen, you've got to stop this crying." He cupped himself around her body, pulling her back against him into the circle of his arms.

She sobbed harder, shivering, trying to twist away, but now she was too weak to do much more than struggle feebly.

He ran his fingers again across the terrible scars. Once he had seen the back of a man who had worked on a chain gang in Georgia. The man's back from shoulders to buttocks had been ridged with white scar tissue. It had been a sobering sight on the back of a hardened felon. Its presence on the back of a slender woman made his stomach turn. Meaningless words and phrases flowed from him, protestations, distractions, apologies, admonitions.

Still she sobbed as if she had dammed the emotion up inside her too long. Once begun she could not stop. Gently, he pulled her back against him, drawing his thighs up under hers, pressed his belly against her buttocks, wrapping one arm around her neck, while he kept the other hand moving over her body caressing and patting her, in an attempt to soothe her.

Star cried until her tears were finished, until her throat felt as if the very membranes that lined it had ruptured and shredded. Yet still the dry sobs came and shook her.

Although her mind remained entrapped in a prison of pain and fear, still she tried to fight his hands as he gathered her up in his arms. With an incoherent moan of protest, she tried to wriggle away. His free roving hand clamped on her belly; at the same time his mouth moved close to her ear. His warm breath tickled her earlobe as he continued his monologue.

Suddenly she went limp in the nest he had made for her. Her nails no longer clawed at his wrists trying to free herself.

At first he thought she had finally heard his words through the hysterical weeping. But the stillness of his body told him otherwise. He took his hands away and she lolled forward. Then he did curse roundly.

She had fainted.

He had scared her so badly by taking her into his arms that she had lost consciousness. None of his words, nor his careful stroking and petting had penetrated her fear at all.

He eased himself out of the bed and stood with hands on hips, staring down at the still body. The bruises from the kidnapping had largely faded, but the scars on her back never would. He shook his head angrily. How had she gotten them?

Stooping, he lifted her body and rearranged it on the bed, placing her head on the pillow and straightening out her limbs. When he lifted the thin wrists, he held one to the light. The same types of old scars lay beneath the new bruises on her wrists. Why had he not noticed them?

Whoever had beaten her had tied her up to do it. He muttered a vicious imprecation. Her husband? Her father-in-law? He had a vision of Luke Garner's impassioned face, flushed with hot rage, his fists clenched, specks of white froth in the corners of his mouth. Turn him loose on a helpless woman and he would show neither mercy nor restraint.

Sighing, shaking his head, Chris pulled the covers up around her shoulders. As he drew on his pants, he realized he could barely remember the beginning of the evening. The exquisite sight of her waiting in the bed for him. The eagerness . . . all had been feigned, he realized with sudden intuition. All, a pretext to avoid more pain. Beatings, perhaps.

He clenched his fist. She thought him capable of beating her. But how could she think anything else? He had kidnapped her, tied her, nearly drowned her, used her.

No, she could not think that he would be gentle with her. He was much stronger than she. He had brought her here to the ranch to rest, but she could not know that. He had not told her so. No doubt she believed he had brought her here to please him before turning her in to the sheriff at Crossways.

He flushed angrily. *Had* that been in the back of his mind?

He shivered suddenly. The room was chilly. He was

naked, except for his pants. Taking the lamp with him, he left her to what remained of the night.

Star awoke to sunlight streaming through her window and a throat so sore that it hurt to swallow. One hand shielded her eyes from the bright golden day, the other massaged uselessly at her neck. She was sore between her legs as well, she discovered when she tried to swing her feet over the side of the bed.

The memories of the night before disturbed her as she wearily drew on her clothes. But she had long ago learned to pretend that nothing untoward had happened. When she had lived with Matthew, no one had been her friend. She had never felt able to approach her sister-in-law, Maude, with her lip permanently curled in an expression of disgust at everything Star did and said.

The first time she had been mistreated, she had gone in fear to her father-in-law. Luke Garner had brushed her aside as if she were speaking of a little rough loveplay. Nevertheless, for a time thereafter Matthew had left her alone. Then Luke Garner had discovered her still without child after six months of marriage. His rage at his son had been terrible.

That evening her torment had begun. Matthew had tied her to the bed, stuffed the hem of her nightgown into her mouth, and . . .

She grabbed the brush from the dresser and began to brush her hair with unnecessary violence, brushing the memories away with the tangles. Memories did no good. Flinging it down, she pulled her hair back severely from her face and twisted it up into a hard knot.

Then drawing a deep breath, she strode to the door.

Chris rose in surprise as she dropped down on the bench

165

at the breakfast table. "Good morning."

Duff waved his fork cheerily at her. "Good morning, Star. Papa said to let you sleep, but you didn't want to, did you?"

She shook her head, smiling her answer at the son and grateful that she could use him as an excuse to avoid meeting the eyes of the father. Her fingers trembling only slightly, she reached for the china mug. When Mrs. MacNeil came forward to fill it full of steaming coffee, Star concentrated on stirring sugar and cream into it. The drink soothed her injured throat. So had she done at countless breakfast tables on Tres Santos, in much worse shape than she found herself now.

When she had finished the first cup, her trembling had stopped and her throat felt well enough to speak. "Good morning," she managed.

Her raspy condition made Chris wince. He looked at the eggs and pone on his plate, feeling his appetite leave him. How would she swallow in that condition?

She must have realized her plight herself. "Just coffee, Mrs. MacNeill. I'm not hungry."

The housekeeper swung around and regarded her narrowly. "Poor thing," she commiserated. "You've caught a bad cold, for sure."

"I must have." Star held out her cup for more coffee.

"Does it hurt bad, Star?" Duff was instantly solicitous. "Aunt Neill always fixes me coffee with honey in it when I have a sore throat." He waved his fork toward the stove. "She always fixes me egg in a glass when I'm getting sick." All business and very grown up, he turned to the housekeeper. "You'd better fix her coffee and egg just the way you do for me."

Mrs. MacNeill smiled. "Coming right up, Duff. Does that sound good to you, ma'am?"

Star felt her stomach heave at the thought of "egg in a glass." "Maybe for lunch, Mrs. MacNeill. Right now I'll just drink the coffee. Maybe it's just a hoarse throat and not a cold. It'll be better soon. I really believe so."

The woman looked doubtful.

"Star, you really ought to do what Aunt Neill says," Duff protested.

The man pushed back his plate and stood. "Let her have what she wants," he instructed curtly. "I'll be back in for lunch." With that, he was gone.

At the end of the day they sat together in the living room, the tension tangible between them. At last Chris rose from his desk. "Walk with me," he commanded.

Clasping her hands tightly together, she went for the shawl Mrs. MacNeill had lent her.

Once under the chill stars he took her arm, but kept his eyes straight ahead until they stood beside the corral, staring again at the dark shapes of the horses. "I never meant to hurt you," he began, by way of apology. "I though you were a willing woman. A widow woman . . ." He paused, remembering how she had become a widow.

"Who had killed her husband and now needed someone else to service her," she finished bitterly.

He swallowed. Turning his back to the corral, he faced her, looking down into her upturned face. "Something like that."

She searched the dark silhouette. Then sighed. "I can imagine how you thought that. I appeared to be so willing. You didn't know any different." She shrugged, then wrapped her arms across her body. "I would like to forget it, if that's possible. Forgive and forget."

"You're very generous."

167

"Not at all. I have no choice. I'm here on your ranch for some strange reason . . ."

"You're here to rest and get your strength back. I was pretty rough bringing you in from Mexico. I . . . I've never brought in a woman before. I guess I treated you like I'd treat a man. You weren't as tough as I thought."

"No, a woman isn't as tough as a man." Again the bitterness in her voice.

For a while they were silent. He tried to think of a way to phrase his next question. He cleared his throat, struggling with the question.

She shivered slightly as an errant breeze lifted the ends of her shawl. "If that is all you wished to say—" she began.

He cleared his throat again, before pushing his hat back on his head. The moonlight picked out the expression on his face. It showed her a mouth drawn down, a forehead wrinkled in a heavy scowl. "How'd you get those scars on your back?" he blurted.

She stared up into his face for a full minute, trying to read there his reason for asking. But his angry, forbidding expression did not change. Abruptly, she turned on her heel and hurried back toward the house, leaving him standing alone. This time he did not follow her.

Chapter Eleven

When Star came to breakfast the next morning, Chris' place at the table was empty. Her taut-stretched nerves relaxed slightly as she took her chair and slipped the napkin from its ring. Dark smudges beneath her eyes testified to a long night spent listening in the dark for the muffled sounds of approaching footfalls and the faint scraping of metal against metal as the door handle turned.

"Papa's gone to the lineshack up north. He stays sometimes two or three nights," Duff made a point of informing her as he forked another flapjack. "Usually, I get to go with him. We sleep in blankets and eat jerky and everything." His gusty sigh was intended to tell her how much he had sacrificed for her. "But he told me to stay here and keep you company."

"I couldn't have a nicer fellow to keep me company," Star told him honestly.

He wiped the white moustache of milk from his upper lip. "I am a nice fellow," he agreed, forgoing his disappointment for a sunny smile. "I'll take you to see where the kittens live? You'd like that, wouldn't you?"

"Sounds like a good thing to do."

Duff dashed ahead of her to the stable, his scuffed boots

thudding through the dust. Star followed at a more sedate pace, her eyes scanning the corrals. Humareda and the Alter-Real stallion Santo Estevao, as well as the other horses, had disappeared.

She curled her mouth in wry disgruntlement. Of course, her captor would have taken every saddle horse on the place with him. He had reasoned rightly that she would have no chance of walking away from his ranch. Since he had brought her home in the dark, she had no idea of the distances separating her from the next habitation where she might beg, borrow, or steal a horse.

"Hey, Star!"

"Coming."

She followed Duff into the shadows of the stables. The familiar odors of horse, hay, leather, and dust blended together in her nostrils. The universal smell raised a wave of homesickness that made her stop and blink back sudden tears. Rancho Montejo! Lost to her forever. And a few days more could very well see the end of everything. Her whole body shuddered at the prospect.

"Star . . ." Duff's voice came from the next-to-the-last stall at the end of the aisle.

She clasped her arms tightly across her chest trying to rid herself of the specter of the gallows. Still its cold, pitiless image swayed before her eyes as she stumbled forward.

Duff knelt in the straw, his index finger stroking down the soft fur of first one and then the other of the kittens. "They're getting their dinner," he announced as she came on. "They almost always are."

"They're just babies," Star reminded him. "They've . . ." She stopped in her tracks. One hand groped for the four-by-four that headed the partition between the last two stalls in the stable.

A horse stood in the last cubicle.

Open-mouthed, Star stared at the animal. She was a mare and not young. Her body was overweight and swayback; her legs, knotty where veins strutted beneath the hide.

"That's my mother's horse." Duff supplied the information. "That's old Lizzie."

"I see." Star reached out a trembling hand and touched the muzzle, with its velvety hair gone almost completely white. Duff's mother had been dead five years according to Mrs. MacNeill, but this horse had to have been old when she was ridden.

"Mama wasn't a very good rider. Papa told me so. Lizzie's not good for anything but crowbait, but Papa keeps her because she was Mama's." Duff scratched the mother cat behind the ears.

Star stooped under the rope that formed the only barrier across the entrance to the stall. Eagerly, she ran her hand down the side of the ewe neck. The mare flicked an ear back, but otherwise made no sign that she had a visitor in her stall.

"She's tame as anything." Duff abandoned the kittens and came around the partition. "Want to see me climb all over her?"

Star swung around toward him, unconsciously spreading her skirts as if to hide the horse from his sight. Although the little boy could have no idea of the thoughts racing through her brain, she felt a guilty flush rise in her cheeks. "Maybe some other time." She slipped out under the rope and went down on one knee beside the kittens.

Duff immediately followed her example, pulling Soxy away from the mother cat's side and turning it around to face him. The kitten spat angrily and batted the air with needle claws. "They sure are growing."

"They sure are." Her eyes swept the stable searching for tack. Her scrutiny was rewarded by a dark bulky shape astride an angle beam in the corner. Suddenly her heart was pounding in her ears. Taking a deep, steadying breath, she rose to her feet. "Why don't we let them go ahead and

171

eat their breakfast? Then when they finish, you can take one or two up to the house to play with. Right now, maybe we'd better go see how Mrs. MacNeill's coming with that buttermilk pie."

Duff set the kitten back in the hay where it immediately scuttled back to its mother's belly. Scrambling to his feet, he thudded back down the aisle. "Oh, yeah. I bet it's done," he called behind him.

Star threw another hasty glance at the dark corner. The saddle was covered by a dusty blanket. A bridle and bit hung from a hook imbedded in the corner stud.

Heart pounding, she pressed her hands against her cheeks. Heat radiated from them until she was sure they must be beet-red. What if Mrs. MacNeill noticed something? She must calm herself. With a bit of luck she could be gone perhaps forty-eight hours before Chris discovered her absence. Texas was big, but surely one could not ride for two days across it without discovering other people, a town, a fort, a ranch. She could slip away right after lunch when Duff was put down for his nap.

Suddenly, lunch seemed an eternity away. Fear for her plan made her breath come short. Involuntarily, she increased her pace. Yet someone might wonder why she was suddenly hurrying across the yard. "Race you." She tapped Duff on the shoulder as she jogged past.

She let him dash into the kitchen a couple of steps ahead of her. Mrs. MacNeill looked at the pair of identically flushed faces and sparking eyes before chiding them for running in the heat. Firmly, she set Duff down at the table and gave them both glasses of milk. Star studied the woman closely for some sign that she might be suspicious, but the housekeeper's affability never faltered.

Star lifted the milk to her mouth and drank greedily. If she were to make good her escape this afternoon, she would need all the nourishment she could get.

* * *

The mare's gait had slowed from a lumbering trot to an amble to a dragging walk. Looking back over her shoulder, Star relaxed somewhat. At least the ranchhouse had slipped over the horizon.

From beneath the brim of her borrowed hat, she scanned the semi-desert before her. The western sun beat on her shoulders. The mare shuffled along at a pace that made Star grit her teeth. Humareda's smooth canter would have eaten up the miles.

Nevertheless, despite the slowness of pace, she had another advantage. The bounty hunter would hunt south first. He would never expect her to head due east. In all likelihood, her captor knew of her connection with the Double Diamond on the Concho. Even if he did, he would still reason that she would make a dash for the Rio Grande rather than risk staying in Texas. If she could just reach her sister, Johanna Sandoval would show them all a thing or two.

She sighed. How she wished she were more like the proud women who were her kin! Many men on Montejo still remembered her mother as a straightbacked lady with a rattlesnake headband around her black hat. Star blinked back sharp tears at the memory of the diamondback. Unconsciously, she rubbed the base of her right thumb.

Mirages shimmered all around her until the entire horizon seemed a silver lake. She could feel her sweat soaking her clothing, even as dark rivulets meandered down the mare's neck. The horse stumbled and blew a roller through her nostrils.

"Easy, Lizzie." Star tugged on the bridle in an effort to raise the drooping head. One ear flicked back, then forward again as the mare lumbered on, her breathing alarmingly heavy.

Another half-hour. An hour. The mare's breathing turned into a wheeze. Her sides heaved in and out. Sweat

173

poured off her flanks. Like a wind-up toy whose spring was exhausted, she plodded to a halt.

Alarmed, Star swung down and went to her head. "I'm sorry, old girl," she muttered. "I didn't realize you were so out of condition. Nobody's been exercising you for a long time, have they?" The mare closed her eyes and stood with head hanging, her sides heaving in and out.

Star looked around her helplessly. No shade to speak of, no water, and no more than a couple of miles distance from the ranchhouse. They simply must move on. Unstrapping one of four canteens, she bathed the mare's nostrils and eyes with her handkerchief. She dared not take a drink herself but poured a little of the precious liquid into the cloth and pressed it inside the mare's slack lips. A few drops fell to the bleached, flinty soil, making little darker circles.

The mare made no response to the handkerchief. The water in the soil evaporated as if it had never been.

Replacing the canteen on the horn, Star pushed her hat back on her head and began leading the mare at a fast clip. She could not, would not rest so soon after her start. Surely, relieved of the rider's weight, the animal would regain her breath.

About a mile further on, the breathing seemed to have returned to normal. Star mounted again. Again the progress was repeated, but with less time before the mare could do no more.

Inside the narrow riding boots Star's feet swelled and burned. Wearily, she followed where her shadow led, keeping it always directly in front of her, watching it grow longer and longer stretching away from her tormented feet.

She mounted the mare one more time as the sun sat on the horizon in a flaming red ball. The animal took two shuffling steps, then slowly collapsed at the hindquarters.

Exclaiming in alarm, Star flung herself from the saddle as the mare tilted slowly over on her side. On hands and knees, sick with despair, she watched the horse go down. When the mare lay on her side, Star crawled to her head.

"I'm sorry, Lizzie," she moaned. "I didn't mean for this to happen. It was just too much for you, old girl."

The mare gave no sign that she had heard. Her sides heaved in and out in tortured rhythm. The breath whistled through her nostrils and through her slack lips.

"Oh, God . . ." Sinking back on her calves, Star pushed her hat back off her hot forehead and looked around. Desperation and guilt made powerful emotional drains on her system. She wanted nothing so much as to curl up and cry her heart out.

Around her the sky began to turn purple. The plants lost their gray-green color and turned to black silhouettes. Over her right shoulder a slender crescent moon began to glow. She was afoot for sure now. The only course was to take the canteens and go. Walk until she could walk no farther, sleep, then walk again in the morning.

Despite her own plight, she pitied the horse more. Unbuckling the bridle from the mare's head, she tossed it aside, loosened the girth and dragged the saddle away. If, by some chance, Lizzie should be able to get to her feet in the morning, perhaps she could make her way back to the ranch if she were unburdened. Satisfied that she had done all she could for the ancient animal, Star draped the canteens over her shoulders and walked away. The mare's harsh breathing quickly faded behind her.

A couple of hours later Star staggered to an exhausted halt. Tears she was not conscious of shedding shone on her cheeks. The last few yards had been agony. With every step she felt the unforgiving leather wear more skin from her feet. Weaving to one side, she dropped to the ground beneath a twisted mesquite. Pillowing her cheek on her hand, she lost consciousness.

The first pink rays of dawn struck her face as a mourning dove cooed above her head. She opened her eyes in time to see a horned toad scuttle across the flinty soil. Despite the protests of bruised, strained muscles, she sat up, her clothing damp and clammy with dew, her body trembling. Facing the rising sun, she ate a cold pone of cornbread washed down with the last of the water from one of the canteens.

Experimentally she wiggled her toes inside her boots. The effort made her wince. Crippled she might be, but she was determined to go on. "I'm just going to ignore you, feet," she declared loudly as she climbed unsteadily onto the members addressed. "I'll concentrate on Johanna. If I can just get to Johanna, she'll take care of me. The Double Diamond is built like a fortress. If she and Marcos hadn't been in New Orleans when I was arrested, I would never have been brought to trial. The Concho can't be so very far away. Johanna will help me. Damn. Oh, damn. That hurts."

Murmuring to herself, she limped toward the rising sun.

Chris Gillard came riding upon her before she was aware. Suddenly, she heard the cantering of horses' hooves. She staggered around, weaving back and forth on unsteady feet, to stare into his dark silhouette against the last red rays of the setting sun. The same sun revealed the play of emotions of hope, fear, and despair, all beneath the layers of sweat and dust. She looked from side to side seeking cover, but the land lay almost flat and barren of trees.

He pulled rein on the stallion, slowing him to a walk. The mare Humareda matched his stride. When the horses' heads were a couple of yards from her, Chris drew them to a halt and eased himself in the saddle. Sardonically, he swept her drooping figure up and down with his eyes. "Had about enough?"

176

The cruel words drove like lances into her lungs and mind. He had caught her just as the sun dropped behind the horizon. Another few minutes and the sky would have been dark. He might have missed her. Drawing a shuddering breath, she allowed the straps to slide off her sore shoulders and the canteens to bump on the ground. "How did you find me?" Her face contorted as she tried to ease the pain in her side. "I headed east."

He shrugged. "Lizzie came home. She and I practically bumped into each other as I was trying to make up my mind which way to go. I just followed her backtrail."

Star passed a hand over her mouth to stifle the groan of anguish. She was exhausted, dehydrated, scorched by the sun. Her shoulders were sore; her feet, raw and burning. "And you just came right along until you caught up to me?" Her voice was huskier than usual.

He reached for the makings of a cigarette. "Actually, I've been on your tail for about an hour now." The flare of the match illuminated his face. She saw he was smiling. She was so tired she wanted to die, and he was smiling.

Rage sent the blood sizzling through her veins. Without thought she swung the half-full canteen in the stallion's face. The horse reared, whinnying shrilly.

Relaxed in the saddle, his hands occupied, Chris was thrown off balance. Only the iron grip of his thighs kept him from being thrown. The reins fell from the stallion's neck.

Screaming like a banshee, Star slung the canteen again. It struck the rearing horse in the chest, driving him to the side. Darting forward almost under the iron-shod hooves, the desperate woman grabbed Humareda's lead rein.

The mare shied too, but the figure doing all the shouting was familiar. She backed slowly. Catching a hold in the flowing black mane, Star swung up into the saddle. With a wild cry worthy of the granddaughter of Masitawtawp, she dug her heels into the mare's sides. Like a black streak,

Humareda tore into the thickening darkness.

Chris cursed the stallion even as he cursed his own carelessness. He had broken most of his own rules where she was concerned. Now he was paying for his lapses. Leaning forward, he caught the trailing reins and brought the stallion under control. Clapping his heels to its flanks, he galloped after the fleeing mare.

The chase in the dark took longer than it would have in light. Star plunged the mare through the sagebrush with the recklessness of sheer desperation. Before her pursuer had gotten his mount under control, she had cut at an abrupt right angle and torn south. Less than a mile, and she pulled up behind a clump of stunted mesquites. The limbs of the trees offered some cover, and there she waited breathlessly, bent low over the mare's neck.

The pounding of her heart and the pumping of the blood in her veins almost drowned out the thunder of the stallion as it tore by. She heaved a sigh, but her relief was only momentary. Unmistakably she could hear the rhythm of the powerful stride break, dissolve into a confused pawing and prancing. He had pulled the mount to a halt. In the sudden silence she could imagine Chris sitting like a statue, alert in the saddle, his handsome head turning to left and right as he strained to catch the slightest sound.

Then he was coming back more slowly. Frustration almost choked her. The stallion would scent the mare. Desperate to escape, she wheeled Humareda and galloped away.

This time the race was a lost one. The stallion's longer stride ate up the mare's lead in great, lunging gulps. Then Chris was directly behind her.

"Pull up!" he yelled.

For answer she lashed the mare across the rump with the reins.

"Damn you. Do you want to kill yourself?"

Even as he spoke, the inevitable happened. Humareda

plunged into a mass of prickly pear cactus. The pain of the spines, driven deep into her forelegs by the force of her run, proved too much even for her gallant spirit. Whickering in panic, she twisted aside, then began to buck.

Good rider though she was, Star was thrown from the horse. She fell heavily on her back. The stars wheeled round in the dark night and then went out entirely.

She regained consciousness beside a small campfire. Groaning, she tried to raise her hand to her aching head but found the movement impossible. A chain clanked dully. She was handcuffed.

Wearily, she sank back against a rough blanket. Feeling utterly defeated, she closed her eyes.

"You almost ruined a good horse."

Her eyes snapped open. Chris Gillard was standing over her, a tall, flat figure. Reddened by the flickering flames from the small campfire, his face was angry; the jaw might have been set in granite.

"Is she all right?"

"Torn up some. I've got the worst of the thorns out and got her rubbed down."

"Thank you."

"You don't have to thank me," he sneered. "I didn't do it for you."

"I know, but I thank you anyway." She closed her eyes.

He squatted down beside her. "In a way it's my fault," he admitted in a surly voice.

She opened her eyes again. "I can't see how. I chose to escape."

"I should have thrown a rope on you the minute I got in range. Never make conversation with an outlaw. That's been my rule. I should have remembered it and abided by it."

She turned her head away. The chain clinked between the handcuffs. "I'm an outlaw," she murmured.

"Right."

She did not look at him again while he rose and busied himself with the horses. Her throbbing body felt strangely light. The pains were not specific, but rather one general ache that throbbed through all her nerves and muscles. Overlaying them, her skin felt feverish, as if the long, exhausting day in the hot sun had somehow baked her and she waited now for her body to cool.

She licked her lips, not surprised to find them dry and cracked. The kerchief around her neck felt suddenly tight and hot. Raising her hands awkwardly, one following the other led by the tiny chain that linked her wrists together, she plucked at the knot.

At that moment she felt the movement of air as he spread his blanket beside her, heard the creak of leather as he laid his saddle on the ground. Then he stretched himself beside her with a faint groan.

Still, she refused to open her eyes. The knot proved stubborn. She was frowning in exasperation when his hands pushed hers aside. "Do you want this untied?"

"Yes."

His question and his nearness compelled her to open her eyes. He lounged beside her, a frown between his eyes, his hands brushing her chin and throat as he worked at the stubborn cotton.

Then he looked into her eyes. They were bottomless, dark and accusing. At the same time he felt the pulse beat in her throat beneath his fingers. How could she be so infinitely desirable after thirty-six hours of hard trail? The sun and wind should have burned her; her hair should have been a snarled mass. Perhaps that truly was her state, and yet she seemed utterly desirable to him.

Gazing into the dark depths of his eyes, Star felt a strange breathlessness that had nothing to do with the tightly knotted kerchief about her neck. She could have no doubt of his desire. Helplessly, she waited for the wave of revulsion that had gripped her for as long as she could remember.

They stared at each other as the seconds passed. A piece of wood crackled and sparks jumped from the campfire. The pale gray eyes became smoky with desire. They scanned her face, saw the heated flush rise in her cheeks, watched her chest rise and fall as she dragged much-needed oxygen into her lungs.

The hands with which he had untied the knot suddenly felt heavy. The fingers like leaden weights pressed against the pulse in her throat. The palms touched the slopes of her breasts and felt her heartbeat increase.

She did not fear him! Neither did his touch repulse her. The wonder and irony of it shook her to the foundation of her being. Intuitively, she knew she could accept his lovemaking. Ironically, the man who had freed her of the horror that the very sight and smell of any man had engendered for two years was the one who would take away her freedom forever. She stared up at him in wonderment; her lips parted slightly.

With an incoherent mutter, he bent his head and kissed her, his tongue caressing the inside of her mouth, drinking from her.

Warmth spread through her as her murmur of pleasure mingled with his own. His kisses seemed to ease the terrible throbbing of her body, or at least to exchange the throbs of pain for pulsations of excitement. Timidly she moved her tongue against his.

Immediately his hands left the knot at her throat and spread to her shoulders, sliding over them and lifting her slightly in his arms as he bent to kiss her deeper and harder. At the same time he hunched his body closer to hers, touching her all along her side. His potency was unmistakable as it pressed against her hip.

The touch of his hard, swollen maleness did not repel her. Instead she felt a sweeping excitement as the warmth in her veins turned to liquid between her thighs.

Yet with the excitement came the sense of anger. He would take her, perhaps even make her feel some of the pleasure that men and women were supposed to feel together. Then he would give her up to Luke Garner tomorrow. Or would he?

As soon as she asked herself that question another formed in her mind. Would he have kept her at the ranch indefinitely had she responded to him? If she had not revealed her true feelings, would he have kept her there in his bed? Would he take her back?

An idea so daring, so dishonorable, so fearsome made her draw in her breath sharply even as his hands opened the neck of her blouse. Did she dare to seduce him? Could she use her body to persuade him not to turn her in? His thumbs brushed across her nipples, and she closed her eyes to hide her deception from him.

"Damnation!" Her body might have been a hot stove so quickly did Chris wrench his hands from her. In a continuation of the same movement he rolled over onto his back on his blanket and threw his arm up across his forehead.

Her eyes flew open at the heartfelt curse. Cold air rushed across her skin where his hands had been. But colder than her skin was the fear that swept her. He would not take her. He would turn away and in the morning he would deliver her to Luke Garner and the hangman's noose.

She could not suppress a moan of fear. She did not want to die. Life, even as Chris's whore, would be better than no life at all. She clasped her icy hands together at her breasts.

He spoke beside her, his voice a little hoarse, as if his throat were clogged. "You needn't worry. I won't touch you."

Opening her eyes, she turned toward him. Her heart pounded with fear. She bit her lower lip to still its trembling. "I'm not the least bit worried," she whispered.

Slowly he lifted his arm away from his face. Propping himself up on one elbow, he searched the dark oval of her

182

face now in shadow as she lay with her back to the fire. His brows drew together in a frown, half-puzzled, half-accusatory.

"I'm not worried," she repeated, her voice stronger. Desperately, she tried to make her stiff lips widen into a smile of invitation.

"Sure you're not!" he muttered sarcastically.

Rather than reply, she extended her cuffed hands to encircle his head. The metal chinked against the back of his neck as she drew him toward her.

The chain against his neck sent a spasm through his whole body. Guilt and a perverse excitement added fuel to the firestorm that seared him. Never had he felt such intense wanting. Yet she had been hurt. She had been stiff with fear when he had taken her before. He would not hurt her again. She was his prisoner. He might not be sworn to uphold the law, but to coerce a helpless woman went against even his rather elastic moral fiber. Firmly he caught her forearms in his hands, ducked his head, and drew her hands from around him. "You don't have to pretend with me," he announced firmly.

A faint unintelligible murmur came from between her lips. Her cuffed hands clasped his cheeks and pulled him down. Slightly off balance, he rolled forward, his mouth coming down hard on hers.

"Hey . . . "

She thrust her tongue into his mouth, tracing the edges of his teeth, embracing his tongue with a hot, eager motion. Her fingers teased the lobes of his ears, stroking them, finding the sensitive nerves behind them.

He could not help responding. His mouth sucked purposefully at her, tasting her sweetness. Eagerly she arched her back and moaned, an unintelligible animal sound from deep within her chest. Her breasts touched his chest. With one hand he located the exciting curve of her waist and slid his palm down over her hip to draw her up to him.

183

She moaned again.

The potent maleness of him swelled almost to bursting at the taste and feel of her and the primal sound from her throat. He was . . . he could not . . . . A tiny whisper of sanity still sighed through his brain. He tore his head violently away from her hands and mouth. He had to clear his throat, so much had every fiber of his body swelled with desire.

"I thought you didn't like men."

Chapter Twelve

Star could not reply immediately. Her own need was shocking to her. As if with each touch Chris Gillard had sent tiny streams of liquid fire leaping through her, she burned with the unfamiliar emotions of a passionate nature released. "I . . . don't . . . feel. . . ."

"Lady," he growled, "you sure as hell feel something. Nobody could fake that well."

Fear streaked across her consciousness. She could hear the echo of Matthew's voice commanding her to feel, demanding to know whether she liked it, insisting that she did. His next move invariably was to wring an agonized cry of confirmation from her.

"Oh, I do." Her voice trembled, then strengthened as she began to babble. "I do. I don't know why I do, but suddenly I do."

He stared hard at her, his brows drawn together. Then an angry curse exploded from him. Violently, he thrust her away. "You don't have to pretend. I won't beat you."

Shuddering, she clenched her hands beneath her throat.

Both were breathing hard as they stared at each other. Each trembled with emotions they denied themselves. Then Chris closed his eyes and drew in a deep breath that flared his nostrils.

While she hesitated, he sat up abruptly, running his fingers through his disordered hair. "I didn't mean for this to happen," he muttered. "I must be going crazy."

Instinctively she knew he would not make another move. She had to do it herself. Yet how did one go about making love to a normal man, a man who cared about a woman's feelings, who even cared about her pleasure?

She raised herself up on her elbow. "No . . . no. I mean . . ." She licked her dry lips in an effort to let the words come out easier. "No, you're not crazy. I've never felt this way before."

He threw her a sardonic grin over his shoulder, one pale eyebrow arched high. "We're all animals under the skin." His look was appraising and faintly contemptuous.

The blood seeped into her hot cheeks. Resentment quickly kindled into anger. How could men be such swine! They would purposely make a woman want them, torment and tease her until her body responded despite herself, and then despise her for her weakness. She bit her lips and turned her head away to hide her thoughts.

He misread her action. "Don't worry," he sneered. "I'll leave you alone. You can slide back down under your blanket."

Her head snapped back around. She could not let him leave her side so long as the faintest hope remained. If she could make love to him, if she could please and satisfy him, he might take her back to his ranch and keep her for a time. With luck, it would be long enough for her to get some sort of message to Johanna. Her life depended on her next move. Black eyes shimmering with the ghosts of unshed tears, she touched his shoulder. "Don't go away," she whispered hoarsely.

He stiffened at her touch.

Moistening her lower lip with the tip of her tongue, she began to open her blouse. "I've never felt this way before,"

186

she repeated, conscious with a sort of detached amazement that she spoke the truth.

Like a statue he sat as she unbuttoned the buttons one by one. With her blouse open on her shoulders, she plucked at the string of her camisole. Slowly she drew the ribbon away in her hand. The garment caught for a moment on the tips of her breasts, but she shook it free with a twist of her torso that made him let out his breath in a sort of sigh.

Uncertain, she followed his gaze. Her nipples stood out tautly. A painful memory made her close her eyes and swallow hard. Matthew had bitten and pinched them in his excitement. Sometimes they had bled and tiny scabs had formed the next day.

Hastily she swept those thoughts aside. Raising her eyes to Chris's face, she cupped her breasts in her palms and squeezed their throbbing tips. At the same time she rose on her knees and offered herself to his mouth.

"Goddamn!" he groaned. "You didn't have to shoot your husband. He just purely died from wanting you." His lips covered one nipple gently, then teased it with his tongue. When she moaned softly, he transferred his attention to the other nipple. His fingers slid down her hip to fumble with the fabric of her divided skirt. Then his hand was beneath the material and sliding upward along her bare thigh.

Her chained hands moved in his fair hair as she felt him rove up over the satin skin between her legs. His fingers brushed the moist, sensitive apex. Drawing in a sharp breath, she waited for the pain to come, the stabbing upward, perhaps with painful scratches of his fingernails or perhaps the pinching. But none came. Instead he stroked her gently and tantalizingly as he continued to caress and kiss her breasts.

She turned her head restlessly. Resentment turned to exultation, which grew as he turned her bones to liquid with his warm mouth. She was doing it! She was pleasing him, giving him such excitement that he would want her and take her back to his own ranch with him rather than give her up. He was not hurting her. She moaned involuntarily at the exquisite sensations created by his mouth on her breast. Panting, she undulated her hips against his chest.

Why, he would love her so well that when he began to tire of her, she might even be able to pay him the reward money to take her back to Mexico!

He drew back for a moment, staring up into her impassioned face, trying to read her motives. Thoroughly puzzled, he shook his head. "I've never seen anybody enjoy it the way you do."

She froze, her face aghast, her hands springing away from his head as if he were hot.

He grinned maliciously. "Truth always has a way of coming out, doesn't it?" His hands tightened as he felt her stiffen, and he began to kiss her breasts again.

Tears did form in her eyes then. Two trickled down her cheeks. She could please him and, so it seemed, herself. But to do so she must lose her self-respect. He would think the very worst of her. She groaned aloud, but not with ecstasy. Somehow his opinion mattered very much.

His long, hard fingers shifted to clasp and caress the sensitive skin where her thighs joined her buttocks. His mouth greedily suckled her breast. Her hips began a gentle dance she could not control. She moaned and licked her lips. Her mouth felt too dry to utter the shameful words that next would come. "W-why not let me help you off with your clothes?"

Reluctantly he pushed himself away from her pulsating body. "Sure, lady," he agreed hoarsely. "Why not? Might as well have the whole show." Letting her skirt fall back in place, he rose, his hands on his lean hips.

She swayed back from him, intimidated by his angry maleness. His eyes were hot in the firelight as he stared at her nipples, shining with moisture and slightly swollen from his kisses. She could feel herself flushing in sudden fear as she glimpsed the expression on his face. Why was he angry? He was getting what he wanted. What every man wanted.

Still he looked and a myriad of strange emotions flickered in his eyes.

She held her breath. Matthew had never looked at her body as if he admired it. Confused, she pulled her cuffed hands down in front of her breasts.

Chris frowned as the silvery metal glinted in the firelight. His right hand made an abortive movement toward the pocket where he carried the key. His fingers brushed the cloth before doubling back in a fist as if he had touched fire.

Star did not see the gesture. Her mind frantically scolded her for not staring at him boldly. He would think again that she had no wish to respond. Reminding herself that her performance was life or death, she raised her hands at the same time she raised her eyes. Curving her lips into a smile, she began to unbutton his shirt.

As each button came free from its hole, she caressed his skin with its silky covering of golden hair. With her first touch, he closed his eyes. She spread her hands as far as the restraints would allow—until her fingers touched his nipples and she felt him shiver.

"My God, lady. You sure do blow hot and cold."

"It's . . . it's more exciting that way," she murmured as she reached around him awkwardly to pull his shirt from his pants.

"I'll do it." With quick, efficient movements he stripped off his garments, letting them drop to the ground beside them. When he was nude except for his boots, he stooped and pulled her to her feet. With hot, hard hands he unfastened her skirt and let it fall from her body. His thumbs curved about her hip bones as his eyes swept over

189

her pale flesh. Sucking in a tight breath between his teeth, he dropped down before her. Roughly, almost angrily, he closed his hands around her buttocks. Her agonized gasp was music as he pressed his mouth to her belly.

He likes what he sees, she thought. It was her last coherent thought as his lips skimmed her thigh. His breath blew hot into the silky hair. In the grip of that delicious sensation she did not have to pretend to stir her hips. They shifted and danced as he worked his magic.

He jerked his mouth away. Tilting his head back, he stared upward between her breasts into the pale oval of her face. His lips quirked at the corners as he rubbed his chin speculatively against the velvet skin beneath her navel. "Shall I kiss you?" he offered.

She stared down uncomprehendingly into his eyes, opaque silver wells that hid their secrets. A shiver ran through her. "No. Let me kiss you."

His grip tightened when she would have stooped. "Has anyone ever kissed you here?"

She hesitated, blood surging through her veins.

"Like this?" His fingers parted the black silk at the bottom of her belly and his tongue touched the swollen sensitive spot.

"No . . ." Her cry was surprise, weakness, shyness, all combined. Her legs began to buckle. He clapped both hands around her buttocks and held her hard while she writhed and twisted. Her cuffed hand fastened in his hair and held him against her.

Her overcharged body could not take such stimulation for more than a few minutes. In almost no time, she convulsed, crying her pleasure to the starlit skies while he held her and suckled her avidly.

When, finally, she hung limp in his grasp, he lowered her to the blanket. Then, without waiting for a sign from her, he plunged into her. Her tight sheath was hot and welcoming. She sighed with pleasure and wrapped her legs around

190

him. As he stroked her, rhythmically and with strength, she felt the same incredible pleasure building. It could happen again! Her lips parted; her eyes stared at the stars overhead. She concentrated with all her soul on the sensations his body created.

His own breath was running hot. "I . . . I can't . . . hold . . ." His words were gritted through clenched teeth. The last word turned into a groan of seemingly mortal agony as he exploded, shuddering and writhing.

At the same time the strength of his thrust touched off another firestorm within her body. She tightened her legs around him and hung on as if he were her only lifeline. They writhed and shuddered together until at last they lay still, entwined around each other.

"I can make love to you now," Star told him shyly, her lips moving against his chest as she spoke. "I don't mind doing it at all."

"I'll say." He lay on his back, staring upward at the stars. At no time in his life had he ever felt so complete. Absently, he stroked her shoulder with his left arm.

"You could take me back with you to the ranch," she went on a trifle breathlessly. Her lips moved against his nipple. "I could love you as many times and as often as you wanted. I . . ."

He sat up abruptly, the movement pushing her aside. He sprang to his feet. "So that's what this is all about."

She roused herself onto her elbows. "I . . . I thought that's what you wanted."

"You want me not to turn you in."

She shook her head in bewilderment. "I thought that's what you took me to the ranch for to begin with. I thought you wanted me to make love to you. When I wouldn't do it was when you decided to turn me in." She held out her cuffed hands beseechingly. "But now that I don't mind . . .

that is . . . that I want . . ."

He cursed her. His words were even and vicious, curdling the blood in her veins. The names he called her eviscerated her, flayed her, until her cheeks and lips turned white as parchment. When he had exhausted his vocabulary, he flung her own words back in her face and laughed at her. "What I need is a real honest woman. I won't ever need the likes of you. No man in his right mind would take up with a murdering whore."

"I am not a whore!" she screamed. "I'm not. Goddamn you! You're just like the rest of them and the worst of the lot." Frantically she stared around her, seeking something to throw at him. She would hurt him. She would kill him if she could get her hands on . . . the butt of his revolver protruded from its rolled-up holster stuffed beneath the saddle. With a primal snarl she dived for it.

He caught her by the shoulders just an instant too late. The Peacemaker slid free and her finger found the trigger. He dropped on her. His considerable weight came down on her hips and legs. An instant later he straddled her, lunging for the gun. She screamed in pain as the rough handling damaged her half-healed ribs. Still she struggled to turn herself and train the muzzle on him.

His long arms and hands quickly covered her arms and directed the pistol into the sagebrush. "Let it go!" he demanded.

"No!"

He let go of one hand to grasp her wrist and squeeze, but the handcuff protected her on his first grip. "Let . . . go!"

"Damn you!" she panted. Her thumb managed to pull back the hammer.

"Drop it!" He shifted his grip and squeezed until the bones ground beneath his fingers.

The thunder of the Colt drowned her scream. In the next instant he had wrested the gun from her grasp and sprung to his feet.

As the echo died away, she drew herself into a ball. Her hands covered her face and pressed against her mouth to extinguish her sobs.

Panting hard, he stared down at the soft curve of her hips and her slender thighs. He was sure she was weeping, but she made no sound. Only the faintest of tremors vibrated her shoulders. His first impulse was to sink down beside her and gather her into his arms. Instead he swept up his pants and drew them on in two brutal jerks. Buttoning them hastily, he thrust the gun into the waistband and swung away into the darkness leaving her lying shattered among the blankets.

A weatherbeaten sign on a post at a crossroads directed them to ride four miles east to Crossways, Texas. A cluster of tumbleweeds gathered around its base like faggots for a burning. Hot south wind tugged at their clothing, dust swirled around the legs of their mounts, sweeping their tails around over their dirty flanks.

Both the horses might have been ridden straight from Huasteca instead of rested for a week at the ranch. The mare's black hide no longer shone in the sun. The stallion's proud neck was streaked a dusty gray by runnels of perspiration.

Struggling to keep her face impassive, Estrella stared at the pointed piece of wood. Only by looking at each letter individually could the traveler make out the name. Her black eyes were glazed. She did not try to read the letters on the gray, wind-scoured surface. In her mind's eye she could see the town, its eight commercial buildings aligned facing north. The jail and the courthouse formed an "L" at the end.

Would Luke Garner still have the gallows beside the courthouse? Solitary, stark, obscenely naked it had stood on the prairie barren of trees. Like the living trees it, did not belong there.

When Chris would have prodded the horses forward, she caught his arm. "Wait." She swallowed heavily, squeezing her eyes closed against the bitter fearful tears. Only with an effort could she bring herself to speak. When she did so, her voice quavered. "I have something to ask of you."

The steely gray eyes beneath the Stetson darkened. After one quick glance at her face he looked away, staring off into the distance. One fist clenched on the reins; the other ground into his thigh. He drew a deep breath.

Hastily she withdrew her hand, closing it over the horn. Her voice deepened, but the tremor was gone. "Oh, you needn't worry. I know if the money I offered you in Saltillo plus four of the best horses in Mexico couldn't bribe you, you couldn't be bribed. I know you'll turn me in."

His face did not relax. He had not spoken to her nor she to him during the day's long, hard ride.

"Likewise," she hastened on bitterly, "I won't waste my breath with a repeat offer of my body. You've made yourself clear on that subject."

He did not look at her. Instead his eyes followed the path of a tumbleweed as it bounced over the pale land some hundred yards away along the trail.

She stared at his profile, willing him to look at her. "I just wanted to ask one favor."

Dark color stained his neck and cheeks. Finally, he turned to face her, his eyes narrowing. At the same time, he shifted uncomfortably in the saddle. The last thing he wanted on his hands was a sobbing woman to lead into Crossways. Some outlaws did cry and beg as they got closer to their destination. Somehow he thought she would have been icy calm to the end.

She read in his face his implacable nature. A tiny flicker of hope died within her, although she had willed it dead long before. She straightened her weary back in the saddle. "Take my horse."

It was the last thing he had expected her to say. His mouth dropped open. His silvery eyebrows shot upward.

"Please. Take her. When you turn me over to the sheriff or to Luke at Tres Santos or wherever you take me, just take the reins to Humareda and ride off as if she belonged to you. I wish I could ask you to take her back to Tomas, but I know that's impossible. You aren't a fool. My brother will kill you if you ever set foot in Mexico again."

"I don't understand. . . ."

She patted the dusty neck and combed her fingers through the tangled, windswept mane. "I can't bear the thought of her being ridden and abused by Luke Garner. She's gentle, delicate. Just like her name. Humareda. 'Cloud of Smoke.' She's been trained to hand and voice commands." The tremor was back in her voice. She leaned farther forward over the mare's neck, now seemingly intent on combing the mane and arranging it until it hung smooth.

"I don't . . ."

"There isn't anyone on Tres Santos who would have any idea how to ride her," she interrupted. "Her mouth is like a baby's. All anyone at that ranch knows is manhandling the stock. Every rider uses a U.S. Cavalry bit with a thirty-two-pound pull." Her voice gathered strength and developed a cutting edge.

"I still think . . ."

"Can you imagine what those gringos do to a horse's mouth? By noon the poor animal is numb. By evening his neck and mouth have been jerked so much that all he can do is hang his head." She left off stroking the mane to face Chris full, her black eyes searching his face earnestly. "Can you imagine her terror? The first time they touched her with a quirt, she wouldn't know what they wanted, so they'd whip her some more. She'd rear and fight them . . . you know what would happen."

In her own mind she was remembering her experience in

the household of Luke and Matthew Garner. Tears stood in her eyes. She had not been able to save herself. Automatically, she massaged the base of her thumb. Sympathetic pain shot up her arm as she felt again the sadistic pressure, heard again the bone snapping like a dry stick. Sweat glistened on her forehead.

Chris moved uneasily in the saddle. The delicate features beneath the black hat looked more drawn than ever.

She blinked. Humareda would at least be saved from the horror. Star did not know what fate awaited the mare in Gillard's company, but she was fairly certain he would treat her with care. The stallion was proof of his master's excellent training. "Please," she whispered, focusing on Chris's face, only a degree less strained than her own.

Chris bit his lip. He half raised his hand in protest.

"Please . . ." Her voice was stronger. She was begging now.

He tightened his jaw grimly. He wanted the mare, of course. But his soul quailed before the manner in which he would acquire her. He had expected to buy her off Luke Garner with some of the reward money, or buy her from the sheriff afterward. To have the condemned prisoner offer him her most prized possession cut deeply into his sensibilities.

Her passionate eyes searched his face. "Think of the wonderful colts," she urged.

He sighed. The sigh was more than capitulation to her request. Despite the violent scene last night, his conscience bothered him. He had behaved badly, his own attitude, in part, precipitating the sordid scene. Grimly he acknowledged that she might easily have construed the idea that he had taken her to his ranch to use her, and that after she had refused him, she had become his prisoner once more.

Other doubt crowded into his mind. This woman did not behave like an outlaw, certainly not like the men whom he had brought in for murder. If one discounted last night's explosion of rage, her days at the ranch had had an air of normality. Her clear, open gaze, her quiet, delicate manner, her care and attention to his son, a thousand things confirmed her innocence at the same time they cast into doubt her guilt. Even her silent study of the landscape as they rode through it had taken on the air of communing with nature. This woman savored every moment of her life. She hated no one. Only under great provocation, in the heat of the moment and to defend herself, could she have taken a human life.

Chris Gillard could not have told how he had arrived at this conclusion. He only knew that it was true, and with that knowledge came shame and self-condemnation. He cursed the day he had ever taken this job. For a certainty, this must be his last.

"Please . . ."

"All right," he muttered grudgingly. He extended his hand across his body to grasp hers in a handshake that sealed the bargain.

Relieved, Star smiled tremulously into his face.

At her smile, Chris's stomach tightened. His conscience smote him viciously. "Let's get on," he snarled, heeling his mount down the trail.

Star saw the gallows before they reached the first building on the street. A tiny sound slipped from between her tightly clamped lips. Chris shot a glance at her, his own gut twisting. His first impulse was to grab the mare's reins, wheel the stallion away, and gallop hell for leather back to Mexico.

But he did neither. Both stallion and mare plodded steadily along until they were alongside the first building. Nearer they rode. Nearer the gray rough boards that formed the crude steps, the rough plank platform, the upside down "L" with an angle piece in it to give it extra support.

Star felt the sweat trickle between her breasts. In her mouth was the taste of burning brass. The noose swung slowly in the prevailing wind, its course a small circle beckoning. Despairingly, she fixed her eyes on the dusty earth between her horse's ears. Her last hope gone, she rode tamely at the side of her silent captor.

The heat of the early afternoon had abated somewhat. A man who stepped through the door of the cafe stared at them as they rode past. His mouth dropped open. He tossed his cigarette into the dirt behind them and sprang down from the boardwalk. Catching up the reins of a mean-looking mustang, he swung into the saddle and wheeled the horse for another look. Satisfied with what he saw, he raked his spurs across the animal's sides and sent it galloping out of town.

Chris swung around in the saddle to scowl ferociously after the departing rider.

"Looks like you won't have to ride out to Tres Santos to fetch your bounty money," Star remarked bitterly between clenched teeth. "Luke Garner will hear in just a few minutes."

Chris's face contorted, then smoothed into impassive planes. "Saves me a trip," he nodded.

"You'll be able to complete your business and get on to the next hunt without wasting any time."

The tired horses halted at the hitching rail outside the jail. Chris swung down and reached up for Star. She stared at his outstretched arms. Suddenly a wave of anger swept her. How could he offer to assist her as if he had taken her out for a Sunday ride? His politeness was a mockery. Angrily she threw her left leg over the horn and slid down on Humareda's right side.

When she slipped under the the hitching rail, he met her on the other side and took her arm. She jerked it angrily away. "I can walk in under my own power, gringo. It's too

198

late to run away now." Her sudden twist put a strain on her bruised torso and newly damaged ribs. Her voice rose in a gasp on the word "now," causing Gillard to throw her a glance of real concern.

Sternly she reminded herself that the mask she had assumed only a few weeks after entering this town as a bride must be in place again. Her face must reflect nothing. With her body straight, in her worn dusty clothing, her shoulders back, her head erect, she mounted the porch to the door of the jail.

Doubling his hand into a fist, Chris sprang up after her. Like a schoolboy remembering his manners, he opened the door and stepped back to allow her to enter.

Chapter Thirteen

The sheriff raised his hat off his eyes to stare blearily at the figures in the doorway. He jerked his scuffed boots off the desk and pushed himself up to stand behind it. His careless movement knocked over a bottle he had concealed beside his chair. With a clink it fell on its side and rolled across the floor of the office. Contemptuously, Star's black eyes followed its path. When the label came uppermost, she recognized it as a four-bit whiskey Matthew had scorned as too raw.

Gillard's eyes also flicked across the bottle, then back to the unshaven sunken face with its network of reddish-blue lines radiating outward from the swollen nose. Scornfully he surveyed the rest of the unlovely minion of the law in Crossways.

A sweat-greased shirt and vest with a battered silver star hung over the thin shoulders and hollow chest. A little potbelly pooching above a low-slung belt confirmed the sheriff's love of alcohol. The man swiped his hand across his mouth. "What can I do fer y'?"

Chris strode to the desk. "Got a prisoner for you, sheriff."

"Sure." The man swayed slightly forward, then backward. His speech was slightly slurred. "Sure. Be right glad to accommodate y'." He pulled his belt up over his belly as he rocked unsteadily to the side. Nodding and muttering, he staggered out from behind the desk. The belt slid down again into its accustomed position when he reached for the keys dangling from a hook on the wall behind his head. He frowned at the man and the woman, his expression puzzled.

Chris ground his teeth. "Prisoner for you, sheriff," he repeated.

The rheumy eyes stared from Chris to Star. Suddenly, recognition began to dawn. The law of Crossways wiped a sweaty hand around the back of his neck. A slow, malicious grin split his mouth, revealing filthy brown-stained teeth. "Hey! You really got her! By God, Luke Garner's gonna be tickled pink to see this little *puta*." Eagerly, he reached out to grasp Star's arm just above the elbow.

Impassive before the insult, Star, nevertheless, flinched away from the roughness of his grasp and the foulness of his breath.

Chris, on the other hand, reacted angrily. Like a striking rattler, his fist struck out to fasten the front of the sheriff's shirt. The man's weight rose on tiptoes as Chris hauled him upright. "Watch your language!"

"Hey. I only said . . ."

"I heard what you said. It's not the truth. So button your lip."

The man flushed angrily. Releasing Star's arm, he caught at Chris's wrist with one soiled, calloused hand. "Take it easy, fella." He made a groping motion at his side with the other hand.

Instantly, Chris grabbed for his wrist. "Keep your damned hands to yourself."

The man grunted in surprise and alarm. "Hey, now,

fella. I'm just doin' my duty. Just take it easy."

"You take it easy." Chris gave the sheriff a hard shove as he released the greasy shirtfront.

The man staggered, then scuttled behind the desk. His eyes darted from one to the other, clearly puzzled by the bounty hunter's strange attitude.

Satisfied that the man was cowed, Chris swung around. Star had stepped back out of the fray. The top button of her shirt had come loose where the sheriff's grasp had disarranged it. His first impulse was to lead her out of the jail. He could take her to the rooming house two doors down, get her a room, tie her to the bed if need be, until . . .

Reason made him step back. What would he do next? He had brought her in for a bounty, after all. He glared at her in turn as fiercely as he had glared at the sheriff. Grimly, he stepped forward and closed the blouse, buttoning it securely. He felt her breasts heave beneath his knuckles as she drew a deep breath. Cold sweat bathed his face, but he drew the key from his pocket to open the irons on her wrists.

Working in uncomfortable silence, he kept his eyes down, even though his gut twisted at the sight of the angry red weals that lay across the silvery-white scars around her slender wrists. Swinging back around, he eyed the sheriff, who now stood with hands hanging at his sides, his face knotted into a puzzled scowl.

Finally, Chris shrugged. "Just lock her up without opening your trap," he growled.

The sheriff's eyes popped. He looked from one to the other. Then, shaking his head, he scooped up the keys and stumped round the desk. "Come on." He reached for Star again but thought better of it in time to draw back hastily. Gesturing with the keys, he allowed her to proceed at her own pace toward the door that led to the two cells at the back.

At the door Star squeezed her eyes together tightly. Her

shoulders lifted in a last deep breath of free air. Then she looked back at Chris Gillard. "Don't forget." Her husky voice was deeper than he had ever heard it.

For a moment he looked blank. Then he remembered. Humareda! "The cloud of smoke." He smiled bleakly.

"Thank you."

She passed through the door. The sheriff followed her and closed it.

Fists clenched, a sinking sensation in his belly, Chris Gillard heard the various sounds of metal striking against metal as she was locked in a cell.

"Y'all want me to write you a receipt?" The sheriff ambled back through the door, locking it behind him. Awkwardly, he dropped into his chair and scooted it up to the desk.

"Save it," Gillard snapped. "I'll pick it up later." Turning his back, he left the office.

Star pressed her back against the bars of the cell as claustrophobia clawed at her throat. The six-by-six cubicle was bare, except for a stained pallet of filthy ticking along one wall and a bucket in the far corner. Moreover, the atmosphere of the cell was hot and still and incredibly foul-smelling.

Her stomach quivered in protest as she pressed her hand over her nose and mouth. Raising her eyes, she sought the source of air. In the back of the cell one small window, some four inches high, a foot long, located fully a foot above her head, allowed light and flies to enter. Blue-bottle flies swarmed noisily around the bucket in a corner.

As the purpose of the container and the source of the stench dawned on her, Star whirled around to press her face against the bars. Her stomach heaved as she gagged repeatedly. Her eyes spouted tears, her body shuddered with the renewed pain from her ribs and the necessity of controlling herself so as not to befoul the cell further.

When finally she managed to quiet her shuddering stomach and draw light, even breaths, she was huddled on her knees in the farthest corner from the bucket. Her first impulse was to shout to the sheriff to come and take the foul mess away. Then she smiled grimly. Common sense told her that any requests she might make would be useless. Luke Garner paid the sheriff. Her confinement would be as hideous as possible. Her only hope could be that it would be mercifully brief.

Wearily, she twisted round on the rough plank floor, her shoulder pressed into the corner formed by the bars and the adobe wall. Oppressive heat surrounded her. The adobe at her back was hot and dry, the cell bars warm. As she rested her forehead against one, she stared downward at the filth ground into the wood. Dark splats marked where tobacco had been spat on the floor. Here and there were the remains of cigarette butts, many in the center of a circular scuffmark, and tiny twisted fragments of paper and scraps of tobacco, along with the gray smudges of ashes.

She must have dozed, or perhaps lost consciousness entirely, she decided when next she knew herself. The cell was dim.

Most of the flies had swarmed away as the sun had set, but the cockroach population had awakened and begun to skitter back and forth across the rough plank floor and up the sides of the bucket.

The stench no longer bothered her. Her sense of smell was mercifully numb. But her flesh crawled at the sight of the shiny-backed brown insects, their antennae waving, their bristly legs flickering as they ran through the filth. She clenched her fist against her mouth in an effort to stifle the whimper that quickly became a sob before it slipped from between her tightly compressed lips.

In a few minutes the cell would be completely dark. She would have to sit here while they crawled across her body. To stand all night long was unthinkable. She was almost too tired to move now. Only an effort of will kept her seated in a huddled ball in the corner, when she longed to sprawl facedown on the pallet, no matter how filthy it might be.

She shuddered weakly, burying her face in her hands.

The sound of a key in the lock brought her to attention. Hand over hand, she pulled herself upright as the door swung open. The sheriff's shape blocked a part of the light. "Forgot to give you your water for the night," he rasped, swaying where he stood. His steps unsteady, he made his way across the short space.

A cracked crockery pitcher swung from his hand. He chuckled when he saw her pressed against the bars with unnatural tightness. "Roaches kinda gettin' to y', huh?"

With conscious motions, he stooped over to set the pitcher down in front of the window at the bottom of the cell. "Brought y' some water," he repeated. His back creaked noisily as he straightened with a grunt and pulled his belt over his belly.

He waited while she knelt and drew the vessel inside the cell. Thrusting his hands into the hip pockets of his pants, he rocked back and forth on his feet. "Sent a boy out to tell Mr. Garner y'all was here. He was havin' supper. Sent word back to keep y' locked up tight and he'd see y' in the mornin'. So that's what I'm gonna do. Y'all hungry?"

Actually, she was very hungry, but a glance at the murky water in the pitcher plus the condition of his grimy hands discouraged her. "No, thank you." Her voice was a whisper he had to incline his head to hear.

He nodded then and trudged back the way he had come. "Well, goodnight then." He paused in the open doorway to rub the back of his neck with his hand. "Roaches don't bite none," he chuckled at last. "Course, there might be some stingin' scorpions in that pallet." His guffaw at that remark ended in a violent fit of coughing. Before it was over, he had closed the door behind him, leaving her alone in the dark.

The rooming house two doors down from the jail had a corral and shed behind it. Chris Gillard led the horses directly there, watered and fed them, and at last tossed two bits to the Mexican squatted in the shade watching him. "Rub them down, *por favor.*"

"*Sí. Gracias.*"

Draping both pairs of saddlebags across his shoulders, he entered the rooming house. A neat gray-haired woman, her spectacles clamped firmly over the bridge of her nose, stared critically at the newcomer. After a moment she passed a cardboard-backed tablet across the polished desk and spoke while he signed his name with the stub of a pencil. "That'll be four bits a day for room with meals, dollar and a half a week, five dollars a month. If you want a bath from time to time, that's twenty-five cents extra. There's a bathhouse out back. Manuel hauls water for it."

"Sounds good, ma'am."

"The name's Rosa McGloin."

Her eyes of the sapphire shade called Irish blue measured his tall form, his silvery shock of cornsilk hair, and his even, tanned features. Her mouthed narrowed sternly as she adjusted the gold wire rims of her spectacles. "No whiskey or women in the rooms."

"No, ma'am."

Evidently, he had passed muster. Her critical surveillance relaxed into a small smile. "Would you be liking that bath now?"

He nodded following her eyes down his filthy shirt and pants. He ran his hand over his jaw. "And a shave."

"Manuel's little boy Hector makes a fair job of that while you bathe."

"Much obliged, Mrs. McGloin." He resettled his saddlebags on his shoulders and peered behind her down the narrow hall.

She jerked her head over her shoulder. "Room's at the end on the right."

He nodded again. He was halfway down the hall when her voice caught him. "There's no prohibition against having a drink in the bathhouse."

He grinned over his shoulder. "Thank *you*, ma'am."

Within an hour he was folded into a steaming tub, the lower half of his face covered with lather. Between his drawn-up knees, he squeezed a bottle of dollar whiskey.

"Now, *señor*."

"Wait a few more minutes, *muchacho*," came the lazy reply. "Let the lather soak in good. Give me a chance to get a few more swallows of this down me." To demonstrate, he tipped the bottle up to his lips. A gusty sigh slipped from him as he lowered it.

Hector giggled. "I come back soon, *señor*."

"You do that, *muchacho*."

He was almost asleep with the half-empty bottle between his knees when the Mexican youth returned. "I shave you now, *señor*?"

Starting sleepily, he nodded. "Sure, *muchacho*. And wash my back."

The addition of another kettle of hot water brought the steam rising again. Chris sighed with pleasure and tilted his head back against a rolled towel that Hector positioned over the edge of the tub.

Delicately, he scraped the razor up the side of Chris's neck. "Is it true, *señor*, that you are the one who brought the Señora Garner back from Mexico?" he asked in a soft voice.

"Yep." Chris' eyes flew open as his smile faded. He stirred uncomfortably in the warm water.

"Are you a ranger?"

"No."

"I would like to be a ranger when I grow up, but it is not for Mexicans." The boy's razor deftly skimmed Chris's upper lip. "Of course, I would not like to bring in a woman. My father says that I am a man and that men . . ." He paused. A moment later he cleared his throat.

"What, *muchacho?*" Chris prodded softly, although he was fairly certain that he did not want to hear what Hector was going to say next.

The boy frowned and shifted uncomfortably, his *huaraches* squeaking. "*Nada, señor*. My mother says I chatter like a *chachalaca*." With a final swipe, he laid down the razor and reached for the towel soaking in a bucket of hot water. Wringing it out, he spread it over Chris's face. "When you are ready, *señor*, I will stand on a stool and pour water over you to rinse you."

The boy's words had broken Chris's peace. He pulled the towel off his face and wiped his neck and throat with it in swift, economical motions. "Go ahead and do it now. I'm getting all shriveled, and the water's cool, besides." Careless of the water he sloshed on the floor, he rose to his feet.

Hastily, Hector hopped up onto the stool from which he bent, lifted the bucket of hot water, and poured it carefully over the tall man's shoulders. When the bucket was empty, he hopped down to fetch a towel.

When Chris was dry and dressed, he held out a fifty-cent piece to the youth.

"I am paid by Señora McGloin." Hector shook his head, but his eyes looked longingly at the shining silver.

"Then give me some information." Chris hunkered down level with the boy's eyes. "Tell me what the town thinks of a man who brings in a woman."

Hector blinked. He looked from the man to the coin and back again. "I cannot tell you what the town thinks, señor." He paused carefully. "I can only tell you what my mother says. A woman must be very badly afraid to flee from her husband or to wish to do him harm. She says this is so because a woman has no chance against a man."

"Not even with a gun?"

Hector hung his head. "I cannot tell, señor, but I do not think so. My mother is afraid of guns."

Later, dressed in clean clothes, his boots shined, Chris stepped out onto the dirt street of Crossways. The half-empty bottle of whiskey dangled from his hand.

The stars glittered coldly in the dark. No moon dimmed their diamond fires. A bat eeped a few feet above his head, as it wheeled close to the side of the building to catch an insect. A chill skittered up his spine, raising the hair on the back of his neck. He hated bats.

The jail was in darkness, as were most of the buildings in town. Thank God, he could not see the gallows. He shivered again as a screech owl hooted mournfully from somewhere in the dark.

Only the door of the local cafe stood open to throw a dim light on the dirt street. Probably not a whore to be found in this whole county, Chris thought morosely as he took a sip from the bottle.

Last night he had no need of a whore. Chris's loins tightened at the thought. She had been so exciting, rising on her knees to offer him her firm, beautiful breasts. He had enjoyed pleasing her with his mouth, feeling her writhe and tremble in his arms, her belly vibrating against him. Then when he had taken her, her legs had wrapped around him so powerfully that he had died of pleasure long before he had intended to. She had been with him then, too, her flesh surrounding his, gripping him so tightly that he had climaxed almost at once, like a boy with his first woman.

He had known no other woman except Star for months now. He wondered if he could find a whore. His mouth curled as he dismissed the thought as repulsive. He really did not want anyone. Unless, of course, he could have her again.

Last night she had been more than any man could ever have wanted. A man could burn, not just warm himself, in all that Mexican fire. He couldn't help but admire her, now that he had had a chance to calm down. He really couldn't blame her for thinking that he would take her back. Hell! What else was she supposed to think? He had been as randy as a stallion ever since he'd gotten her across the border.

She was a desperate lady. And yet so gentle with his son . . . he shook his head. Her last concern had been for her horse. She had grit to go for that gun. What had Hector's mother said . . . a woman has no chance against a man.

"Hell!" Angrily, he dropped off the porch of the rooming house and all but ran toward the lighted door of the cafe. Surely to God there'd be somebody there to take his mind off Estrella Garner y Montejo.

The occupants of the cafe hardly glanced in his direction as he entered. A fat man in a large apron, filthy across the middle, wiped scratched glasses methodically with a cloth scarcely less soiled than the apron. He stood behind a bar that consisted of two one-by-twelves laid across two oak barrels.

At a table in the center of the room beneath a hanging lantern four men sat playing cards. Their hats were pushed back on their heads; smoke from their cigars rose in wreaths around their faces.

A fifth man lay slumped over a table near the bar. His face was turned away from the room. As Chris entered, the man snorted and sat up. His bleary eyes searched the room without interest. "Whiskey," he croaked. "How about some more whiskey, Jedlicka?" His voice took on a pleading note. "Jedlicka! I've slept some now."

The big man behind the bar ignored the request. He eyed

the half-full bottle in Chris's right hand. Chris swung the label uppermost. The man nodded as he set one of his freshly polished glasses on the bar. Chris splashed a couple of ounces of whiskey into it.

"More whiskey," came the plaintive voice.

"Y'all have had enough, Doc." The barkeep's voice rumbled out of his big belly. "Why don't you just mosey on out of here now that you're awake."

"Hell! I haven't had nearly enough. I tell you, I can . . ." The man at the table angrily pushed back his chair. Whatever he was about to aver was lost when he toppled out of his chair and sprawled on the floor.

The barkeep leaned over the edge of the one-by-twelves. "Doc, go home."

The man rolled over and lurched to his feet. Staggering to the bar, he placed himself nose-to-nose with the barkeep, shouldering Chris accidentally aside. "Now's the time that I need it most. I don't sleep without it." He clutched the edges of the boards. "You know, Jedlicka," he quavered. "I don't sleep without it."

"For God's sake, give him a drink and shut him up," one of the men in the card game complained.

The doctor spun around with a fatuous grin. Both elbows hooked over the bar in back, supporting his wobbly legs. "You're a real pal, my friend," he called loudly.

"He's had enough," Jedlicka protested.

"He'll never get enough until it kills him," another one commented.

"You're right," the one called Doc nodded, spinning back to face Jedlicka again. This time his feet slipped out from under him. Chris steadied him by the elbow to keep him from falling flat and hitting his chin on the bar as he fell. Too drunk to know what he had avoided, he shook Chris's arm off and leaned forward earnestly. "Jedlicka, you have to help me to get this." He looked over his shoulder. "My dear friends there playing cards implore you in my name. I will never get enough until it kills me. And I am taking so long to die." He seized his pulse in surprisingly competent fingers. "So damned long." He smiled eagerly at the card players.

"I ain't givin' him any more!" Jedlicka folded his hands. "Any of you gents wants to pay for his drinks, he can drink all night, but not for free."

The men at the table suddenly evinced great interest in their cards. The one who had spoken first even went so far as to pull his hat a little more firmly over his eyebrows to shade his eyes.

The drunk's eager smile faded. He looked from the unresponsive backs of the card players to Jedlicka's adamant face. Lastly, he located Chris, who had moved to the other end of the bar. "How about you, stranger?" The doctor turned a singularly charming smile on Chris. "You care to buy a man a friendly drink?"

Nodding to Jedlicka, who slid another glass across the bar, Chris poured a shot of whiskey into it.

"To your good health and my demise." The man swept the whiskey off the bar and into his throat in one deft motion. Pulling a clean handkerchief from his pocket, he wiped his lips daintily. "I don't suppose there would be another where that came from." He cocked one bright blue eye.

Chris smiled back. "You've probably had enough if you hurry right home."

The other snapped his fingers as if he had just lost a throw on the dice. "Too bad. Looks like I won't die tonight." He staggered away from the bar, straightening himself with considerable effort. Then with a studied air of the very drunk, he walked carefully in a straight line across the floor to the door. "I bid you all goodnight." He smiled again in Chris's direction, although it was doubtful that he could see at whom he smiled. Then he lurched out the door; his fumbling footsteps died away in the night.

Turning back to the man called Jedlicka, Chris poured

himself another drink. Checking his bottle by the light of the flickering lantern, he discovered it to be only a quarter full. He should have been as drunk as the man who had just left, but he felt nothing except a deep depression. He lifted the glass to the light and stared critically at its contents. Sighing, he set it on the bar untouched. "Got anything to eat around here?"

"Some beans and tortillas," the barkeep shrugged. "Cook's gone home. There's some cheese left from the free lunch. Maybe a pickle or two."

"I'll take some of everything," Chris grunted. Carrying his glass and bottle with him, he retired to the table just recently vacated.

The barkeep laid a tin knife and fork beside a tin plate layered with the victuals—beans on the bottom, topped by tortillas, a slab of rat cheese, and finally a huge green dill pickle. "That's all we got," he said, stepping back and wiping his hands on his apron.

Chris's mouth watered as he dug in. He had not bothered with food today in his haste to get Star to Crossways. When he had thrown her into the saddle that morning, he had handed her a piece of jerky and taken one for himself. They had gnawed as they rode. He found himself famished.

The pickle was so sour it made his mouth pucker, but the first bite of beans made him sigh with pleasure. Either Jedlicka or his cook cooked a savory pot of *frijoles con chiles*.

Using the last piece of tortilla to mop up the last drop of liquid, Chris stuffed it into his mouth. The last swallow of whiskey washed it all down. He sat back in his chair, his hands on his thighs, a drowsy feeling stealing over him at last. He felt that he might be able to fall into his bed at the rooming house and sleep.

The lantern was guttering low as two of the card players rose and stomped out into the night. The other two remained only long enough to settle their bets before calling their thanks to their host and departing.

Throwing another dollar on the table, Chris called for another bottle of whiskey. As the barkeep brought it, he lingered curiously beside his last customer. "You the bounty hunter that brought in Star Garner?"

Chris felt a chill up his spine. His right hand dropped to his thigh. Curtly, he nodded.

Jedlicka's forehead creased in a frown. "Where'd you take her?"

"The jail."

"Funny. I didn't get no call for a meal. Usually get a call for a meal when there's a prisoner. I was all set, too. Get paid two bits by the county." The big man scratched his head disappointedly and moved away. "I guess sheriff forgot to feed her."

Chapter Fourteen

Although the passage between the jail and the general store was fairly wide, the ground was uneven. Blinded in the blackness, the man set his boot on a clod that turned under him. Off balance, both hands full with a sack and a bottle, he blundered against the adobe wall, bruising his shoulder. Feeling an utter fool, Chris Gillard cursed softly.

He was still cursing when he rounded the corner and came to stand beneath the first of two slits high in the adobe wall at the back of the jail. Shrugging irritably, he stared up at it. Slightly above his head, it appeared as a deeper blackness against the dark gray of the wall.

Suddenly embarrassed by the offerings in his hands, he glanced hurriedly from left to right, then grinned ruefully. No one was out at the time of night to see him.

No. He was the only damn fool in Crossways. Leave, he counseled himself. Turn around and go back into the rooming house. The job is done.

In the morning he could collect the second half of the

bounty from Garner and ride on his way. He'd be another five thousand dollars richer, plus the added bonus of the Paso Fino mare. At the thought of Humareda, he groaned softly. His conscience lashed him furiously. His fists tightened around the objects he carried.

"Star!" he hissed viciously.

No sound came from behind the adobe wall.

"Star!" He tried again more loudly. "Estrella Montejo?"

He was about to move on. Then a faint noise within the cell reached his ears, a sound of rustling, like a something moving among corn shucks. "Star Garner," he called a little louder.

Her husky voice answered him out of the darkness. *"Quíen es?"*

"Chris Gillard."

Silence greeted his name.

"I . . ." He swallowed. "I've brought you some supper."

Again the silence, then he heard the same rustling. "S-supper . . . ?"

"I'm setting it in the window. Can you reach it?" Putting the bottle down beside his foot, he poked the sack in through the narrow opening.

Again came the movement within the cell and with it the sound of her breathing. Then she gave a soft sound somewhere between a sign and a moan. When she spoke, her voice was strained. "I can't reach it. The wall's too thick."

Rising on tiptoes himself, he pushed it farther until he felt her hands pull it from his grasp. "It's just beans and tortillas," he apologized.

Inside the cell Star's fingers trembled as she eagerly fumbled at the knot in the top of the rough cloth. The combined scent of onions, chilis, and pinto beans was making her weak. Her stomach grumbled urgently and her mouth watered. At last the sack came open.

216

Feeling in the dark, her scrabbling fingers encountered the flat, limp corn cakes and thrust one into her mouth. With a sigh of relief, she leaned back against the wall to chew the leathery bread. Despite her hunger, the dry tortilla was torture to her parched throat. She began to cough and choke helplessly. Tears started from her eyes.

"Here." Chris's voice called to her outside the jail again. With a soft clink a bottle slid down the adobe wall. "Don't let it break," he warned anxiously. "It's full."

In the hot, odorous blackness she uncorked the bottle and swallowed the whiskey neatly. Like liquid fire it slid down her throat. Her breath, drawn in at the pain, wheezed out as some of the alcohol choked her. More tears stung her eyelids.

Outside the cell Chris Gillard heard the sounds of her distress and chuckled. "Goes down smooth, huh?"

"Oh, yes," she wheezed again. Her voice was unnaturally high as she wiped the back of her hand across her cheeks. "I'm strangling, but it's good."

"Eat some beans," he advised when the sounds of her distress began to abate.

She needed no encouragement. Alone in the darkness, she ate the food with her fingers, sternly repressing thoughts of the dirt she could not see, the filth around her.

Only after her first pangs abated did she pause long enough to take a breath. Even then one arm curved protectively around the sack and its contents. With a shudder she glanced around her in the impenetrable blackness. Her fertile imagination could visualize batallions of roaches and rats massing to overwhelm her.

The bottle clinked companionably against the adobe beside her shoulder. Swallowing the food in her mouth, she uncorked it and drank again, this time with less pain.

"Nothing like a good drink of whiskey." Chris's voice came from somewhere above her. She glanced up. He must be standing beside her. Only the thick adobe wall separated

217

them.

He had brought her food and now was waiting patiently for her to eat. She had no way to repay him for his kindness. "Why don't you have a drink with me?" she suggested almost shyly. "I'll never be able to finish this whole bottle."

He hesitated only a moment. Then the bottle clinked up the side of the wall. Through the thick adobe came the sound of movement, the rustle of clothing. "Don't mind if I do," he acknowledged. Then he chuckled. "Here's looking at you." He must have seated himself against the wall right at her back.

Despite her predicament she smiled. More slowly now, she folded a tortilla and used it to scoop up a mouthful of beans. "These are very good," she remarked politely.

He made a snorting sound. "You're too hungry to be any judge. They came from the cafe down the street. They're just beans. Just better than nothing is about the most you can say for them. Here comes the bottle."

This turn she took an extra-large swallow, relishing the burning sensation, its edge taken off, she supposed, by the beans. Leaning her head back against the wall, she welcomed the faint buzzing that began about her ears. With her senses dulled, she might be able to get through this night without losing her reason.

She took another swipe at the beans. "This stuff really tastes good together," she commented woozily.

He chuckled again. "Almost anything tastes good when you wash it down with enough dollar whiskey."

"Is this dollar whiskey?"

"Couldn't you tell?" He sounded offended.

"Of course." She took another swallow and let it burn down her throat. "It burns all the way down to the middle of my chest." Her head rolled on the wall as she sent the bottle on its way. "Your turn."

He pulled the rawhide cord up carefully and slid down

218

the wall again. "Cheap whiskey," he informed her, as if he were making a profound pronouncement, "burns all the way down to your belly."

His voice came right next to her ear. She realized dimly that they were sitting back to back with no more than a foot or so of adobe between them. His head was probably resting against the same brick as hers. Unaccountably, she raised her hand, brushing her fingertips down the rough surface.

Suddenly, she had to know. "Why are you here?" she asked.

He did not answer for a moment. She had decided he was not going to when at last his voice came, flat and emotionless. "Just doing a man a favor. The fellow at the cafe asked me to bring this over."

"Liar," she chided. "If you were doing someone a favor, you'd have come in the front door."

"You don't believe me?" His incredulity sounded feigned. "The man who owns the cafe said that the state paid him twenty-five cents for every prisoner's meal. He was real upset because the sheriff had forgot to order yours for you."

"So you paid him the twenty-five cents for my meal and brought it to me."

"I wouldn't have wanted him to be out his twenty-five cents. Besides, I paid a dollar for the whiskey," His voice was brusque. She could tell from the sound that he had risen to his feet. "Here it comes."

Something with tiny claws skittered across the floor of the cell. She took a long drink in hopes the whiskey could obliterate the sounds of scratching and gnawing.

The silence grew until she thought perhaps he had gone. Something brushed against her knee. "Chris?" she exclaimed. "Chris!" Her voice quavered.

"I'm here," came his voice, deep and reassuring. "I'm right here." He was seated again with his head beside hers.

"What's wrong?"

She laughed shakily. "This cell has a lot of critters that think they have first claim."

"Oh," he muttered.

"I'm not going to worry," she asserted, with more courage than she felt. "I'm bigger than they are."

"That's the spirit," he encouraged heartily, at the same time clenching his fists in guilty frustration. He had seen the inside of enough jails to have a very vivid picture of the conditions she endured.

She did not answer. Instead they sat together back-to-back in companionable silence. The cell began to cool off slightly as the heat of the day escaped into the atmosphere. At last he cleared his throat to blurt the next words in an overloud voice. "One thing I don't understand."

"What?"

"How could you have murdered anyone?" His words rushed out upon themselves. "You behaved like a big sister to Duff. You made arrangements to have that pretty little mare of yours taken care of with the noose right in front of you. The only time you ever even went for a gun was when I was cussing you out blood raw and when you were being attacked. I've known men who've shot people for looking cross-eyed at them. They'd never take that kind of abuse, and no jury in Texas would ever convict them."

Star let her head fall forward onto her chest. The base of her thumb began to throb. Suddenly she was shaking with fear and pain and overwrought nerves. A deep, gulping sob ripped out of her throat before she could suppress it.

"Star? Estrella?" Chris called, alarmed at the choked sound. "Are you crying? Aw, don't cry. Quit that." He scrambled to his feet. "Here comes the whiskey again. Now stop that crying." He slid it back to her.

She clutched the bottle with both hands as it swung down by her ear. Desperately, she turned it up to her lips. Dizzy now with the increasing amount of alcohol, she shook her head. In the darkness tears trickled slowly down her cheeks, but she compressed her lips tightly so no other sound came. At last, drawing a deep breath, she weighed the bottle. It was almost empty. Wetting her lips with its remainder, she sent it back up. "Finish it," she whispered against the wall, hoping the muffled words would not betray her weakness.

"Star," he asked again, "are you sure you don't want to answer my first question?"

She wanted badly to unburden herself in the darkness of the night. Like the confessional it would be, he the priest, she the penitent. But he was the bounty hunter who had brought her in. What good would it do to open up all the old wounds? Her body felt warm and relaxed. The crawling creatures and the filth of the cell seemed far away. The prospect of seeing Luke Garner again, the noose swaying gently in the wind at the head of the street, both dimmed before the gentle drugging of her senses. Even the pain in her ribs had been laid to rest.

"Star, are you still awake?"

"Yes." Her voice was only a whisper.

"But you won't tell me why you did this?"

"What good would it do? Tomorrow morning, bright and early, Luke Garner will be here, and by noon I'll be dead. Just say that I was too stove in by the ribs to think about a gun."

"Not too stove in to make a break or two," he reminded her.

"Just forget it." Her voice was slurred. With eyes closed she leaned back against the cell wall.

A long silence followed. Perhaps he had gone away. Suddenly she hoped not. She was not sleepy, despite the alcohol. The thought of the noose had set her nerves tingling. "Why did you become a bounty hunter?" she asked softly. If no answer came, she would know she was alone.

"Needed to make a lot of money in a hurry," came back the instant reply.

"And have you made a lot?"

"I've got the ranch."

She smiled grimly in the dark, thinking how many wanted men Chris Gillard must have brought in to earn that much money. Luke Garner's hatred ran deep. He could certainly afford to pay for the best. "Is ten thousand dollars a lot of reward?"

Her words lanced at Gillard's conscience, already pricked and sore from his own reflections. "Enough," he replied.

"How much?"

"Why do you want to know?" His voice sounded surly.

Ruefully, she chuckled. "A girl likes to know how much she's worth. It's a matter of pride."

He sat silent for so long she thought he was not going to answer. "It's the most I've ever gotten. Most of the time the rewards are a hundred or five hundred dollars," he replied at last.

Now it was her turn to be silent while her emotions warred with one another. At last she relaxed. "Well, I'm glad to know I'm worth so much—alive? I hope that will be enough for your purposes. It's really quite a lot of money. May I ask what you intend to do with it, I mean, now that you already have the ranch?"

"Breed horses. Turn that ranch out there on the Pecos into the best."

"Humareda," she whispered.

He did not hear her. His enthusiasm carried him along. "It's right on the stage lines. The army's built forts all along there. Good horses are money. When Duff gets a little bigger, he'll help me. Together we'll show them. We'll show everybody."

She did not miss the determination and bitter defiance that underlined the last statements. "Yes."

"That land is good for horses. The Comanches run their horses on it. They're tough and strong. It's got good grass and good water." He stopped abruptly, embarrassed at his emotional outburst.

Neither spoke for a moment. At last she cleared her throat. "I wish you luck," she said sincerely. "You really ought to make me your last criminal. Your next bounty might be too expensive to collect."

"I've been thinking about giving it up," he replied seriously. "I just wanted to get a real big stake, so Duff wouldn't have to do without."

"And I'm real big?" she asked curiously.

He shrugged. "They only paid five thousand for Jesse James."

"I'm more wanted than Jesse James," she murmured. "I'm twice as dangerous as Jesse James." How Luke must hate her. Suddenly his angry florid face rose before her. He would laugh to see her hang. And she was sitting and talking to the man who had brought her to this. Sudden rage almost choked her. "Perhaps you'd better go," she blurted coldly. "I feel very sleepy and tired. The whiskey has relaxed me. Thank you for it and for the food."

He could hear the dismissal in her voice. The camaraderie had vanished, leaving in its place the stilted politeness of people who do not like each other at all. "Goodnight, then." His voice came from several feet above her head. He had risen.

"Goodnight," she whispered as she listened to his boot heels crunch away over the rough ground. "Good-bye."

Chris Gillard walked several hundred yards out into the brush. His head ached and his mouth tasted sour. Ten thousand dollars would enable him to buy the breeding stock he needed. Indeed, his breeding program would be immeasurably speeded by the colts from Al out of Humareda. . . .

He flung the bottle with all his might into the brush, hearing it crash into splinters on a rock. Sweating, his chest heaving, he wiped his hand across his face and stared upward at the cold stars.

Luke Garner drove into Crossways in a black buggy. Squeezed in against his considerable bulk sat the thin-faced Maudie, dressed in pale dove-gray, a black bonnet shielding her face from the sun. Six grim-faced outriders followed the buggy, pistols tied down on their thighs, rifles in their saddle boots.

Reared back in one of the several rockers on the front porch of the rooming house, Chris Gillard watched them come.

At the sight of the hunter, Garner guided the buggy over to the porch, pulling up the horse next to the railing. "Got her, did you? Brought her back alive?"

"See for yourself. I'll be coming round for my money before noon, if you'd meet me at the bank."

"Oh, I intend to see for myself," Garner grinned. His front teeth had moss-green stains halfway up toward the gums. The sight of those teeth made Chris realize that he had never seen Garner smile before. The heavy face almost instantly slumped into its accustomed scowl, the face of a hard-bitten man, bitter and humorless. The contemplation of revenge had been its only pleasure.

Garner's expansiveness of spirit manifested itself in a heavy-handed joviality. "Maudie." He nudged his daughter hard in the ribs. "You remember Mr. Gillard."

Politely, Chris tipped his hat to the woman crowded alongside the corpulent body. "Ma'am."

Her face and frame seemed to have lost flesh since he had seen her last. Of course, he had only been with her for a few minutes, not enough to really study her. Still, she seemed more angular, her fingers, where they wrapped around the handle of her parasol, more knobby and thin.

In the uncompromising sun of the Texas morning, her skin looked dry and weathered, with an unpleasant, muddy sallowness. The gray of her dress deadened the tan that might have been attractive under other circumstances. Her hair, barely visible slicked back under the bonnet, seemed to have no color at all.

"Mr. Gillard," she replied stiffly. Her mouth drew down as if she had tasted something sour.

"Hell, Maudie." Garner jabbed her again with his elbow. "Be nice to the man. This here's the *hombre* who got Matthew's killer for us."

Her lips quirked upward in a stiff smile. "Thank you," she murmured, inclining her head slightly.

"I'll go long to the jail now." Garner's grin flashed again briefly as he remembered his destination. He lifted the reins but did not bring them down on the rumps of the horses. "Come out to the ranch tonight for your money," he instructed as an afterthought. "I don't cotton much to banks. Useta know a fellow who robbed 'em. He didn't have sense enough to come in outa the rain. Never trusted them after that." With a mirthless bark that might have been a laugh, he slapped the reins down on the horses' backs and guided the buggy on down the street.

Rosa McGloin had come to the door of the rooming house, her arms folded tightly across her bosom. From behind Chris, her voice carried softly. "Poor girl."

He rocked backward slightly without turning his head. "Miss Garner."

"No, Mrs. Garner."

His boots eased down deliberately onto the porch. "Did you say 'Mrs. Garner'?"

Her Irish blue eyes flashed obstinately. "I most certainly did. You aren't from around here, mister. You don't know anything about any of these people or about anything that went on here."

"I don't have to know anything but that the jury found her guilty," he defended himself.

"That poor girl didn't know what she was getting into when she married that twisted, bunged-up excuse for a man. Oh, he was handsome enough. Much better-lookin' man than Maude is a woman, for all that he was her twin. But he was mean. Mean clean through. I've been out here all my life and I'm here to tell you that every once in a while a fella just turns mean. When that happens, his folks are the ones who bear the brunt of it until usually he pulls some crazy stunt and kills himself. Once in a while, someone kills him. And then it's a blessing and a relief for everybody."

"If Luke Garner felt so much relief, he wouldn't have offered such a reward."

Rosa McGloin's face turned red. "Luke Garner's back is up. He's just like a lot of tough men who've made their lives out here. He won't let anybody get away with anything that's his. Whether he wants it or not."

Chris Gillard rose from the rocking chair, his tall, lanky form dwarfing the small Irishwoman, but not daunting her in the slightest. "Are you telling me that Star Garner isn't guilty?"

She sniffed irritably and adjusted her glasses on her nose. "Jury thought so. That's not for me to say. All I'm saying is that she might have had a reason." She dug her hands into her hips and stared at the couple dismounting from the buggy. "I should've kept my mouth shut."

"You didn't, though." Chris spoke softly, his bleak eyes on the rope swinging in the wind.

She turned to go back into the rooming house, then paused with the screen door open. "Why don't you hunt up Doc Foster if you really care to know what happened? Otherwise, just forget all about it and collect your money." Her mouth snapped to in a stiff line. The screen door slammed behind her, putting a period to the conversation.

Chris ran a hand across the back of his neck as he looked up the street and down. Doc Foster? The man who had begged a drink off him last night had been addressed as Doc. Could he be the one? Or someone else? Surely this town could not support two physicians. He shrugged. Even if he could find the doctor immediately, the exercise was pointless. The hanging party might start at any minute.

He glanced feverishly at the jail, his eyes raking its front. Five of the outriders lounged around the buggy and the porch. A sixth had accompanied the Garners into the jail. On the porches that formed the boardwalk of the street, men stood or sat or leaned. They made a pretense of talking to each other, but their eyes drifted constantly to the closed jail door.

Cold horror settled into the pit of Chris's stomach. The door might open any minute now. The sheriff would lead her out. Small, slender, her hands cuffed behind her, her head up. Would she be blindfolded? Chris felt his stomach heave. In another instant he was going to vomit over the side of the porch.

He could not watch this. Yet he could not leave. She should not have to face her death alone.

Luke Garner climbed out of one side of the buggy. The father did not help his daughter. Instead, he heaved his body out to stagger slightly on his feet as his bulk tipped sideways. The springs of the buggy bounced crazily.

The woman in gray extended her gloved hand to one of the riders who had dismounted and tied his horse at the hitching post. Without effort she stepped down and allowed him to lead her to the porch and help her mount the high steps. The sheriff opened the door for them before they could reach it and backed aside obsequiously.

At the sound of Garner's deep rumble, Star Garner y Montejo climbed to her feet in her cell. Not long now, she thought. With trembling hands, she smoothed her matted hair as best she could and attempted to pull on her black gloves. Her fingers, like icy sticks, refused to obey her brain's commands. Defeated, she folded them and thrust them back into her waistband.

Futilely, she brushed at the wrinkles in the filthy rumpled clothing. Its condition, as well as the state of her own unwashed body, embarrassed her. She was sure that the stench of the cell had permeated her skin.

The humiliation of it all, the horror of her impending death by hanging, brought her near to tears. That would be the final humiliation, she thought. To be led sobbing to the gallows before Garner and her sister-in-law, the townspeople and the Tres Santos riders. A Montejo knew how to conduct herself with dignity . . . she would not give the gringos the satisfaction of seeing her beg.

The door of the cellblock swung open to admit Luke Garner. His bloodshot eyes found her instantly, standing upright in the center of her cell. Immediately, behind him came Maude, her handkerchief pressed over her nose and mouth.

In two steps the big man had stalked across the intervening space to the bars and grasped them in his hands, wrapping his bloated fingers tightly around them. His cold eyes surveyed her slender figure, noted how it swayed slightly where she stood. He surveyed the contents of the cell, the thin cornshuck mattress, the bucket in the corner, the filthy floor.

Garner grinned for the second time that day. "Brought you down a peg or two, didn't I?"

Star gave no sign that his words surprised her. Her hand hidden in the folds of her skirt clenched into a tight fist as she struggled to keep her feelings hidden.

Garner stared at her a long minute, his grin widening, his eyes glittering. Then he took a deep breath. Dropping his hands from the bars, he pushed his coat open. His thumbs latched into the belt at his waist as he began to rock

228

back and forth on his heels. His eyes never left off surveying her, from the dusty, mud-caked boots to the matted black hair.

Star's skin began to crawl as she felt him insolently undressing her with his eyes, picturing her naked body beneath the ruined clothing.

At last he sniffed the air, his eyes slid off her and back to the bucket around which the flies were just beginning to buzz. "Phee-oo-wee," he mocked. "Sure does smell rank in here. Don't hardly see how a high-toned Spanish señorita like you could stand it in here all night long. Seems like you'd a fainted and fell down or some such thing as that. Ain't that right, Maudie?"

Maude's eyes had been avoiding her sister-in-law assiduously. Now she glanced briefly at her without meeting her eyes. Hastily she backed to the door of the cell block. "Papa," she whined, her voice a nasal twang from the handkerchief pressed against her nose. "Papa, is this really necessary? Just tell the sheriff. . . ."

"Just hold your horses," Garner flung over his shoulder at his daughter. "You don't tell me to tell the sheriff nothing. You understand. I didn't ask you to come along on this party. You dragged yourself along. So now you can just shut up and listen." He swung his heavy grizzled head back to the silent woman in the cell. "Come on up to the bars, señora, so I can see you better. The sheriff don't have this place lighted very well."

Star could scarcely comprehend his words. Terror and weakness were making her head whirl. Blackness threatened to rise up and overwhelm her at any moment. Heedless of Garner's command, she tottered sideways until her shoulder found the wall of the cell. There she leaned her temple against the dry adobe and closed her eyes.

A deep frown creased the flesh between Garner's eyebrows. "Tom!" he called to the sheriff. "She don't seem very feisty. Was she off her feed last night?"

The sheriff shuffled his booted feet. "Well, to tell the truth, Mr. Garner, she didn't eat nothin' last night. It was late by the time I got all the paperwork done." He hunched his narrow shoulders as if to ward off a blow. "I figured you'd just want to take her right out this morning and hang her. I just . . ."

Garner grinned again. "Nothin' to eat, huh? You gettin' hungry, señora?" He stepped back from the bars. "Open this cell," he snapped to the sheriff.

Star's eyes flew wide. All the color drained from her face. The moment had come. They were going to drag her out and . . .

The key grated in the lock. The sheriff swung the cell door back. Maude Garner crumpled the handkerchief as she let it drop from her face. Two long steps and the sheriff grasped Star by the upper arm.

"Just bring her to the door of the cell," Luke ordered. "I want to see her up close. Not back in there in the dark."

The sheriff steered her to the door, stationing her so she stood only a couple of feet from her tormentor. Sweat glazed her forehead. Her face was pasty white, her lips bloodless.

Her heart was pumping so madly Garner could see it move beneath her shirt. His bloodshot eyes fixed on her, he chuckled malevolently. "Scared to death, señora. Purely scared to death. You look like hell. You purely do. God damn, but you look bad. All dirty and scrawny and about to puke you're so scared. The sight of you does me good." He turned to his daughter, who had come up behind him and was staring with avid curiosity. "Don't the sight of her like this do you good, Maudie?"

Maude backed hastily away from her father. "For God's sake, hang her," she shrilled. "Hang her and get it over with."

Garner's mouth snapped to like a trap. Angrily he swung back around to address the sheriff. "Just put her back in

230

that cell, Tom. For now she can just stay right there. Don't worry about her none. In fact, just play like she's not even there anymore."

His eyes flicked to the cracked pitcher on the floor outside the bars where the prisoner had placed it in the hopes of getting more water. Clumsily, his booted foot swung out. The pitcher shattered against the adobe wall.

Hastily the sheriff pushed Star back into the cell and locked it.

Garner recovered his ponderous balance by grabbing hold of the cell bars. "Now, sheriff, you just let her stay right here for a while. You just hand me those keys and play like you ain't got no prisoner back here. Think you can do that?"

The sheriff stared at the key ring in his hand, then back at Garner's profile as the rancher stared the prisoner up and down. The hate in the man's mottled face made the sheriff quail. "Sure thing," he mumbled, pressing the keys into the outstretched hand. Without a word of protest, he sidled out of the cellblock.

Garner threw him a contemptuous look. "There goes a man with his tail between his legs," he confided to Star. "He ain't gonna stick his head in here again. Nobody's gonna come for you except me." He dangled the keys in front of her eyes.

She stared at them, her black eyes dilated with fear, her head whirling.

Garner whirled on his daughter. "Get out of here, Maude!" he bawled.

Like a gray shadow, she scuttled through the door.

He stepped forward, his face within inches of the bars. "Now it's just you and me," he drawled evenly. "Now you think about this. It's gonna get mighty hot today. That bucket's gonna get mighty ripe. You just got one hope, and that's me. You think about that."

She did not move, as mesmerized as a bird before a

231

snake.

"You think about that," he repeated. "I don't have to come back at all. *Comprende?* So you'd better pray that I do. And while you're prayin', you'd better make up your mind to be a changed woman by the time I come back."

With those cryptic words, he strode out of the cellblock, locking the outer door behind him. In the dim cell, Star slipped to her knees, then to her hip, and finally, to her side, to lie with her body pressed against the bars.

Chapter Fifteen

The door of the jail swung open.

Chris Gillard straightened instantly from his slouched position against the porch of Rosa McGloin's boarding-house. One hand closed around the post on which he had been leaning. The other dropped to the butt of the Colt Peacemaker slung low on his right hip. His muscles, which had been gradually tightening as the tension mounted, now jerked to almost painful alertness. He could not have told what he would have done in the next moment, so wildly were his emotions spinning.

But no small bedraggled figure in the remains of a white silk blouse and a black riding skirt was led out. The riders who had been lounging around the jailhouse steps climbed to their feet exchanging puzzled glances. One of them leaped to take Maude Garner's arm to assist her down the steps and into the buggy.

Behind her came her father accompanied by the sheriff. Garner was doing the talking. The sheriff merely shuffled along in his wake, nodding his head. His instructions concluded, Garner spoke curtly to two of the riders, who stepped back up onto the steps and stationed themselves on either side of the jailhouse door.

The sheriff swung around, staring angrily at them, then swung back toward the rancher. His rumble of protest faded before Garner's curt dismissal, delivered as he was swinging into the buggy. The lawman put his hand on the dash, but Garner shot him a warning look before lifting the whip from its socket and pulling the reins off the brake.

Chris stepped off the porch at McGloin's into the path of Garner's buggy as it rolled smoothly down the street. Immediately the rider beside the buggy reined his mount in front of the bounty hunter. The buckskin mustang neighed as the heavy bit snagged its jaw, and it pawed the ground within a few feet of the toes of Chris's boots.

"Get back there!" The rider's hand closed over the butt of his revolver. Smooth and fast as a coiling rattler, he drew the gun and leveled it at the bounty hunter.

Unimpressed, Chris held his ground, his gray eyes steely. "Satisfied, Mr. Garner?"

Garner pulled the buggy to a halt. "Hatch, you damned fool, this here's the man who brought her in. You done saw him just a few minutes ago. Don't you remember anything?"

Angrily, Hatch hauled the nervous mustang back. His eyes remained locked with Chris's.

"You done a real good job bringing her in, Gillard," Garner said with false heartiness. "She looks like she's been dragged through a knothole, but she's all in one piece." He turned to his daughter. "Maudie, you remember this now. It always pays in the long run to hire the best. If you want a job done, hire the expert. You won't be disappointed." He glanced significantly at the foreman, who backed his horse farther away from the conversation.

Chris waited impassively while the man finished his

lecture. "I'm glad you're pleased, Mr. Garner."

"I'm pleased," Garner snorted. "Damn right, I'm pleased. I hired the best and I expect to be pleased. Seeing her in that jail is worth every penny. . . ." He broke off in midsentence, his eyes narrowed as he stared at the head of the street. "My God! Run for cover, boys!"

Even as Chris swung to face the danger, he drew the Colt from its holster. Garner hefted himself out of the buggy with surprising speed for one of his weight. Three of his men went for their pistols.

The first shot spanged by Chris's ear as four riders at the head of the street spurred their mounts forward. The buggy team twisted nervously in their harness. One horse reared against the shafts, shaking his bridled head in terror as more of the riders around him fired at the oncoming charge.

Maude screamed as the buggy tilted precariously. Hatch reined his horse around the buggy and reached over into it. Her arms went around his neck for him to drag her out. As the charging riders swept by, he spurred his mustang and deposited Maude onto the porch of Rosa McGloin's rooming house.

Chris aimed the Colt but immediately eased back on the hammer. The thundering horsemen were led by Don Tomas de Montejo.

The don's face contorted in fury as he caught sight of the man who had tricked him and kidnapped his sister. As his vaqueros galloped on toward the jail, he whirled El Espectro on his hind legs and charged back toward the boardinghouse. His pistol level, his mouth open in a ululating cry, he bore down upon the bounty hunter.

Chris dived for the space beneath the porch of the boardinghouse as the buggy team panicked. The buggy rocked drunkenly as the team fought against the brake. In the meantime, the Tres Santos riders wheeled their horses to fire shots that spanged harmlessly off into the desert as their plunging mounts destroyed their aim.

As Tomas reined the magnificent stallion to the side, the brake released and the team bolted in front on him, almost knocking his mount down in their terror-stricken dash for safety. Almost unseated as the gray staggered back, the don was forced to pull leather for all he was worth. Cursing fervently in a mixture of Spanish, English, and some language Chris did not understand, the don struggled furiously to get his horse under control.

The sheriff and the two riders remaining at the jail began firing from the porch. The attack faltered as the vaqueros were caught in a crossfire. One man screamed in pain as he was slammed forward over his saddle by a forty-five slug that shattered his shoulder blade.

His two compadres caught him under the arms, righted him in the saddle, and galloped their horses between Jedlicka's and the general store out of the hail of death from the Texans.

Throwing a furious frustrated look around him, Don Tomas wheeled the curvetting El Espectro. Heedless of the bullets, he galloped the horse after his men. Above him on the porch, Chris heard Hatch's gun explode. Tomas jerked half around in the saddle as blood splattered as if by magic across the shoulder of his white shirt.

Chris rolled from beneath the porch and sprang to his feet. "Mine!" he shouted even as Hatch aimed again at the figure cutting across their path.

Taking careful aim, Chris put his slug into the four-by-four that held up Jedlicka's porch just as Tomas flashed into the alley after his men.

From behind Chris came a shrill cry of disappointment from Maude, blended with a snarl of disgust from Hatch.

Garner's foreman leaped from the porch and ran to the head of the alley too late. The attackers' retreat was screened by a cloud of dust.

Hatch swung around, his face contorted in angry frustration. "Son-of-a-bitch!" he thundered, stalking back down the street toward Chris. "Jumping up in front of me and yelling 'Mine!' I'd 'a had him with a second shot. He'd 'a been buzzard bait."

Garner stomped out of the depths of Rosa McGloin's, his brows darkening. Maude rose from behind the chairs on the porch. "Hatch," she interceded. "Anyone can miss."

"He'd 'a been dead."

Conscious of Garner behind him, Chris met Hatch's accusation unmoved. "You bungled your shot," he pointed out. "He should have been dead before I ever got a chance at him, instead of reeling in the saddle."

Hatch's face turned livid. "You . . ."

"Break it off!" Garner lumbered down the steps. "Hatch, go rustle up that team. We took the fight out them. Damn Mexes won't be back any time soon. With two of 'em shot up, they'll have to hole up somewhere and rest a spell."

"They rode right down the middle of the street!" Maude exclaimed. "Of all the nerve."

All along the porches, people were coming out to stare incredulously at the street. Garner looped his thumbs over his gunbelt and glared at the row of buildings. His heavy face was florid with rage. "Somebody told them there was gonna be a hangin'," he declared. "Somebody got word to that don. If I find out who, I'll see he don't ever say nothin' to nobody again."

Maude came down the steps as Hatch led the buggy up. "You'd better go back in there and get her out and hang her, Papa. Put an end to this once and for all."

The rancher shot her an angry look. "Button your lip, Maudie. I'll do what I damn well please about this. Hatch, you stay here in town, just to give the sheriff a hand. I don't think they'll be back anytime soon, but you never know. If there's trouble, send Booger on the double."

Hatch nodded shortly, his eyes still blackly accusing Chris. "Hell of a bounty hunter, missing a shot like that," he muttered.

Chris shrugged. "Anytime you'd like to test my marksmanship," he offered significantly.

But Garner jerked his thumb in the direction of the jail. Hatch swung into the saddle and rode up the street. "Come out to the ranch tomorrow," Garner ordered as he climbed into the buggy.

Chris tipped his hat and stepped back as it rolled away. The sheriff came hurrying down the street but stopped as the buggy gathered speed. Three of the outriders followed it as Hatch dismounted at the jail.

Standing in the street until the party was out of sight, the sheriff became aware of the people of Crossways standing on the porches watching him, their faces grim. He tugged his hat low over his eyes, but even its shadow could not hide the dark red that mottled his face. Shoulders hunched, he hurried back up the street and entered the jail.

"Good Lord, deliver us all," Rosa McGloin prayed fervently as she stepped from the shadows of the rooming house living room with a Sharps buffalo gun cradled in the crook of her arm. "I thought the Comanches were come for sure. All I could think of was getting McGloin's rifle and finding a place to brace it."

Chris smiled faintly at her white face and wide, shocked eyes. "Did sort of sound like it, didn't it?"

"Exactly, even to the screeching. Lord help us, but that man in the white shirt sounded just like one of Quanah

Parker's Quahadis. My blood just ran cold. I thought for sure I'd heard the last of that."

Chris put his arm around the trembling woman and helped her to the rocking chair. "They weren't after the town," he reassured her. "That fellow doing the screeching was after the prisoner in the jail. He's her brother."

Rosa leaned her head back on the chair. "Well, if that's true, I say more power to him. Luke Garner's bound to do away with that poor girl. It's a thousand wonders she wasn't already walkin' up them gallows steps when they came riding in. . . ." Abruptly, she clapped a hand over her mouth and began to rock furiously.

"That's probably what Montejo was expecting and hoping," Chris agreed, without appearing to notice Rosa's behavior. "Probably a lot of people were expecting the same thing."

Rosa stopped rocking. "Wonder why Garner didn't hang her? Are you sure you got the right woman?"

Chris nodded his head. He hitched his thigh up onto the porch railing and gazed speculatively at the jail. "I'm sure." Pulling the makings from his shirt pocket, he rolled a cigarette.

They sat in silence for a moment. At last Rosa climbed shakily to her feet. Heaving a deep sigh, she wiped the perspiration from her forehead with her apron. "Well, I just don't get it."

"You mean why he didn't hang her?"

"Yes. Why didn't he?"

Chris drew the last of the smoke deep into his lungs. The nicotine brought a welcome temporary release to his strained nerves. He flicked the butt into the street in the direction of the disappearing buggy. As Rosa opened the screen, his voice caught her. "What was the name of that doc?"

One eyebrow rose quizzically. "Foster."

"Where might I find him?"

"Probably in his house down at the end of the street, the first one on the left as you ride into town. But don't expect him to answer his bell. He's most generally asleep this time of the morning."

"With all this noise?" Chris asked incredulously.

Rosa sniffed expressively. "Drinks," she explained.

"I think I met him last night."

"If you were in Jedlicka's, you did."

"Might take him a bottle down there for a special treat," Chris remarked out loud.

The Irishwoman's eyes sparkled. "You'd have to get him to talk mighty quick, or else you'd better ration the stuff. Otherwise you'd never get any information. He'd pass out on you too quick."

"Oh, I'd hold the bottle." Chris looked down the street. "Notice Jedlicka's is open this morning."

Her face reflected her contempt for the venality of her fellow merchant. "He never misses a chance to make a penny. There was *supposed* to be a hanging this morning. He figured he'd get some business from the gawkers. As it is, he got more than he bargained for. Probably half the men in town are in there right now, cussin' and discussin'. He'll be right happy to sell you a bottle too."

"I'll be spreading sunshine wherever I go," Chris mused, his face innocent.

"Get away from here," Rosa chuckled. "I don't have time to waste on a fellow with a tongue like yours. Did you say you were a tinker?"

"No, ma'am. Just a poor horse trader." Chris doffed his hat and swept it elaborately across his chest.

"Same thing. In Ireland you'd be a tinker. Tongue like warm sorghum." Her smile firmly in place, she disappeared

240

into her boardinghouse.

The bell pull did not work after the first good yank. Neither did repeated knocking arouse anyone. The place might very well have been deserted. At last, blowing on his knuckles, he walked down the pairs of one-by-twelves that served as the crude walkway from the front porch around to the back of the house. After his knock at the back brought no answer, he twisted the knob. The door swung open easily.

The room into which he stepped was obviously a kitchen. A dry sink piled with dirty tin cups and plates stood beside a potbellied stove. A coffeepot, its bottom badly smoke-blackened, stood on the burner. On the oilcloth-covered table sat a crusted pot with the handle of a spoon sticking out of it. The door stood open into the next room.

Unhesitatingly, Chris went through it into a small dining room. Light streamed through a tear in the windowshade, revealing a table and sideboard, both thick with dust. A long streamer of spiderweb stretched from the bottom of the hanging lantern to the top of a chair back. Doc had evidently given up on housekeeping.

As he opened the door into the living room, Chris heard the sound of labored breathing. One hand dangling limply over the back of a leather couch signaled the location of the occupant.

Making no effort to walk quietly, Chris rounded the couch.

The rhythm faltered on a tiny snort. The doctor's hand flipped over the edge of the couch and swiped at his mouth. One eye slitted open. "What in hell do you want?"

Chris grinned slightly, his head cocked to one side. The light was not so dim that he could not recognize the man

241

who had begged a drink from him the night before.

The doctor's eyelids blinked with an effort, as if they were stuck together. He swiped again at his face.

He still wore the suit he had worn the night before. Irrelevantly Chris noted that it seemed not much worse for wear. The doctor lay on his back as if at attention, one hand placed precisely across the front of his chest, his legs stretched straight out, heels together, toes turned outward. His hat rested on the floor at his side. "I asked what the hell you wanted."

Chris hoisted the bottle by the neck. "Oh, just came to pass the time of day. Brought you another bottle."

The slitted eyes widened slightly, then narrowed again. A coated tongue flicked out from between cracked lips. Then the eyes closed. "That's bullshit," the prone man remarked mildly. "Nobody ever comes to see a doctor to pass the time of day."

"Here's the proof."

The other hand moved. Trembling fingers reached inside the breast pocket of the suit to withdraw a glasses case. Cursing mildly at his fumbling ineptitude, he finally managed to extract a pair of gold-rimmed spectacles. These he perched on the end of his thin nose to stare intently at the man and the bottle. A pained frown deepened between his eyebrows. He licked his lips again.

"Jedlicka's best whiskey," Chris declared, a pleasant smile curving his lips.

The doctor rolled his eyes toward the window. "Too early in the morning for Jedlicka to be open."

"He opened up for the hanging."

Doc Foster met his unwelcome visitor's eyes only for an instant, before flickering away toward the window. One hand passed trembling over his lips and chin. With a heartfelt groan he swung his legs over the side of the couch and sat up, his hands hanging limply between his knees. "Poor woman," he murmured hoarsely. He looked at the bottle meaningfully.

On the table beside the couch was a cloudy water glass. Chris uncorked the whiskey and poured a generous shot.

Doc Foster tipped it to his lips and downed it without blinking an eye. "Poor woman," he muttered again.

"Why 'poor woman'?"

The doctor shook his head glumly. "Terrible way to die. Strangling at the end of rope. Did that damn fool get it right? I've tried and tried to tell him how to do it, but he's too damn stupid to learn. He may not be dumber than an old dog, but he's not any smarter than one, either." The water glass hung limply between his knees as he stared at a fixed spot on the floor.

Chris perched on the scratched oak arm of the couch. "But she was a coldblooded murderess. She killed her husband, poor Matthew Garner, Luke Garner's crippled son."

The doctor shook his head tiredly. Without comment he held out his glass for another shot. "Find yourself a glass, my friend," he said. "I hate to drink alone. Although I do not let loneliness interfere with my main pursuit in life."

"What's that?"

"Death." The man downed the whiskey at a gulp. "My own," he added impassively.

Chris raised one eyebrow. A picture flashed through his mind of the doctor stretched out like a corpse on the leather couch. He grinned. "You picked a long way to go about it."

"Ah, but a pleasant one." The doctor cradled the glass as he settled his aching head carefully upon the worn leather. "And relatively painless. Only the living with the failure of each successive attempt is painful. Death will be painless."

"Hanging's not pleasant," the blond man agreed.

"No," the doctor agreed morosely. He thrust out his glass again. "How about another drink?"

Chris pretended not to hear for a moment. "I always thought hanging was quick."

Doc Foster nudged his arm with the glass. "Goddammit. Give."

"Tell me about hanging."

"No!" Foster growled.

"Tell me." Chris prodded gently as he splashed a thimbleful of dark gold liquid into the glass.

Foster drank it down, this time grimacing as if it burned all the way to his gut. "If the drop's not far enough . . . if the knot's not right . . . God! It's a mess. The person takes a long time to die. Hours. God! A light little thing like her . . ." he shuddered. His eyes narrowed. "I hope there's still plenty left in that bottle," he observed pointedly.

"Plenty," Chris promised.

"Then I beg you to keep it flowing. I need to get quite a way's down the road before nightfall. Your advent with your bottle into my house has been a pleasant diversion."

"But if she's a murderess . . ." Chris steered him back onto the subject, sensing the whiskey had let the doctor's tongue loose to babble.

The doctor clutched the empty glass. Suddenly restless, he rose to his feet, steadying himself by pushing off from the couch arm. Listing only slightly to the left, he began to pace the room. He moved as if he had followed this same route night after night, glass in hand. When he spoke, he no longer spoke to his surprise guest. "Matthew Garner," he whispered. "She was supposed to have murdered Matthew Garner."

"So the jury found."

The doctor made a rude sound in his throat. Angrily he

244

tossed the remains of the glass of whiskey down his throat. "Maude said she did. Testified that she saw the whole thing."

"Why should she lie?" Chris filled the doctor's glass as he paused in front of the couch, his brow furrowed, his eyes staring into the past.

"Hell, I don't know. Probably didn't. But I wouldn't call it murder." The doctor shook his head. "No, I wouldn't call it murder."

"What then?"

The man paused in his pacing. "Just who the hell are you?" His depression dissolved into belligerence. "Just who the hell invited you in here in the first place?"

Chris Gillard rose. His white-blond crest topped the doctor's thinning sandy-gray strands by six or seven inches. His level gray eyes looked down into the other man's. "I'm the bounty hunter who brought her back from Mexico," he admitted softly.

The doctor's face did not betray any emotion. He merely stared. The silence in the dusty, stuffy examining room was heavy. At length, the doctor shrugged his shoulders. "Hell of a way to make a living," he remarked, turning away to resume his pacing. "Hell of a way. Why, that's worse than doctoring. Once in a while I get lucky and actually save someone. But you . . . ?" He shook his head.

"Tell me what you meant about it not being murder," Chris prompted, catching the wavering glass as the man wandered by.

The doctor grinned mirthlessly. "Conscience bothering you, is it?"

His face impassive despite the doctor's direct hit, Chris poured himself a drink and set the bottle on the table. "Maybe."

"A lot like doctoring. You got a hell of a way of making a

245

living. How come you aren't looking for a way to die?" He paused to stare intently into the face of his uninvited guest.

"Maybe I am," Chris admitted soberly. "I guess I am, but I hope to make enough money to buy me a share of life before I cash in my chips. I'm a gambler."

"Whiskey is a sure thing," the doctor growled as he held out his glass for another drink.

"But slow. Not quick and clean." Chris filled both their glasses and dropped down onto the padded stool the doctor kept beside the examining couch.

The doctor did not answer. Instead he pulled aside the windowshade. Sunlight lanced in, making him throw up a hand to shield his eyes.

"Tell me about Matthew Garner," Chris prodded. Had the doctor noticed that the noose was still in place, swaying in the wind?

Foster snorted in disgust. "Damnedest fellow. Little and thin. Like Maude. Have you seen Maude?"

As Chris nodded, he extended the bottle. The doctor came to get his refill, forgetting the window and the street outside for the time being.

"I guess the mother must have looked just like those twins. Lord knows they don't look like Luke. He's a big hoss. You've seen him. He hired you, I suppose." He did not pause in his monologue for confirmation. His words flowed out unbidden, as if someone had opened a spigot. "Matthew was just like I said. A small man. Pale. He most certainly had a goiter, but I was never allowed to examine him for that. Colloid enlargement of the thyroid, eyes just beginning to protrude from choking effect. Classic symptoms."

"Was he crippled?"

"Did Luke say he was?"

"No, but I've heard . . ."

"Well, he was. But Luke couldn't stand the thought of that, either. And it wasn't a real problem. Or it shouldn't have been. One leg was a couple of inches shorter than the other. A special shoe would have handled the whole matter. Just like salt brought in from Corpus or somewhere would have handled the goiter. Why, that shoe wouldn't even have had to have been all that specially made. The kid broke his leg when he was about six. I set it for him, but somehow it got injured again." He glanced in Chris's direction.

Although the bounty hunter gave no sign, the doctor bridled angrily. "Oh, I know what you're thinking. I know. You and everybody else suppose I was drunk and messed it up."

Chris shrugged. The only trouble with pumping information from drunks was that they strayed too far from the subject. "I wasn't thinking a thing," he interposed mildly.

His words did not reassure Foster, who shook his head. "I never heard the straight of what happened, but somehow that leg was reinjured in the cast. Damnedest thing. Anyway, it didn't grow for a while. I was afraid it wasn't ever going to grow again." He dropped down on the couch with a creak of springs. He took another drink of whiskey.

"Don't get too comfortable until you tell me about Star Garner y Montejo," Chris warned, setting the bottle on the floor behind him.

"I don't know what set Luke on that Mexican don's sister. I heard it had something to do with horses that the don was breeding. And I could see that. Luke likes to have things nobody else around here has. But why not just buy the horses? Why marry that boy to a Mexican señorita? Specially one of those convent-educated ones. He couldn't appreciate what she was like. So delicate. So sensitive."

Chris's eyes narrowed. He stirred restively. His own conscience pricked him. At the same time he recognized

247

that so far as Star Montejo was concerned, the sensitivity was well-concealed. Yet, was it really? He could remember. . . .

"That boy was a swine!" The doctor interrupted Chris's self-castigation.

"What did he do?"

"I'd hate to tell you the number of times I've patched up people who got into fights with him. He really felt bad about being small and bunged up the way he was. He'd fight people just to prove that he could beat them up. If he beat them, he beat them bad. If he didn't beat them, then Luke'd send some of his riders after them, and Matt would watch and grin."

A horrifying suspicion reared itself in Chris's mind. "That doesn't mean he would hurt his wife," he insisted without much hope.

"Doesn't it?" The doctor held out his glass. He might never have consumed a drop, so cold sober did he appear at that moment. "Doesn't it? Listen. You hit a kid that's smaller and weaker than you are and you teach that kid to hit things smaller and weaker."

"But surely . . ."

"I think the only reason that boy married that girl was because his father insisted that he do it. I wouldn't be surprised if Luke Garner got right nasty about it. Now, there's a man who could be mean. And he didn't care much for Matthew. Right disappointed in him because he was so small and crippled."

"His own son?"

"Not just his son. I got called to the ranch one time to take care of Mrs. Garner, Luke's wife, just before she died. There was a big bruise on her cheek. . . ."

"Did you ever see Luke hit Matthew?"

"No, but others did. Jedlicka's was always full of talk

248

BUSINESS REPLY MAIL
FIRST CLASS   PERMIT NO. 276   CLIFTON, NJ

POSTAGE WILL BE PAID BY ADDRESSEE

ZEBRA HOME SUBSCRIPTION SERVICE
P.O. Box 5214
120 Brighton Road
Clifton, New Jersey 07015

about how Luke used to slap his son around a lot. Luke'd get drunk and tell everybody how his son was useless and crippled. I can imagine what might have happened out there at Tres Santos if Matthew told Luke he didn't want to marry that girl."

Suddenly, he belched. One hand covered his mouth apologetically. "I shouldn't be talking like this. Violating my H-Hippocratic oath." A tear rolled down his cheek.

Chris rolled his eyes in disgust. The doctor was becoming maudlin. If the utmost care were not exercised in giving the man the rest of the whiskey, he would pass out with his story untold. "It's all probably exaggerated." Chris patted the doctor's shoulder consolingly. "Mrs. Garner probably fell. The boy was probably just mischievous. Men say a lot of things when they're drunk."

"Maybe so, but I just can't get it all out of my mind."

Chris watched as the doctor pulled out a handkerchief to mop his face. The silence lengthened. At last Chris tightened his grip on the doctor's shoulder. "Did they call you the night of the murder?"

Chapter Sixteen

Foster wiped his hand across the lower half of his face. "I'm the only doctor around," he replied, steadying himself a bit and taking a sip from the whiskey. "Hatch. He's the foreman out at Tres Santos. He's a real surly bastard, too. Never could . . ."

"What happened?" Chris interrupted quickly. "Was Hatch sent to bring you?"

"In the middle of the night," Foster nodded. "He came tearing in with the buggy. He dragged me out of bed and away we went like the devil was trailing us. Got to the ranchhouse. Shambles. My God! That place was a madhouse. I'll never forget it." His eyes were suddenly clear, focusing on the scene in his mind. From the slurred and maudlin speech of a few minutes ago, his voice had changed to become crisp, clear, and undeniably accurate.

"There was Matthew bleeding from front and back, shot clean through. I did what I could, bandaged him up, but one lung was gone, his ribs were smashed, and his heart might have been nicked. The loss of blood alone would have killed him."

He shook his head at the futility of life. "Luke was raging like a mad bull. Roaring and cussing and throwing himself around. Maude had her brother's head in her lap, talking to him. Every so often, she gave a scream like a banshee. With every breath he drew, Matt's blood would trickle out from his nose and mouth and she'd bend over and wipe the blood off his face with her hair. I've never seen anything like it before or since."

Chris took a drink from his own glass, his own equilibrium upset by the vivid description. To doubt the man was impossible.

"Blood all over the place. Like a slaughterhouse. I tried to get Hatch to take Luke to another room. Hatch just stared at his boss and backed off. Then I tried to get some of the women to help me get Maude away from him and into another room. They just sobbed and ran. Nobody'd touch any of those people."

"Where was Star all that time?"

"Who?"

"Estrella Garner y Montejo? The murderess. Her name means 'star.' "

The doctor took another drink. "Well, sir. That was the strange thing. She was the only person in that room with a semblance of sanity. She might have been the only sane person on the whole ranch. I'd be willing to swear to it, if anybody asked me to swear. She was huddled down in a big leather chair over by the fireplace. This was in the part of the ranchhouse that Luke had specially set aside for the honeymoon couple. That place is like a fort up there, and they had their own apartment."

"The murder didn't take place in the main part of the house?"

"You haven't been up there, have you?"

Chris shook his head. "No. I was hired in El Paso. Luke hunted me down."

"Wait till you see it. It's a damn fort. Perched up there

on a cap rock with a wall around it. I don't have any idea how many rooms it has in it. Probably more than in the whole town." The doctor swung his arm wildly.

"So the murder took place in the couple's apartment, and it's part of a big house," Chris prompted wearily, extending a supporting hand under the doctor's arm.

"Right! Right in their living room. Not the living room in the main part of the house."

"So where was Star?"

The doctor paused, frowning in his effort to get his thoughts organized. He pointed a trembling hand at a dusty corner. "She was huddled down in that chair. I bandaged Matthew, as I've said. Then I tried to get Luke to settle down. He wouldn't. Just kept roaming and raging. Then I tried to get Maude to let go of Matthew. I knew he probably didn't know anything by that time. But she could at least let him die in peace without moaning and weeping over him.

"Finally, I went over to the girl. Her hands were folded in her lap and I figured she was praying. Holding her crucifix and all. I asked her if she was all right and she nodded. God! She looked like the death angel herself. She had on a white silk robe that was splattered from neck to hem with blood. There was even a streak of blood on her face."

Chris swallowed numbly. So her guilt was confirmed. He had half convinced himself that she was an innocent wrongly accused.

"I thought she might be hurt, so I helped her to her feet and guided her toward the bedroom. As I turned her around, I saw she had blood on her back too." The doc was sweating now. The whiskey glass rested half-full on his knee.

"In the bedroom I asked her to remove her robe. Her pupils were dilated, so I guessed she couldn't hear what I said. I reached over and pulled the sash loose and eased it off her shoulders. The bloodstains on her front were someone else's. I guessed they were probably Matthew's. But when I turned her around and got to her back, it was a different story. She'd been whipped with a quirt all across her back and shoulders. She had rope burns on her wrists, too. Someone had tied her up and whipped her. I'd swear to that on a stack of Bibles."

Chris drained his whiskey and rested his head in his hand. Somehow the doctor's confirmation of what he had already guessed made it that much worse.

The doctor did not notice. "She didn't flinch as I bathed her off and put some ointment on her. There were old scars under the new places, but she wouldn't say a word. Never made a sound. Must have hurt like sin. Pain like that can penetrate almost the deepest state of unconsciousness, but she didn't make a sound. I take care of an Indian now and then. I thought they were the only ones who can close their minds to pain like that.

"Finally, I got her to lie down. I was covering her up and was about to leave the room when I saw that she was still clasping her hands. I reached over and patted them, thinking I'd tell her to say a little prayer for me. When I touched her, she screamed."

Chris leaned forward. "What was wrong?"

"I examined her hands. Her right thumb was broken and dislocated back over the top of her hand. Someone had almost torn that girl's thumb right off."

As the heat in the jail cell climbed in the blazing afternoon, Star lapsed into a kind of stupor. Too hot to sleep, trapped within the haze of heat exhaustion, all senses save the sense of touch became distorted. Sights, sounds, smells undulated around her as the heat waves acted as temporary barriers.

Early in the day she had heard the sounds of shots and galloping horses. Her curiosity had been aroused; but since she could not see out and since no one had come into her cell, she could not satisfy it. After a while, she had lapsed back into an apathetic huddle.

Now, in the hottest part of the afternoon, her lips dried and cracked as the very saliva in her mouth was absorbed immediately. The delicate membranes shriveled. A taste of burning brass settled on the tip of her tongue when she licked her lips in an effort to relieve their pain. She was rapidly dehydrating.

Absent-mindedly, her fingers rolled round and round the base of her thumb. If only she could remember, she might not feel so tortured. The idea that she would go to her execution not remembering whether or not she had killed Matthew bothered her. Her head rolled despairingly against the bars. To be accused of something so horrible as shooting a man to death and not to be able to remember had tormented her for months.

Perhaps being in contact with the Garners again might provide some kind of key. Eyes closed tightly, she concentrated. Her last supper with them had been a disaster. Luke had begun immediately demanding the answers to embarrassing personal questions. *"Why ain't you got her pregnant, boy? By God, I'm thinkin' I've got a mule on my hands as well as a cripple."*

He had gone on and on with that theme. Matthew had sat through it all drinking straight whiskey, eating nothing. With each question, with each insult, his face had turned a darker red. His eyes had glinted like hellfire.

Then Maude . . . what had Maude said?

Something about the problem not being Matthew. *"Maybe it's her fault?"* she had spat, her nails curving like claws into the tablecloth. *"Maybe she's the one to blame?"*

Luke Garner had looked at her speculatively before shaking his head. However, Matthew had seized upon the idea. His eyes had threatened terrible things even before the meal was over. With a crushing grasp on her wrist, he had all but dragged her to their bedroom.

There he had slapped her twice across the face. She had
careened across the room! The gun had been in its holster
hanging from the back of the chair. When he had come for
her, she had seized it; but he had been too strong. He had
struck her again and again at the same time he wrenched
the gun from her hand with a force that . . .

Or had he? She could not remember. The blows had all
but knocked her unconscious. She could remember. . . .
She could not remember. . . .

Her head throbbed painfully. The heat was like a band of
hot iron about her temples, squeezing. When she tried to
open her eyes, they felt swollen shut, their lids stuck
together without the beneficence of tears. Why did Luke
not hang her and get it over with?

Hang her . . . hang her . . .

A fantastic and horrific vision unfolded on the back of
her eyelids. She was no longer alone in the foul cell.
Matthew sprawled beside her, his hand clutching her shoe,
his chest covered with blood. More blood trickled from his
mouth. He was dead. Yet his hellfire eyes were wide and
alive, accusing.

"I don't remember," she whispered. "I don't remember."

Painfully, she tried to struggle to her feet, but Maude
placed a taloned hand on her shoulder and held her down.
Wildly, she stared up into the face of her sister-in-law.
"Your fault," she snarled. "Your fault."

Star gasped in pain as tiny streams of blood from
Maude's talons flowed sluggishly down the white silk of her
nightdress. Impossibly, she was in her nightdress. as she
had been the night when . . .

"I don't remember. . . ."

A wind blew from the top of the gallows, swaying the
noose in lazy circles. Luke Garner stood beneath it, his face
a mask of evil, grinning, gloating at her terror and helpless-
ness. Her hand hurt. Her head hurt. In wracking her brain

to remember the events, she had roused devils that threatened to drive her mad. And the madness was filled with pain. Her head, her mouth, her hand . . .

She sucked in a deep lungful of the superheated air and screamed. The sound was terrible; wrenched from her dry throat, it did not sound like the voice of woman. Rather it was the howl of a tortured animal maimed in a trap and despairing of escape. It was an animal no longer cautious, an animal with nothing to lose, proclaiming its agony to the world.

Luke Garner's guards outside the small jail stirred uneasily and hunched their shoulders as if to ward off blows.

The scream had the effect of releasing Star from the delirium into which she had sunk. With it she managed to open her eyes. Blurred images gradually focused into sharp lines. The bars of her cell materialized in front of her eyes. She felt the filth ground into the floor beneath her hand. From the dimness of the cell she judged the time to be late afternoon.

The broken water pitcher lay in shards across the narrow hallway. Tormented by her agonizing thirst, she licked her lips in painful awareness of the condition of her mouth both outside and in. Her own discomfort had brought her out of the stupor. She closed her eyes in misery. How much more could she be expected to endure?

Luke Garner had taken the keys to the cell and dismissed the sheriff. Perhaps he meant her to suffer and die a slow, agonizing death by dehydration. If so, her death would not be long in coming. Another twenty-four hours and she would know nothing. Already her senses were distorted by the merciless heat.

She thought about Chris. Did she dare to hope that he would perhaps come one more time with food and drink? The possibility cheered her considerably. She should move to the wall of the cell, so she would hear him when he came.

The dark part of her mind jeered at her even as she

grasped the bars to pull herself up onto her knees. Bitterly she admitted to herself that he had probably collected his money and ridden away by noon. A twinge of pain ran along her ribs as she staggered to her feet. She was a fool to move and cause herself more pain. He wouldn't come again.

Still she straightened doggedly and moved to the back of the cell, sliding down its rough wall directly beneath the window. Was her imagination turned to wishful thinking, or did the bricks seem a little cooler? She glanced upward. "Please," she whispered. "Please come, Chris Gillard. Please come just one more time."

"She needs your attention now, Doc." Chris interrupted the doctor's protests that he be allowed to return to sleep.

"She's dead."

"No, she's not."

"You told me . . ."

"You assumed that the hanging had taken place."

Doc Foster wiped his hands across his face. "That information was bound by the *Hic*-Hippocratic oath. You tricked me."

Chris shook his head in annoyance. "That's not important now. Star is still alive, but she needs help. She's sitting over in a filthy cell right this minute in this sweltering heat. Her ribs are cracked. You're probably the one man who could get her out and into this office where she could rest easy." Surreptitiously, he slid the bottle with its last couple of ounces of whiskey behind the back leg of the couch.

The doctor stared blankly at his tormentor. Behind the ravaged face, a terrible struggle raged. Then, with a visible effort, the doctor straightened his shoulders. Taking a deep breath, he shuddered as he tried to throw off the effects of the alcohol. "I'll need coffee," he rasped. "The sheriff would probably throw me in the cell next to hers if I showed up in this state. Come on." He led the way into the disordered kitchen where he motioned to the stove. "You'll have to fix some coffee. Make it hot and strong. I'm going to stick my head under the pump."

Sobered sufficiently to speak without slurring and stumbling over his words, the doctor accompanied Chris to the jail. When they arrived their way was barred by Hatch. His expression narrowed as he heard the request to enter the jail. He rested his hand on the gun butt in its holster.

"Boss's got the keys," he stated unequivocally. "Nobody gets in . . . or out. Prisoner might try to escape and you might miss her, bounty hunter." He stood like a statue in front of the jailhouse door.

"We'll get the sheriff to let us in," Doc Foster blustered.

The man shrugged. The other Tres Santos man eased to the side of the porch, placing Chris and the doctor between himself and Hatch. Hatch grinned nastily and reached for the sheriff's chair. Dragging it in front of the door, he seated himself in it and tilted it back against the wall of the jail.

The calculated insolence made Chris grind his teeth. He was within an inch of knocking the chair out from under the foreman and going in anyway when Doc caught his arm and pulled him aside. "Let's go find the sheriff and get the straight of this," he begged. "No sense starting a fight if you don't have to."

In Jedlicka's they found the sheriff making his supper of a mound of beans and a pitcher of beer. He scowled as the bounty hunter approached. "I'm off duty," he mumbled.

"That might well be," Chris replied evenly, "but Doc Foster here has something to say."

The sheriff's grim gaze slid to the doctor, who had hung back and now sidled along the bar toward him. He sneered nastily around a mouthful of food. "Doc," he cautioned.

258

"Don't give me no trouble tonight. How's about y'all just turnin' right back round and goin' home?"

Doc Foster attempted an ingratiating smile. "Now, Pete, I'm not here to make trouble. I just want to help you avoid some. I understand that you've got a wounded prisoner in the jail cell. I expect I'd better take a look at her. The state pays to have prisoners given medical attention same as food," he finished pointedly.

The sheriff stirred uncomfortably. His eyes dropped to his plate. "Don't be worryin' about her," he mumbled noncommittally. He took a hearty swig of beer to wash down the beans.

"Why not?" Chris Gillard's voice was soft, but edged.

"What the hell difference does it make to you?" The sheriff backed his chair away from his plate. His conscience did not need the prodding of others to sting him about leaving his prisoner, a woman at that, all day long in a cell without food or water. Furthermore, he had not bothered to feed her the night before, preferring to pocket the money the state paid for the meal. The last thing he needed was people poking their noses into his business. "She's Luke Garner's responsibility, anyway," he growled.

"I could have sworn she belonged to the state of Texas." Chris took a step that put him in front of the doctor.

The sheriff had not forgotten Chris's rough handling in the office. He pushed himself up and put the chair between himself and the bounty hunter. "Garner offered the reward," he insisted uneasily, thrusting out one hand as if he might ward off the criticism that he saw implicit in their presence. "The state sure didn't want her enough to offer one. He paid for her. He's got her locked up now. I'm out of it." So saying, he tossed a couple of quarters onto the table and strode from the room.

"Well, that's it. Poor lady," the doctor sighed, his weak will fully prepared to yield the battle. "Whatever Luke Garner's got his fist around, doesn't get loose." He ambled

259

over to the bar. "Jedlicka, a whiskey, please."

Chris Gillard caught him by the shoulder. "That's it, is it? That's as far as you're prepared to go."

The doctor hunched forward over the bar, his eyes fixed on the glass. "I don't see that I can go any farther. You heard the sheriff. She's Luke Garner's problem. . . ."

"An innocent woman may be in pain. I'll back your play."

He slapped his hand on the bar. Jedlicka poured a shot of whiskey into a glass. The doctor tossed it down without blinking. "I can't do anything more. She's Luke Garner's. . . ." He trailed off lamely as he held out the glass to the bartender. His hand shook slightly.

"Damn you!" Chris spun away and stalked to the door of the cafe.

The doctor downed the second shot of whiskey as if it were water. He pulled his hat low over his face. "I've got to live in this town after you're long gone and forgotten," he murmured.

Shaking with anger, Chris turned to Jedlicka. "What time will you send the meal over to the prisoner?" he barked.

The man shook his head regretfully. "No meals ordered." His eyes did not quite meet those of the young man. Quickly he turned his attention to polishing the bar. The doctor slid forward his empty glass and Jedlicka filled it without hesitation.

Muttering a foul oath, Gillard strode out, his boot heels striking the porch like distant pistol shots. Equal parts of anger and frustration galled him as the hot Texas sun cast his shadow beneath his feet. Star was over in that jail with only a little water, no food, in pain, alone. He had been thirsty himself. He knew the agony of only a short time in the desert without water. Strong men staggered in circles, their tongues blackened and protruding. Thank God he had brought her food last night.

He stared hard at the jail. Hatch still remained at his post. The other man had disappeared. Chris's eyes narrowed. Hidden out somewhere, he guessed. His eyes scanned the street. No buildings across the street, but the board front of the store next to the jail could hide a man. Or an alley. His skin prickled. Was he even now a target if he made a move toward the jail?

His first impulse to charge Hatch and break into the jail was instantly quelled. Alone in Luke Garner's town, he would be quickly dispatched. He must wait for nightfall and pray that she would not be too weakened by her ordeal.

Shortly after sundown the black buggy rolled up the street alone. At the sight of it, Chris withdrew into the shadows of the boardinghouse living room. One hand on his gun butt, he used the other to brush aside Rosa McGloin's lace curtain to peer out.

Hatch pitched the glowing cigarette away into the dark and walked to the edge of the porch. Behind Luke, he entered the jail and closed the door firmly.

While Hatch fumbled to light the lamp, Luke waited, impatiently jangling the keys in his fist. The floorboards creaked as he shifted his weight from side to side until the match, struck against the base of the lantern, ignited the kerosene on the wick.

Even before the foreman had replaced the chimney, Garner lumbered across the office, inserted the key in the lock to the cellblock, and threw back the door. The same foul odor borne on a wave of overheated air blasted him in the face. Despite his stoicism, he stepped back a pace, blinking rapidly as the onslaught of vapors irritated his eyes. An unpleasant smile crooked one corner of his mouth.

Motioning Hatch to precede him with the lamp, he followed the man into the hall in front of the cells. Its rays barely illuminated the back of the cell, revealing the still figure crumpled beneath the window.

"Estrella," Garner called. "Estrella Montejo."

The figure stirred feebly, moaned. With one hand she touched her tortured lips; with the other she tried to push herself into a sitting position.

Garner moved closer, his eyes trying to discern her expression in the dim light. Inserting another key in the lock, he opened the door of the cell. "Drag her out, Hatch," he ordered.

As Hatch bent over her, Star managed to open her eyes for the first time since the two had entered her cell. His unfamiliar face slipped in and out of focus as she blinked her eyes. Then his hand slid under her armpit and tugged her upward. Supported by that hand, her back propped against the wall, her knees trembling, she licked her lips as best she could. "Water," she managed to croak. "Please. Water."

"Haul her on outta there," Garner called impatiently.

With rough hands Hatch shifted Star's limp body, so that she lay half across his hip. His hand closed over her tender ribs.

She moaned and flinched in pain.

"What's the matter?" Garner growled.

"Don't know," Hatch shrugged. Experimentally he pressed his hand against her abused body.

His callous roughness wrung a cry of pain from her accompanied by the croaking words, "Please don't. My ribs."

"Says she's got hurt ribs," Hatch reported as his fingers tightened deliberately again, eliciting another whimper. "Must be cracked, 'cause they don't feel broken."

Garner shrugged impatiently. "Don't just stand around feeling her. Drag her into the office." He led the way while his foreman struggled with the fainting girl and the kerosene lamp.

Star was almost unconscious from the rough handling

when at last she was allowed to sink into the sheriff's chair. There she sat with head bowed, breathing carefully while her pain subsided, and the torturous dryness of her skin and the pounding of her head resumed their sway. At last she carefully raised her head.

Luke Garner hiked one hammy thigh up on the edge of the sheriff's desk and contemplated her with satisfaction. "Bout whipped, ain't yuh?" he remarked in a conversational tone.

She swallowed, her eyes dull with deprivation. "Water," she whispered.

"Not yet."

His words registered at last, as did his identity. Until that moment she had not recognized him, nor known whose mercy she depended upon. With recognition came pride, despite the overwhelming odds. She would not beg again. Firmly she clamped her bleeding lips together.

Luke Garner's affable expression faded somewhat. He had expected to find her thoroughly cowed. To see her cower, to listen to sobs and pleas would have been a show to gratify his soul. Of course, he intended that she would do exactly as he had planned despite whatever she might say.

Through a haze of pain Star focused on his face, reading the innate viciousness of the man. He would give her water if he intended her to have some. Otherwise she would be wasting her breath. Beyond clinging to the few remnants of her pride, she could think of nothing to do. In despair she dropped her head.

Garner stared at the midnight-black hair matted and snarled like the tangles of a witch. "Get out." He jerked his head in the direction of the door. Hatch went gladly.

When the door closed, Garner moved the lamp to the edge of the desk. Roughly, he pushed her shoulder against the back of the chair and tipped up her face so that the light revealed her features in uncompromising starkness. "Now just hold steady, just like that," he commanded.

"Don't make a move. I wanta see your face clear while I tell you what you're gonna do."

Satisfied with her posture, he pulled a cigar from the inside pocket of his vest and lighted it by the lamp flame. Blowing the acrid blue smoke toward the ceiling, he studied her. She might have been a waxen image, she sat so still. An ugly image, he nodded with satisfaction, one that had run out her string. He could do anything he wanted to her.

"Now let's take a look at what we've got here," he said at last. "You killed my son." He rolled the cigar between his fingers. "He wasn't worth much. I admit that. Crippled up the way he was, not hardly bigger than his twin sister, he wasn't hardly worth killin'."

Star's eyes listlessly followed the blue smoke curling above his head in the heat that rose from the lamp chimney.

Garner bent forward and tapped her cheek with his finger. His face was within a foot of hers. "Did he ever get it up with you without beating the tar out of you first?"

Revolted by the coarse question, her eyes flashed in anger. Her hands clenched around the arms of the sheriff's chair.

Noting her reactions, Garner ran his hand down the front of her body. "You gonna answer me, or do I have to squeeze those ribs?"

Star closed her eyes to shut out the sight of his face. "Never," she whispered at last.

He shrugged as he drew back. "Tough," he admitted. "Some women like it occasionally, but a steady diet gets too much." He stared at the cigar before putting it to his mouth again. "Couldn't get you pregnant, neither," he remarked through the smoke, his eyes slitted against its sting. "A real useless critter."

Star coughed slightly as the atmosphere thickened. The pain lines deepened across her forehead.

"Don't have any idea what's comin', do you?" he chuckled.

She shook her head slightly. One trembling hand rose to press against her temple.

"Keep lookin' at me," he snapped.

Obediently, she dropped her hand back onto the chair arm.

"Now I got two choices, as I see it. I can hang you and marry Maude off to someone who don't mind frost in bed while he sires me a grandson to carry on the family when I die." He puffed on the cheroot and blew the smoke over Star's head.

"All in all not a bad idea, except for a couple of important points. Not real sure that Maude can have children. Her brother couldn't. And then her husband might not take kindly to being passed over. Might get the idea that he had the right to my ranch. Might even get the idea to hurry me along before that grandson—always supposin' that there was one—got big enough to take over."

In her tired mind, Star could only hear the ringing in her ears. The words made little sense. She closed her eyes against the throbbing pains.

"Open those eyes," he snarled. His hand closed over her chin and shook it slightly. "Look at me when I talk to you!"

Although the effort exhausted her, she managed to comply.

He did not take his hand away. Instead he increased the pressure. "That's one choice. The other . . ." He smiled affably. Suddenly his hand released her and patted her gently.

"Now listen real good while I tell you what I'm gonna do. I'm healthy. I'm strong. I'm in the prime of life. I've had two legal kids and a couple of bastards. Least that's what their mothers say." He straightened his shoulders and grinned maliciously, waiting for her reaction.

Star stared at him dully, not fully comprehending what he was saying.

When he got no response, he grunted in disgust but hurried on. "When I first got this idea, I asked myself where could I get a wife who wouldn't give me no backtalk ever? Never did like a woman to give me a lot of backtalk." He paused significantly, but again she showed no reaction.

Then he played his best card. "Finally, I had a brilliant idea. You killed my son. You'll give me another son." His grin spread from ear to ear. "You'll marry me."

Chapter Seventeen

"You're crazy. I'd rather die."

"You don't have no choice," Garner declared smoothly. "I paid for you. The sheriff does what I say. I'm gonna take you out to the Tres Santos tonight with a stopover at the church. You're gonna be my wife before this day is out."

The horror of his statement combined with his presence hulking over her had the effect of driving the last touch with reality from Star's mind. The tight hold she had maintained almost constantly over herself for the last two years shattered. The pupils of her eyes dilated as she stared into Luke Garner's face. She giggled suddenly. Her giggle grew into a laugh, husky, almost guttural as it rasped from her dry, painful throat. Tears stood in her eyes, then overflowed to trickle down her cheeks.

From the time she had married Matthew Garner, throughout her marriage, with its sadistic beatings as preludes to the act of copulation, inherent pride had never allowed her control to break. During the mockery of a trial when she could offer no defense, she had remained calm, an icy numbness paralyzing her mind. During the months at Rancho Montejo, after her brother had engineered her escape with bribes, she had closed her conscious mind to the horror of her recent past. Only during the night had she experienced periods of terror, as grotesque nightmares interrupted her sleep time and time again.

Her strength was at its lowest ebb, almost totally depleted from the pain of her injuries at the onset of the kidnapping. For the last thirty-six hours she had been imprisoned without proper food or water in quarters medieval in their cruelty.

She could no longer see Luke's face, nor comprehend his hideous threats. A darkness closed in around her. She feared the darkness, but could not stem its rolling tide. She began to scream.

Garner's eyes narrowed. He had seen two or three hysterical women in his life, as well as at least one hysterical man. Unemotionally, he slashed his heavy hand across his body in a bearlike swipe that connected with her cheek.

Her screaming ended abruptly as the force of the blow drove her head sideways and her body slammed against the chair arm. That pain more than his blow left her gasping for breath in agonized, whimpering cries.

Hand at the ready he loomed over her, waiting unemotionally to handle any subsequent outbursts with his superior strength.

Wishing for death with every fiber of her being, Star raised a trembling hand to her abused cheek. Outside it was fiery hot, while inside her mouth she tasted blood where the tender membranes had split against her teeth. Oblivious of everything except pain, she wondered why she could not faint. Other people did. Usually women managed the act with some degree of regularity. Why did she seem doomed to suffer the kind of endless torture under which the damned must surely writhe?

Satisfied that he had stifled the hysterical outburst, Garner let his eyes roam round the room. A water barrel stood in the corner. Sliding off the desk, he strolled over unhurriedly and lifted the lid. A tin dipper hung inside. Again unhurriedly, he carried the battered object partially filled across the office to the suffering girl.

"Here!" He nudged her shoulder with his free hand.

Despite her determination not to, she cringed away. The movement brought her ribs into contact with the chair arm, wringing another whimper from her.

"Hey! Don't be so skittish. I've just got some water for you," he explained. "No need to get all excited and scared and hurtin' yourself some more."

He held the dipper to her lips, allowing her to taste the water. Then, grinning sadistically, he moved it out of reach of her clutching hands. Contemptuously he tossed the remainder onto the floor in the corner. "No more."

She moaned helplessly when he turned up her chin again. "Now you're gonna get more in a minute." His voice made a mockery of soothing her. "But you gotta promise to stop throwing those temper fits. Don't do nobody no good. I want that baby and I'm gonna plant it in you healthy and strong." He nudged her chin until he was staring into her tortured eyes, reading her pain with grim satisfaction. "Savvy?"

Scarcely knowing what she did, she attempted to nod. Her chin moved infinitesimally against his fingers.

"Good." He released her to go for more water. "Now don't put your hands on this dipper," he ordered her. "You gotta learn right from the start who's boss." When he held the dipper to her lips this time, he allowed her to drink several small sips before pulling it away and tossing the contents again on the floor.

Resuming his seat on the edge of the sheriff's desk, he leaned forward. "Now listen to orders. First off, we're gonna walk down to the church and get that padre awake."

She shook her head in faint protest, but he raised his hand. "You don't need to worry none about me beatin' you. I'm all man. Don't need nothin' but a woman's body to get my pleasure. I'll pleasure you, too," he added generously. His mouth curved into a travesty of a real smile, the first she had ever seen on his face. "You don't need to be scared so long as you do what I tell you to. You Mexican señoras are raised that way, anyway. Shouldn't be no problem for you."

She shuddered visibly. The few drops of water he had allowed her had done little to assuage her thirst. She longed to locate the water barrel, but dared not turn her eyes from his face.

He studied her in silence. "You gonna marry me tonight?" he grunted at last.

As though pulled by a chain, her head dipped fractionally.

"Say, 'Yes, sir.' "

"Yes, sir," she croaked.

"Want some more water?"

"Yes, sir."

He raised his hand to her bruised cheek and patted it gently. "Good girl. Now go help yourself to that water, but plan to stop drinkin' when I tell you to. Don't want you foundering like a horse."

She started up. His hand dropped to her shoulder. One tangled eyebrow rose. She looked up into his eyes. "Say, 'Yes, sir. Thank you, sir' "

"Yes, sir. Thank you, sir."

His hand dropped away. As she rose unsteadily to make her way across the office, his hand patted her backside familiarly.

When she had drunk a dipperful, he called to her. "That's enough. Now turn around and come back over here and sit down. I got one more thing to say."

When she was seated in front of him, he deliberately

270

stubbed out his cigar on the sole of his boot. "Did you hear all them gunshots this morning?"

She frowned, trying to remember. Vaguely, she remembered the noises, but when they had ceased and she had heard nothing more, she had forgotten them.

"Your brother," Garner told her succinctly.

"Tomas?"

"Yeah. Somebody musta told him I was gonna take you out of the jail, 'cause he come ridin' into town and was gonna shoot the place up and grab you back again. Only he got shot hisself," Luke told her callously.

Her hands flew to her throat. She felt as if a great weight were pressing down on her, suffocating her. "Tomas," she quavered again.

"He didn't get killed," Luke assured her. "Just wounded. Course he may crawl off and die somewheres. You never can tell about bullet wounds. But the last time I seen him, he was ridin' off."

She relaxed fractionally, but her eyes never left his sweaty face.

"I'm just tellin' you this so you know that he's been around. Now I'm warnin' you. If you try to put up a hassle about this marriage in front of the padre, I'll bring you back over here and keep you here until your brother gets hisself together enough to try it again. And this time I'll be waitin' for him. Savvy?"

"Tomas," she whispered softly. Tears stood in her eyes.

He looked down at her with a self-satisfied air. "So you ain't gonna say anything to the priest."

She wrapped her arms around her body. "I won't say anything to the priest," she promised.

In the semidarkness of the candlelit church, she stood dumbly in the clutches of Garner's foreman, Hatch. He had dragged her from the jail and supported her as the three, followed by the two other Tres Santos riders, walked together behind the building rather than down the deserted street.

Hatch's hard fingers, like carved pieces of wood, bruised her arms just above the elbow. In this manner, he held her in a slightly arched position. The strain was making her body ache damnably; her breath came in tiny gasps. She and Hatch stood waiting at the back of the church, while Luke Garner shifted from side to side a few feet up the aisle. Another Tres Santos man waited at the altar for the priest to throw on his cassock and get himself ready.

A small moan escaped her as she twisted wearily in a futile effort to relieve the pain.

"Hold still, gal," Hatch cautioned in her ear. "Lean your head back against me if you want to," he chuckled.

She stiffened instantly. The foreman seemed vaguely familiar, yet she could not remember his being at the ranch the year before. "You don't have to hold me," she whispered. "I'm too weak to run far, and besides I've no place to go."

His hands relaxed fractionally, then tightened again. "Nope. It'd be my hide if you was to even make a break, much less a getaway. But just be nice and I'll ease up some."

The candles and incense in the windowless cavern of the church began to make her light-headed. Bitterly Star cursed her sex, their weak, helpless bodies that men craved as receptacles for their lust and as breeders for their children. Instead of allowing her head to drop back against the musky vest and shirt covering the hard body behind her, she drooped forward, her chin coming to rest on her chest.

Imprisoned in darkness, sick at her stomach, she waited to be married a second time. She did not fool herself by thinking that this marriage would be any less denigrating than the previous one. Although Luke Garner had said he

272

would not beat her as a matter of course, she did not doubt that he would hurt her savagely should she not humiliate herself in every way before his will.

The padre entered the church, his eyes uncertainly searching the dimness. Luke Garner spoke to him, his words an indistinguishable rumble to Star's distorted senses. Then with a motion of his hand, he summoned them down the aisle.

Hatch shifted his grip, sliding down her arms to her wrists, which he promptly twisted up behind her. "Move," he whispered.

When she did not immediately start forward, he twisted a bit harder. Perhaps he was stronger than he knew. Perhaps he sadistically administered an extra twist on purpose. Star arched frantically. Then her breath escaped in a low moan as she collapsed unconscious in his hands.

The argument that ensued between Garner and Padre Toribio never reached Star's ears. Despite requests that turned to orders that became threats, the priest refused flatly to marry the two.

"She must answer for herself, Señor Garner. She must sign the register. In her unfortunate condition she can do neither. The marriage would not be legal in the eyes of God nor man . . ."

"Damn it, padre . . ."

"I shall be glad to assist you by coming to the *rancho* at your request. I will even bring the book so that your marriage can be recorded, but I can do nothing so long as she cannot speak."

Luke Garner cursed angrily. He had no use for religion, but he recognized the necessity of marrying Star legally in order to secure his heir. He doubled his fists and shook them under the nose of the priest, but the man stood firm, his arms folded beneath the sleeves of his cassock.

"This is God's house, señor. He hears our prayers. He also hears your profanation. Be warned."

With a final curse and a shake of his fist, Garner strode out the way he had come; the other Tres Santos riders melted after him into the darkness.

Hatch, who had inadvertently caused the delay, breathed a sigh of relief that his boss had not realized his foreman's maltreatment of the intended bride. More gently, he allowed her upper body to fall back across his arm as he lifted her feet off the ground with an arm beneath her knees.

She could not have weighed a hundred pounds, he estimated, as he carried her up the aisle. He might very well have broken her arm. He was damn lucky Luke had not figured out what had happened.

Outside in the shadows, Chris Gillard waited. He had seen the party come out of the jail. Gone cold with fear for Star, he had eased his gun from the holster. Too many guns surrounded Luke and his captive. He could not hope to outshoot them and rescue her. Still, he would not let them hang her without a fight. Even as he had taken aim at Luke's broad target, the party had turned away from the gallows.

Now as he watched and waited in the darkness, they left the church. Luke Garner strode out first, his chin thrust forward pugnaciously, his fists clenched. The two riders followed close behind him. Last came the foreman Hatch, bearing the body of Star in his arms.

Chris started forward, then pulled himself back. At least he could relax for now. If she were dead, they would have left her body in the church. She had walked in under her own power. Chances were she had fainted.

Frustrated at his lack of power to help her, he watched Star's body being loaded into the buggy. The bright moonlight revealed her white face as Hatch passed her up into Luke's arms. Deep shadows marked her cheeks and eyes. Chris felt a surge of pain deep in his gut. He had brought her to this. She had escaped after shooting a man who according to Doc Foster had beaten and abused her. Hell!

If she hadn't shot him, someone else probably would have before very long. She had probably done everybody a favor, according to Rosa McGloin.

As the buggy pulled out, Chris sprinted for the stable behind the boarding house. Slipping a line into the hackamore around the Alter-Real's head, he swung up onto the horse bareback and followed the procession at a safe distance through the night.

The horses threw their necks against their collars to pull the buggy up the last stage of the torturous rise to the ranchhouse at Tres Santos. There it sat on the high caprock that had remained after the ancient sea shrank and fell away to become the Gulf of Mexico. The bluff's precipitous slope provided the ranch's first line of defense against marauding Indians. Some hundred yards above the sluggish river, a four-foot adobe wall encircled the bluff to form its second line of defense. With shrewd practicality, Luke Garner had planned the wall to be high enough so that a horse couldn't jump it but low enough for a man to rest a rifle on.

On the inside of the wall the ground sloped upward again for another hundred yards to a two-hundred-foot-long adobe wall, eighteen inches thick. Above the crest of the mesa, the wall rose thirty feet to a crenelated parapet. A bizarre replica of a feudal stronghold, it protected the inhabitants of Tres Santos while it dominated the countryside for miles around. Tonight, because Luke Garner was not at home, torches flamed at twenty-five-foot intervals. Their leaping, flickering lights outlined the house and bathed the faces of the travelers in a hideous red.

A double gate of shaggy mountain cedar had each pole sharpened to a point at the top, so no one could climb through the small open space below the arch. Like the teeth of hell, it swung open as the buggy approached.

Star roused from semiconsciousness to clasp her hands tightly together in her lap. Pain began in her thumb and spread up her entire right arm until she was massaging it frantically, unconscious of what she did. Eyes glazed with fear, powerless as a felon dragged to the gallows, she felt her heart stop beating for an instant as the dark shadow of the gateway arch engulfed her.

Then the buggy circled around the inner court and pulled up in front of a smaller gate. In a horrible nightmare of remembrance, Star could almost imagine that her dress was the white lace she had worn as a bride and that the man beside her was Matthew. Closing her eyes, she bit back a sob as the horses halted.

Hatch swung down beside the buggy as Luke Garner climbed out with much grunting and sighing. For an instant Star sat alone, her mind flirting with the insane notion of grabbing the reins and whipping the horses into a run.

With a slight motion of her head, she threw the thought away. The solid cedar gates, bound with lead and barred with iron, were already swinging closed. Like a medieval fortress, Tres Santos kept its people behind double walls on a mountain height. Impregnable to outside forces, it would also serve as a prison from which no one could ever escape.

"Come on outa there!"

Unsurprised by Luke's rude command, she silently put aside her thoughts to climb from the buggy. Luke stomped up the steps through another set of double doors, which swung open as servants came out with kerosene lamps to light his way. By their light Star could see clearly the doors as she remembered them, things of beauty, things of irony. Hand-carved and very old, they were, according to Maude's boast, the doors of El Apostol Santiago, a two-hundred-year-old Spanish mission, long abandoned.

In her grimmer moods, Star had wondered at the irony of doors to a place of worship, of sanctuary, being used as doors for a place of torment and vileness. For only a fleeting moment was she allowed to remember them before Hatch's hard hand in the middle of her back pushed her through them.

Two women stood in the living room. Maude's expression changed from astonishment to anger as Star staggered forward, impelled by Hatch's rough hand. Maude's slitted gray eyes flung daggers at her father's face, but Luke Garner would not look at his daughter.

Instead he motioned to the other woman in the room, the Mexican housekeeper, who came forward obediently. "Bathe her and put her to bed," Luke Garner ordered shortly. Without waiting to see them leave, he crossed the wide room to the sideboard where his whiskey was kept.

Her dark Indian face impassive, Emilia Uribe put her arm around Star's shoulders to guide her from the room. The girl made no demur when the housekeeper led her from the living room of Tres Santos.

Pouring himself a water glass full of whiskey, Luke Garner turned to face his daughter, his expression one of distaste at the sight of her.

Blinking and gaping in shock, Maude stood stock still in her long gray robe, too surprised to interfere as the two women left the living room. Dark circles ringed her gray eyes; her hair straggled limply over her shoulders and her flat chest. As Emilia closed the door softly, she managed to find some part of her voice. "Have you lost your mind?" she rasped. "What's she doing here?"

"She's here," Luke growled at his daughter. "And she's staying just as long as I want her."

"My God," Maude's voice rose shrilly as hysterical rage began to build. "What are you saying? She murdered Matthew. Murdered your own son, my twin brother, in cold blood. And you walk in here calmly in the dead of night and tell Emilia to bathe her and put her to bed."

"Don't know so much about cold blood." Luke turned

his back on the avenging harpy to pour himself another drink.

"She did!" Maude screamed. "She did! Oh, my God! Matthew's blood covered the front of her gown. He was so . . . close to her when she shot him. She shot her own husband."

"Shut up, Maudie," Garner warned, pointing one finger at her and keeping the others wrapped tightly around the glass. "You and I both know that Matthew got what he was asking for."

Maude's face contorted in madness and ferocity. Blood surged beneath the sallow skin until the veins strutted and writhed about her temples. "Oh, God," she moaned. "Oh, Matthew, my brother." She clasped her arms around her lank body and swayed from side to side. Her bloodshot eyes never left her father's broad back as he hung over the liquor bottle on the sideboard. "You can't do this!" she cried. "You can't do this!"

Swinging her arms wildly, she gestured toward the picture of Matthew, a huge framed photograph hanging between arched black draperies on the wall. "Look at him!" she cried. *"Look at him!"* In a frenzy she pulled the picture down. The nail spanged from the plaster and the black material floated limply to the floor.

Startled by the noise, Luke spun around, the whiskey slopping over his fingers. His eyes narrowed angrily as Maude thrust the portrait in front of his face.

"Look!" she cried again. Tears streamed down her cheeks as she encircled the portrait in her arms and pressed her own face against the edge of the frame.

But Garner did not spare the picture more than a passing glance. Instead he scanned the distraught figure of his daughter. What he saw disgusted him. Her thin, straggly hair, which she kept covered during the daylight hours, was liberally streaked with gray. Her red, contorted face bore no resemblance to the somber, thin face of the boy in the picture. Furthermore, her screeching voice grated on his nerves as she raved at him, senselessly protesting, arguing, cursing, accusing.

Tired to death and sick to his stomach, he poured himself another drink, a large glassful. Pushing her ungently aside, he dropped down into the big leather chair. He was getting too old for these kinds of hours. The day had been long and exhausting. He could not put in a day from before dawn until a couple of hours after midnight without feeling its effects. He did not have too many good years left, despite his boast to his daughter-in-law. Taking a sip of whiskey, he stared morosely at the spot on the floor as he closed his ears to his daughter's harangue.

Finally, Maude ran out of breath. With a last hiccuping sob, she laid the picture face up on the table. As she straightened away, she became aware of pain in her head, so intense that her trembling fingers pressed to her temples did nothing to alleviate it. Staggering across the room, she at last gained a straight leather bishop's chair beside the wide adobe fireplace.

"Are you through?" her father inquired when she had seated herself.

"Why?" she whispered.

"I'm not going to try to talk to you until you're ready to listen with your mouth shut. Are you ready to listen?"

She shot him a look malevolent in its hatred. "Yes."

He took a long drink of whiskey. "She took my son. She's gonna give me another one."

"Oh, my god." Maude's voice was only a breath of sound. "She'll shoot you, too."

He rolled his head on the chair back. "She won't do no such thing. She'll do like she's told. You can order her around all you want to. Don't mean nothing to me. Just don't hurt her till after that baby is born. We can always hang her later," he added placatingly.

Maude took a deep breath. "You are going to marry your

son's widow?" she whispered, aghast.

He stirred uneasily. "That don't make no difference," he maintained. "A woman's a woman."

Maude clasped the arms of the bishop's chair until her knuckles turned white. Her short blunt nails clawed ineffectually at the leather. "Why have you got to have another son?"

"Hell." Luke Garner threw her an accusing look. "I ain't worked all my life to see it all fall apart when I die. I want what's mine to last for a good spell. I want a man to leave this ranch to."

A frustrated groan escaped Maude. She clenched her fists and leaned forward imploringly. "You have me," she gritted.

"You ain't a man!" her father accused brutally.

"No, I'm not. But I've followed your every step for years. I've gone with you everywhere and watched you. More than Matthew ever did. You know that. You do!"

He shook his head. "Was that what you was doin'? I thought you was just makin' a nuisance of yourself."

His words shoved her back against the black leather. Her eyes glistened in the lamplight. Silently, she stared at her hands to hide the tears. She swallowed hard. "I could marry. . . ."

Her father's look was withering. "You don't stand a chance. I ain't got that kind of money to buy a husband for you."

Then the tears did start to trickle down the thin cheeks, gone white now and oddly pinched. "I'm not so bad when I'm fixed up. I could attract a man. I know I could. I just don't have a chance to meet anybody out here on the ranch all day long."

His eyes took on a crafty look. "You could go somewheres if you wanted. How'd you like a trip to San Antone? Or Fort Worth? Or even New Orleans?"

For an instant she looked at him with something like

280

hope in her eyes. Then her expression changed. Her tears dried on her cheeks as her face twisted with hatred and pain. "You'd like that, wouldn't you? Send me off and leave the way clear for you to wallow with that bitch. I wouldn't have anything to come back to. It'd all be gone. I'll stick." She rose from her chair on her last words. Her fists clenched and she screamed the words at her father. "And damn you both to hell. No one is going to take what's mine."

Garner lumbered up from his chair and crossed the room with astonishing speed in a man so heavy. His right hand swiped at his daughter as earlier in the evening it had swiped at his daughter-in-law. The force drove Maude back into the chair, which would have fallen over backward had it not been stopped by the wall behind it.

With a screech she threw up her hands, but he batted them down and struck her twice more. "You don't have a thing," he growled. "You don't have a damn thing! You hear me!" He struck her again, splitting her lower lip.

She screamed like a rabbit caught in a trap, a high-pitched shriek cut off by another blow.

"Not a thing on this place is yours. It's mine. I built it up and I'll give it to whoever I damn well please. If I want to give it back to the Indians, I'll do that. If I want to leave part of it to you . . ." he paused significantly ". . . and part to my son, I'll do that." He waited while her sobbing abated. "But I can kick you out anytime I damn well please. Savvy?"

She pulled her trembling hands down from her face and looked at him through drowned eyes. The bruises began to swell immediately on her face.

He stared at her remorselessly before tossing the remainder of the whiskey down his throat.

The silence grew in the room, until at last Maude straightened in her chair, clasped her hands together in front of her and hunched over them.

Garner nodded his satisfaction at her cringing posture. He did not see her gray eyes flash like sabers glinting in the lamplight. Death looked out from beneath the streaked brown hair disarranged by his blows.

When he had filled his glass, he came back and clumsily patted her on the shoulder. His anger was over. His daughter was suitably humble. He had come on a bit heavy-handed, but females forgot who was boss occasionally. They weren't long on brains. She had ceased screaming and weeping now and sat in shivering silence, only occasionally making a tiny coughing sound.

"Come on, Maudie," he said placatingly. "You ain't gonna lose a thing. In fact, you gained that sister-in-law back again to torment. Oh, I know how you and Matthew used to gang up on her. You and him always could make a match for anyone." He clenched his fist as he tried to call back his son's name. Damn! He should not have mentioned the two of them together. That would just make her feel worse.

However, the woman in the chair did not move. A muscle tightened in her jaw, but her disordered hair hanging about her face concealed it from her father. The color raised by the blows burned her cheeks. Her lip hurt like blazes. A drop of blood fell onto her lap staining her robe. Hastily, she covered it with her hand.

Her silence began to bother Garner. "Think of it like this, Maude. It'll be like she's havin' your baby for you. You can raise it after it gets here. But you won't have to get married to some guy who might take you away from Tres Santos and your old father. Instead you can stay here on the ranch, be your own boss. You'll be just like you've always been."

Still she gave no evidence that the idea was acceptable to her.

"Come on, Maudie. Loosen up." He shook her shoulder with false heartiness. "Here." He poured another whiskey

for himself and one for her in a lead crystal glass. "Here!"
He brought it to her and thrust it into her hand. "Here's to
the new baby. My new son. And to his Aunt Maudie."

Composing her face as best she could, Maude Garner
raised the glass to her lips. The whiskey stung like liquid
fire.

Chapter Eighteen

In the dark beside the sluggish river, Chris stared upward at the flickering torches. Sick to his stomach, he watched the gates swing open and close again behind the buggy and the riders. Within those walls her life was in constant peril.

Possibly Luke Garner had taken her out of the jail in Crossways to hang her at Tres Santos. In his hill fort he was safe from another raid by her brother. Even if Luke did not intend to hang her, the fact remained incontrovertible that someone in that house had killed Matthew Garner. That someone might want to be rid of his widow as well.

He shivered slightly as a coyote yipped somewhere in the darkness. Another answered and then another, their mournful songs like lunatics celebrating their escapes from some madhouse.

Chris had brought her back into a madhouse. He was as certain of that as he had ever been of anything in his life. Good people like Rosa McGloin testified to Matthew Garner's cruelty. The son must have learned it from the father. And Star was at the mercy of someone like that.

"God help her."

The empty night swallowed up his prayer but did not swallow his fear. What was happening to her now? Was she even now hungry or thirsty? In pain? Terrorized? A cold sweat stood on his forehead. She had found for the first time some small joy in her own sensuality. Was some man even now using his superior strength against her? Chris had never thought much about rape. Now suddenly it became a damnable sin.

Wearily, he pulled the saddle from the stallion and stretched himself out in a thicket of mesquite scrub and cactus. The last time he had slept under the stars, she had been with him. She had begged him not to take her to Crossways, had bargained with her body. With a groan he swiped his hand over his face.

He was seven kinds of a fool. Pray God he was only that and nothing more.

Her dark Indian face impassive, Emilia Uribe took Star's arm across her plump shoulders. The girl had no strength to resist when the housekeeper led her from the living room of Tres Santos.

However, when she turned into the hall that led to the wing that she had shared with Matthew, Star began to tremble. Despite her deadly weariness, each step was an emotional wrench. Her teeth chattered in sudden chill, and her knees threatened with each step to give way and drop her to the floor.

Ignoring her charge's condition, Emilia managed to draw her into what had been the couple's sitting room. The heavy leather-covered furniture, the chairs and couch, the massive oak tables and bookshelves were just as they had been furnished for the newlyweds. Beneath their feet a huge black and white rug made of the hides of piebald steers covered the floor of living limestone. A rack of long horns was mounted above the adobe and rock fireplace. All in all, it should have been a comfortable room, a room that reflected the life of the successful Texas rancher.

Yet Star felt only rising nausea as chills racked her body. In this room Matthew had died. His blood had spattered over everything. How had Emilia managed to get it clean? At the door to the bedroom she had shared with Matthew, she balked. Shaking like a leaf, her eyes dilated, she gasped in an effort to draw in breath.

When Emilia would have pushed her forward, she shook her head. "No. *No!* Not in there. Not in there!"

"Do not be foolish, señora." Emilia spoke for the first time. "Señor Garner says . . . you heard what he say."

But Star was too hysterical to listen to reason. Instead she grasped the door facing with both hands and held on like a child. "No."

With a shrug the Mexican woman relented. "Lie down then on the couch, Señora Garner," she sneered ungraciously. "But you gonna get cold and your back gonna be stiff."

Taking advantage of the temporary reprieve, Star flung herself across the room and slumped down on its smooth leather. The couch was a fairly comfortable piece of furniture, despite its stiff springs. Beneath its smooth, well-tanned upholstery was considerable padding. Star rested her head thankfully on its smooth rounded back.

Emilia clasped her hands together under her apron. "What you want me to do for you?"

For a full minute, Star stared blankly at the dark, flat face.

Emilia clamped her lips in a severe line. "Can I bring you a cup of coffee?" she prompted.

Star shook her head, her eyes straying round the room. At last she spoke, her voice withered and dry. "Water," she whispered. "A whole pitcher of cool, clean, clear water. Then bring some bedding to make up this couch here."

After she had drained a second glass of water and Emilia

286

had the bed linens spread and turned down over the couch, Star braced herself against the arm. "Now," she murmured.

Obeying reluctantly, Emilia knelt down to draw off the dusty boots. As the first stocking was stripped away, the housekeeper could not suppress a gasp. She clapped both hands to her pudgy cheeks. "*Pobrecita*, señora, your poor feet . . ."

With a kind of detached curiosity, Star inspected the swollen, blistered extremities. Her boots had not been off since she had left Gillard's ranch. She had walked uncountable miles before he had caught up to her. He had taken her directly to Crossways where she had been so repulsed by the terrible condition of her cell that she had been too intimidated to remove even a single article of clothing.

Her teeth caught in her lower lip as she wriggled her blistered toes gingerly. "The rest of me is probably in worse shape, Emilia, if you can believe that. I haven't had my boots off in days. Same with my clothing. My ribs are every color of the rainbow. Just like my wrists." She held them out for inspection, revealing the deep purple bracelets left by the manacles.

Emilia made a clucking noise with her tongue even as she cradled Star's high-arched foot in her hand. "You need a good bath before you go to bed. You sit here and rest. I get you some hot soup and put Juanita to work filling that bathtub with hot water. You just rest. I be right back." So saying, she heaved herself up off her knees and hastened out the door, leaving Star sitting numbly, too tired to worry about the plans Luke Garner had revealed to her.

The clock in the hallway outside the main room of the ranchhouse was striking three when Emilia finally slipped a cotton nightdress over Star's thin shoulders. The rough unbleached muslin gathered with ribbons and trimmed

287

with Irish crochet at throat and wrists was unfamiliar to the girl. Matthew had never allowed her to wear nightclothes, preferring her body naked and defenseless should he desire her in the middle of the night.

"This *camisa de noche* used to belong to my daughter Sarita," Emilia explained as she brushed Star's midnight-black hair free of dust and tangles. "When she married, she wanted more fancy things. This one was almost new, so I just keep it. It's too short for me, *si?* But you are little. Of course, it is too big. You're way too thin."

Star raised her tired hand, intercepting the brush in midstroke. "*Gracias*, Emilia," she whispered. "I thank you so much, but I'm just too tired to sit up another minute. *Por favor*. Let me lie down and go to sleep."

But when she would have stretched out on the couch, Emilia stopped her. "Why not in the bedroom, Señora?" The housekeeper gestured to the door through which Star had refused to pass. She swept her hand wide. "Here is where El Señor Matthew . . . all the furniture here was replaced. Everything here new. All the furniture. The bedroom will be like home. Same furniture as when you left. You sleep comfortable in big wide bed."

Star had not known the furniture in the sitting room was new, so exactly had Luke replaced it, but she would not have cared. The sitting room was the room in which Matthew died, but since she had little memory of that night, she had few associations here.

In the bedroom was the bed that had served as her torture rack. She did not doubt that Matthew's clothes, his belts, his spurs, his riding quirts were all in place in the closets. The memory of the instruments of torture made her shake. The sight of them would drive her mad.

"No!"

Emilia's smile disappeared. She shrugged her shoulders.

"I'll sleep here perfectly well," Star insisted.

Emilia looked doubtfully at the couch.

"I've been sleeping on the ground and on the floor off and on for two weeks. The couch will feel like heaven. Tomorrow you can fix me another room to stay in."

Almost as soon as her head sank to the feather pillow, Star fell into a stupor. So deeply unconscious was she that she did not hear the door open nor Luke and Maude enter.

Star's thin hands clutched the sheet at her breasts. Her loose black hair spread in waves around her. One long skein slipped off the edge of the couch to hang almost to the floor. The flickering light from the lamp held in Maude's hand revealed the drawn, troubled face.

Garner felt his body righten slightly. A crafty smile turned up one corner of his mouth. There was life in the old boy yet. "She looks better now that Emilia's got her cleaned up, don't she?"

"She looks like hell," Maude observed succinctly, bending close. "Her sins are showing in her face. She killed Matthew. She's a murderess."

Luke Garner's eyes narrowed. Was Maude about to start raving again? She was going to have to get rid of that kind of talk. He cleared his throat significantly. "Wish I'd told Emilia to forget about nightgowns," he rumbled. "I'd like to pull down that sheet right now and see what I'm gettin'."

Maude gasped. His crude words drove her away from the couch. "For God's sake, Papa . . ."

He took the lamp from her. "Get on back to bed, Maudie. You've stayed up too late tonight."

She backed away from him, fumbling for the doorknob. "Are you coming?"

He followed her, menacing her with his bulk. Almost lazily, he reached out his big hand to grasp her chin. His fingers pressed hard against her skin. "Maudie, I don't need you to tell me when to come to bed. Understand?" He felt her nod, though her head did not move. "Furthermore, I don't want to hear you call her a murderess no more. You've said all I want to hear on that subject. Savvy?"

She gulped.

His hand punished her jaw cruelly. "Now. Go to bed." He released her.

She jerked the door open enough to slide around its edge and flee down the hall.

Luke lingered. The hand that had punished his daughter now grasped the sheet to pull it gently from the sleeping woman's grip. Small mounds rose upward beneath the rough cream-colored cloth of the nightgown. He petted one, prodded it gently with his fingers. Fumbling, he finally located the nipple, feeling its nub of flesh at the center.

The nightgown's ribbon tie presented no resistance to his questing fingers. Likewise, the gathered neckline gave way as he tugged it clumsily. A slow grin spread his lips back from his teeth as he stared down at the smooth skin of his daughter-in-law's throat and breasts.

Beneath the outward curve of his belly, he felt himself stir and harden. A slow, pleased smile spread across his face. By God! He wasn't dead yet. He could get himself another son. This time, he wouldn't have one off a shivering, mealy-mouthed wretch like his first wife. He'd have one off this girl. Her daddy had been half-Comanche and half-Mexican, and her mama had been Texan. Good blood. A good mix. He wasn't a horsebreeder for nothing.

His fingertips grazed the tempting nipple, stroked the small, firm mound.

Star stirred. Her hands flexed as if searching for the covers he had dislodged.

He'd better leave her alone. She needed rest tonight to get her strength back a little. If he treated her good, she wouldn't fight him so hard. Once the baby came, she'd raise it right. Give it some manners, some dignity, some sense. She'd make his new son into an upstanding man.

She'd made a bargain. She'd stick to it. If she didn't . . . well, holding her brother's safety over her head had been a smart move. He'd treat her right and not hurt her. He didn't need to beat and hurt her to excite himself. Just the sight of Star excited him.

As if she felt his eyes on her, she stirred, drew a deep breath. Her breasts rose in the lamplight.

Brushing his good intentions aside, he reached for her breasts with both hands. His bloated fingers tweaked the nipples.

Her black eyes flew wide, instantly alarmed, instantly fearful.

"Now, don't get . . ." he began.

She screamed. Her hands clenched into fists, she struck at him, struck at his hands. "Get away!"

In a frenzy, she rolled off the couch, even as he backed away from her, hands raised to placate her.

Screaming in horror, she scrambled up and sped toward the door.

"Now, hold your horses . . . !" he thundered behind her.

His words could not penetrate her mind. Endurance and control at an end, she fled down the dark hall. A door opened on her right and Maude stepped out, a lamp held high. The angle of the light turned her thin face into a witch's smirk. Star screamed again.

Barefooted and bare-breasted, she flung open a door to the inner court and burst out into the arms of Hatch. As she crashed into his hard form, she screamed again and tried to dodge past him.

The nightgown slipped from her shoulders. The rough material covering his hard chest scratched her bare skin. She screamed again and went for his eyes with her fingernails. He clapped long arms around her and gathered her into a crushing grip.

"Hold her," came a gruff voice behind her.

Wildly, she twisted her head to locate her pursuer even as she flailed at Hatch's cheeks with her fingernails. "Let me go! Please. For pity's sake! Let me go!"

"She's clawing me!" Hatch snarled.

"Bring her in here." Luke Garner strode past the struggling figures.

Hatch spun Star around and clamped one arm across her breasts, the other around her waist. "Seems like I'm always handling you, gal," he whispered through clenched teeth as he pressed her forward.

Still screaming, she struggled violently, oblivious of pain, imbued with unnatural strength. But the foreman was stronger. Despite her wildest struggles, she was borne down the hall to a lighted doorway where Garner's silhouette waited.

"Hold her tight!" he commanded harshly.

Hatch's forearm shifted from her breasts to her throat and pressed harder, turning her screams into choking groans.

Garner lifted a glass of cloudy liquid.

"No! No . . ."

"She's clawing the hell out of my arm."

"Open up."

She flailed her arms at him. One hand knocked the glass away, sending it crashing against the wall, its contents splattering.

Luke Garner scowled. "All right," he grunted. "We'll do it the easy way."

Hatch's forearm tightened. She could feel his thigh beneath her buttocks lifting her up on tiptoe, so she writhed ineffectually with no base to launch her blows.

Garner tipped the laudanum bottle to her lips, forcing the tiny neck between her teeth. At the same time Hatch's forearm pressed upward, preventing her from twisting her head away. A tiny amount of the bitter liquid slid back over her tongue and down into her throat. She gagged once, then swallowed reflexively.

Garner grinned. "Hold her, Hatch. She'll get easy in a minute." He lowered the bottle and turned back into the lighted room. Hatch relaxed fractionally.

Suddenly, Star was incredibly tired. The laudanum could not be taking effect so soon, but she could no longer resist the exhaustion of her own body. In the darkness of the hall, she went limp in his hands.

Chuckling philosophically, the rider swept her up in his arms. "Where you want her stowed, boss?" he called.

"End of the hall on the right," Garner growled over his shoulder as he poured himself another drink.

Down the dark hall Hatch carried his unconscious burden. The long black hair framed her pale face in the light from Maude's door as he strode past.

"Whereabouts?" he asked.

"Two more doors," she responded angrily. As she watched the man carry Star, she ground her teeth. Something must happen to her soon-to-be stepmother. The way the woman threw herself around, an accident was inevitable. Or perhaps she was suicidal. Violent people often were. Maude closed the door thoughtfully.

Chris presented himself at Tres Santos shortly after breakfast the next morning. He was passed without comment through the various gates. Emilia admitted him to the hallway, where he stood hat in hand while she knocked on the door to Garner's office.

"Come in, Gillard," Garner growled. His tone was a warning that his expansive mood on the day before had cooled. Dark pouches sagged beneath his eyes. His entire face looked puffy and swollen. A glance at the hands that held several sheets of paper revealed their trembling. He had not been long out of bed. "Come for your money, I guess."

"That's it." Chris looped his thumbs into the belt that passed around his waist.

Garner did not ask him to sit but regarded him sourly.

"Did she give you any trouble?"

The bounty hunter hesitated. Why should Garner ask? "Not much," he said at last. "She got hurt. Cracked some ribs right at the start. Knocked the fight right out of her." His cool words tore him apart. The memory of her ordeal tore at his belly and quickened his heartbeat.

Garner snorted, nodding his head slowly. His brown-speckled skin showed through a bald spot on his crown. "She didn't seem much hurt to me."

He must have had a rough night, Gillard realized, suppressing a smile. Knowing Star as he did, he could imagine the fight she had given them. "Cracked ribs can be mighty painful."

Garner nodded again, even less heartily than before. Squinting slightly, as if light pained him, he let his gaze run speculatively up the long figure standing alertly in front of him. "You had a real easy job," he accused nastily.

So that was the problem. He did not want to pay the rest of the money. Chris relaxed fractionally. Garner did not suspect his real reason for coming here. "I made it look easy," he declared.

"Hire a professional if you want the job done right," Garner muttered. One hand pulled open the righthand drawer of his desk and withdrew a thick brown envelope. Speculatively, he turned it over and over. His hands trembled like leaves. Abruptly, he slapped the envelope down on the desk and thrust his hands out of sight in his lap. "There it is," he growled. "But I want that mare the woman rode up here."

In the act of reaching for the envelope, Chris paused. "What mare?"

"Don't play coy with me. Hatch saw the two of you ridin' into town day before yesterday. You was ridin' a big stallion. She was ridin' a little black mare."

"So?"

"So. That mare's my property."

"If she doesn't belong to the woman I brought in, then she belongs to Tomas de Montejo," Chris pointed out reasonably.

Garner's face reddened. "I don't guess it's any of your business to make a judgment like that, but I'll act like you have a right to know," he drawled. His hands came out on the desk clenched in tight fists. "Those horses was the reason I had my boy marry that Mex gal. I was cornerin' for a deal on them when my boy got plugged. Now that's all in a cocked hat. But I'll get at least one out of this."

Chris stared blankly at the man. Could this be the man so determined on revenge a month ago that he had almost suffered a stroke? Now he spoke of his dead son as if he were of no more importance than a stranger. The gallows was still built in town, but Star was not hanging from it. What had happened in the past couple of months to cause this change?

Luke Garner raised his head when Chris did not answer. He smiled humorlessly, his lips hardly quirking at the corners. "To tell the truth, Gillard, I want that horse worst way."

Chris shook his head. "I earned that horse," he said slowly. "My cover to get on the ranch and get that woman to ride with me was as a horse breeder and breaker. I was paid for my services with that horse."

Garner's eyes narrowed. His mouth thinned to a lipless trap. "Not *that* horse. You ain't foolin' me about *that* horse. Maybe you was given a horse. You might even have been given a Paso mare. But that mare belonged to that Mex gal. That's her special mare."

Chris straightened. His hands dropped from his belt to hang loosely at his sides. "I earned that horse," he repeated. "And you owe me five thousand dollars."

"I ain't payin'. I was payin' for a criminal to be brought to justice. Since then I've found out she did what she did by accident. My boy's death was a pure accident. Pure and

295

simple. So the job warn't dangerous at all."

"How do you figure that?"

"Well, you weren't bringin' a killer in. You were just bringin' a scared little girl back to her family."

"Her brother's *vaqueros* fired real bullets at me twice."

Garner spread his hands. "I'll give you the money for the horse. Hell! What do you want with the mare, anyway? She's too small for you. Fact is, she's too small for me. I want her for Star. See, she's gonna stay here at the ranch for a while and get better. You roughed her up pretty good, just like you said. I figure she'll be happier if she has her favorite horse to ride."

Chris stared in disbelief. He rubbed the back of his neck with his hand. "Well, that's sure good news for Señora Garner. She was afraid you were going to hang her."

Garner nodded. "She was real pleased last night when me and the boys went to the jail and got her out. We brought her out here and put her back in her old room."

"I'd like to see her," Chris said softly.

"What for?" Garner's eyes narrowed suspiciously.

"To apologize. I didn't hurt her any more than I had to, but I'm sorry about her breaking her ribs and having to spend the night in jail. It's a shame she had to go through that."

"Yeah," Garner agreed. "A damn shame."

"Why didn't you just come right out and say something day before yesterday?"

Garner scowled. "I just found out."

"Lucky for her," Chris remarked. "How'd you find out?"

"Doc told me."

"Oh."

In the ensuing silence, Garner picked up the envelope again. "Let me have that horse," he resumed, "and you can have this."

"I'd like to see Señora Garner."

The rancher's face turned red. "Well, you can't see her. She's restin' now. You dang near killed her bringin' her in, and then that dang fool sheriff didn't treat her right. So she's pretty well done in."

"I was acting under your orders. Now pay me," Chris insisted firmly.

"Hell, no!" Garner slammed his clenched fist down on the desktop. "You get the hell out of here. I've paid you all I'm going to. You'd better be gone before sundown. After sundown on Tres Santos ain't exactly healthy for strangers. They've been known to have bad accidents."

Chris Gillard's steel-gray stare moved slowly over Garner's florid face and bulky frame. Then he reached for the brim of his hat, pulling it down more firmly over his forehead. He did not say another word as he strode to the door.

"You'd better get the hell out of the country," Garner yelled after him. "Get the hell out of my reach. And remember. I've got a mighty long arm."

Chapter Nineteen

"Gillard! Christopher Gillard!" A voice hissed his name from a corner of the inner court.

His hands paused in unlooping the reins from around the hitching post. A hedge of velvety gray-green sage grew along the front of the family's quarters in the compound. At the corners of the courtyard it had not been cropped but allowed to grow to its natural height. From behind one of these thick clumps Maude beckoned.

Glancing around warily, Chris walked toward her. "Miss Garner." He tipped his hat politely.

"Do you want to see Star?" she began without preliminaries.

He did not answer immediately. One pale eyebrow rose in amazement.

"You needn't look so surprised. I overheard the conversation between my father and you," she admitted. Maude's lower lip was swollen; a tiny scab bisected it vertically. A deep discoloration marked the side of her jaw. As he frowned at her, she raised one hand to cover the spot.

He hesitated fractionally, guessing that Luke Garner had worked her over. He shuddered to think what condition Star would be in. His instincts warned him that whatever motive Maude could have for taking him to Star, it could have nothing to do with Star's good, or his own for that matter. Still, she was his only chance. "If it wouldn't be too much trouble," he said at last. "I hope she's all right."

Maude looked at him appraisingly, taking in his height and breadth of shoulder. The tip of her tongue swiped across her bruised lip. "Of course. I don't know whether she'll be conscious or not. She might not know that you've been to see her." Maude's voice never varied in tone. She might have been reading the livestock reports from the local newspaper.

A muscle jumped in Chris's jaw as he struggled to maintain control. "Why not?"

"She got hysterical last night." Maude's gray eyes studied his reaction to this information. When his face showed no more than a tightening of his jaw, she shrugged. "My father drugged her. She's sleeping it off."

"I can't imagine anyone getting hysterical over being told she wasn't going to be hanged." Chris probed delicately for some kind of explanation.

Maude shot him a gray glance. Callously, she flicked a spot of lint from her sleeve. "Do you want to see her or not?"

Chris rested his hand over the butt of his Colt. "I want to see her."

"Then come with me." Her gray skirt flapped around her ankles as she led him to a door facing the courtyard at a right angle to the main living area. Producing a key from her pocket, she threw her shoulder against the stubborn door. With a protest from the hinges, it creaked open.

"We never use that outside door," she explained. "Wait

here." She disappeared around a corner in a hall.

He stood in some sort of entry, unfurnished except for a small chest with a layering of dust on its scarred top.

Warily, he looked around him. His right hand never left the butt of the pistol. In less than a minute, Maude was back. "This way."

She led him to a room spartan in its furnishings. A large brass bed was pushed against one wall. Against the other was pushed a huge ornately carved mahogany wardrobe. The atmosphere was stuffy in the extreme. Hot sunlight streamed through an uncurtained window located above shoulder level beside the bed. A band of it cast its fire to the foot of the brass bed, which in turn cast a mirrored reflection on the adobe wall. All this Chris took in at a glance before focusing on the occupant of the bed.

Star had thrown her covers back. Her white nightgown clung damply to her body. Her flushed face was beaded with perspiration. She looked incredibly fragile lying there.

Although its intricate curlicues wound up and up the wall, the bed was low, less than two feet off the floor. Chris went down on one knee beside it. With fingers that trembled, he brushed a strand of damp hair back from her temple.

Star stirred restlessly, muttering something. In her sleep her hands clasped across her breasts in a gesture he had observed before, during their travels. Her left thumb and forefinger massaged the base of her right thumb.

His jaw tightened against the sympathetic pain that lanced through him as he recognized the reason for the movement. Without thinking, he closed his own warm hand over hers in an effort to comfort her.

Despite the laudanum, his touch penetrated the layers of fog enclosing her brain. The reassurance of gentleness relaxed her. The dream that always lurked at the edge of her sleep world receded. Moving her right hand, she gave it into his clasp.

The gesture was like a plea. In Chris Gillard's life as bounty hunter, he had done much of which he was not proud. He claimed no parents, no friends. He had encased himself in a hard shell that only Duff could penetrate. Until this moment. Now Star pulled herself into his heart with her small hand.

His grip tightened on the slender fingers as he sought to reach her through the sense of touch. "Star," he whispered. "Star." He lifted her hand to his lips. His other hand touched her cheek.

"Is she out?"

He had forgotten Maude Garner standing restively behind him. Her dry voice pulled Gillard back to the present.

"Seems to be," he replied. "What did your father give her?"

Maude approached the other side of the bed. "Probably laudanum. There was some around here, as I remember. Matthew used it for his leg."

Feeling his fingers trembling, Chris laid them firmly against Star's cheek to turn her face toward him. "She's so hot," he complained, looking upward to Maude for help. "Should she be this hot?"

Maude draped one arm over the brass bed. Chris could smell the acrid odor where the perspiration ringed her blouse at the armpit. "Probably got a touch of fever. Also that laudanum makes a body sweat as it wears off."

Chris dropped his eyes to hide his revulsion. Her callous disregard for the helpless woman as well as her personal repulsiveness made his stomach heave. "Señora Garner," he whispered, bending low over Star's ear.

For a second the black lashes fluttered against the fragile magnolia of her cheek.

301

"Señora Garner," he spoke more loudly.

As if weighted, the lids lifted. For a few seconds the black eyes stared unfocused at his face, their pupils enormous.

"Star," he called softly.

Even as her eyelids were closing, she recognized him. He was sure. Then the door of her eyelids slid to, imprisoning her behind them. But not before they had sent him a silent message. Despair, fear, then hope. A silent plea. He could not fail to read the message. In his hand her small one tightened almost imperceptibly, struggling to retain her grip.

Sweat broke out on Chris's forehead. If she had screamed at him at the top of her lungs, he would have heard no more clearly. He steadfastly returned the grip, tightening his fingers around her hand with gentle cruelty, squeezing the bones until they made a tiny cracking sound. At the same time he bent nearer. Had he penetrated the laudanum fog?

A slight lift to the corners of her pale lips was his reply. She had felt his answer! He had given his pledge.

Gently he placed her hand on her breast. He straightened the disarranged nightgown and pulled the covers up above her waist. He took a deep breath that shrugged his shoulders. "I guess I can't get anything out of her tonight." Impassively, careful to show no emotion, he faced the thin woman in gray on the other side of the bed.

Maude's pale gray eyes narrowed; she studied the bones of his face, his tanned skin, the golden-blond hair in the V of his shirt. "Maybe you'd like to stay until she wakes up?" Although her voice rose slightly at the end, her sentence was more a command than a question.

Chris stared at her skeptically. "Maybe," he replied at last. "But I guess I'd better be moving on." Lifting his hat, he ran his hand through his sweat-damp hair before replacing it, tugging the brim down firmly across his eyes.

His hand was on the bedroom door before she spoke. "Of course, I would be willing to pay you something for your time," Maude interposed. "Wait for me in that old office and we'll talk."

One hand hooked over the butt of his gun, Chris looked around warily at another sparsely furnished room. A dusty desk with a scarred top, a hard straight oak chair behind it, a three-shelved bookcase with glass doors comprised the total furnishings of the room. The floor was bare of carpets; the walls, bare of pictures. He looked curiously around him. If this were an office, not much business had been transacted here in a long time.

He felt rather than heard Maude enter and close the door behind her. Slowly he turned to face her; one side of his mouth quirked upward. "Your move."

She ducked her head and went around him. Calm as a man, she seated herself at the desk and laced her fingers together on its top. "I want to hire you." Her voice had taken on a harsh, grating sound.

"To do what?"

She flushed, her high cheekbones stained with the first color he had ever seen there. "Do you . . . er . . . happen to have a smoke?"

"You surprise me," he remarked. "I didn't think ladies smoked." He pulled the makings from his vest pocket.

"Matthew taught me," she replied, not quite meeting his eyes. "Would you roll it for me?"

While he complied, the silence deepened. Deftly he twisted the ends and held it out to her. While she put it between her lips, he struck a match off his boot.

"I don't really have anyone on the ranch that works for

me," she said, when the gray smoke curled round her head. "That woman killed my brother Matthew." She ran a finger across the surface of the desk. It came away gray with dust. She grimaced. "This used to be his office. Now it's gathering dust. She killed him."

Even though Gillard shook his head, she hurried on. "Even if *she* didn't, *someone* did. I need protection. I need my own man. Anyone on this ranch could have done it. If he killed my brother, then I might be next."

"I don't work cheap."

"Oh, money is no problem," she insisted. "My father has always let me spend what I wanted to."

"But you've never hired a guard before," he reminded her.

"That's true. But I think in this case he'll agree to let me hire you." She inhaled deeply. Her gray eyes narrowed. "He wants that mare."

"You did listen."

She did not bother to answer. "How about it?"

Chris hesitated. He longed to be gone. Off the ranch and out of the county. Whatever Maude could pay him would be little compared to what he could earn bounty hunting.

Suddenly, he imagined his hand was still warm from Star's. He remembered the silent plea in her eyes. If he could remain at the ranch within sight and call of the house until she had regained her strength, he could take her back across the Rio Grande. The sight of her perspiring face, the feel of her thin hand had wrenched his heart. Mentally he squared his shoulders. He was committed. "How much?"

"Hatch gets two dollars a day. He's the foreman."

"I make five dollars a day and expenses."

"Five dollars?!"

"Either that, or a flat fee based on how dangerous the job is."

"But there's no danger here."

"You're hiring me to protect you," he pointed out reasonably. "If there's no danger then you don't need me."

She dropped the cigarette on the floor and stubbed it out beneath her foot. "I want *you*," she insisted with peculiar significance.

He waited.

She glared at him. "Five dollars," she capitulated.

"I'll move my things from Mrs. McGloin's."

"Do that," she sneered. "However, the bunkhouse is too far for me to call for you when I need you. You couldn't protect me properly. There's an identical room across the court from this one. You can sleep there. It backs up on my room." She paused significantly.

"You want me to sleep in a room next to you?"

"Where you can protect me." For the first time in the interview, she smiled. Her teeth were small and dingy. Everything about the woman was gray. "You can report to me each morning and check on me in the evening. I'll tell you your duties for the day," she paused delicately again, lifting an appraising eyelid, " . . . and the night."

"Now just a minute . . ." Revulsion made his belly twist. This thin body and colorless face hid something else.

"For five dollars a day I expect twenty-four-hour attention," she interrupted.

His hand closed over the doorknob. "I'm not . . ."

"Nobody knows who killed my brother. You'll never convince me that she didn't do it. But . . . there's always the chance that she didn't. Then who did? And who is the next victim?"

She had voiced his own thought. He dropped his hand. His gray eyes glittered like polished steel.

She smiled. "Gillard," she hissed. "Part of your duties *will* be performed at night."

"Yes, ma'am." He kept his voice expressionless as he tugged his hat down on his forehead and closed the door quietly behind him.

When Star regained consciousness, she was violently nauseated. Emilia brought a pan, but it was unnecessary. She had nothing to give. The housekeeper held her head until the spasms ceased and she rolled back shuddering on the sweat-soaked sheets.

For the next forty-eight hours Emilia coaxed and begged her to try to eat. Her efforts were in vain. Star refused more than a few bites of food at any single meal. In the hot stuffy room, the perspiration dried on her body until a red rash erupted here and there on her skin. Her hair came loose from its knot to hang in ropelike strings.

Twice Luke Garner came to stand over her, frowning hotly. On the third afternoon, he stood over the bed, his eyes blazing with anger. The soiled gown sticking damply to her figure revealed her to be thin to the point of emaciation. "Goddamn!"

The housekeeper jumped and cowered back against the wall on the other side of the bed.

"Get her up!"

"But, señor . . ."

"Get her up, I said. Tonight she's gonna come in and eat at the family table. By God, I'll see that she eats."

He stalked out slamming the door, and Emilia came forward apologetically. "I must get you up, señora. You heard him."

Star turned her face into the pillow. "Please just go away, Emilia. If you go away for a few more days, I'll be dead."

"*Por favor*, señora. Do not say those things. You are young. You have a long life to live." Without waiting for

306

Star to comment, Emilia thrust her arms underneath her patient's shoulders and lifted her to a sitting position. "I leave you for a minute. When I come back, I bring clean clothes. Juanita will bring warm water. Then I give you bath and get you dressed. You will feel better *muy pronto*."

At seven o'clock that evening, Star appeared, dressed in clothes she had left behind her when she fled. Not meeting the eyes of the Garners, father and daughter, she seated herself at her accustomed place at their table. Instead, her eyes flickered over the chair at her side, the one Matthew had always sat in when he had come to supper. It held no particular terror. He had been missing many times, not bothering to come to dinner, staying in town drinking. Only in her bed had he been a terror.

She raised her eyes defiantly. At her left at the head of the table sat Luke and across from her sat Maude, her expression unforgiving, her lips drawn back in a malicious sneer.

Garner, on the other hand, chuckled with satisfaction. "You been sick long enough," he opined. "Nobody ever got well by stayin' in bed. People die in beds." He stared hard at her frail form that nevertheless held itself erect in the high-backed chair.

Emilia had pulled the midnight-black hair back into a thick chignon at the nape of the graceful neck. The style accented the classic bone structure that needed no ornamentation or softness to disguise slight faults. The forty-eight hours of semi-starvation in bed combined with the deprivation of the time spent in the jail had drawn her skin tightly across her bones and lightened its normally healthy tan color to a dark magnolia cream.

"You look too white," Garner grumbled. "Don't she

look too white, Maudie?"

His daughter nodded indifferently. "Perhaps I need to take her out for a buggy ride tomorrow. The two of us can drive over the ranch with an escort. I've hired your bounty hunter as my escort, Star. I hope you don't mind."

Star stared at her incredulously, not sure whether to believe her or not. Deep within her, memory stirred. Gillard's face swam out of a laudanum-induced haze then vanished again. Perhaps he had not been a dream. "Why should I mind?"

Even as she spoke, Maude motioned to a someone behind Star's chair. "No reason. I've instructed him to wait for me tonight while we eat."

Luke Garner raised his grizzled head from his contemplation of his daughter-in-law. "What the hell . . . ?" he began.

"I hired him to work for me," Maude interrupted. "To protect me," she explained.

Luke's face flushed dark red. His mouth contorted. "Well, I told him to get the hell off this place," Garner jerked his napkin from around his neck and flung it down beside his plate. "What in hell do you need protecting from, anyway?"

Maude smiled smoothly. "Someone killed Matthew," she reminded him. "Whoever it was might want to kill Matthew's sister."

Their argument went on and on. Chris moved around the foot of the table, while still remaining in the shadows in the corner of the room. Star closed her hands tightly around the arms of her chair. Until that moment she had believed him to be gone. She had accepted the fact that she was alone. He had taken Humareda with him and she had rejoiced in the knowledge that the mare was safely beyond Garner's hands.

308

The first day at the ranch her father-in-law had cursed her vituperatively as she lay in helpless weakness, still partially ill from the effects of the laudanum he had administered by force the night before. Fortunately, she had been too oblivious of the problem to be overly upset by his anger. Now she remembered. Garner had cursed her because she had let the mare go to a bounty hunter who was long gone out of the country.

Now Chris Gillard stood tall and impassive at the foot of the table, his white-gold hair combed and trimmed, his steely gray eyes cooly regarding her as they had when he had first seen her.

Hopefully she searched his face for some sign that he would help her. With a sinking feeling she realized she could detect nothing of the man who had brought her food and drink during her long night of incarceration in the Crossways jail. Nowhere did she recognize the horseman to whom she had given her mare.

Instead his mouth was curved in the hard line that she had seen the night she had prostituted herself to make love to him, tried to bribe him with her body, only to be humiliated and unmercifully cheapened by his rejection. A wave of weakness born of despair swept her. She raised one hand to her forehead as her eyes fell to the food on her plate.

Observing her sister-in-law's reaction, Maude chuckled. "Oh, my goodness. I forgot. Star, how thoughtless of me. I don't suppose you and Gillard have much love for each other, do you? I just didn't think."

From his place at the head of the table, Garner muttered something unintelligible under his breath.

"Why don't you wait outside in the court, Gillard," Maude ordered with a smirk. "Emilia, you may take these plates away and bring the main course. Star doesn't seem to care for your soup."

"Well, she ain't alone there," Garner barked. "When I sit down to eat, I want it *on the table*." He slapped his hand down beside his plate to emphasize his displeasure. "And what's more, Maudie, I don't want no hired hand of yours hanging round here where we're being a family together." He threw Star a quick inquiring glance. "If you want to hire a man, Maudie, that's okay. But he don't come up to the house and stand around while we're tryin' to eat. He stays over in the bunkhouse until you're ready to ride with him. Clear?"

"Of course."

"Good. How much is he costin' me?"

But Maudie pretended not to hear his final question, which was murmured *sotto voce*. "Emilia," she called. "You may serve the roast."

The heavy meal of venison, potatoes, pinto beans, and squash washed down with coffee completely defeated Star. Each bite of vegetable seemed to stick in her throat. The venison haunch roasted dry was tough and leathery. After a halfhearted attempt to cut a portion with her knife and fork, she gave up and pushed it aside. The coffee was stronger than she liked and boiling hot.

Once she glanced at Luke sitting at the head of the table, his face bent over his food. In his left hand he held a hunk of bread for a scoop. On his fork in his right, he piled up large bites of meat and beans and stuffed them into his mouth. The freckles dotting the bald spot on the top of his head moved with the rhythm of his chewing.

Her appetite gone, she gave up pushing the food around her plate and put down her fork. Reaching for her water glass, she glanced across the table at her sister-in-law. Maude, who had seen Star look at Luke, glared back maliciously. Star clenched her hand over the arm of the chair, wondering again why she was sitting here.

Emilia stepped forward to take her plate. "I have made some nice flan just for you, señora," she murmured. "I bring it to you now, *Sí?*"

With a grateful smile, Star nodded.

Two portions of heavy pecan currant cake were brought on a tray for Luke and Maude and a single portion of the light pudding for Star.

"What's that?" Garner growled, pointing to the golden-yellow custard topped with rich brown caramelized sugar.

"A dessert for Señora Garner," Emilia explained nervously, holding the tray back from his stabbing fork. "It is very light, Señor Garner. You wouldn't like it much. It is right for someone who has been sick."

"Bring it here," he insisted, gesturing with the fork again.

Reluctantly, the dismayed housekeeper set it in front of him. With a scowl, he dipped his spoon into the center and tasted it. His face wrinkled. "Baby food," he sneered. He dropped the spoon with a clatter. "Never put any color in those cheeks with that kind of pap. Give her a piece of cake."

"*Sí, señor.*" Emilia's face settled into a mask of disgust and frustration. Picking up the ruined dessert, she carried the tray out.

Why was I not allowed to die? Star stared bleakly at a spot above Maude's head. I cannot endure this for weeks, much less months or years. What if I do become pregnant? I cannot leave my baby alone here, yet I cannot bear to live for the rest of my life with this.

"The priest'll be here next week," Luke informed the two women. "He'll be a-bringin' the book and everything. Gonna tie the knot legal. My son's gonna be born in the church." He slapped the table with his hand. "By damn,

311

he's gonna be registered just like a stud in a stud book."

Star winced as the plates and silverware vibrated. Maude sneered as her full water glass slopped over.

Luke stared critically at the woman on his left. "Hope he don't look too Mex."

The magnolia skin blanched whiter. Her eyes looked daggers at him. "Why do you want to marry me?"

"I done told you that," was the instant reply. "You took my first son. It's only fair and proper that you have another one for me."

"Excuse me." Maude flung down her napkin and scraped back her chair. Her normally flat voice dripped with sarcasm. "Gillard and I will go for a ride in the moonlight."

"What're you up to, Maudie?" Luke cocked his head to one side as his daughter rose.

"Me?" Maude pushed the chair back hard against the edge of the table. "You needn't worry that I'm 'up to' anything. You told me that you didn't have enough money to buy me a husband. You're getting a wife. Of course, you may not get your son. If Matthew couldn't get her pregnant, she may not be able to get that way."

Luke's face flushed angrily. "Shut up and go if you're goin', Maudie."

She stalked to the door. "He's going to let me ride that black mare of his," she threw over her shoulder at Star. "He promised."

Luke Garner pushed back his chair. Pressing his knuckles down on the tabletop, he heaved himself up. "If that don't beat all," he growled. "She's been hangin' around listenin' at doors again. She's gonna get that mare off that guy, and he'll think it was his idea." He came around to put his hand on Star's shoulder. "You'll get your mare back after all, and you'll have your sister Maudie to thank."

"I don't feel well," Star murmured, trying to shrug out from under him. "I need to lie down."

"No, you don't." His hand tightened painfully. "You can sit up as well as lie down. We'll go on in the living room and you can sit down in my wife's rocker. That's where I want you. After a while you can go to bed, but I want you to get used to sittin' there with me in the evenin'."

"I'm really too tired."

"Should have eaten more when you had the chance," Luke replied callously. "Go long with you now." He patted her backside familiarly.

For over an hour she sat in a ladder back rocker with a thin hide cushion tied over the slats. The woven bottom had been replaced by one of cowhide. The hair retained heat and prickled the backs of her thighs through the thin cotton of her skirt and petticoat.

Luke read the San Antonio paper as well as the local paper from front to back, reading aloud items he found particularly interesting. His odorous cigar smoked in a stand between his heavy chair and hers.

At last he allowed the paper to droop lower and lower until it lay across his face shielding it from the light. A stentorian snore rumbled from beneath it.

Staggering slightly as she pushed herself out of the rocker, Star brushed against the cigar stand. The foul stub fell to the floor. She trampled it beneath her shoe as if it had been vermin.

Her companion did not move. His snores rumbled on. His belly rose and fell rhythmically.

Tiptoeing across the room, she opened the door. At the same time she carefully lifted it by the knob so it would not scrape noisily along the floor. Once in the hall she fled to her room, pushing open her door and collapsing against it when she closed it behind her.

313

Reaction threatened to overcome her. Panting and trembling, she staggered dizzily to the window and managed to tug it up. The soft night breeze billowed the curtain over her as she slumped down on her knees and leaned her face on the sill.

She sat there for a long time, slipping in and out of consciousness until the faint buzzing in her ears subsided. Gradually night noises, the chirp of crickets, the hoots of a pair of screech owls, the squeak of a bat began to sort themselves out.

She was about to push herself wearily to her feet when she heard voices. At first she thought they came from outside. But the courtyard was empty. She stared out. Several windows were open for coolness. All were dark.

"Everyone's asleep." Maude's dry flat voice rose irritably.

"Maybe so. Maybe not."

Instantly, Star stiffened. Christopher Gillard had spoken with her through jail walls. She would recognize his voice anywhere.

"Kiss me." Maude's voice commanded imperiously.

"I don't. . . " Gillard's words were interrupted. Silence conveyed the futility of his protest.

"Harder," the command was a breathy sigh. "Again. . . ."

Chapter Twenty

Nameless, violent emotions raged through Star's body. Emotions she had not thought herself capable of made her hands curve into claws. Reflexively, she clamped her teeth together so hard that pain shot through her jaws. Swaying where she stood, her sense of hearing peculiarly acute, she listened as clothing rustled faintly.

Again Maude moaned, an importunate sound. Star heard a muffled expletive, Chris's voice.

"Touch me." Maude groaned. "Harder, damn you. Harder!" Her command ended in a sharp gasp.

The soft curtain brushed Star's hot face. It fell away, then billowed out again, this time brushing her with dampness. Tears were starting in her eyes. Slow, hot droplets trickled down her cheeks. Angrily, she turned away. Her limbs were trembling, her stomach roiling as twin demons of anger and jealousy left her peculiarly dizzy. She took a couple of uncertain steps and fell full-length across her bed. To muffle her sobs, she buried her face in the pillow.

Star woke clawing frantically at a hard hand pressed

315

across her mouth. Kicking out with both feet, she encountered a hard-muscled thigh where it pressed against the side of the bed.

"For God's sake, Star," an irritated whisper tore through her panic. "It's me. Chris."

The sound of his voice coupled with his name reassured her. She fell back in a welter of covers. As he felt her resistance ebb, his hand slid away from her mouth to gently cup her shoulder.

"Chris?" Her normally husky voice rose to a child's hoarse whimper.

"Ssh. Yes." He patted her as if she were indeed a child. "I'm here."

Instantly Star closed her hands around his wrist. Still befuddled by sleep, dizzy from her violent effort, her head pounding horribly, she clung to the only person who might bring her some measure of comfort.

His other hand fumbled in the darkness. The calloused fingers touched her cheek, then her hair, smoothing the escaping tendrils back from her temple. Gently they brushed away the trails of moisture left by her tears.

Their faces were close—only inches apart in the warm darkness. He could see her eyes glistening in the white oval of her face. "You've been crying," he accused softly.

"No . . ." Her voice quavered on the denial.

"You shouldn't be, you know." He squeezed her shoulder. "I'm here to take you back to Mexico."

A hoarse, muffled sound escaped from deep in her throat. Her fingers tightened convulsively around his wrist.

"Ah, don't, Star," he whispered. His lips touched her forehead. "Don't cry. Don't cry." He kissed her again. His mouth brushed her eyelids, her temples, the corners of her eyes. His cheek pressed against hers, warm and slightly scratchy. As her senses became charged with his nearness, the pounding in her head disappeared as if by magic.

At the same time that her hungry body responded to his masculinity, her mind gave up its struggle to think clearly. Her deep, shuddering breath drew his scent into her nostrils. Her eyes followed the line of his silhouette as his body leaned over hers, his arms braced on either side of her shoulders. His weight pressed in on top of her.

She was totally surrounded by him, all her senses tingling with his presence. She bit her lip as a wave of longing rippled outward from the center of her belly.

His lips moved down to the lobe of her ear, nibbling the tender flesh, taking it between his teeth as he exhaled against her cheek. "Star." One hand covered her breast, finding her nipple erect, the aureole swollen.

Quite suddenly, she remembered. "You were with Maude," she accused, struggling for sanity. "You've just come from her b-bed." Her fingers, which had been pulling him toward her, doubled into fists to push and pummel against his shoulders. Her back which had been arched to raise her breasts to his caressing fingers, suddenly bowed backward into the mattress.

Somewhat to her surprise, he fell away from her. The springs creaked as he sank back onto the bed. His arms fell limply to his sides. "How could I forget?" he remarked bitterly to the hot night.

"I heard you . . . working . . . for her now." She uttered the words with bitter disdain.

"Yep," he agreed in the same flat tone. "I'm for hire. Just meet my price."

"Get out!"

"No!"

"If you don't leave immediately, I'll scream."

"Go ahead." He sighed wearily. "I'm just thinking that I'd like to get myself thrown off this ranch right now. I could forget about the whole crazy lot of you."

"You were with her."

"In the dark, in her bed."

"My God . . .!" She started up.

Suddenly, he rolled over. His hard hands grabbed her shoulders, dragging her back against him. "Listen to me!" His voice was panting, harsh. "The only way I could stay on this ranch was to whore myself. Do you understand what I'm saying? I whored myself for you. I climbed on top of that . . . that . . ." Words failed him. He swung his head to the side, swallowing convulsively. "But that's not important. What is important is that if you were able, I'd take you out of here tonight."

"Liar."

"No lie." His mouth was hot against her ear. The beginnings of his beard scraped her neck raw. *"No lie."* One palm ran down over her breast to the fragile slenderness of her rib cage.

"Keep your hands off me!" she snarled. "Isn't one woman a night enough for you?"

His teeth clicked together only a couple of inches from her ear. "Forget about that," he warned angrily.

She twisted futilely in his grasp. "I'll forget about it when you're gone. Let me go. You even stink of her."

"Will you calm down? I did what I had to do to wait for you."

"For me?" She twisted her head, trying to bite him. "That's a damn lie."

His temper snapped. One arm whipped round her rib cage and squeezed hard.

Her breath whooshed out of her body in a whimper of agony.

Instantly, he ceased the punishment. "It isn't a lie. But now you do see what I mean. You'd never make the border."

She panted shallowly as the pain receded. She had never hated anyone so much in her life as she hated him at that

318

moment. He was right. "I made it here," she denied obstinately.

"You were in good condition by comparison." His fingers traced the pathetic hollows between her ribs. "Listen, Star, you have to eat to gain strength enough to escape." He stretched her body out on her back and positioned himself on his side, his head supported by his bent elbow.

When she opened her mouth to protest, he put his hand over it. "You know it's true. Feel yourself the way I feel you." His hand left her mouth to move over her body, but with the difference that he now sought out tense muscles and bunched nerve endings rather than spots where she would be aroused sexually.

Her anger cooled as his skillful hand found pain she did not know she had. Her tears dried. Long before he had finished, she was emotionally depleted and unutterably weary. With his touches had come the realization that he was telling the truth. She was too done up to ride. But was he equally truthful about his reason for being there? Had he stayed to rescue her, only to find her in such bad condition that she could not stand the trip? Or did he merely torment her with false promises, while Maude promised him even more money than he had been paid by Luke Garner? If so, why was he here in her bed risking being thrown off the ranch?

He had lied before. He had deceived her and her brother and delivered her into Texas into the hands of the Garners. She was too weary to think of all the possibilities. Rolling her head away, she stared into the blackness.

His voice brought her back. "Listen to me. I couldn't get you twenty miles in your condition." He ran his hands up and down her sides. Impersonally as a doctor, he brushed lightly over the damaged, tender spots. "I can put my finger between every one of your ribs." His hands dipped lower to the pitiful cradle of her pelvis. "Your hip bones feel like they're about to come right through the skin."

Irritated by his criticism as well as by his presumption of her body, she stirred restively. "Did Luke put you up to saying this to make me eat? The minute I get strong enough, he'll force me to marry him."

"What?"

"Oh, didn't Maude tell you? I thought everyone on the ranch knew. He saved me from the gallows to give him a son to replace Matthew."

"And you agreed?"

"*Goddamn you!* After what you've done tonight, you find that hard to believe?" Suddenly galvanized into action by his implied sarcasm, she struck at him in the dark. The flat of her hand caught the side of his head. It stung his ear but stung her hand more. He caught her wrist and held it to prevent her from doing more damage. Nevertheless, she would not be silent. "Damn you! He came to the jail to tell me I owed him a son. I hadn't had a drop of water to drink for . . . over . . . twenty-four . . . hours." Her words faltered to a halt. She tried to swallow a sob. "It was pretty bad what he did to me," she finished wearily.

Beside her Chris cursed foully. His grip on her wrist turned into a caress. What a hellish mess! With danger all around them, they lay in the darkness unable to trust each other. He ran a hand over his face, thinking that he had never been more tired and knowing that he had much more to do before he could ever rest.

"I finally agreed to do what he wanted in exchange for a dipperful of water." Her voice trailed off into a disgusted mutter. He had to bend so that his ear almost touched her lips. Her words were largely unintelligible, but he caught the word "Diamondback."

When she fell silent, Chris patted her shoulder. "You won't marry him," he vowed.

She shook her head. "Liar," she whimpered softly. "Liar.

Liar."

Once more his lips came down hard on hers. He thrust his tongue into her mouth, bruising her with his force. The pain brought her fully awake again for just a moment. His hands tightened roughly around her shoulders. "Remember," he commanded. "Eat lots of good food. Get strong. When you're strong enough, I'll come for you."

"Liar," she insisted. Her voice was the merest breath of sound expelled between bruised lips.

He rose wearily from the bed. The whole weight of the day crashed in upon him. He could have dropped where he stood and not stirred for twenty-four hours. He headed for the door, then returned and caught up her hand again. "One more thing," he muttered. "I'll be here every day. But don't look for me. Understand. *Don't look for me.* If you happen to see me, look the other way. If Maude throws us together, pretend you hate me. Understand." With a squeeze of his hand he was gone, his spurs clinking faintly as he tiptoed across the hardwood floor.

Almost unconscious, she turned his words vaguely around in her head. Hate him. Of course, she did. Yet how her heart had leaped at the moment when he had bent over her! What strength she had felt as she clung to his wrist. Like a fool she realized that she longed to believe him, to grasp at the straw he held out to her. He had told her to eat to regain her strength. In the darkness she ran her tongue across her lips. Her stomach rumbled softly. She *was* hungry.

With a wry smile, she closed her eyes, letting her head roll on the pillow. She was a fool. Not only did she long to trust Chris Gillard, but his visit had stimulated her physically. The stirrings of quickened breathing and of racing blood had made themselves painfully known to other parts of her body with their sudden urgent demands.

Rolling over, she reached for the water carafe on the

bedside table. Pouring herself a glass of water and then another, she drank them both in an effort to fool her stomach. In that she met with little success. She was in for a long, hungry wait until morning.

Outside in the darkness of the hall, Chris paused to listen. Not a sound could be heard throughout the house. All its occupants slept soundly, except for the girl whose room he had just quit. He stooped to unfasten his spurs. No one must know of his visit. With them in hand, he tiptoed stealthily down the hall.

As he disappeared, the door of Maude's room opened a bit wider. Her white-robed form stepped out into the dark hall. Her angry breath hissed in and out of her nostrils. So furious she was shaking, she whirled back into her own room.

Her heart almost stopped as a figure threw a long leg over her windowsill and stepped into the room. Hatch lunged across the room at her. "Whore!" he snarled.

She staggered back against the door. "Get out!"

He caught her by the shoulders with hands that bruised her flesh. "I've done what you wanted."

She twisted angrily. "Let me go."

"You promised me. . . ."

She brought up her hands in front of her body and slashed outward with them. "I paid you to do a job," she spat. "I've always paid you."

"It's more than that." His voice grated out of his throat. His wiry arms snapped round her body like steel cables. One hand grasped the braid of hair to pull her head back. His mouth ground down on hers, smashing her lips against her teeth.

In the darkness their violent groans and pants went on and on as each strove against the other. Suddenly, with all his strength, his hand slapped the flesh of her buttock. When she opened her jaw to protest, he thrust his tongue into her mouth, driving it into the back of throat. Even though she gagged and choked, he did not relent.

Only when she made a whimpering sound of submission, did he lift his head. "You want me."

"Hatch . . ."

His hand raked the nightgown down from her throat, tearing a broad strip from the middle. "Down on your knees." His hand around her braid forced her while his other hand unbuttoned his fly.

"Hatch," she moaned.

"Beg for it," he chuckled.

"Please."

He followed her down, forcing her legs apart, driving into her. His brute force made her cry out, but when she closed her mouth she sank her teeth into his shoulder.

A few quick thrusts and he was through. He gasped, groaned, then slumped across her. Less than a minute later, she shuddered to her own climax.

At last with a groan, he pushed himself off her.

"Monster," she hissed. "You hurt me."

He chuckled. "Can't get too rough for you, can it, Maude?"

"You're crazy."

He ran his hand up her body to her throat, closing his fingers around it. "Don't go near that bounty hunter again," he warned. "If you want him alive, leave him alone."

"He can take care of the likes of you," she sneered.

Hatch snorted contemptuously as he pushed himself to his feet and buttoned his pants. "He couldn't even hit the Mex who came to rescue your sister-in-law. He doesn't stand a chance." He bent down and pulled her to her feet. "Now I want you to get to bed like a good girl. You should sleep real tight now." He patted her buttock.

While she stood swaying, her nightgown hanging in rags

323

from her shoulders, he stepped out the window through which he had come and disappeared into the night.

The next day and the next, Star ate and rested. A curious lassitude invaded her body as her emotions swung from desperate hope to blackest despair. Emilia fretted and scolded. The housekeeper took to appearing at odd moments with rich milk concoctions.

Luke Garner watched his intended bride closely, his brows drawing down farther and farther over his eyes as she showed no improvement. Each evening he insisted that she sit with him while he read the paper.

On the fourth evening of her stay at the ranch a thunderstorm blew in from the southwest. Rain mixed with hail pounded on the roof. Lightning forked across the sky and thunder boomed, rattling the panes of the windows. The fireplace in the living room smoked as the wind switched erratically from south to southwest to west.

Surrounded by a faint blue haze, Star began to cough. Luke dropped the paper in a crumpled heap. Speculatively, he stared at her, noting the acute slenderness of her wrists and hands where she clutched at the shagreen book.

Aware of his scrutiny, Star's fingers began to tremble. Abruptly, she closed the book and faced him.

He cleared his throat noisily. "Maudie was sure after you tonight, warn't she?"

Star laid the book down on the table between them. "Can you blame her? She hates me. She hated me before because I married Matthew. They were so close. You might expect that she would be furious at what you intend to do."

"Oh, she's mad all right," he nodded, lighting up his cigar. "But I kinda think there's more to it than that."

Star pressed her fingertips against the center of her forehead, massaging lightly. "Why should there be? That's

324

certainly enough."

Luke exhaled a cloud of odorous smoke that thickened the haze in the room. "You don't look a bit better," he accused. "You still look peaked and holler-eyed. I'm gettin' Doc out here next week if you don't pep up."

She shrugged. "If you want to, but it's not necessary. He can't do anything. I didn't get in this condition overnight. I won't get out of it overnight."

Luke puffed rapidly to keep the cigar lit. "Could be Maudie's jealous?"

Star nodded slowly. "You're her father and she loves you. She hates me. She probably just doesn't want you to make a mistake."

He grimaced. "Oh, I don't mean she's jealous of you and me. I mean she might just be thinkin' you had some interest in that Gillard fella."

"Gillard." Her voice was devoid of expression. "I hate him."

"He took his own sweet time gettin' you here."

Instantly, she was wary. "I fought him every step of the way. Tomas chased him. A couple of outlaws tried to rob and kill us."

"Maybe so, but he said you gave him that mare."

She looked at her hands, thinking fast. "I did," she said at last.

"You did? Why?"

"I offered her as a bribe. If he'd let me go, he could have the mare."

Luke chuckled. "And the son-of-a-bitch took her anyway."

She shrugged.

"How about that!" he marveled. "I thought he was too good to pull that kind of deal. Come to find out he's human, too. Makes me feel a damn sight better about havin' him around." He pulled hard at his cigar and blew a

325

thick stream of smoke into the air.

Star's eyes began to water. "I think I'll go to bed now." Without looking at her father-in-law, she rose from her chair. The acrid smoke was thicker when she stood.

However, before she could leave, Luke heaved himself awkwardly from his chair. His big hands closed over her shoulders, turning her around in his arms. She winced at his touch.

He was much taller than she; her head barely reached his shoulder. His fingers tightened, then relaxed slightly as he felt the extreme fragility of her shoulders through the fabric of her blouse. Shuffling his feet forward, he brought his ponderous belly into contact with her slender form. "Hey," he muttered, scowling. "How's about a little kiss for the bridegroom?"

She went white to the lips. "I . . . I . . ."

His face was brightly flushed. A fine dew of perspiration stood out on his upper lip. Chuckling nervously, he rocked back and forth on his heels. "Oh, I know I ain't young no more. And you're a right pretty girl. When you get a little fat on your bones, you're gonna be fine. Now I'm a good man. I never hurt no woman. You're gonna like what I can do for you." He rubbed his belly suggestively against her. "Don't you be afraid now. Just give me some sweet sugar."

Disgusted beyond her wildest imaginings, Star shuddered convulsively.

He pretended not to notice as he caught hold of her chin in one hand to turn it up to him. He smiled, exposing stained, uneven teeth, then pooched out his lips. She stared aghast at the moisture glistening on them and the prickling grizzled hairs on the skin around them. His breath smelled powerfully of cigars and the night's meal, a heavy stew redolent with onions and garlic.

She tried to pull away, pushing his shoulders with her hands, but he would not be denied. As sexually demanding as Matthew had ever been, Luke Garner plundered her mouth with his tongue. At the same time one hand dropped from her shoulder to close over her buttock and grind her lower body hard against his.

She began to struggle in terror. As he dragged her in tighter, her hands were crushed between their bodies in his bear-hug embrace. Little whimpering moans of protest escaped around the edges of his questing mouth. Her whole body felt as if he were squeezing the life out of her between his arms and his belly.

The door opened.

"Oh!" Maude exclaimed loudly. "Pardon me. I didn't have any idea I'd be interrupting something like this."

Luke whirled around, breathing hard. Clapping his fists tight against his hips, he scowled angrily at his daughter. "Goddamn it, Maude. What the hell did you expect to find? Don't tell me you don't have sense enough to knock?"

"To come in the living room?"

"When a man and his bride's courtin' . . ."

"Well, I never thought you'd be doing stuff like this at your age."

Star took advantage of their exchange to slip through the door. Then she picked up her skirt and ran down the hall toward her bedroom.

"Wait up, Star," Luke bawled after her. "Don't run off embarrassed like. Maudie, damnit all . . ."

When Star did not stop, he turned to Maude. "By God, you knock before you come bargin' into this room. I'm gettin' me a new wife. I want some time to get 'er warmed up."

"You'll never get her warmed up. But she'll end up cooling you off. You'll be dead," Maudie warned. "She killed Matthew. . . ."

"Damnit . . ."

Star closed the door to her room to shut out the sounds.

When Star came down to breakfast the next morning, Luke was waiting for her. Characteristically, he rose very early, before dawn, and went out to breakfast in the bunkhouse with the men. A premonition of what was coming shot through her.

"I'm gonna send Hatch for the priest," he announced abruptly. His dark eyes fixed on her, judging her reaction.

She caught hold of the edge of the table. "I'm . . . not . . . strong."

"Strong enough," he growled. "Don't take no strength to lie down on your back."

She winced in embarrassment, a bright flush rising in her cheeks.

"Hatch can't go," Maude interposed shortly. Her face was almost as red as Star's, her anger barely suppressed. "He's doing some work for me."

Luke cursed mildly. "I thought that's what you hired this bounty hunter for. You done already sent Hatch away once this month. He come back limpin' and stove up. He's the foreman. I need him to run this ranch, not fetch and carry for you."

"Why don't you just wait for him to come back?" Maude suggested. "He won't be gone but a day or two. You've got no reason to rush."

But Luke shook his head like an old bull. "Who'd you send with him this time?"

"Nobody."

"Good thing. Whitey didn't make it back from the last trip."

Star's scalp prickled. Her mouth went suddenly dry. Concentrating on her hand, she reached for the glass of water at her plate, satisfied that her fingers did not tremble. As the hot flush of color drained from her face, she sipped the water slowly.

"Whitey wasn't any loss," came Maude's callous estimation.

"Ornery and crazy to boot," Luke agreed.

"Hatch'll be back day after tomorrow," Maude assured her father. "Star can rest another couple of days and eat lots of nourishing food. Right, sister?"

Star met the other woman's eyes. "Right, Maude." At least now, she knew whom to guard against.

Chapter Twenty-one

Star heard the door click as the knob turned. Staring across the room illuminated by the full moon shining through the window, she could see its light reflect off the facets of the glass doorknob. Every sense was alert tonight.

She had forced herself to eat everything on her plate at three meals today. Then when Emilia had come with a drink before bedtime, she had firmly refused it. Now, lying wide awake and nervous, she was convinced that the "drink" she had been brought each night had contained a dose of laudanum, probably at Luke's prescription.

The muscles beneath her skin twitched and tensed as they reacted to every slightest sound.

The door opened. For a split second, his tall figure was outlined in the door before he slipped inside. She sat up in bed extending one slender hand toward him. "Chris!"

He shut the door silently behind him to cross the room in swift strides. When he reached the bed, his hand fumbled and caught hers, gathered it in against his chest. "Are you all right?"

"Chris," she whispered urgently. "Maude tried to kill

us."

She felt him tense beneath her fingers. "How'd you find out?"

"You're not surprised."

"I heard talk at the bunkhouse. Hatch and another man went off a couple of weeks ago on orders from Maude. Hatch came back creased; the other man didn't come back at all."

"His name was Whitey. Luke reminded Maude this morning at breakfast that Whitey hadn't come back from the last job that she sent him on."

Chris whistled softly. "Maude sent riders out to kill us. They must have been waiting, perched on a peak somewhere. When we crossed and rode up from the river, they must have seen us coming."

"But why did they try to kill you, too?"

Chris shrugged. "No questions, no witnesses. You and I would have just disappeared off the face of the earth. No one would have known anything about what happened to us."

Star began to shiver uncontrollably. "Chris . . ."

Kneeling on the bed, he gathered her into his arms. "Don't think about it. It didn't happen. They got more than they bargained for when they caught you."

She would not be soothed. "Maude hates me. I knew she loved Matthew out of all reason. But why send them? Luke was bringing me back to hang."

Chris kissed her forehead. "But he didn't. Maybe that's what she was afraid of. Maybe he'd let slip that he was thinking about marrying you himself."

His words brought a fresh wave of fear and remembrance. "He wanted Hatch to go for the priest. Maude said Hatch would be back in a couple of days. Oh, Chris, what am I going to do? I can't marry him in a couple of days. I can't."

"Ssh. No." He kissed her forehead again, her temple,

331

her cheek. His hand rubbed soothingly over her back. He felt her warmth through the thin batiste nightgown. He felt himself stir and tighten, but he sternly forced his mind to other things. "No. I've got to get you out of here. You'll have to come as you are. Something is wrong. You should be looking better, stronger. Instead, you're thinner than ever."

"Someone has been drugging me at night," she whispered fearfully against his neck. "My first guess would be Luke. He wants me to get better so fast. But now I'm not so sure. Maybe Maude . . ." Her hands clutched at his shoulders. "I fall asleep at night right after Emilia brings me a drink. I thought it was just hot sweetened milk, but I didn't drink it tonight and I'm not sleepy."

In a single expletive he named Maude.

"Why, Chris . . ." She mocked him softly. "She's your boss."

His lean frame stirred in irritation, gathering her even closer against him. "We'll leave tomorrow night," he said with sudden decision. "It's going to be hard on you, I know. But you're not going to get better in this house. Both the horses are rested and getting fat just standing around in the corral all day eating. With them under us, Tres Santos doesn't have anything that can catch us."

The thought of riding Humareda again made Star's spirits lift. She drew back in his arms. Her breasts brushed against his chest. "Will you really take me?" she breathed. Her hands touched his cheeks as she tried to see his face in the darkness.

Her nearness was affecting him powerfully. He must get up from this bed very quickly. "I promise," he murmured, his voice hoarse.

"I believe you." She lifted her mouth to his.

She was so unutterably sweet that she almost unmanned him. "Star. I have to go."

"Yes," her mouth moved against his. One hand slid from

332

his cheek through his hair to caress the back of his neck.

"Star," he breathed uneasily, "I don't want you to think that I came for this. I don't have to be paid."

"No." Her other hand slipped over his ribs gently pressing him down beside her.

"You don't owe me a thing." Even as he said the words, his kisses became longer; his tongue teased her eager mouth. Suddenly he was trembling and throbbing. "Christ!" he exclaimed, attempting to pull away.

She held him firm. "Don't talk. Please don't talk. I've been so afraid, so alone, so long. I don't understand what's happening, but I need . . ." Her voice broke as she lifted her mouth to his.

His arms closed round her. His tongue was warm and thrusting; his breath, hot; his mouth, sweet. The perfect passion they had experienced when she had let herself go before rekindled now and burst into a sheet of flame. She moaned, pushing her body urgently up to his, her nipples diamond-hard points through her thin nightgown.

"Star," he breathed as he shifted his hold to cup the back of her head and lower himself gently on top of her. His lips kissed her earlobe, breathed meaningless syllables into her ear, trailed tiny nibbling kisses across her arched throat.

"Oh, yes," she begged. "Oh, yes."

". . . didn't come for this," he insisted, as with her own hand she slipped the buttons at the neck of her nightgown and bared her breast to his lips.

"Oh, please," she whimpered, as his hot mouth suckled her. A faint cry escaped her as he set his teeth over the hardened nipple and bit gently. In the grip of intense pleasure, she writhed and whimpered beneath him.

Swiftly, his hand covered her mouth. "You must not make a sound," he whispered. "No one must hear you."

Her eyes wide in the darkness, she nodded against his hand. At the same time her body arched upward, pushing her pelvis up against his belly.

"Do you really want me to make love to you?" He was panting slightly. She could feel the hardness of his muscles against her thighs.

Again the nod.

"Even though you can't make a sound?"

She nodded, setting her teeth as wave after wave of desire made her weak. Her limbs were utterly pliant; the center of her body, hot and moist. Gently he removed his hand. While he stood up to strip off his clothes, she wrestled her nightgown off over her head and lay back quivering. She had never wanted to be naked with a man before. Now she wanted the oneness of their flesh above all things. "Chris," she breathed, when he seemed to take an inordinately long time to come to her.

"Here." He stretched himself beside her, raising his head on his bent arm. Lazily, with only one hand, he began to explore her. Never had she dreamed that a woman's body had so many places where pleasure lay so near the surface. His fingers trailed along the tender sides of her breasts, then cupped them from below and squeezed, savoring their exquisite firmness. Her nipple ached as his thumb pressed down upon it, denying it at the same time he stimulated it.

Each time his hand moved, she drew in her breath at the terrible intensity of her sensation. When his lips again suckled her nipple, she caught her lower lip in her teeth to contain the cries of pleasure rising in her throat.

Sliding beneath her buttocks, he squeezed them, lifting her slightly, pulling tight the skin over her belly, making her achingly aware of the rushing heated blood through her veins.

Her body vibrated as he tormented her, but how different from the excruciating agony Matthew had wreaked on her flesh. When Chris's fingers slipped over the mount of her belly into the wet softness that lay below it, she opened her mouth. Hastily he covered it with his own, dropping a hot, seeking kiss to still her involuntary cry.

"Chris," she moaned into his mouth.

His fingers did not stop. They lifted her higher and higher, tauter and tauter. Just when she was sure that she could bear no more, he drew away from her. Her eyes flashed open, "Oh, please . . ."

"Too soon," he breathed, his lips brushing her ear. His calloused fingers, dark by comparison to her magnolia skin, traced the contours of her body, keeping her in a state near to madness.

Tossing her head from side to side on the pillow, every nerve in her body craving release, she moaned his name again and again.

"Do you need it so much?" he whispered. "Do you want it so much?"

"From you," she moaned. "Only from you. You. The only m-man." She stammered as pleasure lanced through her body again. His knowing fingers moved in her secret places, forcing her to continue her frantic dance.

"Why me?" he breathed.

"K-kind . . . gentle . . . your touch . . . Ooo-o- . . ."

With each word she arched body against his hand, seeking the ultimate pleasure she could only guess must be waiting for her somewhere.

"Are you ready?" he teased, his teeth nipping the breast thrust upward as she stretched, catlike, shivering with longing.

"Yes. God . . . yes . . . Oh, Chrisss . . ."

He reared up above her, grasping her buttocks in his hands and opening her legs with his knee. Poised in readiness, he admonished her again. "Not a sound."

"Oh, no," she promised through set teeth.

Like a lance, he drove into her body. Despite her promise, a sliver of sound, faint, low, burst from wellsprings of feelings deep within her body. It was not a sob and not a laugh, yet somewhere in between, as if delight had touched sorrow and mixed with it.

In his own fierce excitement, he could not stop. The demand of her flesh passionately enfolding his was too great. Slipping backward, he began to move again, stroking long, slow, exquisite strokes into her enveloping sheath, which vibrated against him in matching rhythm. His hands clenched her buttocks, holding her firmly to receive each thrust.

"Chris," she sobbed as the spasm came again. "Chris." Over and over she hissed his name to urge him onward. Her body flowered beneath his; she could feel the petals of her being opening to his caress. Love, she thought. How she longed to say the word! He would think her a fool, would find some reason to reject such an emotion. Perhaps she was, but she knew she loved him. Loved this tough, gentle man. This hunter. He had ridden into her life and carried her off. Now he came to her in the night when she needed him.

Again the unbearable tension. Her spine arched. She flung her head back onto the pillow, her mouth open in a soundless scream of ecstasy.

Her lunge had the effect of engulfing him more deeply than ever. He had no more control, nor did he wish to have. He clenched his hands about her buttocks as tightly as he clenched his teeth to contain the howl that accompanied the bursting of his own exquisite pleasure.

Afterward they floated down together, his arms clasped warmly around her body, his palms and splayed fingers covering her midriff and one smooth hip. Her hands nestled in the fur of his chest. She pressed her face against his neck and drank in his hot scent with every light breath. For a moment in time each knew himself complete in the other.

At long last, searching shyly for some way to thank him, she kissed his warm, damp skin, tasting the salt upon her lips.

In return, his lips touched her forehead. "I can't

begin. . . ." He swallowed, gathering her closer. "I didn't come here to seduce you. You must believe that."

"Oh, I do," she whispered. "If anyone did any seducing, I did. I seduced you. Except that I didn't really, did I? I think it was a matter of mutual . . . need."

He was silent for a long while. The hand on her midriff pressed her slightly, as if to urge her on.

"And caring . . . ?" she breathed, a question in her voice.

Again there was no answer, only the pressure.

She stirred restively. Bitterness at his silence had begun as a tiny taste in her throat had gradually begun to spread. Mentally, she chided herself. What had she expected him to say? He had brought her here. He was being well paid. Certainly he was being paid now. Possibly he was tired of being a bounty hunter. Perhaps he had almost enough money? Perhaps he was merely making connections with Texas ranchers? Or gaining experience?

Her limbs relaxed in warm abandon. She yawned, despite her disturbing thoughts.

"You're tired," he observed.

"I feel so warm and relaxed," she admitted. "I might even sleep tonight."

His chuckle was a mere brush of air against her ear. "Anything for a lady. Just send for Doc Gillard anytime."

The small hand pressed against his chest tweaked some of the golden hair it nestled in.

"Ouch!" He caught her wrist in the darkness and carried her fingers to his mouth. There he bit the tip of one. "I don't stand for abuse, lady. I give as good as I get."

At the word abuse, the old memories flooded her. "You don't know the meaning of the word," she breathed bitterly.

Instantly sympathetic, he kissed her palm and gathered her in against him again. "Tell me about it," he commanded. "Tell me and get it out and over with. Sometimes it helps to remember a nightmare. Then it turns out to be

337

just a nightmare."

Involuntarily, she began to massage her right thumb. Her whole body tensed. "Oh, it was no nightmare. The house itself is a nightmare. You can't imagine how its atmosphere frightens me. Because of what happened here, I expect to see him at every turn. He enters every room and comes up behind me. I can't bear to sit with my back to a door."

Abruptly, she fell silent. Where he had held a warm, pliant lover in his arms, he now held a taut, shivering girl. "Star," he prodded gently. "You must have had some idea of what he was. What or who made you marry him?"

She hid her face in his neck. Her voice was muffled. "I-I hate to talk about it or even think about it. I'm so ashamed I could die. The reason sounds so silly, so childish."

He waited, holding her gently, supporting her weight on his chest.

The breath she drew was more like a gasp. "I had to get away from home."

He paused in his stroking. "But why should you want to leave home? You're a woman."

She raised her head. "What difference does that make? A woman can want to be free the same as a man. Even though I was educated in the convent, Mama didn't consider that enough. She wanted me to have everything." She dropped her head back down onto his shoulder. "Mama wanted to give me the things my sister Johanna had lost by getting married when she was seventeen years old. So as soon as I was out of the convent, she took me on a Grand Tour. We went to New Orleans and New York City and Paris. When we came home, she got sick. The doctor said cancer. He proposed an operation, but she refused. I couldn't stay at Huasteca after she died. It was like a prison. So I went to stay with Johanna on the Double Diamond."

"And exchanged one boss for another," he muttered, half

to himself.

She paused, her voice flattened to self disgust. "Just about. So when I met him, he seemed so kind. And no fortune hunter. He wasn't exactly handsome, but he seemed to be willing for me to do what I wanted to do." She shook her head sadly. "It was all an act. His father was after him to get married. He took one look at me and saw a stupid, innocent fool with a rich family too far away to protect her."

She waited for his condemnation, but he remained silent. When he did not condemn her, she finished swiftly. "I thought he was so kind that he wouldn't care if I did things on my own sometimes. I thought my love for him would grow. I walked right into his arms. It was like walking into hell."

His stroking fingers slid over her shoulders and down across her back. Where her skin should have been smooth as velvet, he encountered the network of tiny crisscrossed ridges.

"Star, tell me about the scars. Tell me why you rub your thumb."

A choking sound burst from her. "M-Matthew liked to . . . he . . ."

"Don't be afraid. That's all behind you now."

"He beat me. He tied me to this very bed," she whispered, her voice quivering and convulsing as she sought to control herself. "He wanted to hear me scream. He . . . he couldn't have sex with me unless he hurt me first. The first night was awful. Terrible. After that he apologized . . . several times . . . but I stopped believing him."

Chris's arms tightened around her. Impotent rage kindled within him. To lie still and listen to this story of torment and know that he could never do anything about it was almost more than he could bear. "Go on," he grated.

"I went to Luke. But then Matthew really hurt me. I threatened to leave, tried to escape, but Luke caught me and brought me back. And then Matthew beat me harder. Maude . . ."

"What about Maude?" Chris urged gently when she stopped uncertainly.

"Sometimes she would w-watch. Smiling. Sometimes they would leave me on the bed after he'd finished with me and they'd go into the other room. I could hear them laughing. And . . ."

"What?"

"And sometimes I'd think I'd hear them . . . moving. . . ." She shuddered again, her whole frame spasming in his arms. "Sometimes I'd think they were . . . making l-love."

Like a dam bursting, her tears wet his shoulder. Terror and agony, resentment and rage burst from her. Her hands clutched his arms now, hanging on to him as if to a rock.

"Why didn't you get word to Tomas?"

"At first I was ashamed to. The women in my family are all so brave and clever. My mother broke horses and branded cattle. My mother and older sister led a cattle drive to Colorado. They fought off Comanches and Yankees. They wouldn't have let anybody treat them like that."

"Your enemies are easier to fight than your husband," Chris pointed out reasonably. "You should have gotten help."

"I tried every way I could think of. I sent messengers. They never came back. I tried to get townspeople to go for me. Everyone was too scared. I even gave a soldier my mother's necklace. He said he was going to be stationed at Fort Concho. My sister owns a ranch on the Rio Concho, a hundred miles north of here. But that was the last I ever saw of that."

"No wonder you don't put much stock in gringos."

She shook her head. "I don't put much stock in people. My mother was a gringo."

Chris lifted her hand to his mouth. His lips moved over

the skin of her thumb like a benediction. "What happened the night Matthew was killed?"

Instantly her finger knotted into a fist. She pushed with her other hand against his chest. "I can't remember."

"Why not?" he pursued.

More tears started from her eyes. "I can't remember," she repeated. "I've tried and tried. It's all a blank after a certain point."

"How would you feel if you remembered you had killed him?"

She went still in his arms. Then her voice came out of the dark like a knife. "I'd feel proud. At least then I wouldn't have to be ashamed that I'm the Diamondback's daughter."

"The Diamondback?"

"My mother's ranch in Texas was the Double Diamond. The men along the Concho called her the Diamondback. They didn't like her very much, but they respected her. After her first husband was killed, Mama gave the ranch to my sister and came to Mexico to marry my father."

"And you're ashamed to be her daughter?"

"Yes."

"I seem to remember when I came to on the banks of the Pecos, you had killed one man who tried to rape you and wounded another."

She shook her head. "You don't understand. Mama would never have let them get close enough to get the drop on her."

He realized he would never convince her. "Tell me what happened up to the point you can't remember."

She pulled herself out of his arms and sat up in bed. Drawing her knees up tightly against her chest, she wrapped her arms around them as if she sought to make herself as small as possible.

He, too, sat up, leaning back against the headboard of the bed. The moonlight bathed his upper torso in pale silver light, gilding the hair on his chest.

Restlessly, she tossed her hair to one side before she laid her cheek on her drawn-up knees. The same moonlight revealed her troubled face turned toward him. Her magnificent dark eyes were wide and shining with tears. "Matthew was furious about something. Someone had said something to him. Probably Luke. It wasn't unusual for Luke to insult Matthew. He did it all the time. Matthew would just pretend he didn't care and then come and take it out on me. He was always saying things to me."

"Like what?"

She shivered. "Like 'half-breed.' My father was Mexican and Comanche. Like 'women are like dough, made to be pounded.' "

"How could you have even gotten close to him before you married him?"

"I wonder about that myself sometimes. But he seemed like a nice young man. Father was killed in eighteen seventy-seven fighting for the Porfiriato. Mother saw me married and the ranch prospering under Tomas, but she's gone too now." She drew a long, regretful breath.

"So you were on your own."

"Yes. That night he came bursting into the room drunk as I'd ever seen him. He didn't even try to tie me to the bed. He just started beating me. He had a braided quirt with a triple-forked tip. He kept hitting me and hitting me. I suddenly knew he was going to beat me to death. I had fought him before, but never like this. I think the pain went away for a minute. I knocked him off balance. There was a gun in the drawer of our desk."

Her teeth began to chatter. Her face in the moonlight was like a death mask. Sweat glistened on her forehead. With staring eyes she looked into the darkness at the corner of the room, as if the nightmare had returned in the flesh.

"I dragged the drawer open as he caught me round the waist. Everything in it went flying all over the room. He

342

was laughing in my ear. 'Fight me,' he kept saying. 'Fight me!' I was terrified. I knew he was going to kill me." She looked at Chris. "Do you believe me? I know he was going to kill me."

Gillard never faltered before the inferno in her eyes. "Go on, love," he whispered.

"He was always unsteady on his feet. He wouldn't wear a special boot. I managed to push him over the desk. Then I threw myself on the gun. It was an old Smith and Wesson forty-five. God knows where it came from." She began to rub her thumb. "I couldn't get the damn thing cocked. He grabbed my thumb. My thumb. He broke it." Tears streamed down her face. "He laughed when it broke," she cried, like a small child hurt beyond bearing and desolate with despair. "He laughed."

Chris realized he was sweating with the horror of her story. This woman was more than special to him. The pain she had endured made him writhe inwardly with helpless anger at the dead man. If Matthew Garner had been within the reach of his hands, he would have torn the crippled weakling limb from limb.

"I don't remember," she continued. "I was almost unconscious from the pain. Suddenly the gun went off. I can't remember pulling the trigger. I thought I dropped it when he grabbed my thumb and broke it. Maybe it exploded when it hit the floor. Maybe we kicked it in the fight. I'll never know." The last words were uttered in a dry-leaf whisper.

Murmuring meaningless words of sympathy, Chris tugged her stiff, bent figure into his arms. She was cold as ice, a light, clammy dew of perspiration coating her naked skin. "It's all right," he whispered. "What does it matter what happened? He deserved to die. He was a twisted sadist. People like that are no use to anybody."

"He was a human being," she murmured.

"Sometimes a human being goes bad, just like a horse or

343

a steer. With loco horses, you can shoot 'em. With loco steers, you can slaughter 'em. Everybody thinks you did the right thing. Why should you feel any different about what you did?"

"But I can't remember," she moaned.

"Then try to forget," he instructed. "If you ever need to talk about it again, tell me. Eventually, all the horror will fade away and it'll be just like something that happened to someone else a long time ago."

"But do you think I killed him?" she whispered pathetically, not sure whether she wanted confirmation or denial.

Chris kissed the top of her head. "I sure hope you did. You'd feel a damn sight better about being your mother's daughter if you did. Now I want you to stretch out again and go to sleep." While he spoke, he began to unfold her body. Carefully, as if she were a fragile doll, he straightened her limbs and lowered her to the pillow.

Lifeless now that her story was told, she allowed herself to be laid back, her black hair gathered by his gentle hands into a long skein that he draped over her shoulder onto her breast. Massaging each thigh and calf, he stretched out her long slender legs, ending with the narrow feet.

"Your toes are cold," he chided, as if she had gotten them that way on purpose.

"I'm sorry," came the lifeless answer.

"Your hands, too," he continued, chafing them between his palms.

Quickly he pulled the sheet over her and drew up a blanket from the end of the bed. Slipping in beside her, he folded her in his arms, warming her as much as possible. In a very few minutes he could tell by her even breathing that she was asleep. Still he held her until the perspiration dried on her body and her skin regained its normal warmth.

At last, fearing discovery if he stayed too much nearer to daylight, he rose and put on his clothes. He stood beside the bed, buttoning his shirt and studying her face in sleep.

His face was closed now, wiped clean of the fierce responses he had betrayed during her story.

He stood there for a long time. At last, with a sigh, he bent to kiss her forehead gently. She did not stir. Adjusting the cover more warmly around her, he left as silently as he had come.

Chapter Twenty-two

Chris Gillard did not return to his bed. Instead he moved
like a shadow to the stables, where he saddled the Alter-
Real. While the guards on the watchtowers dozed, he led
the big horse down the steep road. Occasionally a small
shower of pebbles or a single larger stone would rattle away
beneath the iron-shod hooves. Chris froze, holding his
breath in anticipation of discovery.

The bar across the lower gate was ridiculously simple to
slide back. Although the gate grated on its hinges, his exit
was made in deepest shadow. Once beyond the wall, he
mounted and rode slowly until he came out into the flat.

Drawing a deep breath, he turned the big brown bay
away from the trail to Crossways and headed north. The
pair cut across rough country toward Sonora, the stallion's
lope steadily eating away the miles. As the hours slipped by,
Chris's eyes ached from scanning the moonlit earth for
prairie dog holes and dry washes that might cause his horse
to break a foreleg.

At last, dull-headed with exhaustion, he rode into Sonora

as dawn was breaking. A small cafe swung open its doors, its lamplight throwing a yellow rectangle on the dirt street in front of him. There he dismounted to drink a cup of coffee before asking directions to the telegraph office.

With the telegraph pad and pencil in his hands, he paused, his face bleak. He was breaking the silence of six years. He had been only nineteen years old when he had ridden away. Would his plea be answered? He shrugged. Star had brought him to this pass. He was going begging to his family, whom he had vowed never to speak to again.

He could hear his father's angry voice. "You have had a place at V.M.I. ever since you were born."

Rand Gillard, with his hair-trigger temper, had planned that his second son should be a soldier. Virginia Military Institute, with its nearly half a century of tradition, would train Christopher to be a leader of men.

"Surely your girl can wait for four years, Chris," his mother had interposed, striving for a reasonable tone as she stepped between the two angry men. "That's hardly any time at all. It'll pass before you both know it."

Chris had shaken his head positively, his jaw set in stubborn lines. "Christine and I am getting married immediately, Father."

Rand's eyes had narrowed. "So the little piece of trash has trapped you, has she? Are you quite sure you're not taking the blame for someone else's mistake?"

With a wild lunge at his father, Chris had shouldered his mother aside, knocking her down into the big chair from which she had risen. Ignoring her shocked gasp, he had clipped his father across the jaw with a wild swing. Caught flat-footed, the elder Gillard had gone down heavily.

"Chris . . ." His mother's outraged cry had not stopped him. Standing over his father, his fists clenched, he had declared that Christine was not pregnant, that his father

347

had defamed a lady.

Rand had wiped a smear of blood from the side of his mouth. His blue eyes blazing, he had thrown off his wife's arm. "Time will tell about that, won't it?" he had sneered mockingly.

"But you'll never know," Chris had declared. "Neither of you will ever know, one way or the other." With his mother's pleas ringing in his ears, he had walked out of the house in which he had been born, taken the horse his grandfather had brought him back from Spain, and ridden away.

At nineteen, stubborn pride had ridden him hard. The fact that his father had guessed right without a moment's thought had not made the pill less bitter. Christine was pregnant.

They had married in San Antonio the next week. But Chris had not chosen to make a home there. Both the MacPhersons, his grandfather and grandmother, and the Gillards, his mother and father, were too well-known there, as well as all over the civilized state of Texas. In stiff-necked pride, Chris had moved his wife to the frontier outpost, Fort Lancaster. From there he had begun to make the only living he could think of that could make him large sums of money quickly. His first bounty had paid for his wife to have new clothes and a roof over her head. The second had paid Mrs. MacNeill's wages for a year. The third had paid for Duff's birth.

He would always remember his grief and guilt. His wife, so young and thin, her big eyes glassy with pain. She had survived, her body torn so that she was never the same again. For almost a year she had lingered, a semi-invalid, recurring infections subjecting her to fever and chills as the torn tissues refused to heal.

Before she died, she had begged him to make his peace, but he had refused. With her dead he would probably be welcomed back into the family, especially because of Duff. But his pride was too great. Why subject himself to their pity and their self-righteous attitudes?

He laid the pad down, his frown deepening, as he stared out the dirty window of the telegraph office. Probably he could handle this himself, without their help.

He clenched his fist. Who was he fooling? Star Garner was accused of murder, held prisoner in a mountaintop fortress in the middle of the Texas desert. Her jailer was a sadistic old man who might very well have killed his own son. Even if Luke had not killed Matthew, someone in that place had. That someone might make an attempt on Star's life anytime. In fact, one attempt had already been made.

Determinedly, he brought the pencil point to the paper, where it hovered only an instant.

To whom should he address this? Not his father, that unbending soldier. Nor his mother, who had always been occupied with the politics of the state. Of course, as a matter of courtesy, he should address it to La Patrona. His grandmother would be almost seventy. A pain caught him behind the eyes. Tears. He had firmly tamped down all family feeling in order to make this self-imposed exile bearable. Now he remembered the tiny white-haired lady with the soft gray eyes. His grandfather, an immigrant from Scotland in the days while Texas was still part of Mexico, would be seventy-six. If he were not dead.

His eyes misting, Chris printed the letters. "La Patrona Mercedes-Maria MacPherson y Carvajal, El Rincon, Camino de la Bahía, Goliad." The letters swam slightly, but he brushed the back of his hand across his eyes and wrote on. "Need your help. Please send family lawyer to Crossways, Texas, immediately. Christopher Stewart Gillard."

He stared at it. His anger and resentment were long over.

349

Suddenly, he felt good inside. Christine was dead. Their life together had been too short for him to assess whether or not their marriage would have been a failure. But they had produced Duff. His son was a wonderful boy. He deserved to know his grandparents and—God willing—his great-grandparents.

He slid the paper to the telegrapher, plunked down a silver dollar, and sent a silent prayer heavenward as he listened to the tapping of the keys.

"Chris Gillard disappeared in the middle of the night," Maude informed her father at breakfast.

Garner paused, a huge bite of egg and beans on the way to his mouth. An angry scowl darkened his face.

"But he left that mare in the stall. I think I'll saddle her up today and take a ride." This last statement was addressed to Star, with calculated maliciousness.

A tremor of fear sent its icy chill down Star's spine. Alarmed by Chris's disappearance and concerned over Maude's interest in Humareda, she ducked her head before the other woman's assessing stare.

Luke, on the other hand, felt no such trepidation. Instantly, the scowl disappeared from his face to be replaced by a considering look. A heavy drop of egg yellow slid from his fork and splashed on the soiled tablecloth. "Wonder where the hell he got off to?"

"Maybe Star knows. She got awfully friendly with that bounty hunter on the way here," Maude sneered.

"How would I know where Chris went?"

"*Chris*, is it?" Maude pounced upon the use of the name. She glanced significantly at Luke. "You've always been careful to call him Gillard. Maybe there's more between them than you thought, Papa? After all, they spent a lot of nights alone together."

Luke set his fork down deliberately. His body instantly snapped alert. "Is that the truth, girl? Is there more to this that I haven't got wind of?" His voice had changed to a harsh growl.

Slowly and carefully, willing herself to be calm, Star looked from father to daughter. "Not at all. The man's a liar and a thief. He lied to my brother and to me. He brought me into jail in handcuffs. I was in the habit of calling him Chris when he worked for Tomas. When you called him Chris, Maude, I just slipped back into the habit."

Maude's mouth twisted into an unbelieving sneer. "I'll just bet."

Without another word, Star pushed herself away from the table. Flinging down her napkin, she addressed her father-in-law. "You really are going to have to do something about Maude, Luke. If you expect me to live here congenially with you, she can't call me a liar to my face."

"Now just a minute . . ." Maude began angrily.

"Nor can she continue to bait me about my horse. I gave Humareda to Chris Gillard because I didn't want her to fall into the wrong hands. At least he knows how to take care of valuable animals. If he left her here, then she belongs to me. No one . . ." Here she glared at Maude directly, "no one is to ride her without my permission. And I don't give it."

Maude's mouth dropped open as Star swept from the room. Her anger kept her going down the hall. Once in her room, however, she trudged over to the window to stare disconsolately at the courtyard. Had Chris left Tres Santos under his own power, or had something terrible happened to him? Had Hatch really been sent on a job for Maude? Or had he been hiding somewhere, waiting to catch Chris

351

alone and kill him? The men who had ambushed them that night had only delayed murder for rape.

The door opened behind her and Maude strode in, two spots of color high in her cheeks. "Don't you tell my father to 'do something' about me," she snarled. "I do what I like. I say what I like. My father doesn't care."

"Then you shouldn't pay any attention to what I say," Star countered smoothly.

Maude blinked. "Well, I don't. That is, I just . . ."

"Then just get out. Don't come into my room without knocking." Suddenly Star realized she was fighting mad. Throwing her chin up proudly, she advanced into the center of the room.

Maude swayed but managed to hold her ground. "I'll come and go where I damn well please."

"Your father has already had something to say about that."

"This is my house and my ranch."

"The other night your father told you to knock before you came into the living room. I'd step lightly if I were you."

Maude clenched her fists. "You bitch! You sweet-talking bitch! I don't have to listen to you."

"Good. Go!" Star took another step.

Maude looked as if she would burst with anger. Her face bright red, she swung on her heel and charged out, slamming the door behind her.

Star swung round in the center of the room. A slow, triumphant smile curved her mouth. At least Maude now knew that Star would not take her insults without retaliating.

Some time later, she answered a knock at her door. Luke Garner stood on the threshold. "Can I come in?"

She looked nervously around her. The door to her

bedroom stood open. Had he come to make another clumsy attempt at romance?

Following her glance, he shook his head. "I just wanta talk."

She stepped back.

"You don't like what Maude said, do you?"

Star crossed her arms in front of her chest. "She's your daughter. This is her home. I told you she'd resent me."

"I don't owe her nothin'," he declared belligerently. "Not a thing more. She don't have to stay here, if you don't want her around, I can send her to San Antone or New Orleans or someplace like that."

Star stared at him incredulously.

He swung his hands out to the sides as he strode past her and began to move aimlessly about the room. Not quite meeting Star's eyes, he spoke with a defiant tone in his voice. "Both them kids got plenty all their lives. My wife died and I just went on and took care of them. Matthew was all crippled up, but I thought I'd marry you to him and he'd get interested in breedin' horses and you'd be good for him. You was all ladylike and pretty, even if you was a Mex. You'd have a baby and I'd get me a grandson that'd be big and strong."

She could not believe her ears. The night in the jail when he had told her of his grand plan for a son, she had thought she was beyond surprise. Now he revealed a callousness of character with a sublime ability to excuse himself for anything that might be construed as a mistake.

"Now, since you're gonna have me a son, I can see that you've gotta have peace and quiet. No two ways about it, if you and me are gonna live here, Maudie's gotta go."

"But she's your daughter," she repeated incredulously.

"She is that, so I'll do right by her. She can go to New Orleans. I'll get a woman to go with her, help her buy some new clothes. She might dress herself up so she looks halfway decent, not wear so much of that damn gray. It don't look good on her. If she'd wear some bright colors, some fella might get interested in her."

"But you can't treat her as if she doesn't have any feelings," Star argued, while one part of her listened incredulously to her defense of Maude. "You can't do that to her. This is her home. She expects to live here for the rest of her life. I'm the intruder here. Oh, of course, she hates me and doesn't want me around. You have to . . ."

Luke swung around with an irritated look on his face. He stabbed a forefinger at her in warning. "What I was gonna have to do was to buy that mare off that bounty hunter. But now he's gone, so I don't have to do that. Now all I have to do is get that priest here and get us married and get on with my plan for this ranch. Hell, I'm not gettin' any younger."

"Luke," Star put out a hand to intercept him as he strode to the door as if to get on with the business. "You can't treat Maude that way."

He paused at the door. "You're sure a lady," he remarked. "You'd defend your worst enemy if you thought they'd maybe get a rotten deal." He shrugged. "She'd throw you a rock if you was drowning."

Star tried one more time. "Luke," she pleaded. "Give up this whole idea. Don't hurt Maude and don't hurt me anymore. Send me home and be happy on your ranch."

He scowled. "You won't have to worry none about Maude nor your mare. I'll take care of it all. And you'll like bein' my lovin' wife. You'll be just as happy as a woman can be. With any luck, you'll get pregnant right off."

Star awoke to the pressure of a hard hand across her mouth. Slashing with her nails at the wrist, she kicked out ferociously with her legs.

"Star! Star! It's me."

She could not hear him. She had been kidnapped and almost raped. She had been jailed and starved and threatened. Her mouth opened wide and her teeth champed down on the fleshy heel of his hand.

Cursing vividly at the pain, he dropped on top of her, using his superior weight to hold her still. "Star! For God's sake . . ."

At last his voice penetrated her consciousness. "Chris . . . ?"

He raised his hand. "Yes."

"What . . . ?"

"I've come to get you," he whispered. "We're leaving here right now. Tonight." Clasping his hand where she had bitten him, he rolled over and sat up, on the side of the bed. "Remind me not to sneak up on you in the dark," he chuckled ruefully.

Instantly she rose on her knees, one hand on his shoulder. "Did I hurt you? Oh, I didn't mean to. I didn't know it was you."

He squeezed her fingers. "Don't worry. I understand. I've been hurt a whole lot worse than a little girl like you could ever do. I probably deserve whatever you do to me."

"Oh, no . . ." She leaned around his shoulder.

He caught ahold of her and tugged her around until she lay across his lap. "You're right. You've hurt me. You need to kiss me and make me well." Deliberately, he covered her mouth with his, hugging her tight, enjoying the woman softness of her, still warm from sleep.

The embrace lasted only for a moment. Then he lifted his head with a reluctant sigh. "We've got to be off."

"Are you sure you want to take me on?"

His answer was a swift, almost painful squeeze. "Señora,

355

I wouldn't have hung around here in this lunatic asylum for the last week if I hadn't been sure. You've got to make just one big effort, then, with any luck at all, the day after tomorrow night, we'll be in San Antonio."

"San Antonio?"

"I figure they'll expect us to try for the border or maybe my ranch. We'll go the way they least expect us to go." With that he kissed her again swiftly, and stood her on her feet.

She clung dizzily to his arm for a minute.

"Easy does it," he admonished.

"Oh, I'm all right. I just have to get my balance. You stood me up too quickly." Bracing herself, she walked carefully to the chest.

From the bed he watched her pull the gown over her head. He could just see her pale silhouette in the moonlight bathing the room, but his imagination tormented him. As she reached for her pantalettes, her breast swung forward. He moaned softly.

"My God, you're beautiful." His voice was a husky drawl. "Lord!" He shook his head in wonderment as his hand, drawn by desire he could not resist, stretched out to touch her body. The tips of his fingers rested on her shoulder, slid down the satin slope of her breast. She shuddered as he found her nipple, coaxing it to excited erection. He lingered only a moment before he continued his slow journey over her waist, tracing her hip bone. . . .

She caught her breath in an ecstatic gasp.

Her gasp was echoed in his sigh as he pulled his hand back. "Later."

She tugged the garments on haphazardly. Suddenly realizing her fingers were shaking, she glared at him in the darkness. "Why did you touch me?" she groaned.

He flashed a grin in the moonlight, although his voice sounded hoarse. "I just didn't want to be the only one wanting."

While she was trying to think of a word bad enough to call him, he held out a sheepskin jacket for her to put on. Then, with his arm around her waist, they slipped from the house. Keeping to the shadows, he led her down the hill. Beyond the lower wall, beyond the gatehouse, two horses waited.

"Humareda!"

The mare whickered softly.

"Oh, you beauty!" Star pressed her cheek against the mare's neck before turning to Chris. "I can't believe it. Maude announced that you had gone, cleared out, and left Humareda in the stable. If she told the truth, then how did you get her out?"

He shook his head. "Too long a story. Up you go." He held the bridle for Star to mount, then vaulted into the saddle of the stallion. Cautiously, they walked the horses down the steep trail.

"I can't believe this," Star muttered. "It's too easy."

"They didn't expect me back," Chris guessed. "Garner's getting careless. His men are eating and drinking too much before they go on watch. He probably doesn't check on them, so they don't bother to keep awake."

"Is that how you got out so easily?"

Chris did not bother to answer. His attention was distracted by the sound of hoofbeats coming up the trail toward them. The slope was purposefully denuded of all cover, so that no Indian war party would have a chance to sneak up close. "We're going to meet someone," he cautioned.

"Who could be coming at this time of night?"

"I don't know, but I'll bet he's not a friend. Let's go!" He struck the mare on the flank with the flat of his hand at the same time he shouted to the stallion. The big horse took

357

the lead, charging down the trail at breakneck speed with the mare clattering behind him.

Behind them lights flashed on in the darkness.

"So much for getting away unseen," Chris yelled.

In the fort behind them the alarm bell began to toll. Then they were face to face with the rider coming up on the trail toward them.

Hatch! Star recognized his startled face as they flashed by on either side of him. He balanced an object before him in the saddle and made no effort to draw his gun.

Along with the ringing of the alarm bell, Star could hear faint shouts as the trail leveled out at the bottom of the escarpment.

Chris hauled the stallion's head up and around. "Head east!"

At first as they galloped along, Chris pulled rein on the stallion. Before they had gone very far, however, he realized that, though smaller, the mare had no trouble keeping the pace. The Alter-Real was tired, calling on reserves of strength that would swiftly be exhausted. Anxiously tuned to the first signs of distress in the horse, Chris led the way across country for several miles. Finally when they came upon the stagecoach road, Chris raised his arm for a halt. "Let 'em blow," he advised. "How're you doing?"

"I feel freer than I've felt in months," Star smiled. With an unrestrained gesture, she swept off her hat and let the lifting breeze catch her hair. "Of course, I'm not free. There are still charges against me."

"Don't worry about them," Chris advised. "I've got someone working on those." Even as he spoke, he prayed that his words were true. They might very well be false. His parents might construe the request for a lawyer to be to get him out of trouble. They might refuse on general principles, figuring that he deserved to be punished for being involved in a crime.

She eased herself in the saddle. "How can you do anything? I still can't remember whether or not I killed him." Her voice had a hollow sound. "I might have shot my husband. I truly don't know. I know I tried to get the gun that night. . . ."

"Let's talk about that later," he interrupted. "I'll tell you my tale, and you'll tell me yours."

Alternately galloping and walking their mounts, they rode east into the bracing morning breeze. Before their eyes the panorama of the Texas dawning spread out on three sides. Midnight black bespangled by stars gradually turned to grayer black. Around them darker clumps against the blackness metamorphosed into clumps of sage, tumbleweeds, and Spanish dagger. A grove of salt cedars rose tall and dark green out of a wash. They broke the flat plain of the horizon like bushy black giants against a pearl-gray sky.

In their shadow Star and Chris paused again to rest. Little by little the earth's rim turned a blushing pink, then orange, then burning gold. Like a blazing ball, the sun burst over the horizon before them. Suddenly all was light. Silhouettes cast shadows. Gray objects turned every shade of yellow, green, and brown. The earth became a blend of umbers and ochres. The brilliant colors on the horizon turned to clean-washed blue.

Feeling the Alter-Real's mighty barrel heaving beneath him, Chris cast a speculative glance at his companion. Her face was as white as pearl in the clear light. "Tired?"

"Yes," she nodded. "But I'm holding up fine." When his eyes swept the horizon, she surreptitiously shifted in her saddle. With her right hand she pressed her aching ribs. She could not remember how her body felt when it was free of pain. Sinking back in the saddle, she eased her feet from the stirrups and spread her legs out straight. Underneath her, Humareda drew a deep breath and shifted from one hip to the other.

"Tired, lady?" Star patted the arched neck beneath the mane.

The rising sun gilded the stubble on Chris's gaunt cheeks. He, too, was tired. For the last forty-eight he had not been to bed. He had been moving constantly, except for a couple of hours holed up in the middle of the day for a brief rest and meal.

Nevertheless, he managed a smile as he caught Star's speculative glance on him. "Not too much farther now," he promised. "I've got a cache of provisions staked out and a couple of fresh horses. We can rest, eat, and then give these two a rest." He patted the stallion's sweat-stained neck. "He's just about worn slick over so many miles."

"Then let's go."

Chris caught her arm hastily when she would have urged the mare forward. "Listen. Do you hear something?"

She froze. A soft wind blew soundlessly through the mesquites; a screech owl called fitfully. She shook her head. Then, even as she shook it, she heard the sound of hoofbeats coming fast.

Providence had led them into the grove, the only place of possible concealment in the whole flat panorama.

Chris swung off the stallion. "Get down. We'll take our chances here. Maybe they'll be riding too fast to look for us."

Trembling, her teeth chattering with tension, she dismounted. Chris led the horses deep into the grove while she followed. Standing together, their hands on their horses' muzzles, they watched four men gallop by. The lather dripped from the necks of their horses. Their handkerchiefs were drawn up over their noses and mouths to filter some of the dust. Nevertheless, the brands on the flanks of their mounts were all too clear.

"From Tres Santos." Chris confirmed what she already suspected. "The hunt is on. Damn! They'll find the horses."

A cold, odd cast seemed to be steeling his features. Shivering, Star recognized the man beside her. The face of the friend and lover he had shown her briefly in the past days was replaced by one infinitely more familiar, the hard, calculating bounty hunter.

"What will we do?" she whispered.

"No choice now, señora," he murmured. "Follow me and ride like you mean it. If the going gets too rough, sing out and I'll take you up in front of me. But we have to get the hell out of this area. Damn shame Hatch saw us last night. Our trail didn't have time to get cold." He dug his heels into the stallion's sides and whipped the reins across the sweat-stained flanks. The magnificent animal bounded forward.

Star leaned forward, speaking to Humareda's ear. One hand stroked her mare's damp neck. "My life depends on you now, lady."

The ears flicked back as the mare listened.

Star lifted the reins. "Give me everything you've got. I can't go back to Tres Santos ever."

Chapter Twenty-three

"What are we going to do?" Star's voice quivered slightly. Her body was so weary that her legs trembled from hip to ankle. The pain in her ribs had dipped lower to encompass one whole side of her body. In an effort to cushion her ribs, she had strained all the muscles beneath them. She tried to maintain a stoical expression, but the frown line between her eyebrows deepened.

"You can wait here while I scout ahead," Chris told her firmly. "If we get lucky, they won't have found the horse and supplies."

"Should I come with you?"

He shook his head firmly. "You can't see your face, señora. You look like you're ready to break. If they find the horses, then I'll have to backtrack anyway, so you might as well rest here. Take advantage of the time. Don't try to be so damn tough. Even if your grandfather was a Comanche, you don't have anything to prove."

He began to strip the saddle off Humareda.

"What are you doing?"

"I'm going to ride your mare. Without the weight of the

saddle, she shouldn't be too burdened. She's fresher than Al." With that, he grabbed a handful of mane and swung himself up. "Try to get some rest," were his last words as he rode off.

She was tired. Star admitted as much to herself. Moving stiffly, she loosened the saddle girth and pulled the bit from between the stallion's jaws. Then she sank down on Humareda's sweaty blanket and pillowed her shoulders and cheek against the fleece lining on the saddle. A nap would do her a world of good.

She awoke to the vibration of hoofbeats. Sitting up quickly, she was ready when Chris rode in, his face bleak. "They found the supplies and mounts," he told her tersely as he put the tack to rights on both horses.

"What shall we do?"

"Hole up. You don't suffer from claustrophobia, do you?"

She frowned. "Not that I know of."

"Let's hope you don't. Mount up." He reined his horse's head to the left, guiding the rested stallion through the sparse clumps of purple sage and prickly pear. "I'm going to hide you in a cave."

"How romantic," she murmured, without much conviction.

They rode north for about an hour. The semi-desert country became rougher and rougher. Instead of table land, gullies and ravines began to cut its surface. Bleached, flintysoil reflected the light back to blind them. Every plant had a spine; every animal, a fang or a horn, including the toads. Doubling back and forth with seeming purposelessness, Chris led them at last down the side of a ravine that deepened into a canyon.

"Are we lost?" Star asked doubtfully.

"No. Almost there."

What appeared to be a dark shadow on the land from

across the canyon proved to be a narrow opening in the hillside. It was totally invisible from above and below. Star hesitated, but Chris guided his horse inside, his belly pressed against the horn to keep from being dragged off by the jagged edge of the opening.

Inside, a rocky trail led down a steep decline into a large open chamber. Water dripped methodically from a small orifice high up in the wall. From a second outcropping, it trickled down over the limestone to gather in a small, cloudy pool. A narrow shaft of blazing sunlight spilled through the opening into the interior where it was quickly diffused. Most of the cave remained in a pale twilight.

"How did you know about this place?" Star asked, amazed. Her impressions of a cave had somehow associated themselves with cold. The interior of the chamber room, however, was amazingly warm and very humid. Wearily, she wiped her arm across her forehead.

"Some friends and I went hunting mule deer out this way before Duff was born. We wounded one and trailed it. It led us right past here. We camped here and explored for a while. Unless you know it's here, I doubt if anyone could find it." He preceded her down the steep trail and jumped down the last couple of feet to the floor of the cave.

Star looked around her in awe. "It certainly is strange. It's as if the whole side of the mountain was hollow." She put out her hand to touch the rough limestone face by her shoulder.

"It goes for miles under the mesa. We found four skeletons in it."

Instantly, she drew back her hand. "How cheerful!"

"Yep." Chris held up his hands to catch her waist and lift her down the big step to the floor of the cave. "Watch yourself. I don't have any idea how deep that is."

She glanced inquiringly between his hands, then shuddered as he swung her across a narrow crevasse, whose scar appeared dark and bottomless beneath her feet. "Good God. Did you really try to find out?"

"Sure did. Our ropes weren't long enough."

"Oh, my."

"We found one skeleton in here," he continued conversationally. "It was really old. An Indian burial with all his possessions. We left him. He's over there in the corner under a limestone shelf. Would you like to see him?"

"Not especially." She shivered, despite the heat.

"Have a drink." He unslung the canteens from his shoulders and offered her one.

"You said you found four skeletons."

He took a drink from the canteen and pressed his lips together as he stared around him. "Yep. Real tragedy. A woman and a man together and a child off by himself."

Star gave a low moan of pity. Fearfully, she glanced around her, expecting momentarily to feel the walls close in or the opening to disappear. "But this doesn't look big enough, nor dangerous enough to get lost in," she protested.

"This is only the outer chamber. We'll leave the horses here. If we get any luck at all, nobody will chase us until we can get a good night's sleep. If someone does chase us, hopefully he'll lose our tracks and won't have heard of this place."

"And if they find us?"

"If they find us, we can go farther back into the cave. Over to the right there's a crawlspace that leads into the channel of an ancient underground river."

"A c-crawlspace . . ."

He patted her shoulder. "Don't get worried. We probably won't have to use it at all. Just stretch out here by the water and rest. I'll unsaddle the horses and we'll pad the rock."

Stubbornly, she rose. "We'll both unsaddle the horses and then we'll both stretch out. You're probably exhausted.

You haven't seen your face recently, either."

He rubbed a hand across his chin, rasping the stubble. "Pretty grimy, huh?"

"The grime doesn't make any difference. It's the dark circles under the eyes. You look like you've been beaten."

He shrugged as he hauled himself up over the crevasse and turned to look down at her. "Tell you what? You stay down here. I'll pass everything down to you. It'll make it easier for both of us."

She came just to his knees. Folding her hands like a small child, she nodded. What else was she to do? The crevasse, although no wider than a foot and a half, did not have a visible bottom. Chris might be kidding. On the other hand, he might not. She nodded. "If you say so."

She watched while he mounted the steep slope, his heels digging into the loose dirt to keep from sliding backward. He started to unhitch the girth from the mare, then suddenly he froze. His head turned to one side, listening. The stallion whickered softly.

Galvanized into action, Chris jerked the tack off the horses and slung it into a dark corner. Spinning, he shouldered the saddlebags and vaulted down the steep path, taking several jumps that brought her heart into her throat. "Come on," he commanded, taking her arm to pull her over to the back of the cave. "I heard someone coming."

They stopped, facing the foot of what seemed a solid wall of bisque-colored limestone. He pointed at the ground. "Crawl through. Hands and knees. Keep your back low, so you don't bark your spine."

"Where?" she asked bewildered. She had the feeling, as she stared helplessly at the wall, that he must have made a mistake.

With ungentle, urgent hands, he shoved her down to her knees. "Through here," he indicated.

Staring into the gloom, she realized she was looking into

a deeper blackness. The slot was some two and half feet high at its highest and several yards wide. Its edges tapered to mere slits at the floor level. Elbows bent, legs trailing behind her, she obediently pulled herself forward into the pitch blackness. Under her splayed fingers the ground was suddenly soft and damp. When she drew back in repugnance, she banged the back of her head against stone. Primordial terror flooded her mind. The rock above her would collapse at any moment and crush her. She would die with her face in the muck.

"Hurry," he hissed.

She could not move.

"For God's sake!" A stinging slap on her rear angered her. "Don't freeze on me now." His face was just behind her shoulder. He was wedged in the slot with her. "Go on! Damn you! Crawl!"

Pushing, prodding, cursing her, he drove her ahead of him. For a space of time, not unlike eternity, she crawled with her hands and knees squishing in the damp clay, her head bumping against the rough rock above it. Once her backbone scraped painfully against a sharp protrusion. Her thoughts, nervous as mice, scurried back and forth. What if he had forgotten the way? What if there had been an earthquake since he had been in it? What if the passage suddenly ended with her face against a blank wall?

Tears trickled down her cheeks as she blundered her shoulder into a rock outcropping. The passage was too narrow for her to turn around in. She would have a nearly impossible time backing out. Her nose and throat were clogging with tears. Perspiration soaked her and stung her eyes.

"Last bit," he breathed just behind her, his voice gentle now, though strained. "Go on, Star. You can do it. All the way down, sweetheart. It opens up just behind this wall. I promise." The hand that had slapped her rear now patted it

367

encouragingly. "That's a good girl."

The mud of the cave floor smeared her chin. Obedient to his voice, in inky darkness, she scrambled forward on her stomach. Suddenly, there was nothing above her head. She pushed herself upward hesitantly and stood. In the damp, oppressing blackness she waited, shivering as nervous rigors racked her and her eyes stared round her uselessly.

She heard him heave to his feet with a heartfelt groan. She heard him curse, then a match rasped against tinder. Light—blessed light—drove the darkness away for a few minutes. He handed her the metal box.

"Don't worry," he smiled. She could see his face lighted from below. "We've got plenty of matches. Light another one and keep lighting them while I see what I need to see." He stooped and pulled a saddlebag through the opening. Helpfully, she bent with him, trying to keep the light in the work area.

He extracted two candles, each about five inches in length. Her hands trembling, she held the match to the wick of one and watched its power drive the darkness back a few inches further.

He drew a deep breath and leaned back against the wall. The candlelight revealed deep grooves in his face, confirming what Star already knew. He was nearly exhausted.

"Now," he said solemnly. "Let me tell you what we found out about this place."

They stood in a chimneylike area, its ceiling lost in the darkness that pressed down from above them. Directly opposite the slot through which they had crawled, the space was bisected by a vertical curtain of rock. To the right appeared to be a well-trodden path. Downward, to the left, a tumble of rocks seemed to bar the way.

Trying desperately to control her thoughts and guide them away from claustrophobia and premature burial, she leaned back against the wall under which she had just crawled. Sternly, she stemmed the impulse to close her eyes. Best take advantage of the light while it lasted.

Chris dropped down wearily beside the candle. Sitting tailor fashion, he draped his hands over his knees. "Now listen. This is tricky. If something should happen to me, bear left and . . ."

"Don't tell me!" Star held up her hand imperiously. Her eyes were wide with fear. "If something should happen to you, I'll know exactly what I'll do. I'll sink to the ground and cry my eyes out."

He grinned. "After that, look at these two passages."

Grimly, she followed where he pointed.

"The one to the right leads on for miles. My friends and I never got to the end of it. And when you're coming back along it, it has another fork that will branch up and lead you for miles to a dead end. The river must have surfaced there and then dried up for ever, or maybe changed course somewhere north and west of here. Who knows? Just remember, though. You'll never find your way out if you get to wandering around in there. So the rule in this cave is bear left and stay down."

"Bear left and stay down." Star recited the instructions like a catechism. "You don't think I'll really have to remember those, do you?"

He grinned wanly. His breath made the candle flame flicker, distorting his face. "I hope not, but you never can tell."

They were silent for a minute. Then he shook himself. "Now if you go to the left here and climb over the rubble, you'll come out in another room sort of like the one on the outside, except it's different. There are all sorts of creatures in it."

"C-creatures?!"

"I'll show you," he rose lithely.

"Not right yet," she begged. Weariness made her tremble. Slowly, she allowed herself to slide down the wall to a sitting position. "Could we stay right here for a while?"

"I'm a slave driver," he acknowledged. He dropped down beside her and put his arm around her shoulder, gathering her in against his shirt. Through the dampness and the smears of clay, his heart beat strongly. "We'll both rest. Probably by the time our nap is over, they'll have searched this place and be gone."

She allowed her head to droop to his shoulder. "You don't really believe that, do you? They'll find the horses immediately."

He rolled his eyes upward into the blackness. "They were overhead on the top of the mesa. I could hear them, probably through crevices in the rocks. There may be a narrow opening somewhere up above the big chamber. They may not even come over the ridge and down into the ravine."

Star shuddered violently. "Luke Garner will follow me till one of us is dead," she muttered. "He's like a bulldog. Once he gets an idea, he doesn't let go."

He hugged her tighter. "Don't worry. If they find this place, a possibility which is highly unlikely, then they may not bother to look in. If they look in and find the horses, they'll probably think that I had spares hidden here and ride on after us. If they search the cave before they go, they'll be highly unlikely to find this crack. After all . . ." He broke off. She had fallen asleep on his shoulder as he spoke.

He caressed her cheek, ran his hand over her temple, and smoothed away some damp tendrils of hair. Positioning her so that she rested more comfortably against his body, he reached over and snuffed out the candle. The very faintest of lights shone dimly under the crack in the stone at his right hand. Closing his eyes, he drifted off into exhausted slumber.

The sound of voices disturbed him. A man shouted, his voice booming hollowly in the antechamber. "Nobody here."

"Gotta be. The horses are here."

Instantly he was alert. Glancing to his right, he could see no light. Several hours must have elapsed. Outside it must be late evening or night. He grinned into the blackness. A search party would have no chance of finding the entrance to the rest of the cave with no light.

He strained his ears to listen. The outer chamber remained silent for a brief space. He was beginning to relax when he heard a voice deeper than the rest. "They must be around here somewhere. Neither one of 'em would leave these horses."

Luke Garner had spoken. How had he gotten here? How had their trail been discovered?

Chris rolled his head against the slimy stone. What had he done to tip the party off that they were riding this way? The telegraph in Sonora? The message had requested a lawyer to be sent to Crossways. But the message had been sent to Goliad. He cursed under his breath. Someone must have figured that he might make for home.

"Nobody here, boss."

Again the rumble of Luke's voice cursing virulently. Footsteps followed the wall of the cave. He could see a faint light. Someone must be carrying a lantern. More conversation. More orders. The many voices argued loudly, making their words indistinguishable.

"We'll wait for light." Luke spoke from not far away on the other side of the wall. "A couple of you fellas get out and keep watch. Scout around while you're at it. Maybe they ain't here. If not, then maybe there's another way out. Might give us some notion of which way they've gone."

371

"Don't make a sound," Chris whispered in Star's ear as she stirred in his arms.

She tensed against him. "Why not?"

"Luke."

"Oh, God."

He took her hand. "We'll move into the next chamber and wait in there. We can light a candle then."

"Move in the dark?" Her voice quavered.

"Sure. Just take my hand and feel along the walls with the other."

They accomplished the climb over the rubble with surprising ease. After Star discovered that she could not see her hand in front of her face, she closed her eyes. She found playing blind man's bluff less terrifying than keeping her eyes open and being unable to see. She stumbled and had to catch her balance several times, but in a remarkably short time Chris let go of her hand.

"Wait a minute," he whispered. A match scratched against tinder. She opened her eyes to the candle glow.

"It's even hotter than outside," she complained softly. "Whatever happened to cool caves deep in the earth?"

"I don't know anything about them," Chris whispered. "This is the only cave I've ever been in. I guess everything's hotter in Texas."

"There's a hollow mountain above Huasteca. It's cold, or so people say. I've never been in it. You have to ride burros or walk to the top to go down in it. I never could see the point."

"You can go explore there next month," he suggested. "Now that you've got something to compare it with."

"Do you think I'll ever be back there again?" she muttered disconsolately. "Or if I do, will I have anything to go back to? Maude got around to telling me that Tomas was shot trying to break me out of jail."

Chris shot her a quick look. "He was only wounded. It didn't even knock him out of the saddle. He rode off under his own power."

"Any gunshot is serious. Sometimes men bleed to death inside. No one knows until they just fall over. Sometimes men die later from gangrene." Her voice quivered.

He caught her arm. "Don't worry until you know what you're worrying about. Look here. This is a living cave. Let me show you some of the creatures that live here."

And creatures they were, strange cousins to the creatures of light. He led her a few yards farther into the cave to a pool into which water dripped constantly. He pointed at its faintly cloudy depths. Silvery fish swam and darted beneath its surface.

She bent to see them. "They look . . . strange."

"They're blind."

"Oh, no."

"They don't need eyes down here."

"They must have been in here for hundreds of years."

He nodded. "Probably swam in the underground river." He set the candle on the ledge. "Look here."

"Oooh. What is it?"

A pinky-white insect with a transparent shell poised on the rock beside the candle. Its body measured less than an inch, but its antennae must have been at least three inches long.

"Guess."

"It looks like a cricket," Star mused.

"It is, but it doesn't need anything to protect it from the sun, so it's lost all its color."

Star shuddered violently. "I really don't want to see anymore," she begged. "I can see something like that happening to me. Maybe I'd get blind and transparent, if I lived in this world."

He chuckled softly. "I don't think that's a possibility."

She shivered again, despite the heat.

"Would you like to bathe?"

Her mouth dropped open. Had he lost his mind? Bathe in there with those blind fish? The thought of it made her skin crawl. Still, she was embarrassed to admit her silly fears. Instead she asked, "What about Luke?"

"It's night outside," he assured her. They're camping in the cave waiting for us to come back. We'll just wait them out."

She swallowed uncomfortably, staring at the surface of the water. "What about the fish?"

"They're just ordinary catfish. We caught one. They won't bother us."

"But . . ."

"You're hot and tired and covered in damp clay and bat guano."

"Bat guano . . . !"

"There are bats up there." He pointed straight overhead. "They're all outside now, but they'll be flying in later." He hunched his shoulders. "I hate bats. Nasty flying rats. That's how we'll know when it's daylight. The bats will come in."

"Oh, God . . ."

"Come on," he whispered. "Let's at least get clean." Without trying to persuade her further, he stripped his shirt out of his jeans and began to unbutton it.

She sank down with her legs crossed tailor fashion and leaned her head on her hand. Beside her, she heard the rustle of his clothes, the soft thud as he pulled off his boots. And then he came down on one knee beside her.

"You'll feel better," he promised. "I'll even blow out the candle if you feel embarrassed."

Fear of the dark sharpened her voice. "Oh, no."

When he unbuttoned her blouse, she did not push his

374

hands away. He pushed the straps of the camisole down. "Now stand up," he instructed.

Like a puppet, she allowed him to help her up. On his knees, he unfastened the waistband of her skirt and sank back on his haunches to pull all her garments off together. She rested one hand on his bare shoulder while he pulled first one boot off and then the other.

When she was nude, he looked up into her face. "Star . . ." he whispered. She shivered at the hoarse tone of his voice. Gently, tentatively, he ran his hands up the outsides of her thighs. Her skin was smooth as silk under his palms.

Clasping her hips, he pressed his face to her belly. His lips kissed and caressed the smooth skin. His tongue flicked sensuously through the fine invisible hairs that arrowed down its center.

She drew her breath in through bared teeth. "Why are you doing this? We could be found at any second," she protested weakly.

"What better time?" he muttered, his mouth moving lower into the dark soft hair at the top of her thighs.

"Shouldn't one of us keep watch? Or something?"

He shook his head back and forth, stroking her belly as he did so.

"But . . . oh, Chris . . ."

He ran his hands up over her waist to cover her breasts with his palms. She leaned against him as he rubbed her in a circular motion until the nipples hardened. Her fingers caressed the nape of his neck, finding the tightly bunched nerves there and massaging them.

"You feel so good."

"You too."

He knelt up so that he could take her nipple in his mouth. The hairs of his chest tickled her lower belly and mingled with her own softness. She pushed against him harder as he took the hardened tip between his teeth and bit it gently.

"Oh, please," she whispered.

"Please what?" Again he nipped her. His hand attended to her other breast, squeezing it, taking the throbbing tip between his thumb and third finger and matching the efforts of his mouth.

"Ooo-o-oh . . ."

When she was dying with wanting him, he rose to his feet. "First we bathe," he decreed. Taking her hand, he led her to the edge of the pool.

Chapter Twenty-four

The water, too, was warm. The pool was really a basin only a few feet deep in its middle. From the ceiling a drop of water formed at slow intervals and fell from the tip of a stalactite.

Star sat on the edge, her feet extended down into the gently sloping bowl. One hand dabbled at the edge. The other arm she kept across her breasts. Her initials doubts about the pool itself had combined with her shyness to keep her from joining Chris in the water.

Although the warmth would have given heavenly relief to her tired, sore body, she did not quite dare to slide farther down into the water beside him. The idea of being in the same water with him struck her as more intimate than being in the same bed. She shivered as a hot curl of desire made her breasts tingle and her belly tighten.

Chris had no problems with shyness. She watched his strong, broad back enviously as he waded out to midthigh, then slid forward smoothly into the water. A couple of gentle sidestrokes took him to the other side of the basin, where he turned his body around with lazy grace and regarded her. "See how easy it is?" he called softly.

She glanced hastily at the candle, now a bare inch of white. It would be out before very long. They would be without light. Somehow that darkness did not seem so terrible as it would have been before they had taken off their clothes.

"Come on," he urged.

She slid a little farther into the basin until the water rose up around her waist. Their movements made it ripple like balm across her abused skin. She could not remember when she had last had a bath in any kind of peace. Had she really only been kidnapped less than a month ago?

She did not realize her eyes had taken on a dazed, unfocused expression. Chris kicked once, straightened out in the water, and floated toward her. His arms circled her hips as his head nudged against her chest.

Relaxed in the water, she allowed herself to sink back on her elbows. He cushioned his head between her breasts. His lips touched, then claimed her nipple. She moaned ecstatically as he lifted her buttocks. Practically weightless in the water, she floated up against his chest. The warm water swirled over and between their fevered skin as they moved.

She wanted him badly, more than she ever had before. Like the petals of a flower blooming in the delightful warmth of the pool, she let her thighs fall open to cradle his hips. When he entered her with a sigh of contentment, she accepted him with an answering sigh.

Though danger waited outside for them, though the candle guttered out, they paid no head. She clasped him close and matched his rhythm with her own. Like black velvet caressing her skin, the absence of light made all her other senses more acute until she did not need or miss her sight.

He shuddered to his climax first, unable to contain himself, losing his control completely, making the water churn with his plunges. "I'm sorry," he gasped, his cheek against hers, his chest crushing hers, his heart pounding wildly. "I didn't . . . that is, I couldn't . . ."

She stopped him with her mouth. Her thighs contracted around his hips as she locked her ankles together. Wrapping her arms around his neck, she held him inside her while she began to move against him. Her buoyancy in the water aided her in prolonging and deepening her movements.

"Ah, Star . . ." He clenched his teeth in the real pain of ecstasy protracted, his engorged staff impossibly stimulated.

"Chris," she begged. "Oh, Chris. I need . . ." She pushed upward frantically, the core of her femininity writhing tightly against him. "Chris!" A deep sob tore out of her throat, to be followed by another and another as tiny explosions of pleasure became bigger and bigger pleasures.

He held her by the shoulders, his forearms supporting her head out of the water while her own sensuality, unrestrained for the first time, swept her to uncharted realms.

Finally, they lay together in the darkness. The water undulated only slightly as they breathed. The silence was infinite, except for an occasional plopping sound as the interminable, inexorable drops fell from the stalactite.

"Is this heaven?"

"I think so," he replied. "Angel's arms and all that."

"I don't have my 'arms' around you."

"I'm not complaining." He nuzzled her contentedly and tightened his arms fractionally.

She felt his breathing even. He had drifted off to sleep in the warm water. Slowly, she transferred his head from her cheek to her shoulder. He did not stir, except to mutter unintelligibly.

She stroked her hand down his spine, feeling its distinct knobs. He had gone without rest for forty-eight hours. No wonder his body was so lean when he made such demands on it. She allowed her legs to float free in the water and wiggled her toes. She was tired, too.

"Want me to wash you in all the places you can't reach?" He spoke seductively against her neck.

"I thought you were asleep."

"I was, but somebody kept running her fingers up and down my back."

She flushed, glad of the darkness and the warm water. "I didn't mean to disturb you."

"I'm perfectly agreeable for you to disturb me like that anytime. Half a dozen times a day."

She pushed at his shoulder. "We should get on with this bath. I'll bet my toes are getting all wrinkled."

He laughed softly and pushed away from her; his hand slipped down her arm to close round her wrist and drag her into the center of the pool. "Can't have wrinkled toes," he agreed. In the pitch darkness he began to scoop water up in his hands and pour it over her shoulders and her breasts. She, in turn, cupped her hands and ran them over the hard muscles of his chest and his belly.

His body was so hard and lean, yet his muscles curved in ways that excited her as she had not thought possible. Drawing deep breaths that were meant to be calming, she ran her hands over him and reveled in his shape. When they were finally finished, she waded out of the bowl reluctantly.

Finding their clothing proved less easy, and Star was giggling softly by the time she had managed to sort out her different pieces and dress herself. At last she was clothed, except for her hose and boots.

"Time to go back to the other room." His voice came out of the dark, its tone regretful.

She sighed. "I can't believe that I hate to leave."

"I can," he murmured, taking her in his arms. "You're really something in the dark."

Somewhat embarrassed by a compliment on her sexuality, she hid her head against his chest where she savored the peace of his heartbeat.

"But I'm going to make you a promise." He cupped her head in his hand and smoothed her hair. "The next time we make love, it's going to be in the blaze of noon. I want to see the lovely expressions on your face when you lose yourself."

Then she did flush. Her arms tightened around him. "Maybe we'd better get out of here," she agreed. "They might be gone."

The distinctive odor of mesquite smoke drifted faintly around them. Their pursuers must have built a fire and camped in the outer chamber. "What are they waiting for?" Star hissed in Chris's ear.

He shrugged. "Who knows? Give them a few more hours. When nobody comes, they'll go on."

"But . . ."

"We can outwait them," he reminded her smoothly, gathering her in his arms and cradling her head on his chest. "We've got water to drink and a bit of food left. They don't have water, except what they've brought, and they don't really know we'll be back anytime soon."

She sighed, tired to death of it all. "If you say so, we'll wait," she agreed. "Tell me about yourself. You've done so much in your life," she commented.

He squeezed her breast, not minding the change of subject. "I've bounced around some," he admitted.

"Tell me about your greatest adventure."

He chuckled, his chest vibrating beneath her ear. "Do you want a bedtime story?"

She nodded.

"Well, once I was down in Wild Horse Desert with my grandfather. My grandmother, everyone always called her La Patrona, was dead set against us going because Grand-

381

father hadn't been feeling too well, but he was just as determined that she wasn't going to tell him what to do. Anyway . . ."

She closed her eyes. Before he had finished the sentence, he heard her even breathing.

"But you're not sure they've gone?"

He lit the remaining candle. "You won't be alone in the dark. And I'll be careful," he replied. "No matter how pleasantly we pass the time, we still can't stay holed up in here forever. I'm getting hungry."

"How unromantic!"

"Ma'am, we bounty hunters got to be practical."

So long as he stayed at her side, he kept the darkness away. Now it closed in around her, despite the tiny light. Trying not to notice it, she kept her eyes firmly fixed on the slot through which he had crawled. She would not remain here for very long. Better to take her chances in the light than to stay in impenetrable darkness.

The candle burned to half an inch. He had not returned. Something had happened! Her fertile imagination took hold. Taking a deep breath, she lowered herself to the slot and stuck her head under the ledge. Again the blinding panic. She could feel the tons of stone hanging above her, pressing down upon her. She snatched her head back so fast that she scraped it on the sharp rock.

Tears trickled down her cheeks as she clapped her hand to her scalp. Damn this place! And damn Chris Gillard for bringing her to it and leaving her here in the dark! "Damn! Damn! Damn!"

The warm, even temperature of the cave suddenly seemed to fill her nostrils with a sensation akin to drowning. A faint rustling, squeaking sound reached her ears. Nervously, she glanced up into the darkness. She could not see more than a couple of feet above her. The ceiling might be there within reach, or twenty feet up or a hundred. She had no way of knowing where the bats were.

Holding her breath, she lowered her face to the slot again. Listening with every nerve strained proved nothing. The stone effectively distorted the sound waves. Still, she could not stay here alone. He might not return. She glanced at the candle. It would gutter any minute now.

Suddenly, she knew the way to drive herself from this prison. She took a deep breath of the fetid, humid air. Leaning over before thought made her a coward, she blew the candle out.

With her bridges burned, she completed the movement, thereby flattening herself on the spongy floor. Tears she did not know she shed continued to run down her face as she thrust head and shoulders into the narrow passage and felt the stone envelop her.

The way going out was surprisingly easier than coming in. Air, much cooler by comparison, blew in her face. Within a few feet she discerned a pale glow. Unmistakably she heard the sounds of people arguing, voices raised in anger. He must be in trouble. He had walked out into danger for her sake. Concentrating on his face, she crawled rapidly and easily back through a passage that had been an endless torture going in. In less than ten feet she reached the outer chamber.

Just before she stuck her head out, she hesitated. Angry voices reached her ears.

"I tell you she's already on a stage for San Antonio," came Chris's voice, hoarse and groaning.

"Damn liar!" Luke Garner's expletive was followed by the nauseating splat of a fist striking flesh. "Where'd you hide her?" Then he raised his voice. "Search every square inch of this cave, boys. He came out of somewhere, and that's where he's most likely got her hid."

"No."

"Then you tell us!" Garner growled.

"Stagecoach . . . San Antone . . ." Chris's words ended in an agonized grunt as the foreman Hatch drove a fist into his solar plexis.

The tears dried on Star's cheeks as they suddenly flushed angry red. Her first impulse was to scream a command for them to stop. Instantly she clamped her jaws together. At least, she must size up the situation. They did not know for sure that she was behind them.

Panting, his breath coming in groans, Chris kept insisting that he had put her on the stagecoach. Star crawled to the edge of the slot. She heard the crunch of gravel beneath boots and drew back.

The boots stopped only a few feet from her. She pressed back against the wall. The man went down on one knee and peered under the ledge. He could not help but see her. His grizzled mouth leered. "Hey, boss," he called.

Star pushed herself forward. "Thank goodness, you've found me," she exclaimed. "Help me up."

The man's grin faded somewhat. Puzzled, he glanced over his shoulder at Garner.

"Help me." Star extended her arms imperiously. Without further hesitation, he took her hands and helped her to her feet. "Luke," she called. "Oh, Luke."

Luke Garner spun around; a stunned look spread across his face.

"Luke! You've come for me. I was sure you would."

"Star?" Luke stared at her in disbelief. The other men looked at each other. Their eyes shifted back and forth among the three major participants in this drama.

Star started up the incline, her hand outstretched toward Luke. "He had me tied up in that cave throughout the whole night," she complained loudly. Her voice echoed shrilly through the chamber.

384

Chris Gillard looked at the face of the man holding him on one side. The man was staring at the girl with his mouth open. The hands around Gillard's arms relaxed.

Suddenly Chris wrenched free. Leaping back, he jerked the guns from the holsters of both men. Before they could move they were effectively disarmed and Chris had flung himself away.

"Hey!"

"Get down, Star!"

Luke wheeled back around to face this new nemesis. Star spun and kicked with all her might at the man climbing the steep incline right behind her. He was caught while negotiating the bottomless crack in the trail. Head down he moved, with most of his weight on his back foot.

Her boot heel landed squarely on his nose with a sickening crunching sound. He let out a gurgling scream and fell backwards, his hands clapped to his face. As he fell over on the incline and began to roll, she dived after him, clutching for his gun. She dragged it from the holster even as he rolled away down the slope.

She cocked the pistol, an antique Colt, and rose ready for battle.

Faced with Chris's two-gun stance, Luke's men jabbed their hands toward the ceiling.

Furious at the shift of power, Luke went for his own gun. "Son-of-a-bitch!"

"Stay down, Star!" the bounty hunter yelled. But his words came too late.

"Luke! No!" She had already started up the steep path directly behind the rancher.

"I'll kill you. . . ." From a crouch Luke, fired point blank. The sound reverberated in the chamber, exploding in Star's ears, the vibrations driving her backward. The rubble on the path slid away beneath the heels of her boots. Her arms flailed the air trying to find a hold, then she

385

staggered and went down heavily on her side.

At the same time, a stunning blow caught Chris in the hip bone. Once when he was a boy, a horse had kicked him in the belly. But this was with ten times the force. It flung him back against the wall and left him paralyzed. His eyes glazing, he slid down its rough surface. Blood gushed instantly from the wound. He could feel its hot river covering his whole left side.

He could not see; he could not think. Indeed, he could scarcely breathe. He could not even raise his hand to feel how badly he was wounded.

"Goddam bounty hunter!" Luke declared. "That'll settle your hash."

Star rolled over on her back, stunned for the moment. *The room whirled around her. Excruciating pain shot upward from her thumb into her brain, deadening all power of motion. Conscious of everything around her, she watched the tableau from her past with crystal clarity. And in that moment of total recollection, she knew with absolute certainty that she had not killed Matthew Garner. Through tears and pain she watched him die and could not lift a hand to save him, even had she wanted to do so. Furthermore, she could not defend herself if the killer should turn on her. Wounded as she was, she could not defend herself even with a gun. . . . even with a gun . . . even with a gun.*

The room dissolved, but the smell of gunsmoke and the strange silence were the same. She lay on her back, staring upward at the rough ceiling of the outer chamber of Four Skeletons Cave.

Matthew had been dead a long time, but *she had not killed him*. Rolling over, she climbed to her feet, doggedly clutching the rider's gun.

"Get his guns, Hatch." Luke's voice drew her attention back up the steep slope. Dazedly, she stared up at his broad back. Like a great bear, he stood out among the smaller men.

The shot! Someone had been shot. "Chris!" Rolling over onto her hands and knees, she scrambled clumsily up the steep slope. "Chris!"

Luke Garner wheeled to intercept her, but she waved the gun at him. "Get out of the way, damn you!"

Before her brandished pistol he stepped back, hands raised in an effort to calm her. Hatch was down on one knee beside the body in the act of wresting the gun from Chris's lax grip.

"Get away from him," she ordered. "Leave him alone."

The foreman cast a quick glance over his shoulder. Possibly he did not see the gun. Possibly he thought that one of the other men, or even Luke himself, would take the gun away from her.

"I said, 'Get the hell away from him!'" The anger and determination in her voice twisted the man around on his haunches too late. Star lunged up the last few feet and swung her pistol at the foreman's head. He reeled back from a glancing blow that knocked his hat sailing and grazed the top of his skull with the barrel. With a harsh grunt, he sprawled clumsily in the dust and rubble beside the wall.

With his body out of the way, she got her first clear view of Chris. "Oh, my God." She dropped to her knees beside him.

The entire lower half of his body was bathed in the horrible shiny red liquid. It ran from him in a red river that pooled under him and trickled in a bright stream down the slope. As she stared at him, trying to take in his condition, his leg spasmed uncontrollably as the agony built.

Biting her lip against rising nausea, she worked the kerchief from her neck and pressed it to the blackened hole in his jeans.

387

"Ain't gonna be no use." Luke's voice betrayed his satisfaction. "He's gutshot. Never get him out of here."

Star shuddered at his diagnosis but pressed hard on the spot. Her fingers found the hip bone, still intact, so far as she could tell. If the bullet had gone to the right of the bone, Chris's chances were slim to none. But if it had burned down the outside of his hip, he had a good chance.

While she worked, the foreman sat up holding his head in his hands. He blinked several times, then burst into a string of vicious curses.

Star caught up the pistol from where she had laid it beside Chris's leg. "One more word and I'll use this," she promised with deadly seriousness.

Hatch cut off his curses in midstream. He stared into her face, then dropped his eyes. Rubbing his hand over his head one last time, he reached across the floor to retrieve his hat.

Satisfied that he would do nothing more, Star motioned to one of the other men. "Bring me a canteen."

While one of the men climbed out of the cave, she unbuckled Chris's belt and unbuttoned the blood-soaked trousers. When she pulled aside the material, the sight of his torn flesh nauseated her. She wiped the back of her hand across her eyes but managed to steady herself.

"He's done for," Luke Garner averred, leaning over her shoulder to inspect the wound.

The man returned with the canteen. Coldly Star reached for it, ignoring Luke's complaints that she was wasting the water. One quick slosh encouraged her. The wound was more a gash than a hole. Pouring more water over it, she swabbed with a bandanna. A gash it was, about two inches long, through which the bullet had entered. She pulled his body toward her. He had another bullet hole in the heavy muscle at the top of his left buttock.

Dizzy with relief, she closed her eyes and breathed a

silent prayer of thanks. Chris was alive. Provided that his hip bone was not shattered, he stood a good chance of recovery. But she must get the bleeding stopped.

The man who had brought the canteen dropped down beside her. "How's it lookin'?" he asked in a kindly way.

"It's going to be all right," she replied, a positive note to her voice. "If I can just get this bleeding stopped."

Even as she spoke, Chris stirred. His eyes flickered open, stared blindly at the ceiling. Then the pain hit him. His face contorted. His hands clenched around handfuls of pebbles in the path. "Goddamn!" he groaned.

"Chris." Star bent over him. "I'm going to pad your wound with kerchiefs and buckle your belt tight across it. Can you stand it?"

He stirred feebly, trying to feel the area of the wound with fingers that had trouble carrying the message back to his brain. "H-how bad am I hit?"

"Not too bad. The bullet's gone clean through."

He sighed, then whispered, "Through what?"

"The flesh of your hip, I think."

He took a deep breath. "Get that belt around it, then."

"Can you help me?" Star turned to the man who had fetched the canteen. "Can you get a blanket from behind the saddle on the black mare and tear it into strips?"

He doffed his hat. "Sure thing, ma'am."

Luke bent over her. He had lighted a cigar, and its odorous smoke made her gag. "So he ain't dead. Too bad. Would have saved me some trouble."

She raised her head. "Be glad he's not dead, Luke. That would have caused you more trouble then you realize."

"Hell, he kidnapped you."

"We'll talk about it in a minute." She heard the rip of blanket. Then the man was beside her. "Chris, can you sit up?"

He was trembling so badly that he had no control of

himself. He was sure he had wet his pants, but fortunately the blood and dimness hid his embarrassment for the time being. He made a try with arms like rubber. Finally, he managed with her help to brace his shoulders against the wall of the cave.

"I've got to pass this around your body at least once." Her face was gray-white and her voice quavered, but her hands were steady as she pulled the long strip of blanket around his hips and made a pad out of both ends across the wounds. Efficiently, she stripped his belt from its loops and adjusted it into position. "Now," she whispered. "This will hurt."

His forehead was beaded with perspiration, yet his mouth was dry. "I don't know anything that doesn't at this stage," he managed to whisper.

She pulled the belt tight and buckled it.

Whirling dark spots filled his vision, nausea welled in his throat, but he did not lose consciousness. The tormented nerves sent message after message to his brain and he absorbed them all through a gray haze.

"Now," she said, from a long way off, "lie back and wait for it to ease a little."

As if he had waited for her permission, he lay back and slipped thankfully into the black tide.

Her crude nursing done, Star climbed shakily to her feet and faced Luke Garner. "Have you lost what little sense you ever had?" she demanded, her hands on her hips, her feet planted wide apart between him and Chris's fainting body.

Luke blinked. The rest of the men shifted uneasily. The big man threw out his chest and clamped down hard on his cigar. "He kidnapped you and stole them horses," he stated flatly.

"No one was kidnapped, and no horses were stolen, and you know it."

"You was gettin' ready to marry me. . . ."

Star felt no pity for his vanity. "You were on the point of forcing me to marry you, but you can't do that anymore."

Luke's face turned hard, his jaw set pugnaciously. "You want to go back to jail, huh?"

"I'm not going back to that jail, Luke. Not now, not ever. You'll never send me."

"And why can't I? That was our agreement. You owe me."

She shook her head. "That was when I couldn't remember what happened to Matthew." She took a step toward him, placing her face very close to his. "Now I know."

"You know?" His face hardened. "You want to tell me about it?"

She drew a deep, shuddering breath. The men around them shuffled their feet as they listened with avid curiosity while pretending not to. "He's dead and gone, Luke. He was sick. You've admitted that to me yourself."

Luke's face turned brick-red. He flung the cigar to the floor and crushed it with his boot. "Goddamnit, woman. If you didn't kill my son, then who did?"

A groan from Chris interrupted the conversation. She hurried back to his side.

"We've got to get out of here," he muttered.

"Just rest easy," she begged.

"N-no . . . dangerous for you." He pushed himself up to a sitting position. "Damn." Sweat broke out on his forehead.

"For heaven's sake, lie back."

But he would not be deterred. "Got to get you to San Antonio."

"Chris . . ." She put her hand on his arm. "Luke believes me when I say I didn't kill Matt. You're wounded. You'll never make it to San Antonio. We can go back to Crossways."

He caught ahold of the front of her blouse with his bloodstained hand. "*No!* You've got to get to San Antonio." Their faces were only inches apart. Both were pearly white, his beaded with sweat, hers haggard and thin. Both might have been twenty years older than their chronological ages. They had been through so much together, suffered both in flesh and spirit together. Comrades and something more, they stared into each other's eyes.

She wrapped her fingers around his wrist. The stains on her fingers mingled with the stains on his hand. She looked into his eyes, and her heart turned over with pity for his pain. "It's all right," she promised. "I swear it's all right."

"No," he insisted. "You can't go back there. You can't get near any of them. You didn't kill Matthew Garner, but somebody did."

Hastily, she glanced over her shoulder. "Be careful what you say," she whispered.

"No. You be careful. You know who did kill him. And that person maybe already knows you know."

Chapter Twenty-five

"Ain't nobody gonna hurt her," Luke sneered belligerently. "She's gonna come home with me where she belongs. She made a bargain, and by God, she's gonna live up to it."

Chris ignored him. His face was calm, the lines smoothed out. His eyes, like smoke-stained steel, fastened on Star's face. "I can make the ride out of here," he insisted.

She looked at him uncertainly. "You're hurt."

"Not badly."

She put the back of her fingers against his cheek. His skin felt warm and damp underneath the bristles of his beard. "I don't intend to set foot onto Tres Santos," she promised. "I'll move us both in with Rosa McGloin."

He shook his head impatiently, dislodging her fingers. "You can't go back there," he insisted. "You're in danger."

"You've lost so much blood. . . ."

The abrupt movement of his head had jostled the tight grip he held on himself. His vision blurred. When he looked back at her, her features seemed to swim and then to fade from his sight. A fuzziness encroached on the edges of his vision, until only her face remained framed in a halo. He swallowed. ". . . about to pass out," he whispered. ". . . not long . . . shock . . ."

She bent over to catch his words, her face only a couple of inches from him.

He gripped her hand with failing strength. "Don't . . . panic. Wait. Promise?"

"I promise."

Slowly, he slumped to one side, his hands sliding laxly down to lie palm up in the dust and blood. Calling his name, Star thrust her hand beneath his shirt. He was alive; his heart beat strongly, but erratically. She gripped his shoulders and eased his way on down into a more natural position. Then, dashing away tears of relief, she rose to face Luke Garner.

His jaw thrust out belligerently at the expression on her face. "If you're through moaning over that bounty hunter, maybe you'll tell me who killed my son?" he snarled.

Star shook her head wearily. "Luke, let it rest. You can't bring him back." She put out her hand. Her fingertips almost touched his forearm. "Do you really want to?"

He raised one eyebrow, glanced suspiciously at her hand, then back at her face. "What're you up to?"

Instantly, she drew back, doubling her hand into a fist. Her shoulders stiffened. "I lost my head," she replied coldly. "For a minute there I actually felt sorry for you, so I was trying to be nice."

"Then be nice. C'mon back like y' promised and . . ."

"No." She shook her head sharply. "No. I never intend to set foot on Tres Santos again."

The expression on his face turned ugly. "What if I call Hatch over and have him drag you out of here and throw you on a horse? If a rock or somethin' falls on this varmint's head in here, cain't nobody be blamed for that. Sure as hell not my fault."

"You wouldn't dare." Her voice quivered.

"No way nobody could prove a blessed thing," he reminded her nastily. "Me and my boys say he was fine when we left him. Maybe he falls and kills hisself when he's leavin'. Shouldn't oughta come in here in the first place. Lotsa accidents happen in caves."

She took a tight grip on her emotions. No longer could she be terrorized by this man. "You're bluffing and you know it. You don't want me to tell all about what happened in front of a judge and jury. Besides, he's already got a bullethole in him. You can't say that was an accident."

"He's not going to get the chance to do either," came a voice from behind her.

"Chris!" She dropped down beside him, relief in her voice. Luke's threats had convinced her that they must get away. "I'm ready to go on to San Antonio if you're strong enough."

He clenched his teeth together. "I'll make it. Give me a hand." His bloodstained fingers clutched at her shoulder.

"No . . . wait. . . ." But he was already pushing himself up, bracing his back against the wall of the cave.

Luke Garner watched them for a moment before motioning to Hatch, who leaned against the mouth of the cave, surveying the proceedings. Pushing himself off the rock, the thin man ambled over.

Chris watched him come, his face reflecting his pain despite his best efforts to control it. "Pick up the guns, Star."

"Luke . . ." she warned, as he took an intimidating step toward her.

"I'm gonna have a son to replace Matt," he snarled doggedly. He stabbed a thick finger in her face.

She caught up the revolvers and pressed the handles into Chris's hands. With a grunt he stood away from the wall, his weight on his right leg, his left merely touching the ground for balance. "Then you're going to have to look somewhere else, Garner."

"Put them guns down."

"Not on your life. Star! Get the bridles on those horses. Don't go between me and this lardbucket. I'd hate to put Doc Foster to the trouble of trying to find a bullet in his gut."

"Son-of-a-bitch! I hired you."

Chris paid no heed to the man. He trained one of the Colts on Hatch, who raised his hands to shoulder height. The other he aimed down the slope at the other two men, who hastily backed away from the horses. "Hurry, Star. My trigger finger might get trembly and I might shoot somebody."

She slipped around behind Luke and hurried down the slope. Humareda took the bit daintily in her teeth, but the stallion drew back nervously, his eyes rolling at the men who edged closer.

"Hurry . . ."

The stallion pawed the rubble of pebbles and loose dirt. "Easy, boy," she pleaded. At last he accepted the bit. She whirled and led them across the slope.

"Can you mount?" she asked Chris nervously.

He shot her an insulted glance. "I'll climb on a horse on the way to my own funeral."

She stared at him doubtfully.

His face glistened with perspiration. Blood welled over the tooled leather belt strapped tightly around his hips. He sucked in his breath. "Take these," he muttered, handing her the guns. For all his bravado the pain was making him light-headed. His legs showed a decided tendency to waver at the knees.

Shuddering with repugnance, she aimed one blood-stained Colt at Hatch's chest. Of them all, he frightened her the most. Suddenly all her senses recalled with nightmare accuracy the horror of the attempted rape. She could see again his distended organ bobbing in front of her face, feel the cruel hands that bruised and twisted her, smell the sweat-and-urine odor of his body. She swallowed convulsively as her stomach heaved.

A dark, malevolent grin curved his lips. His right hand rose from the butt of the pistol strapped to his thigh. Even as she watched it, fascinated as if it had been a snake, it moved across his belly. His thumb hooked over his belt buckle while his fingers spread downward. . . .

She wrenched her eyes away to his taunting face and cocked the pistol.

The hand moved instantly back to his hip.

"Don't try it," she warned. "It's not dark enough. I wouldn't miss."

His smile changed to a sneer as his sharply drawn breath pinched in his nostrils.

Oblivious of the conflict only a few feet from him, Chris turned the horse to take advantage of the upward slope. Catching hold of the mane, he tried to lift his left leg. A tortured groan escaped his tightly compressed lips.

She glanced over her shoulder hastily, then back at Hatch.

He grinned nastily, even as he raised his hands a little higher in mock surrender.

Drawing a deep breath, Chris set his palms flat on Al's broad back and heaved himself clumsily up. Scrambling weakly, he managed to throw his right leg over and twist himself astride.

There he stuck. The pain from his hip sent his vision

whirling, so that he lay ingloriously sprawled across his horse.

"Chris, are you all right? Can you make it?"

Star was talking to him. Lacing his fingers in the mane, he lifted himself and straightened his trembling arms to brace himself. Sour bile rose in his throat. For a minute he thought he was going to vomit.

"Chris . . . ?"

"All . . ." The word came out on the end of a moan. "A-all right."

"You're sure?"

"Yes. Damnit. Mount up." Exerting all his will power, he managed to take hold of the reins and sit straight, unsupported.

Tucking her own pistol into her waistband, she grasped Humareda's mane and swung up. To clasp the mare's warm barrel between her thighs gave her a feeling of confidence. She met Hatch's mocking stare with cold eyes.

Luke stepped forward, a harsh grin on his face. "So y'all gonna ride out of here to San Antonio?" he sneered.

Chris braced himself by folding his hands over his mount's withers. His eyes were dimming, his whole body bathed in sick perspiration. "Head out, Star," he gritted.

"Hey, Hatch, maybe you'd better tell Mr. Gillard here where you been the last couple of days," Luke suggested.

Hatch nodded. "Yeah. Too bad he left before he could find about the nice surprise Miss Maude had planned for him."

Star hesitated, looking doubtfully over her shoulder at Chris, who shook his head. "Go on," he urged.

"If he don't come back, I don't guess she'll know how to take care of that little boy," Hatch added.

Chris froze in the saddle. His mind blocked out the throbbing in his hip. "What little boy?" he asked through clenched teeth.

"Cute little blond kid," Luke chuckled. "Bout five."

"You're lying!"

Neither man answered. Their mouths spread in travesties of smiles.

"Chris," Star whispered. "Chris . . ."

"You're lying," he repeated, more evenly. His whole body shook with the force of his emotion and the effort of maintaining himself physically in the saddle.

Hatch laughed mirthlessly. "You almost ran us down when I was bringing him the other night. If I'd known who was ripping down the trail in the dark, I'd've sung out. You could've stopped right then."

Chris viciously jerked the Alter-Real's head around and guided the horse down the slope until he was even with the foreman of Tres Santos. His eyes burning, he stared at the thin, saturnine face. "You're lying."

Hatch shrugged mockingly. "That old lady that keeps the boy, she was real uncooperative about me taking him. Didn't seem to believe that I was taking the boy on a trip to surprise his daddy. She made a grab for a gun." He turned toward Luke. "Shame about her. Had to knock her down, boss."

Plainly enjoying himself now, Luke rocked back on his heels, thrusting his thumbs into the armholes of his vest. "Unreasonable people get hurt sometimes," he opined mockingly.

"Think she was the boy's aunt or something. Leastways he kept calling her Aunt Nell or something like that."

"Aunt Neill," Star managed to croak.

Hatch looked over his shoulder at her. "Could have been. Something like that."

Star swung her attention to Luke. Her eyes glinted like obsidian. Her skin seemed to shrink tightly over her cheekbones. "You ordered this?"

He held up his hands placatingly. "Now, Star, you heard me say it was Maudie's idee. She don't always let me in on what she's gonna do. But it usually works out fer the best. . . ."

His excuses were broken off as Chris launched himself from the saddle, coming down hard on Hatch's shoulders. The two men fell to the ground and rolled down the precipitous slope locked together.

"Chris! For God's sake . . ." Star dropped from the saddle and started to run down after them, but Luke caught her arm.

"Let 'em fight it out. They gotta lot to settle."

"No!" She twisted quickly. "Chris is wounded."

"He ain't feelin' nothin'."

Hatch's body came up against an outcropping of rock, just at the lip of the bottomless trench. Chris reared over him, driving his fist into the man's face with a sickening thud.

Star drew her gun and ran down the slope. "Stop!"

Chris did not hear her and Hatch could do nothing. He threw his arms about his head to protect his face from the punches. Wedged between the slope and the rock, with his opponent straddling him, he was getting the worst of the fight.

Star poised helplessly a yard from them. "Chris," she called. "Stop! You'll kill him."

Chris hit him again. His fist split the foreman's eyebrow. The blood spattered from the blow.

"Better drag 'im off, boys," Luke Garner called with a show of unconcern, "afore he kills Hatch."

The two men scrambled forward to grasp Chris's arms and drag him back. Hatch curled his body into a tight ball.

"Don't hurt him!" Star cried, running forward to grab

400

hold of one of the men. "He's wounded."

After one futile attempt to get at Hatch again, Chris slumped in their arms. Suddenly his whole left side, from armpit to knee, was a blaze of pain. The belt had been dislodged and blood trickled into his boot. Yet the pain only served as a stimulus for his anger. The thought of Duff in the hands of the foreman drove the blood pounding to his temples. A red haze covered his eyes.

Luke went down on one knee beside the foreman. "You all right?" he asked.

"He's a dead man!" Chris shouted.

A shudder went through the foreman's body. Carefully, he stretched out his legs and sat up. Swiping the blood from his eye, he stared at Chris, then rolled over and staggered to his feet. His eyes darted everywhere, searching futilely for the gun that had slipped from his holster on the roll down the slope.

Star swung her gun around, training it on Hatch. "Just keep your hands where I can see them."

His answer was a wordless snarl.

Hanging between the Tres Santos riders, more than half his weight supported by them, Chris raised his head. His eyes bored into Luke Garner. "Have you lost your mind?"

Garner shook his head, setting his features into an expression of geniality. "C'mon back to Tres Santos. Most likely the boy's just fine. It'll be just like a family reunion."

Chris swallowed hard. "You kidnapped him," he accused. "There'll be a lawyer in Crossways in a couple of days. He might even be there right now." He straightened and pulled his arms free. He took one staggering step and then another.

Luke looked amused. "You're makin' that up. Where'd a bounty huntin' scum like you come up with a lawyer? Unless he's a shyster."

"I may be the black sheep, but my family takes care of its own. I've already sent for help for Star. They'll come fast enough for the great grandson of Reiver MacPherson, and when they do . . ." He broke off as Hatch lunged away from the group and staggered up the slope toward the opening of the cave.

"Running for it, yella belly." Chris's voice followed him contemptuously. "You've done that before." He threw his arm around Star's shoulder. "Help me," he pleaded. "Help me up the slope."

"But, Chris . . ."

As if she had been a crutch, he dragged her along, using her body to take some of the weight off his left side. She could smell the heat of him. His sick perspiration and blood stained her side.

Beside the stallion he poised, gathered himself, then threw himself across the broad back.

Star did not waste her time protesting. Instead she steadied him with a hand on his back as he struggled to maneuver his right leg astride. His face was bathed in perspiration as he took a clumsy swipe for the reins. Wordlessly, she handed them to him.

She doubted that he realized that she had helped him. His teeth were clenched; his face was set as he endured the tortures of the damned both in body and soul. Without acknowledging the presence of anyone else in the cave, he lifted the reins from the stallion's neck and drove his heels into its side. The great beast plunged up the slope toward the daylight, just as Hatch's figure appeared in silhouette in the cave's mouth.

The foreman had evidently gone for the rifle in his saddle boot, intending to kill Chris. Blinded by the light, he screamed once as the horse plunged into his chest. The ironshod hooves trampled him as the close-coupled body gathered speed almost from a standing start.

Star covered her face with her hands. Behind her she heard Luke swear vehemently.

The other two men lowered their arms and trudged up the slope past her. Star swung herself onto the mare's back.

Before she could send the mare galloping after Chris, Luke caught her bridle. She stared at him with hatred in her eyes. With his free hand he jerked off his hat and wiped the sleeve of his coat across his forehead. "I'm offerin' my men and me as an escort to take y' home." The humidity of the cave and climbing up and down the slope of the chamber room had exhausted him. The long hours trailing through the badlands were hard on a middle-aged fat man.

"You never give up, do you?" She tried to back Humareda away, but he kept his hand on the bridle.

"I want what's mine. Nobody welches on a deal with me. What's more, you claim to know who killed Matt. You warn't gonna leave without tellin' me that, now was you?"

She did not answer him. The mare swung her head up and down, fighting the hand that held her.

Suddenly, Luke let go with a curse. "You'll follow that scum. You wouldn't marry me, but you'll follow that bounty-huntin' scum. Here I was thinkin' you was so special, but you're just a tramp. That's that Indian and Mex blood. . . ."

Wishing she could ride him down as Chris had done Hatch, Star clapped her heels to Humareda's sides. The mare lunged up the slope. She knew that if she stayed one minute longer, she would pull the guns from her waistband and shoot Luke Garner. As she burst out into the bright sunlight, she wondered why she had not done so.

The two men were kneeling beside Hatch, who was stirring feebly. Both Chris and she seemed to be missing golden opportunities, she thought with a viciousness that surprised her. Then she spared them no more concern as she headed Humareda down the steep side of the canyon.

Luke and his men caught up with her in about an hour. She did not acknowledge them, nor was she particularly surprised to see them. They closed in behind her but made no move to touch her. Luke put the nose of his horse on Humareda's rump but said nothing. The mare's smooth-stepping gait ate up the miles.

She had seen no sign of Chris, nor even of his dust cloud, but again she was not surprised. He would ride the stallion to the limit of his strength and perhaps beyond in his effort to get back to Tres Santos to confirm whether what Hatch had said was true or not.

Guilt rode her hard. Indirectly, this kidnapping was her fault. She had asked for his help and he had given it. He could have taken the money offered by Luke, along with the mare Humareda, and ridden away free and clear. Instead, he had stayed to investigate her guilt or innocence. Then he had freed her. She owed him more than her life, and he was paying for it dearly.

They came to the grove of salt cedars where she and Chris had hidden to watch the Tres Santos riders gallop by. Had they really only been there twenty-four hours ago? So much had happened.

The mare was covered in lather. Beneath the soft shade Star paused to let her rest. When Luke proffered his canteen, she accepted it with only momentary hesitation.

"I can't figure why the hell Maude wanted that kid," Luke remarked conversationally.

"Because she's crazy," Star replied flatly.

"Crazy like a fox," he snorted. "She's like me. She don't do nothin' without a reason."

Hatch sat his horse in silence, out of Luke's range of vision. His eyes burned beneath the bloodstained bandage tied around his forehead. His lip curled in a sneer at the words.

Angry and uncomfortable with the pair of them, Star handed the canteen back to Luke and guided Humareda out of the grove.

The western sun was beaming directly in her eyes when riders appeared in silhouette on the road ahead. With a feeling of trepidation, Star shaded her eyes against the glare but could not recognize them. She glanced behind her, but Luke was easing his pistol in his holster. Neither he nor any of his riders knew whom they were meeting.

Humareda, however, lifted her head and whinnied a greeting.

The horse of one of the riders who occupied the center of the road threw up his head and whinnied back excitedly.

Star stared hard at the figures. Almost immediately, they came galloping toward her.

"Estrella!"

"Baby sister!"

Incredulous tears started in Star's eyes as she felt the weight of the world suddenly lift from her shoulders. "Tomas! Johanna!"

They came sweeping down on either side of her. Johanna Sandoval grabbed her sister first, hugging her hard. Even with the intense emotion of her greeting, her calculating Irish blue eyes, her only heritage from her father, swept the men who formed Star's escort. They settled on Luke Garner and blazed furiously.

Star hid her head in her sister's neck, trying to keep from crying with relief. Now someone would back her play when she rode into Tres Santos to help Chris and Duff. She could be sure that she would have a back-up.

Wordlessly, the two sisters hugged each other. Then drew apart. Johanna stared into Star's eyes. "Are you all right?"

Star nodded. "God, you look so good. I can't believe how good you look to me." She hugged her sister again, then turned to Tomas. *"Hermano mio,"* she cried.

"Hermanita!"

"Were you badly hurt?" Her eyes scanned his lean figure for bandages. "I heard you were shot trying to break me out of jail."

"No es importante," came the reply. "A flesh wound only." He flexed his arm to demonstrate that he could use it easily.

"You were lucky," Johanna interposed. "He was bleeding like a stuck pig when he came riding in. Those men hadn't been able to get it stopped."

Star shuddered. She clasped her brother hard. "You've been through so much for me, Tomas. You are the best of brothers. The very best."

Leaving them to their reunion, Johanna moved her horse past Humareda until her fine blue roan stood nose to nose with Luke Garner's horse. "I'm here to see that you leave my baby sister alone," she announced baldly.

Garner gulped. "My son . . ." he began.

Johanna Sandoval made a cutting motion with her gloved right hand. An imposing figure on a horseback, her presence silenced his protests. "We're all sorry about your son," she agreed. "But killing Estrella won't make him come back."

"I ain't gonna kill her."

The riders from the Double Diamond and the *vaqueros* from Rancho Montejo had closed ranks behind Star and Tomas, their hands resting on their thighs close to the pistol butts. At his words they relaxed fractionally. Hatch guided his horse off to the right of the group. Without a word to anyone, he loped his horse down the road.

Johanna nodded shortly. Her black hair was pulled back in a tight mass at the nape of her neck. Little wrinkles beneath her eyes and down the center of her forehead had replaced the breathtaking beauty of her youth with unquestionable strength of character.

Luke Garner shifted his bulk uneasily in his saddle.

"Luke made me an offer of marriage," Star interposed. "I've told him I can't accept it."

"You can't accept any offers right now," Johanna agreed. "You have to come home to the Double Diamond with me for a while. You need to rest and regain your strength." She surveyed her half-sister critically. "You look like you've been dragged through a knothole."

"Just a cave," Star smiled ruefully. "I'll rest just as soon as Christopher Gillard is safe."

"Gillard!" Tomas spat the name. "Christopher Gillard. Was that Stewart's real name. Forgive me, sister. You did not want to take him on, but I insisted. If I had listened to you, this would never had occurred."

"Don't blame yourself, Tomas. If Gillard hadn't gotten me one way, he would have gotten me another. He's the best. Now we have to help him."

"Help him. Have you lost your mind?"

"He helped me. He fed me and cared for me and helped me to escape after he discovered that I couldn't possibly have killed Matthew."

Johanna put her arm again around her baby sister. "I never did believe you did, whether you could remember or not. I knew you couldn't have."

"No," Star admitted, drawing a deep, shuddering breath. "I couldn't have done it. Matthew broke my thumb

407

before I was shot. I couldn't have cocked the revolver."

"If you didn't kill him, then who did?" Johanna looked straight at Luke. "Did you hire someone to kill the good-for-nothing so-and-so and blame it on Estrella?"

"No." Luke held up his hands. "I couldn't kill my own son."

"There's no time to discuss this now." Star interrupted Luke's protestations. "Chris has been wounded."

"Chris?" Tomas asked suspiciously.

"Yes, Christopher Gillard. And he's ridden into danger. I'm gong to ride back to Tres Santos. How about it, both of you? Will you back your baby sister's play?"

Johanna smiled at the choice of words. "Always, Estrella. It sounds like you're not a baby anymore. You sound just like Mama."

Tomas looked at her wonderingly. *"Sí."* he agreed. "You do. You sound . . . wonderful."

Star smiled wearily in return. She did not feel wonderful like her mother. She only knew she had a job to do and she had to do it soon.

Chapter Twenty-six

The parapets of Tres Santos wavered in Chris's vision. The Alter-Real stumbled wearily, its breath coming in stentorian gasps, its proud head hanging low. "Just a little more, boy," Chris muttered, pulling back on the reins and lifting the stallion's head. The horse shuddered. Its hide was caked with dust mixed with lather. Its mouth hung open and ropy strings of saliva trailed from its lips.

When Chris leaned forward to pat the filthy neck, he was forced to acknowledge the horse's condition. In a daze created of pain and fear, he had almost killed his horse. He shook his head helplessly. "God, I'm sorry, Al."

The gate on the lower wall stood open. A single sentinel leaned lazily in the shadow of the gateposts. "Kinda stove in, ain't y', fella?" he observed. "Need any help?"

Chris ran his tongue across his cracked lips. "Got any water?"

The guard came forward with a canteen.

The water was lukewarm and tasted of rotten eggs. Nevertheless, it alleviated his thirst. "Much obliged."

The man recapped the canteen and stepped back. "Anything else?"

Chris shook his head. "Guess I can make it on in. I've made it this far."

The man touched the brim of his hat in agreement and spat a stream of brown tobacco juice into the dust.

Chris pulled his own hat down tighter over his forehead and guided the tired stallion up the most precipitous part of the slope to the big house. The man at the cedar gate recognized him and swung it open for Chris to ride into the empty courtyard.

The windows stared at him blankly. Behind which one was his son? Despair swept over him in a black wave. He could barely sit a horse. How could he search through that maze of hallways and rooms for a little boy? Duff was his son, placed in jeopardy by his bounty hunting. Deal with dangerous people and you put those around you in danger.

A man materialized out of the shadow of the gatehouse to take hold of his bridle. "I take your horse, señor."

"Don't take him far. I don't intend to be here very long."

He eased himself out of the saddle. At first he was forced to hang from the horn. Then, gradually, strength returned to his limbs. His right leg took his weight first; then his left. In a moment he would be able to walk.

Just as he let go of the saddle, the door opened and Maude stood framed in it, a welcoming smile on her face. Her dress was black this time rather than her usual gray. The rusty wool with white collar and cuffs made her skin appear more sallow than usual. At the sight of the ominous brown stains covering the whole left side of his body, she gasped. "Chris! My God! You're hurt. Emilia, come quick!"

Hurrying down the steps, she slipped her shoulder underneath his right arm to support him.

He accepted her aid without comment until they had entered the living room. Then he straightened, taking his weight off her. "Where's Duff?" he demanded even before she could get him to a chair.

"Who?"

"Don't play dumb. Hatch told me that you'd sent him to get my son. Where is he?"

She guided him to a chair, not meeting his eyes. "Oh, he's around here somewhere. Probably playing. But you mustn't worry about him right now. You need doctoring. Emilia!"

He grabbed for her wrist, but she turned away too fast for him to grasp her.

"Emilia!"

"Aquí, Señorita Maude. Qué pasa?" The housekeeper bustled into the room. Her hands flew to her cheeks as she caught sight of Chris's strained posture and pain-wracked face. *"Ay de mi!"*

But when the Mexican woman came forward to inspect his wound. Chris waved her away. "Where is my son?" he gritted.

"Now, Chris," Maude pleaded. "You don't need to be concerned. . . ."

This time when Chris made a grab for Maude's wrist, he caught it. "You sent Hatch to kidnap my son."

"Chris . . ." Maude gasped. "We can discuss this later. Please . . . you're hurting me."

"I'm going to do more than that if you don't get him out here right now."

"I don't think . . . ow!"

"Don't say 'don't' to me. Where's my son?"

But he was weaker than he knew. Maude swung her free hand at the side of his head. The blow itself was nothing, but it knocked his injured side against the oaken arm. Blackness closed in around him and he slumped over the side of the chair in a dead faint.

"Señorita Maude . . ." Emilia began.

Rubbing her wrist where his hand had bruised her,

411

Maude stared down at the unconscious man. Her eyes narrowed and her lips set tightly. "Get some water and bandages, Emilia."

"*Sí.*"

"And get a man to carry him into the south wing."

"*Muy bueno, señorita.*"

Chris woke as the Mexican woman tightened the swath of cotton around his hips. Maude's face hung above him. By mutual consent they waited in silence for the woman to finish and leave.

Maude spoke first. "Would you like some whiskey?"

"Yes." He was surprised at the hoarseness of his voice. Only on the second try could he manage to get the word out.

She picked up a decanter from the bedside table and poured an inch into the water glass. Sitting down on the bed, she lifted his head with one hand and held the drink to his lips.

The raw alcohol burned all the way to his empty stomach where its warmth spread through his chill, still body.

"Want some more?" she asked when he had drained it.

"Please," he murmured.

She filled it again and held his head while he drank it down."

"Where's Duff?" he asked.

She shrugged. "We need to talk first."

His side was throbbing until he could hardly keep conscious. Determinedly, he compressed his lips into a tight line. "Shoot."

"I want a son," she stated baldly, her eyes never leaving his face. "I want to get pregnant."

He gaped at her in amazement.

She set her chin at a firmer angle, as if daring him to

412

laugh or censor. "I may already be pregnant. You made love to me the other night. I was careful to lie very still afterward. I even put my legs up after you left. But I won't know for a few weeks whether or not it took. It might not take the first time."

"You're crazy," he stammered.

She smiled, a mirthless feline grin that showed her small, dingy teeth. "I've been accused of that before. I don't believe it."

"Only a crazy woman would . . ."

Leaning over the bed, she slapped him hard across the mouth. When he lunged for her, his right hand was jerked suddenly back. "What the hell . . . ?"

Laughing richly, she rose from the bed and stepped back out of his reach. A Colt .22 pistol emerged from the pocket of her black skirt. "Lie back down," she ordered.

"Damn you! What the hell have you done?" He rolled halfway over to stare down the side of the bed at his wrist. His own handcuff encircled it. The other cuff was clasped around the iron rail of the bed.

Aghast, he rolled back over to meet her triumphant expression. Knowing the motion was futile, he nevertheless fumbled with his left hand. His holster was empty. She waited until he slid back on the bed, his face contorted with pain.

Smiling maliciously, she slipped the pistol back into her pocket. "Now you just lie there and listen," she commanded. "I've got quite a story to tell you, and I want you to understand."

Face bathed in perspiration, he sank back on the pillow. His muscles flexed and strained from wrist to shoulder, testing the cuffs. He knew them to be chilled steel, but the bed might give. He flexed and pulled again, grimacing with the effort.

She flew at him and slapped him harder. "Look at me!"

413

The blow rolled his head on the pillow. Red fingermarks appeared on his cheek. His eyes blazed angrily.

She laughed and struck him again. "You look so furious. I thought I'd really give you something to be mad about."

He whipped his left arm up to try to wrestle her to the bed, but she eluded him again with a triumphant laugh. "You might as well relax. You can't get loose. The key's hidden in the desk in my office. And if you keep waving that left arm around, I'll call in someone to tie your other arm to the bed."

"Does Luke Garner know what you're up to?"

She shook her head proudly. "No. I'm making this on my own. That old son-of-a-bitch is just about through around here."

She looked narrowly at Chris as if to gauge his reaction. When he said nothing, she moved closer. "I'm going to sit down here on the side of the bed," she told him. "But before I do, you're going to put that left arm under the covers. If you try to make a grab for me, I promise I'll go for your side with every bit of strength that I've got. I don't guess you could take much of that without passing right out."

She waited while he slipped his arm under the covers with obvious reluctance. Then, fairly beaming with heady triumph, she seated herself. "Now," she began, placing her hand proprietarily on his chest. If she felt him stiffen, she gave no sign. "I don't appreciate the fact that you left with that sluttish sister-in-law of mine. But I forgive you. Actually, you did me a favor, helping her get away."

"Then give me my son and let me go. . . ."

She put her hand over his mouth. "Now you just listen to me. You're not to say anything." When she felt his lips close beneath her palm, she smiled. "You've got a nice body." She ran her hand over the hard muscles of his right shoulder, then down under his armpit and along his ribs.

Her eyes never left his face. "A nice body."

He stared at her. His skin crawled as he felt the heat in her hands through his shirt. He had never thought much about how a woman must feel when unwelcome hands intruded over her body. Now one part of his mind recognized the revulsion Star must have felt at having to submit.

Maude's right hand joined her left in running down the side of his arm before moving over to unbutton his shirt. Her fingers raked through the hair on his chest on their way to the flat male nipples. Her pale gray eyes studied his face avidly as she pinched the sensitive flesh.

He scarcely felt the pain in his body, but in his mind the humiliation was terrible. He lay as if on a bed of nails, his body throbbing with wounds and trembling with exhaustion, his mind frantic with worry about his son. Uncaring and oblivious, this bitch was trying to arouse him sexually. He would have laughed had he not been so angry and helpless.

"I was always the sister, the girl," Maude murmured, her own eyes glassy as she continued to stroke and pinch his shrinking flesh.

Looking up into her rapt face, he struggled to keep from yelling and cursing her.

Her left hand slid down his undamaged side to fondle his right hip and slip across his body to the bottom of his belly. Beneath the rough, stained denim, his manhood lay soft and vulnerable.

"Matt got everything. He was a boy. He was going to turn into such a big man. Until he broke his leg. After that he wasn't perfect anymore. He didn't get so much after that." She chuckled softly. Her hand gathered the spare skin around Chris's nipple and pinched it harder, twisting it unconsciously, as if she remembered childhood torments.

"He needed me. He loved me. Me. His sister. Then Star came along and nothing was every the same again." She looked down at the man whose body she had beneath her hands. "I loved him so much," she whispered. Tears streamed down her face. "I loved him so much. I cried so hard the night he died."

"I love my son the way you loved your brother," Chris told her.

She shook her head. "No one loved anyone the way I loved my brother. The only way I can have him back again is if I have a son. We were twins, you know. We spent the first nine months of our lives locked together. We should never have been separated." She raked her claws across his chest like a furious cat.

Chris winced. Desperately he tugged on the handcuffs. The bed shook.

Instantly she came back to the present. "Stop that!" She slapped him hard, rocking his head on the pillow.

His temper erupted. His left hand snaked from under the covers, grabbing for her throat, choking off her fearful shriek. She clutched at his wrist with both hands. For a minute his superior strength defeated her. Then her face flushed red with anger. Clasping her hands together in one big fist, she brought it down in a short, hard chop against his wounded hip.

The intense pain wrung a hoarse cry from his throat. Still he did not relinquish his grip until she had hit him again.

With a snarl of anger she tore herself free from his failing grasp and backed across the room. "You'll be sorry you tried that," she spat. "You'll be sorry, and your precious son will, too."

He struggled up, his face white as parchment. Perspiration dripped down his face. Blood welled from his wound and stained the fresh bandage Emilia had wrapped around him. "You touch Duff and I'll kill you. Woman or not. I swear to God I'll kill you."

She pulled open the door. "You'll do what I tell you to do

if you both ever expect to leave here." With that she slammed the door behind her. He heard the key turn in the lock.

She stormed into her office and slammed its door for good measure. Her eyes lit on the tear-streaked face of the little boy cowering on the floor in the corner. "Come here!"

He pressed back against the wall and shook his head.

"Come here, damn you!"

He hid his face in his hands.

Maude swooped across the office and caught hold of the boy's wrist, dragging him out of the corner and slapping him hard across the side of the face. "When I say come here, you do what I say and make it snappy."

He did not shriek as she had expected him to. Instead, he clawed at the hand that encircled his wrist and kicked at her shins. "Don't have to!" he yelled. "Don't have to! You're not my daddy. You're not Aunt Neill. I don't have to do what you say."

"Why you . . . !" She slapped at him again, but he ducked under her hand and sank his teeth into her wrist.

With a curse she let him go to grab the bruised skin. Duff ducked around her and darted for the door.

"Come back here, damn you!"

His small boots had thudded only a few steps down the hall before she heard a squeal of pain and fear.

"Where you think you're goin', brat?"

She had straightened and smoothed out her expression when Hatch appeared in the doorway carrying the struggling, squirming Duff. "Lose something?" he mocked.

"Hatch!" she exclaimed, her eyes taking in the cut in his eyebrow, the bruise on his jaw. "Where's Luke?"

The man shrugged, squeezing Duff's body until the little boy stopped squirming and hung panting in his captor's grasp. "Ran into a bunch of your sister-in-law's folks on the trail. They was right upset and we was outnumbered, so I didn't hang around to find out what they decided to do."

"W-was there a fight?"

The corners of his mouth quirked up in a mirthless grin. "If you mean did they kill him, sorry to disappoint you. They was still talking when I left."

Maude made no comment. Dropping her eyes, she sat down behind the desk.

Hatch chuckled briefly. "What y' want me to do with this?" He swung Duff's body forward so the boy's legs swung like a doll's.

Maude's mouth curled in distaste. Rising, she came around the desk and caught hold of the little boy's ear. "You," she shrilled, "are going to sit down in that corner over there and not make a sound. Hear me?"

Hatch punctuated Maude's speech with a rib-cracking squeeze.

Duff squeaked weakly and nodded.

"If you move," she threatened. "I'll have Hatch take you out and stake you to an anthill."

Almost out of breath, his heart pounding wildly inside his punished rib cage, Duff could barely nod.

Maude smiled coldly. "Put him down, Hatch."

Callously, the foreman dropped the child. Duff fell on his side, rolled over, and scuttled to the chair. The foreman dusted his hands. "Don't send him to the corner. Send him out."

"He's going to stay right there."

"Send him out." His voice rose angrily.

Their stares locked. Then she dropped her eyes and stepped to the door. "Emilia!" she called. "Come and get this kid." She turned back to Duff. "Run down the hall to meet Emilia."

He needed no urging. Scrambling to his feet, he skirted Hatch's tall, imposing figure and tore out of the door, past Maude.

Hatch motioned to Maude. "Come here."

"I've nothing to say to you."

A frown pulled his eyebrows together. "Come here," he repeated gruffly.

She tried to edge by him and put the desk between them, but he cut her off. His hands closed round her elbows, tighening painfully. "Where's Gillard?"

"I don't know," she lied.

Hatch's smile became murderous. "I think you do." He pulled her tightly against his body crushing her breasts against his chest.

"Hatch, you're hurting!"

"Yeah. And you love it. If I wanted a straight answer out of you, I'd do better to treat you soft." His mouth came down hard on hers, punishing her, driving his tongue in between her lips. He shifted his grip to latch one arm around her waist and bend her back.

She struggled to free her hand, but it was trapped at her side. She tried to turn her head away, but his mouth held her captive. She champed her teeth viciously on his thrusting tongue.

He jerked away, clapping a hand to his mouth, cursing.

She darted behind the desk. "Stay away from me."

Hatch touched his fingertips to his tongue, looked at the pinkish stain on them, then grinned wolfishly. "You don't mean that, Maudie. You can't get what you get from me with anybody else."

She pulled the .22 from her pocket. "Yes, I can, Hatch. I can get more than what I get from you. I can get a baby."

Her words brought him up short. "What the hell're you talkin' about?"

She leveled the pistol at him. "I want a son," she admitted. "I want a boy to pass on the Tres Santos to when I'm gone."

He shifted his weight to the balls of his feet, his eyes

419

craftily appraising her. Her .22 popgun couldn't stop him. It would hardly slow him down, but he didn't want to get shot. A woman with a pistol in her hand was dangerous. Nobody could tell what she would do, because she didn't know herself. Purposely, he kept his voice low and gentle. "You don't need that pistol, Maudie."

"Don't try to get round me, Hatch. I'm through with you."

He held his hands up. "If you say so, gal, but you're makin' a mistake."

"No. I want a boy," she insisted stubbornly.

He extended one hand toward her, palm up. "Is that what you had me take that kid for?"

She shook her head. "No. I want a son of my own."

He grinned. "No problem, Maudie. I'll marry you if you want."

She took a firmer grasp on the pistol. "You'd marry me?"

"Sure thing. Send for the preacher."

A frown creased her forehead. "How do I know you could get me pregnant?"

He stopped. Despite himself, he was shocked. No woman had ever talked to him in such a frank way before. No female professing to be a lady had ever used such a word in his presence. "Now Maudie . . ."

"You don't think I want to get married because I need a man, do you?" she mocked.

He lowered his hands. "You can have both, Maudie. All legal and proper. Hell, I'll even get dressed up for you in suits like Luke wears."

At the mention of her father, her face darkened. "He says I can't get any man to marry me. It would almost be worth getting married to see the expression on his face."

"Yeah, it sure would." Hatch chuckled dryly as he edged closer to the desk. "We could go do it right now before he

420

gets back. Hell, the way he was arguing with those people, he may not be back before tomorrow. We could get you fixed up tonight." He grinned widely.

Suddenly, she noticed his movements. "No . . . !"

He dived under her hand. The .22 went off like a firecracker in the closed room, its bullet singing harmlessly over his back and shattering the chimney of a lamp in a bracket on the wall.

"Drop it, Maudie," he growled. One hand grasped her waist; the other closed round her wrist and pointed the pistol toward the ceiling.

She clawed and scratched at him, but his grasp was torturous. He twisted her body and dragged it across the desk and into his arms. The pistol thudded to the floor. Lying across his thighs, she stared up into his angry face.

He stared down at her, gloating over her fear. "Now." His voice had deepened. "You're gonna do just what I tell you."

She struck at him with her free left hand.

He caught it and twisted it behind her. At the same time, he brought her other arm down and locked both wrists together with his right hand.

Panting and groaning, she struggled furiously, but his strength completely dominated her. "I'll kill you," she promised.

For answer, his free hand tore open her blouse and ripped her camisole down to her waist.

"Hatch," she moaned.

"Yeah, Maudie," he grinned. His hot mouth came down open on her neck as she arched away from him. His teeth nipped the skin, then, his lips pressed against her flesh, he sucked—hard. The blood rose to the skin. He sucked harder as she moaned and twisted futilely. He moved on, leaving a throbbing bruise behind him.

At her breast, his teeth found the aureole swollen, the nipple hard.

"Don't, Hatch . . . ah . . . !"

He bit her cruelly, intending to draw blood. At the same time his hand clenched on her other breast. His fingernails scratched at the peak. The hand beneath her body pushed her wrists farther up her back, arching her higher to receive his punishment.

She twisted and writhed, the pain arousing her despite her protests, which quickly turned to sobs of anguish.

Gradually, her struggles ceased, and her legs dangled limply off the desk.

He drew off her. "Learned your lesson, Maudie?"

Her head fell back over his thighs, her eyelids slitted. "I'll kill you," she promised flatly.

He chucked. "Still makin' mistakes, huh? Still sayin' the wrong things. I'm glad. I'm gonna love teaching you after we're married. I can spend hours at it." Abruptly, his hand released her wrists.

She shuddered. Though she was suddenly free, she was unable to move.

"Put your arms around me."

She hesitated.

He chuckled her under the chin. "Come on, gal, and I'll give you what you want." The hand that had been around her waist pulled her skirt up and kneaded her thigh through her drawers.

She sucked in her breath. Little by little she managed to unwind her twisted arms and lift them trembling to lie across his shoulders.

He smiled. "That's right, gal. That's more like it." He kissed her then, long and slowly, drinking from her mouth. One hand kneaded her breast, while the other pulled the cotton undergarments down and plucked at the hair at the bottom of her belly.

Her sobbing breaths changed in tone. Instead of pain-wracked they became importunate. Her hands curved around the back of his neck.

"Hot for it, ain't you?" he breathed against her throat, his mouth finding the spot where he had bruised her and kissing it.

She sobbed as his fingers slid into the wet darkness of her body. "Hatch," she moaned. "Oh, Hatch."

"Yeah, gal!"

He pulled his fingers out, feeling the soft folds of her flesh squeezing at him, begging him to stay, trying to keep him inside her.

"Now, are you gonna send for that preacher," he demanded, "or do I have to turn you over and spank you until you're bright red?"

"Hatch," she begged, lifting her hips to him. "Yes, Hatch."

Chapter Twenty-seven

"Wait, Estrellita. He's a Texas Ranger." Tomas de Montejo laid his hand on the cantle of Star's saddle and whispered in her ear.

Both hands braced on the saddle horn, she nodded curtly. "I can see the star." Despairing weariness settled over her. She felt like screaming and tearing her hair. Would she ever come to a time when she would not be called upon to defend her innocence? Would a U.S. marshal materialize next in the trail?

"He won't put you in jail," Johanna asserted positively. "We won't let him." She guided the blue roan ahead to meet the ranger, who had turned his horse across the roadway.

Star raised her eyes to the Tres Santos, high and imposing at the end of the road. Her jaw set sternly. She could not allow anyone to detain her. Chris was wounded up there. He and Duff needed her badly. She knew it.

Luke Garner spurred his mount alongside her. "Looks

like you'd better change yore mind fast about marryin' me," he muttered. "Otherwise, I'm gonna let this lawman know just who and what y' are."

Tomas moved El Espectro around behind Garner. The muzzle of his revolver suddenly poked the rancher in the spine. "You will not get the first words out, Señor Garner."

"Now hold on. . . ."

"Put your hands down and smile."

The Texas Ranger stared quizzically over Johanna's shoulder at the large group of men. "Howdy, ma'am." Tipping his hat politely, he waited for her to speak.

While Johanna hesitated, not knowing exactly what to ask without betraying her sister, Luke acted. "Help!" he yelled. At the same time he pulled savagely on his horse's head. The animal crashed sideways into Humareda. The mare was much lighter and smaller than Luke's heavy gelding. She neighed fearfully and went down on her haunches.

"Estrellita!" Tomas made a grab for his sister to keep her from being crushed should the horse be unable to regain its footing.

Luke jerked the gelding's head back around and spurred it toward the ranger. "Arrest 'em!" he yelled. "They're tryin' to kill me."

The ranger drew his gun but held his fire. Luke sawed back on the horse's reins, setting it back on its haunches. "Arrest 'em all," he repeated.

The ranger surveyed him without particular alarm. "What for?"

"Kidnappin' and attempted murder." Luke pointed an accusing finger back at Tomas. "He jus' poked a gun in my back and told me he'd kill me if I said a word to you."

The ranger looked at Tomas, who had climbed down off his horse and was running his hands over Humareda's

425

trembling body. Star leaned anxiously over the saddlebow to pat her horse's neck.

"So you crashed into the lady to get away?" the lawman observed drily. "Don't seem like a gentlemanly thing to do. He could've emptied his six-shooter in your back while you was pulling that horse around. What's your name?"

Luke spluttered angrily in the face of the lawman's calm. Then he recovered himself. "My name's Luke Garner," he gritted. "I own the Tres Santos ranch. That's the biggest spread in this area, mister. That woman there is a Mex from south of the Rio Grande. She's his sister. She's in cahoots with him. They're killers. Arrest them." His anger was making him incoherent.

"Who'd they kill?"

Luke's jaw set pugnaciously. Throwing a triumphant look at Johanna Sandoval, he leaned forward in the saddle. "That there's Star Montejo from Saltillo, Mexico. She killed my son, Matthew Garner."

The ranger did not seem impressed. He sized up the brother and sister as they rode up to the group at last. "You mean that little woman that you run over with your horse killed your son?"

"That's right. She shot him and broke jail. I hired a bounty hunter named Gillard to bring her back, but she bribed him to help her get away. She was gonna kill me this time. I want 'em both arrested."

"Gillard?" The ranger slid his gun back into the holster. "Gillard, did you say?"

Luke hesitated fractionally. "That what he called himself."

"Tall fella, yellow hair, gray eyes, 'bout twenty-five years old."

Luke began to grin. "Is he wanted somewhere?"

"Not exactly."

426

Luke waited, his grin slipping, but the ranger did not elaborate. Luke thrust out his jaw. "Well, what exactly?"

The ranger tipped his hat back on his head. A shock of grizzled brown hair sprang up in front of the brim. 'Well, to tell the truth, I ain't exactly certain. All I know is that Jim Hogg got a message from Mrs. Mercedes MacPherson over by Goliad that her grandkid Christopher Gillard needed help in Crossways. So Jim got ahold of me and Coll Davis and sent us over here *muy pronto*. When Mrs. MacPherson says *muy pronto*, she don't mean any time you feel like it. Jim Hogg was mighty positive about that."

Johanna raised her eyebrows in Star's direction. "Your young man's grandmother told the attorney general of Texas to send a ranger and a lawyer to Crossways."

A faint blush rose in Star's cheeks. "He's not my young man exactly. But he did say that he had taken care of everything. I thought he was just saying that to keep me from being discouraged."

Johanna shook her head. "What were Mr. Hogg's orders other than to get over here *muy pronto*, Mr. . . . ?"

"Josiah Amberson, ma'am. Call me Josey." The ranger tipped his hat and replaced it in its proper position. "Well, we're out here to get to the bottom of whatever Gillard was having trouble with."

Luke Garner bristled visibly, but the ranger continued unperturbed.

"Sheriff didn't seem to want to be too cooperative, but Coll thought he'd stay in Crossways and ask around. I rode out here to see you, Mr. Garner, as a matter of fact, to get your information. Since Mrs. MacPherson's grandkid worked for you last, maybe you can give me some ideas about what we're supposed to straighten out." The ranger's mouth shaped a pleasant enough smile, but his eyes were watchful.

427

Suddenly, Luke was aware of hostile faces surrounding him. He shot a rueful glance at Tres Santos, silhouetted by the western sun. "Damned if I know," he muttered.

Star's hands were damp with perspiration. Heat suffused her body and her heartbeat increased. If she were going to make a play, now was the time to begin. Johanna and Tomas would back her. She cleared her throat, which had gone suddenly dry. "Christopher Gillard was wounded this morning. He's ridden to Tres Santos." She indicated the fort with a wave of her hand. "Luke Garner told Chris that his son Duff was at Tres Santos."

The ranger eyed Luke Garner narrowly. His question went to the heart of the matter. "What's the MacPhersons' great-grandson doing at Tres Santos?"

Luke whipped off his hat and ran his sleeve across his forehead. The whole thing was getting a little bit complicated, and some of it stank to high heaven. One thing remained clear, however. "That ain't important. A crime's been committed here and she's the one that done it." He swept his hat in the direction of Star. "She murdered my son. We was gonna hang her legal and proper. Then she broke jail and escaped to Mexico. Now I want her arrested again."

The ranger looked from one to the other, uncertain what to do. The man looked and talked like the Texas ranchers he was used to dealing with. At the same time he did find his story that this little dark woman had murdered anyone hard to swallow. Clearly, the dark man was her brother, and they appeared to be Mexican. His eyes swept over the men, some dozen or so riders. Several of them were Mexicans; others were hard-eyed Texas cowboys, who watched the blue-eyed woman as if waiting for a sign to move.

Johanna Sandoval smiled thinly. "Why don't we all ride up to Tres Santos together, Josey, and see what Mr. Gillard

428

has to say about all this?"

Luke's mouth dropped open. The suggestion had been his thought. A feeling of triumph welled in him. Here he was outnumbered. There he would be able to tell this Texas Ranger a thing or two. "Sounds like a good idee to me," he agreed.

"Lead the way then, Mr. Garner." The ranger pulled his horse aside for Luke to pass.

As the horses began the ascent, Star noticed the gate to the outer wall was closed. Intuition sent a frisson trailing down her spine. She stared hard at the sun-bleached wall throwing a long afternoon shadow out in front of it. Above it the house loomed, with its parapets at each end and the cedar gate with pickets no Indian could climb over.

The Texas ranger stared at the structure. "That's some sight," he mused. "I don't guess I've ever seen anything like it."

"It's the only one there is," Luke declared, pride unmistakable in his voice. "When I came here, warn't nothin' but varmints and Indians. Apaches on one side and Comanches on the other. If I was gonna make it, I had to have a place to make a stand."

"Looks like nobody could get into it."

"Nobody ever did."

When they were fifty yards down the slope from the lower wall, the gate swung open wide enough to emit a man. Maude stepped out, accompanied by Hatch, a white bandage tied around his forehead. He held a rifle in the crook of his arm.

Luke rode to the fore and raised his arm. "Open 'er up, Maudie," he called. "I'm bringin' home a bunch fer supper."

She put her hands on her hips. "No, you're not! You're not bringin' that slut back onto this ranch," she yelled back.

Luke pulled his mount to a halt to stare at his daughter. His affable expression turned ugly. "Don't gimme none of your lip, daughter. Just open that gate."

"No. She's not comin' back here. I've got the whole thing taken care of."

Luke was suddenly very tired. His back ached from too many hours in the saddle. He wanted a drink and a hot meal and a warm bed to lie in. "Get the hell outa the way," he snarled, waving his arm. "Hatch, open the damned gate."

To Star the motion of the arm seemed slower than usual, just as the motion of Maude as she pulled the rifle from Hatch's arm seemed incredibly slow. Josiah Amberson raised his left hand to call a halt to the party. In what seemed a rhythmic extension of that motion, his right hand swooped down for his Colt .45. Johanna Sandoval made a sweeping motion with her arm. Tomas ducked low at his older sister's unspoken command and wheeled his horse in front of Star. They all seemed to her like people moving through water, every limb gliding with torturous slowness.

And then the rifle blasted her eardrums.

Luke Garner gave a grunt; his huge bulk rocked in the saddle. The ranger's answering shot spanged the wood to the right of Hatch's shoulder as the foreman pushed the girl inside the gate.

The gelding turned halfway around as Luke's arm jerked reflexively on the reins. Star saw his heavy face, gone yellowish-white, a mixture of anger and surprise. On the right side of his vest, low down, blood spread in a bright red circle.

He did not look toward the people he rode with. His eyes

never left the walls before him. Then he jerked the gelding's head back around and sank his spurs into its flanks. A yell of fury broke from his lips. The big horse sprang forward, heading directly up the slope for the gate.

Several men's heads appeared over the wall, their rifles trained on the figure. None of them fired. Luke's long yell, fierce as any Comanche's, wafted fearsomely back on the heads of the people behind him. How much more fearsomely it rang in the ears of the men who saw their boss bent on revenge, spurring his mount toward them.!

Twenty-five yards away from the gate, then twenty. The gelding never slackened stride.

His rifle resting on the wall beside the archway to the gate, Hatch stared mesmerized at the madman who rode toward them at full gallop.

"Goddamn," the man beside him breathed. "The boss'll kill us all fer this."

"Give me that rifle!" Maude screeched, trying to wrest it from Hatch's hands. "Don't let him in. Shoot him."

Hatch lofted the rifle above his head with one hand. With the other he grasped her shoulder. Not for anything would he let her have it. "Get hold of yourself!" he cried.

"He ain't slowin'!"

"Goddamn! He's gonna try for the wall."

The gelding was big, fully sixteen hands, and game. It tucked its forelegs neatly under itself and cleared the wall with its withers. But the height plus the uphill slope was too high for it.

Perhaps Luke's weakness made him bobble, perhaps his weight was in itself too much. The horse's barrel scraped the adobe, the stifle caught. For an instant the horse hung there helpless, squealing in pain and fear, stuck as if a child had placed it astraddle a toy fence.

Cursing viciously, Luke Garner rose from its back and

staggered along the adobe wall toward the archway. Drawing his gun, he took aim at the terrified pair.

Maude screamed and slashed at Hatch's face with her fingernails. "Shoot him. Shoot him! For God's sake, give me the gun!" Almost paralyzed with horror, the foreman stared up into Luke's contorted face. He could see Luke thumbing the hammer back.

At that moment the gelding scrambled sideways, dragging its hindlegs behind it. When its forelegs touched the ground, it began frantically to pull itself forward. One flailing leg swept Luke's feet from under him.

In breathless horror the onlookers saw the big man tumble from sight inside the wall.

"Take cover!" the ranger yelled, not a moment too soon.

As if a spell were broken, Hatch gave the only order he could think of to keep the horsemen outside from entering the fort. His voice broke as it yelled the command. "Fire!"

The men of Tres Santos did not think. Nerves strained to the breaking point, loyalties divided and redivided, they obeyed because they dared not do otherwise. They fired, each determined in his own mind not to shoot to kill. Comanches or Apaches they would have gunned down mercilessly. If only *vaqueros* from Rancho Montejo had been before them, they would not have hesitated. But fellow Texans, two of them women, were another matter entirely. Bullets spanged harmlessly off into the graying sky.

Maude flung herself at the wall, staring over the top of it at the retreating horsemen. "Goddamn it!" she yelled frantically. "Aim, you bastards!"

The ranger's command to take cover immediately proved impossible. Josey himself, whirling his horse around, could see nothing to take cover behind or under. The ground was stripped clean of everything except the lowest grass and cactus. Not a single tree nor clump of sage provided the slightest protection. Luke Garner had planned his fort well. No Comanche could crawl up the slope on his belly.

Unhurt, the riders galloped back down the hill out of rifle range.

"Sangre de Christo!" Tomas exclaimed when at last he pulled El Espectro to a halt. "What happened back there?"

"I think Luke Garner was as surprised as anyone," Star said quietly. "His own daughter shot him."

"But why?" This from the ranger. "Hell, I never seen nor heard tell of anything like that. I couldn't make head nor tails out of what they was saying. You sure that was Luke Garner, the boss of Tres Santos?"

"I'm sure."

Johanna shook her head. "I think we're better off out of this, baby sister. These people are crazy."

Star closed her eyes, tempted out of all reason to follow Johanna's suggestion. Vaguely she realized she was tired to death. Her ribs ached naggingly, but she had been so long with the pain of them that she no longer allowed it to intrude upon her. She was hungry, too. How long had she been riding without stopping for a meal?

Tomas came up on the other side to put his arm around her and draw her close. "Let us go, *hermanita mia*. We can do nothing more. Those people up there. They are not our problem. You come now with Johanna and me. The three of us will go together into town and spend the night. I don't know for sure, but I think that nobody is going to come out of Tres Santos looking for you anymore."

"Luke Garner had a bullet in him before he fell off that wall," Johanna added. "Looks like he's got problems more urgent than making your life miserable."

Star looked at Josey Amberson. The ranger shrugged amiably. "I don't have no warrant for your arrest, ma'am.

433

Fact is, the sheriff in town was babbling away, scared like, 'bout how he didn't have nothin' to do with mistreatin' you. He kept insistin' that he was just actin' under orders."

"Then let us go," Tomas urged.

She shook her head. In the midst of all her friends and family, she sat alone and felt Chris's arms around her. In the darkness and warmth of the cave he had held her safe from her own fears and filled her with such sweetness that she had hated to leave. Deaf to the pleas of her sister and brother, she heard only his voice saying, *The next time we make love, it's going to be in the blaze of noon.*

"I have to go," she said flatly.

"Go? Where?"

"Oh, no, baby sister."

"I have to, Johanna. Please try to understand. He came for me. He and his son are up there. He's wounded. I have to go for him."

"This is the man who put you in danger in the first place," Tomas protested bitterly.

"I know, but he realized he had made a mistake and he tried to rectify it. I can't leave him there to be killed."

"You don't know he'll be killed," Johanna pointed out reasonably. "Now that they know he's got the law on his side, they won't dare harm him. They'll probably be deciding to let him go any minute now."

"I don't think anyone up there is capable of making a rational decision at this moment."

Johanna shrugged. "Surely someone is in authority . . . the foreman, maybe?"

"What do you think?" Star asked the ranger.

Josey shrugged. "Worth a try to ask. They might just let him come out. Y'all could take him back to town and then telegraph for help. I don't know what this is all about, but a man was shot tryin' to ride into his own ranch tonight. I can't give this the go-by and ride on."

"It'll be dark soon," Johanna observed. "We aren't really prepared to spend the night out. We don't have enough food."

"I'll try to talk to them," Josey agreed. "If I can't get anything out of them, then I'll take it kindly if you'd contact Coll Davis and tell him to get himself out here pronto, just as soon as he wires for help."

"Be glad to," Johanna promised.

Josey pulled a white handkerchief from his pocket and tied the end of it around his rifle stock. "I'm hopin' they'll know what this flag's all about," he told them grimly. "But in case they don't, I can drop it shootin'."

"Be careful."

"Sure do intend to be, ma'am. What's the little boy's name?"

"Duff Gillard. He's five."

"Tough. Some people are just too mean to live. Sometimes, like right now, this job gets downright dangerous." The ranger tugged his hat down tighter over his eyes and rode slowly up the trail.

Behind the wall, the men of Tres Santos gathered around Luke's body.

"He's out cold."

"Looks like he hit his head fallin' down the wall. Leastways there's a pumpknot on it."

"He's bleedin' pretty bad."

The foreman went down on one knee beside Luke's body. The heartbeat beneath the vest was strong but erratic. Although blood covered the front of his shirt, his color was good. Hatch stared up into the faces of the men. They were watching him closely. "He'll come to in a few minutes," he said neutrally.

"Hey, Hatch, one of 'em's ridin' up with a flag of truce."

The foreman sprang to the wall. He blinked and rubbed his eyes, then cursed vividly. The last rays of the setting sun, shining between the parapets of Tres Santos, reflected off the lone star on the man's shirt.

"Goddamn," he moaned softly. "Oh, Goddamn."

Wheeling round on Maude, he caught her and shook her hard. Her eyes were glassy as she stared down at Luke's body, the blood trickling over his belly into the dust. "Do you see what you've done?" he shouted.

"Is he dead?"

"Near enough."

"He has to be dead," she insisted. "You're committed now. We don't dare leave him alive."

"That's a Texas Ranger down there."

Her face went white. "How? Who?" She leaned against the wall, her eyes drawn to the star.

Then she looked up pathetically at Hatch. "I didn't know there was a Texas Ranger with him. Where did he come from? Luke's never brought a Texas Ranger home to supper."

"We'll say we made a mistake, mistook him for someone else."

"My own father?"

"Hey! Hello!"

Maude turned to the wall. "Go away!" she yelled. "Get the hell out of here."

The ranger rode a little bit nearer. "Ma'am, I'm here to talk to Christopher Gillard and his little boy Duff. I understand Mr. Gillard is wounded up there."

"He's not here." Maude shot back.

"Beggin' your pardon, ma'am, but Luke Garner told us all . . ." He indicated the group of horsemen waiting out of rifle range.

"He's not here!" she screamed.

"Maude! Hold on a minute." Hatch caught hold of her arm. "What're you lookin' for him for?"

The ranger allowed him a small smile. "His grandmother sent to the attorney general of the state to get him."

"The attorney general." Hatch turned to Maude. "We'd better think this over."

"Not a chance." She leaned over the wall. "Get the hell off this land!" she yelled. "You're trespassing."

The ranger did not move. "Is your father all right, ma'am? He did invite us in. I saw he was shot. Probably a mistake, but we need to come on in and talk to Mr. Gillard. . . ."

"No-o-o-o!"

"For God's sake, Maude . . ." Hatch began.

"You let go of me," she stormed. Her face purple with rage, she turned on the men. "I'm paying your wages. I'm telling you what to do."

They shuffled back, eyes averted.

"Don't be a fool. You can't keep out a Texas Ranger. I'm opening this gate." Hatch turned on his heel. "You cool down and we'll talk. Find out what this is. . . ."

"The hell you will!" Maude jerked a pistol from a holster of one of the men. In one smooth motion she cocked it and pulled the trigger. The slug tore into the center of Hatch's back, slamming him against the gate. At first he thought she had hit him in the back with a rock. Then his eyes widened as blood and pieces of his lung spattered the pale adobe. His hand reached out toward the stain. The contrast of red and light was the last thing he ever saw.

Dropping his flag of truce to aim his rifle, Josey Amberson watched the gate swing slowly open. The man's body collapsed against it and slid down to lie in a crumpled heap

437

that acted as a stop to keep the gate open.

Through the archway, the ranger could see the woman called Maude swing up on her horse and gallop up the precipitous trail to the house. The cedar gate opened to admit her and closed behind her.

For a minute he waited. Then another man appeared in the opening with his hands raised. "Come on in," he called.

"Throw them guns over the wall first and come out where I can see you." While he watched to see that his orders were carried out, he waved the onlookers forward. When they came abreast, he spoke to Star and Johanna. "Maybe you ladies better wait here. It most likely won't be pretty."

Chapter Twenty-eight

"Nobody comes through that gate!" Maude screamed as she galloped in under the arch. "Close it and keep it closed. They've killed Hatch and wounded my father."

"Pero, señorita . . ." The gatekeeper caught her bridle.

"I mean it. Nobody."

He looked doubtfully up at her contorted face. Her sallow skin was underlaid with a sickly gray.

Swinging down off the horse and snatching off her hat, she whirled on the gatekeeper. "What are you staring at?"

He dropped his eyes instantly and led the animal away.

Maude whirled around in the courtyard. On every side of her the windows stared blankly. Her thoughts swung dizzily from fear and guilt to triumph. No one appeared to accuse her. No one dared.

She dashed into the house, slamming the heavy front door behind her. She had escaped them all. Luke would never hit her again. He would never tell her what to do. She was her own mistress. No one could tell her what to do. Striding to the buffet, she poured herself a glass of whiskey and drank it down. The first swallow strangled and burned her, but she drank another with tears spouting from her eyes. No one could tell her not to.

Glass in hand, she tried to think of her next move. She must leave nothing to chance. In Luke's office she could find proof of ownership. Panting with excitement, she ran into his dark sanctum and tore open the bottom drawer of his desk.

Once he had shown her and Matthew the contents of this drawer. The metal box containing the cash and gold, the Colt .45 kept carefully cleaned and loaded, and the leather envelope containing the land grant to Tres Santos. He had taken the parchment out and read it word for word to Matthew while she, Maude, had been grudgingly allowed to listen.

Now she seized triumphantly upon the precious packet. With a hoarse cry torn from the depth of her throat, she unbuckled the leather strap and thrust the papers into the waistband of her skirt. The grant belonged to her now. It all belonged to her.

Throwing herself backward into Luke's leather chair, she took another swallow of whiskey and laughed aloud. She was the mistress of Tres Santos. No one could dispute her title. No one. The ranch, the cattle, the horses. Everything belonged to her.

And she would have a son. She might even have several children. She rolled the glass between her palms, her eyes alight with the prospect. Chris would come to love her eventually. She would be like a mother to Duff. They would both admire and respect her.

Josey and Tomas worked over Luke Garner. Finally, the rancher stirred feebly, his eyes opened and then closed tightly against the pain. "Damn . . . fool . . ." he whispered.

"Just lie still," Josey advised him.

Luke groaned as Tomas pressed a pad against the wound. "Gi . . . me . . . drink. . . ."

Johanna passed a canteen over the ranger's shoulder.

When Luke had taken a swallow he lay back, his face dripping with perspiration. "She shot . . . me," he groaned in a puzzled voice. "Hell of a thing . . ."

"She killed the foreman, boss," one of the Tres Santos men volunteered. "Shot ol' Hatch right through the back just as he was openin' the gate for the ranger."

Luke grunted. He shook his head slightly, despite the awful pain. ". . . crazy . . . don't make . . . no sense at all."

Silence greeted his musings.

His breathing became more labored. "Anybody got . . . any whiskey?"

His request set off a muttering among his men. Finally, one went to the gatehouse and dug out a jug from its hiding place. Pulling the corncob from the mouth, he held it for Luke to drink.

The raw liquor bit like a rattlesnake, but it brought a stain of color back to his cheeks. "How bad am I hit?"

The ranger shrugged diffidently. "Hard to say."

"That don't sound good. In the lung?"

"Lower."

"Hell." He took another noisy swig off the whiskey. His body seemed to shrink and cave in slightly.

Tomas rose. "Let's get Star out of here," he suggested to Johanna. "There's nothing more to be done."

"Star . . . ?" Luke stirred as if he had just remembered her. "Star . . ." he called peremptorily.

Johanna caught her arm. "You don't owe him a thing," she reminded her sister.

"I'm here, Luke," Star knelt beside him.

He looked past her. Suddenly one torch and then the other flamed into light on the parapets of Tres Santos. He sighed. "Don't that look fine?"

She twisted around to see. The flickering lights limned her profile.

"You're sure a looker," he commented before he took another drink.

Her face unsmiling, she turned back to him. "What did you want to speak to me for?"

He coughed as the whiskey hit the back of his throat, half strangling him. When he had recovered, he fumbled for the sleeve of her blouse. "Lean forward," he whispered. "You're too far away."

"Luke . . ." she protested.

He grimaced. "It ain't gonna hurt. I got a favor to ask."

She was conscious of the ranger, Johanna, and Tomas listening intently.

"I wanta give. . . ." He hesitated, patted the pocket of his vest, cursed mildly. "Check my pockets," he pleaded wearily.

Hating to touch him, yet hating to deny him, she patted them halfheartedly. "What am I looking for?"

"The key."

Even as he spoke, she found the long metal object in the watch pocket of his pants. Her stomach heaved as she drew it out sticky and warm from the blood-soaked material. "Here it is."

"Take it."

"What shall I do with it?"

He coughed again. "Go open . . . door in wall . . . at south corner."

"A way into Tres Santos!" she exclaimed.

"Yeah." He shifted slightly and groaned in pain.

"I can take it," the ranger offered.

"No," Luke whispered. "Belongs to . . . Star. Her house . . . soon. All hers . . ."

"Oh, no . . ."

"Sure . . ." He stared up at the leaping torches. "Go on . . . get th' gate open. I don't wan . . . die out here." He closed his eyes, his breath rasped agonizingly.

Star held the long key gingerly. Her first impulse was to

give it to the ranger, despite Luke's request. She almost put it in his waiting hand. Then she drew it back. "I guess I have to go," she said weakly. "It's a chance to find out what happened to Chris and Duff without anyone else getting killed."

"No!" Johanna and Tomas exclaimed together.

"You promised you'd back my play," Star reminding them.

"But, *hermanita* . . ." Tomas began.

Surprisingly, Johanna put her hand on his arm. "No, Tomas. She's right. We did promise. Of course, we did." Her eyes slitted as studied Star's determined face. At last she nodded. "And you have to do it, don't you, baby sister. You have to pay your debts."

His eyes going from one dark face to the other, the ranger felt compelled to intercede. "Miss Garner, I don't know nothin' about debts, but that woman in there's gone plumb crazy. You better let me go into town and get that useless excuse for a sheriff to issue a warrant."

"There's no time for that," Star replied positively. She tucked the key into the pocket of her blouse. "She shot Hatch in the back. He always did what she told him to do. I know Chris isn't going to do what she tells him to. And then there's Duff. Besides, you heard Luke," she reminded them softly. "He wants to . . . be inside."

Johanna calmly unbuckled the gunbelt from around her slender waist. "If you're going to do a job, you need the proper tools."

"For God's sake!" Tomas exploded. "You're both of you crazy."

"Would Mama have thought we were crazy?"

He stopped. Strong memories flooded their minds, special memories to each of the uncommon woman who had borne them. He shook his head sadly. "She'd have gone in the front door."

Star lifted her arms for Johanna to buckle the belt

around her hips. "I'm not the woman she was, but I can still get in."

The Texas Ranger scratched his head. "Never seen the beat of womenfolks fightin'. I tell you what I'll do. I'll go up and talk to the guard at the gate. Talk real loud with a torch in my hand. Everybody'll be watchin' me, includin' them fellas up there by the torches." He laughed softly. "Not that they can see anything anyway. Like lookin' out of a lighted room into a dark night."

Star kissed Tomas's cheek. "You are the best of brothers," she murmured. "I've never wanted for a thing. You've always given me everything."

"I can do this for you," he offered. "I really wish you'd let me."

But she shook her head. As she turned to go, her fingertips brushed down Johanna's arm. "Thanks, sister."

Johanna patted her shoulder. "Good luck . . ."

Star leaned her body into the side of the steep slope. Johanna's last word came to her faintly, like talisman. ". . . Diamondback."

Duff sobbed softly in the corner. Chris swayed where he stood in the middle of the office. Behind the desk, her hands clasped tightly in front of her, her cheeks flushed unnaturally, sat Maude.

Unable to meet his eyes, a Mexican had motioned him off the bed with a pistol and forced him to his knees. Pushing him over flat on his face, the man had unlocked the handcuff from the bed and relocked it around Chris's wrist. Then he had stood back cautiously while Chris climbed unsteadily to his feet.

Now Maude's laugh sounded unusually high-pitched and discordant. Her eyes fairly burned with a feverish light as they darted from his face to Duff and back again. His head ached from the beginnings of a fever. His side

444

throbbed maddeningly with each beat of his heart.

"I own the Tres Santos now," she began. She waved one arm wildly across the desk to indicate the boundless expanse of her domain. "Luke's gone. Matt's gone. It's . . . all . . . mine." Her voice rose as she separated each word with particular emphasis.

"Congratulations," Chris replied huskily. "You can let Duff and me go now. You don't need either one of us if the place is all yours."

Frowning, Maude gave her head a nervous shake. "Maybe you don't realize what that means? It means it's all mine. I can run it the way I've always wanted to."

"Good." Chris regarded her steadily, though pain was making the edges of his vision fuzzy.

Eyes glowing feverishly, she pressed her knuckles into the desktop and stood up. "I need a husband now more than ever. I need sons. I want you to be my husband." She came round the desk toward him. "You didn't realize how serious I was about this until now, did you?" She put her hands on his chest and slid her palms up over his shoulders to cup around the back of his neck.

Her weight threw Chris off balance a step, but she followed him, pressing her breasts against his chest.

"You know you want me," she murmured, her lips only inches from his mouth. "It was good the other night. You remember." Her fingernails clawed at his ribs, scratching the skin despite the heavy cotton shirt.

His eyes met Duff's over her head.

Suddenly remembering the little boy, she twisted half around. "Duff, wouldn't you like for me to be your new mama?"

Duff shook his head sharply. Trembling with fright and fatigue, he made a choked stifled sound deep in his throat.

Maude let go of Chris and strode across the office to Duff. Catching him by the shoulder, she shook him. "Your father should have taught you better manners. Tell him how

445

much you want me to be your mama."

Duff tucked his head lower. "Don't," he muttered shortly.

"Leave him alone," Chris cautioned, striving to keep his voice normal when anger was making him tug futilely at the handcuffs. "He doesn't understand what's happening."

She dragged the little boy up and tugged him across the office to stand in front of his father. Going down on one knee, she held Duff tightly by the shoulders at the same time she never took her eyes off Chris. "Then tell him," she grated. "Tell him right now. Make him understand."

When Chris hesitated, her fingernails dug into Duff's shoulders until he squirmed with pain. "Tell him."

"Duff . . ." Each word came out breathless with anger and acute frustration. "Do as she says. She's a lady. You know you're always supposed to be nice to ladies."

Duff looked angrily from his father to Maude, then capitulated with poor grace. "I'm sorry," he muttered. "I'd like to have you for my mama."

Immediately she released him and sprang up to confront Chris. "You see," she exclaimed, as Duff scuttled back out of reach. "We can be married immediately."

Chris drew a shallow, slow breath. "Let me loose and get the preacher, then."

She kissed him. Put her arms around his neck and pressed her body against him from breast to thigh. The kiss went on a long time. As she finished, she slid one hand down the front of his body. No hardened evidence of desire sprang up beneath her searching fingers.

Stepping back, she smiled coldly before turning on her heel to stroll back around the desk. "Oh, you'd like to be loose, but I don't trust you. You'd pick up Duff immediately and leave. Or I'd have to shoot you. No. I'll have to keep either you or Duff tied up tight until I get pregnant for sure. That could be several months." She frowned in the direction of the little boy. "I admit that's hard on him, but you must see what I'm driving at."

"No," he protested. "I don't. If I give you my word . . ."

"You'd break your word without a moment's thought. After all, what good is a word that's gotten with a gun at your head? No. You'd break that. But not to the woman who carries your child. You'd respect me and be obliged to take care of me. That's the way I'd hold on to you."

Chris's temper exploded. "Let me go! You're crazy if you think you can keep me pinned up like a stud for three months."

She shook her head at him. "I'm not crazy. That's where everybody makes the big mistake. I'm not crazy."

He lunged for her then. With hands chained behind him, weakened from his wound, he charged round the side of the desk. "Run, Duff!" He could not see whether the little boy obeyed his command. Turning his body sideways, he aimed a kick at Maude's face.

She screamed and went over backward, clutching for the .22 pistol in her skirt pocket.

The chair went over with her and Chris's leg came down entangled in its legs. She rolled away from him and came up unharmed. Her face was contorted in an expression of pure hatred. "I'll kill you," she sneered. "I'll kill you. I offered you everything, but you wouldn't take it. I'll kill you and keep your son. Duff will forget you soon enough. He'll have no one but me, and I'll make him mine." Retreating away from him, she aimed the pistol at Chris's chest as he circled the desk.

"Stay back!" she snarled, straightening haughtily. "Or I'll kill you right now."

"Put that gun down, Maude!"

Both figures in the room froze at the command of the voice neither had expected to hear.

"Star!" Maude's gasp of dismay was echoed by Chris's groan.

Star Garner y Montejo stood framed in the doorway,

447

Duff clinging to her side, his tearful face buried in the folds of her skirt.

"Run for it!" Chris yelled. His booted foot struck out again to kick the gun from Maude's hand. It went sliding across the floor into the farthest corner. Maude screamed and clasped her wrist tightly.

Star drew her gun from its holster. "Stop right there, Maude!" she shouted, with more calm than she felt.

Maude shook her head in confusion. Her eyes searched for the gun, then stared from one to the other. "How did you get here?" she snarled at last. "I gave orders that the gate was to remain closed. I didn't hear any shooting."

"Luke gave me a key." Star drew it from her shirt for proof.

"Luke? He's still alive?"

"Was when I left him," Star replied noncommittally.

"But he may not be now?" Maude pounced upon the words.

Star shrugged. "Are you all right, Chris?"

He twisted his handcuffed hands from behind his back. Sweat trickled down his brow and into his eyes. His face was yellowish-white around the mouth. "See if you can find out where she's got the key," he begged.

Star jabbed the gun at Maude. "Get it."

Assuming an aggrieved position, Maude rubbed her wrist where Chris had kicked it. "It's not here. I don't know where it is."

"She's lying," Chris muttered. His head had begun to swim. Rather than fall down he staggered to a chair and dropped into it. Duff ran to him and threw his arms around his father's neck.

"Maude. Get the key," Star repeated.

"You wouldn't dare shoot me. I-I'm carrying his child."

The words stopped Star for a moment until Chris shook his head. "She can't know that. In fact, it's a lie. She just asked me to marry her so I could get her pregnant."

Star looked at Maude pityingly. "Maude. How can you do these things? say these things?"

"I've got to have a child. Don't you see? I've got to. Matthew couldn't. I laughed at him when he couldn't get you pregnant. I laughed and laughed. I was sure that I could. I'm positive I can if this *man* will just cooperate." She curved her nails like claws toward Chris's face.

"Let him go, Maude," Star advised gently. "You can't force a man to make love to you. You can't even force people to like you. You can only make people hate you."

Maude made a triumphant face at her sister-in-law. "But I can keep him from liking you. Matthew might have liked you, but I kept telling him what a fool you thought he was. How you hated his leg. I told him that no one would want to be in bed with a cripple."

Star gasped in horror. "Are you telling me that's why he hurt me so badly?"

Maude shrugged. "Not at first. He liked to be a big man. He really did. I loved it when he was forceful and strong like that." Her eyes took on a glassy appearance. She flung her arms tightly around her body and squeezed herself hard. "Sometimes he'd whip me like that when we were children. It burned like fire, but then it felt so good afterwards. Then he'd hold me and rub me all over. Nobody was ever so good to me as Matthew after I'd let him do what he wanted."

Chris and Star exchange appalled glances.

She caught their looks and grinned. "You just didn't understand how to play the games," she explained with a superior look on her face. "You fought him, so he came to me afterwards. I got the good parts without the whippings."

"He was furious the night he died," Star whispered.

"Oh, my, yes. I had told him he couldn't have me anymore until he got rid of you. I was tired of you getting so much attention."

449

"You came into the room after he broke my thumb." Star could feel perspiration start out on her skin.

Maude stared at her angrily. "So you finally remembered."

Star nodded. "I finally remembered. But I was so far out of the picture, I didn't know what was going on. What did you say to him to make him want to kill you?" Her voice was so low that Chris had to strain to hear.

A peculiarly vulnerable look flitted across Maude's face, a look mixed with fear and grief. "He was going to kill me. He told me he was. I came to him just like always when he had finished with you, but he pushed me down. He had decided that I was taking too much from him. Loving me was taking too much from him. He was going to kill me and then make love to you. He was certain he could get you pregnant in just a couple of tries if I was dead."

"Then why beat me half to death? I was sure he was going to kill me."

Maude threw back her head and laughed richly. "You never understood him. He had to work himself up to things. Especially killing. He didn't have the nerve to just walk in and do it. He wasn't like me. I can just step out of a gate and shoot a man down. But Matthew was crazy." She looked at Chris conspiratorially. "I understood him, you see."

Chris's head swam dizzily. "I can see you do." He slumped back against the chair.

"I saved your life," Star reminded Maude quietly. "When he was going to shoot you, I grabbed for his gun, but he was too strong. He threw me clear across the room. After that I couldn't remember anything."

Maude nodded. "It gave me the time I needed. I shot him with my own pistol. That drunk doctor never even bothered to dig out the lead and see that you hadn't done it."

"And you would have let me hang rather than tell what

really happened. That's why you sent Hatch to kill me before I got back. You were afraid I'd remembered."

Maude shook her head. "You can't blame me for that. I helped you get free in the first place. Who do you think sent word to your brother to come and get you? If you'd just stayed down in Mexico, everything would have been fine. But you've always been a slut. You came back up here to marry my father and take my ranch away from me."

Star took a deep breath. "I've heard enough of this. Get the key to Chris's handcuffs. Don't lie about not knowing where it is. It's in this room. Otherwise you wouldn't have brought him in here."

Maude snarled. "I don't have to do what you say."

"This gun says you do."

"You wouldn't dare."

Star took a couple of steps toward her sister-in-law. Her black eyes flashed. "Listen, Maude. You understand people who have to work themselves into a rage to do something. Well hear this. I've been kidnapped and half-drowned and starved and beaten. I've spent the last twenty-four hours without a decent meal or a decent place to sleep. Right now I feel mad enough to kill you and tell God you died. *Get that key.*"

Maude held up her hands protectively before the fierce almost primal anger she read in the usually gentle face. "All right. Don't get excited." She hurried behind the desk and righted the chair. Sitting in it, she opened the top drawer. The key was there, right where she had left it. Her fingers were reaching for it when suddenly she drew back.

"I forgot," she muttered. "Oh, you're making me so nervous with that pistol that I can't think straight. I wish you'd point it somewhere else."

"Find it," Star repeated implacably.

"Yes. All right." Maude reached down to the bottom drawer. It slid open smoothly to reveal the metal money box, the leather envelope, and the Colt .45. She looked up at Star, a smile on her face. "There's some money here. Would you like that, sister dear? We could divide it and you could be on your way."

"The key."

"Then I guess I'll have to take it all." Expression like a madonna's, she rose with the Colt held in front of her. Her thumb pulled the hammer back, but Star was too fast for her. Fanning the gun with the heel of her left hand, she fired point blank at Maude's chest. The thunderous blast was echoed by Maude's own gun discharging at the ceiling as the force of the .45 at close range flung her backward against the wall.

Chapter Twenty-nine

Father Toribio made the sign of the cross before them.
Chris turned Star into his arms and kissed her with aching
tenderness. By the light of the votive candles he could see
the tears glisten in her eyes. "I love you," he promised. "I'll
always love you."

"And I love you."

He kissed her again lightly, then turned her to face the
assembly. Her sister, Johanna, stepped forward to kiss him
while Tomas kissed Star. Rosa McGloin wiped a tear from
her cheek, while the cowboys and *vaqueros* cheered and
clapped him on the back.

Star bent to kiss Duff's cheek and accept his strangling
hug. "You're really my mama now," he crowed delightedly.

Standing on the porch of Rosa McGloin's after a full
meal, Johanna hugged her sister again. "You really should
come home to the Double Diamond. You both still need
more rest. You've been through a terrible ordeal."

"It's only a hundred miles away." Tomas added his
support to his sister's suggestion. "That's not such a long
trip as you're planning."

"Much obliged to you both, but we won't go anywhere,
not even home, until I take her and Duff to visit my

453

grandmother." Chris shook hands with Johanna and Tomas.

"Are you sure?" Johanna looked doubtfully at Chris's
face, somewhat gaunt after the two weeks he'd spent in bed
at Rosa McGloin's.

The landlady had turned the entire rooming house over
to Johanna and Tomas and had helped in nursing Chris
after Doc Foster had sewn together the jagged edges of the
wound.

"I'm fine. I'm more worried about Star and how she'll
stand the trip with her ribs." He put his arm around her
gently and drew her against his side.

His bride smiled with some irony. "Now he's worried
about my ribs. After dragging me all over southwest Texas
and northern Mexico when they were freshly broken."

His light mood darkened; he looked away. "I won't ever
be able to forget that."

She caught him under the chin and turned his face to
receive a kiss. "Of course, you will. You mustn't think
about it. Think of all the good things that came out of it.
I'm free forever. Before you came for me, I was a prisoner
on Rancho Montejo and in my own mind."

Johanna smiled. "Every person has to fight her way
through a long, dark tunnel to get to the light at the end.
Our mother," she informed Chris proudly, "fought for
years. You only get stronger. After it's all over, you find the
pain has been worth it."

"Our father came through a long, dark tunnel, too,"
Tomas added, "when he was only a child, not much older
than Duff here. You'll have to tell Chris about our family
sometime, *hermanita*."

"Did your father get kidnapped when he was a boy?"
Duff wanted to know.

Tomas smiled down at him. "When he was a little boy,
his father, a Comanche war chief named Masitawtawp, told
him he was dead. None of his people would even look at

him. Then a lady on a medicine horse came for him. She took him away back to her people where he grew up strong and tall."

Chris was looking at Tomas strangely. "I can't believe what I'm hearing," he mused. "My grandfather used to tell me a story. I had forgotten until you brought it up." His face set in serious lines. "You've got to remember, I haven't been home for more than a few months in ten years," he apologized. "My grandmother," he continued hoarsely, his mouth suddenly dry, "was captured by a Comanche war chief. She escaped on a mustang stallion that was the start of my grandfather's herd. Since then, of course, we've branched out into Arabians and Andalusians, but the first horses at El Rincon were all descended from a stallion my grandmother named San Leon."

"El Rincon?" Johanna queried sharply. "Your grandmother lives on El Rincon?"

Chris nodded his head; his eyes closed in pain and guilt. "She brought back a little Indian boy with her. He was gone long before I was born, but I remember my grandmother weeping over a letter she got a few years back. He had been killed somewhere in Mexico. She told my grandfather that Ten Bears had been killed."

Star barely smothered a cry. "Ten Bears was my father."

He shook his head incredulously. "Your father was a Spanish grandee, Don Alejandro de Montejo."

Tomas shook his head. "Our father had many names." He gazed fondly at Star.

"He was my husband's best friend," Johanna added. "Marcos Sandoval was born at El Rincon."

Chris held out his hands in a plea for mercy. "I can't have tried to collect a bounty on the daughter of someone my grandmother loved." His face was pale. "She'll kill me."

"My father was Alejandro Paruwa Sermahno MacPherson Montejo." Star recited the names proudly.

"If I'm not a dead man, then I'll wish I was when La

Patrona gets ahold of me," Chris intoned.

"Well, at least Duff and I will have someplace to stay while you're recuperating," Star laughed.

Riding in the carriage they had rented in San Antonio, Chris kissed his wife very thoroughly. Her lips were warm and sweet, her body eager to respond to his touch. He had teased her unmercifully for the last hour. At last, when she was shivering and moaning helplessly, he knocked on the top of the carriage.

The driver pulled up and Duff's face appeared in the little window behind the box. "Whatcha want, Papa?"

"Your mother and I have decided to ride ahead for a few miles." He ran his hand over the inside of her thigh beneath her riding skirt and leered when she bit her lip and tried to keep her face impassive.

"Gee, that's great. Can I go, too?"

"Not this time," Star informed him breathlessly. "You continue to ride up on the coach with the driver if you like."

Chris sprang down and led the horses to the door. His wife stepped up into the saddle of Humareda. He swung up onto the stallion. "Meet you on the road ahead," he told the driver.

The man tipped his hat politely. Duff waved good-bye as the two urged their eager horses into a gallop.

"You had this planned." Star watched in delight as little shivers of desire went up and down her spine.

Chris unfastened a blanket from the back of Al's saddle and spread it out in the tall grass of a meadow. They were out of sight, but not out of hearing of the Camino de la Bahía. "A bounty hunter has to be prepared for all emergencies," he leered. "Come here."

He held up his hands; she swung her leg over the horn

456

and went into his waiting arms. Holding her by the hips, he lifted her up with an exultant laugh before planting a kiss on her body.

"Chris," she exclaimed happily. "Oh, Chris."

Slowly, he let her slide down his body. "I want you," he said huskily.

"Here?" She looked around her hastily. "But it's broad daylight."

"That's right," he grinned, his hands busy at the front of her blouse. "I promised you the next time I'd make love to you, it'd be in the blaze of noon."

"But your side?"

"Honey, I've got a confession to make." He peeled the blouse down over her shoulders hooking his thumbs in the camisole straps and pulling them down at the same time.

She squirmed while he kissed the tip of each breast, impossibly white and peaked with a dusky rose point. "You mean you've been pretending the last couple of days that you were too stiff and sore to make love."

"Sure have." His hands unbuttoned her skirt in back and pushed all of her clothing down about her knees.

"For heaven's sake, Chris." She caught his hair as he sank to his knees to kiss her belly. "Suppose someone sees us."

He shrugged. "We're married. If anybody happens by, let him go find his own wife." His hands covered her buttocks while his tongue traced circles of delight over her lower belly and into the soft black curls at its base.

When she was shuddering with pleasure, her legs so weak she could no longer stand, he laid her down on the blanket and stood to tear off his own clothing.

Shivering with desire, she cupped her breasts and offered them to him, arching her back away from the blanket. "Hurry," she whispered. "I want you so badly."

When only the bandage covering the wound in his side remained on his body, he came down on top of her.

Stretched out full length, he touched her at all points, his rampant desire hard as steel against her soft belly.

"You are so beautiful," he gasped. "I can't believe that we've only made love at night. I should keep you naked in the sun for hours every day and look at you. You have the most beautiful body."

"I'm so glad it pleases you."

He began to kiss her, his lips trailing over her breasts and down into the cup of her navel. "Turn over," he commanded.

Obediently, she turned in his arms. "What are you doing?"

"I want to kiss every inch of you." His voice was muffled as his mouth moved down her spine."

She gasped as his tongue touched the indentations on either side of her buttocks. "Are you sure you're supposed to be kissing me there?"

He chuckled. "I'm just kissing your dimples. Dimples are made to be kissed." His fingers slid under her into the soft, curling black hair at the bottom of her belly and spread her delicate lips.

She moaned in ecstasy as one long index finger touched the throbbing point of pleasure exposed there. "Chris," she sighed.

"Does that please you?" he whispered. "Do you like that?"

She could not move, and yet she could not help but move. She writhed and danced as his fingers and mouth kindled the fires within her even hotter. Tears seeped from between her tight-closed lids. She sobbed for mercy, or for release, but he drove her higher and higher. Her nipples rasped against the wool of the blanket, her cheeks flushed hot. She was consumed in flames, not knowing herself, losing all sense of identity, being only one helpless, pulsating organism.

When she was sure she would die of mindless pleasure,

she felt his hands turning her again. She sobbed in ecstasy as he lifted her hips to the tops of his thighs and plunged into her to his full length. His rod touched the mouth of her womb. Thrills began to shake her body. She wrapped her legs around him and hugged him closer.

Now it was his turn to groan. She had taken control. He could not pull out of her to stroke her. Her muscles within her stroked him, pulled and released as she moaned and twisted. "For God's sake, Star," he begged, but she did not hear him.

All around her was heat and light and pleasure. Every nerve in her body was attuned to sensation. She shivered and moaned and gasped for breath.

His hands clasped her breasts and squeezed, his thumbs and index fingers giving special attention to the diamond-hard tips. She breathed faster and faster, panting in ecstasy.

He felt her whole body stiffen. Then she screamed. As her thighs squeezed tighter, he burrowed deeper into her body. With that movement his own climax came. With a shout he poured himself into the very mouth of her womb.

Star listened to his even breathing beside her. A few minutes before, the rumble of the carriage had disturbed her own doze. They would have to dress and go soon. Doubtless they would not have to wait, but instead catch up.

Staring up into the clean burning blue of the Texas sky, she pressed her hands against her belly. Today she knew she had conceived. Within her he had planted a seed that would begin to grow from this minute on. The face of her child swam in her inner eye. Turning to Chris, she found him lying on his back with closed eyes, his breathing even and relaxed. The sunlight touched the hair on his chest and clothed him in a mesh of gold. She thought she had never seen anything more beautiful.

She put out her hand to touch his shoulder to share with

him her vision of a beautiful little boy with white-blond hair and smoky gray eyes. Her fingers clenched. He would think her silly or overly romantic. No woman could really know the moment of conception. She closed her eyes, seeing the vision clearly again.

Then Chris spoke to her, and she realized in confusion that her face must have betrayed her. He turned over on his side and propped himself up on his elbow. "What are you thinking about?"

The warm sun behind him created a halo of gold around his head as he bent over to plant a kiss on her cheek. Dazzled by the light and gently secured in the warmth of his love, she shook her head slowly. "My secret."

"Tell me," he whispered, his mouth against her ear.

"No, I don't think so. Not just yet. I want to hold it a while longer."

"I'll bet I can guess." He fastened his teeth playfully in her lobe.

"Guess then," she challenged.

He raised his head and looked at her. His hand covered her naked breast again where the nipple hardened in anticipation. "I should make love to you until you tell me."

She laughed softly. "The only way you could make me talk would be if you stopped making love to me."

"Star," he coaxed. He moved his lips to the corner of her mouth. "I'll bet you were thinking naughty sexy thoughts." His tongue flicked across her lips sending shivers of pleasure all through her.

"You could be right," she gasped breathlessly.

"Insatiable," he teased. "What happened to the woman who faked passion when I met her a couple of months ago?"

Star threaded one hand through his thick golden hair. "She was kidnapped," she growled in his ear. She pushed her other hand into his shoulder at the same time she thrust her hips against his and rolled him over onto his back. A

460

quick wriggle and she was lying on top of him, her naked body pressed to his from breast to knee. Roughly she ground her hips and belly into his, feeling him harden again beneath her.

When he groaned, she trailed kisses down his jaw and along his neck, luxuriating in the taste and texture of him. ". . . and the bounty hunter had his way with her." She rotated the palms of her hands against his nipples while her fingers tantalizingly tugged at the hair on his chest. "Now she's intent on revenge."

He drew in his breath sharply as she shifted her weight from side to side. "God, Star!" Then his body shuddered and stiffened. He chuckled hoarsely. "Be gentle with me."

FIERY PASSION
In every Zebra Historical Romance

WILD FURY   (1987, $3.95)
by Gina Delaney

Jessica Aylesbury was the beauty of the settled Australian Outback. She had one love; her childhood friend Eric. But she could never let him know how she felt—and she could never let anyone but him teach her the smouldering pleasures of womanhood . . .

CAPTIVE SURRENDER   (1986, $3.95)
by Michalan Perry

Gentle Fawn vows revenge for the deaths of her father and husband. Yet once she gazes into the blue eyes of her enemy, she knows she can never kill him. She must sate the wild desires he kindled or forever be a prisoner of his love.

DEFIANT SURRENDER   (1966, $3.95)
by Barbara Dawson Smith

Elsie d'Evereaux was horrified when she spilled wine on the pants of the tall, handsome stranger—and even more shocked when the bold Englishman made her clean it up. Fate drew them together in love and passion.

ECSTASY'S TRAIL   (1964, $3.95)
Elaine Barbieri

Disguised as a man, Billie Winslow hires on as a drover on a trail herd to escape a murder. When trail boss, Rand Pierce, discovers that the young tough is a nubile wench, he promises to punish her for lying—and keep her for his loving.

PROUD CAPTIVE   (1925, $3.95)
by Dianne Price

Certain that her flawless good looks would snare her a rich husband, the amber-eyed lass fled her master—only to be captured by a marauding Spanish privateer. The hot-blooded young woman had gone too far to escape the prison of his arms.

Available wherever paperbacks are sold, or order direct from the Publisher. Send cover price plus 50¢ per copy for mailing and handling to Zebra Books, Dept. 2088, 475 Park Avenue South, New York, N.Y. 10016. Residents of New York, New Jersey and Pennsylvania must include sales tax. DO NOT SEND CASH.

Zebra Historical Romances —
Dare to Dream!

MOONLIT MAGIC   (1941, $3.95)
by Sylvie F. Sommerfield
How dare that slick railroad negotiator bathe in Jenna's river and sneak around her property! But soon her seething fury became burning desire. As he stroked her skin, she was forever captured by *Moonlit Magic*.

SAVAGE KISS   (1669, $3.95)
by Sylvie F. Sommerfield
Rayne Freeman thought he was dreaming. But one moment in Falling Water's arms and he knew he would never betray the ecstasy of their *Savage Kiss*.

SURRENDER TO DESIRE   (1503, $3.75)
by Catherine Creel
When Marianna learned she was to marry a stranger once she reached the Alaskan frontier, her fury knew no bounds. But she found herself falling under the spell of passion's sweet fire, destined to welcome defeat and *Surrender to Desire*.

PASSION'S BRIDE   (1417, $3.75)
Jo Goodman
"Don't make me love you," Alexis whispered. But Tanner was a man used to having his own way. The Captain would keep her prisoner rather than risk losing her to her quest for revenge.

Available wherever paperbacks are sold, or order direct from the Publisher. Send cover price plus 50¢ per copy for mailing and handling to Zebra Books, Dept. 2088, 475 Park Avenue South, New York, N.Y. 10016. Residents of New York, New Jersey and Pennsylvania must include sales tax. DO NOT SEND CASH.